The Forgiving Woman

M.L. Lexi

Titles by M.L. Lexi

The Blind Woman
The Deceitful Woman
The Forgiving Woman
The Grieving Woman
The Guilty Woman
The Loyal Woman
The Noble Woman
The Resolute Woman
The Unfaithful Woman

The Farfalla Family Saga
The Determined Woman
The Persevering Woman
The Invincible Woman

The Fearless Woman Series
The Fearless Woman
The Naïve Woman

Copyright

For every bullied woman and girl
who rises above it all.

Forgiveness is the greatest expression of love.
It fuels our heart, our mind, and soul.
It makes us noble.
It makes us human.

—M.L. Lexi

Prologue

October 1970

SARINA INSTINCTIVELY SENSED, she was going to die.

Writhing in pain, the perspiration beading thick on her forehead as she was rushed to the operating theater Sarina sensed it wasn't going to be the routine caesarean they'd told her it would be.

She was twenty-three and she was going to die, and so was her baby.

How did it come to this?

For the past nine months, she'd done everything to ensure her baby's wellbeing. She'd eaten the right foods, religiously taken her vitamins. She'd exercised and kept her stress to a minimum.

How had it come to this?

On every visit to Dr. Berkeley, Sarina had brought up the questions, the concerns, the fears of a young, nervous, first-time mother-to-be. Each time she'd asked the questions, Dr. Berkeley had assured her everything was as perfect as it could be. Dr. Berkeley told Sarina—with a confidence that left no room for uncertainty—she was fit and healthy. He'd assured her she would face no problems giving birth to the nine-pound baby she was carrying.

Dr. Berkeley had repeatedly assured Sarina everything was fine.

Now, as whitewashed walls rushed past her and the sharp tang of antiseptic, despair, and illness that tinted the hospital hallways latched onto her like the long, bony fingers of death, Sarina dismissed everything Dr. Berkeley had told her as utter bullshit.

Sarina tasted death in the bile rising in her throat.

With the new wave of pain from the surging contractions rolling in one after the other with vicious intensity, Sarina's unearthly, keening cries like those of an animal in deep distress reverberated throughout the brightly lit hallway.

"Is everything all right?" Sarina's face was so pale she seemed almost translucent.

"We have to get you to the operating room, Sarina." The stethoscope looped around Molly's neck, shimmered against her blindingly white nurse's uniform. "Can I call anyone for you, family, friends—the father."

"There's no one. It's just my baby and me, and you didn't answer my question." Sarina sounded more forceful than she intended, but the pain was too much to bear now.

Reaching for Sarina's hand, Molly's olive-black eyes curved into a consoling smile. "You're fine, Sarina. You're in excellent hands. Dr. Berkeley is the best." Crepe-soled shoes silent against linoleum ran alongside the gurney.

"Is my baby okay?" Sarina's anxious face contorted in agony.

"Exhale through your mouth," Molly instructed when Sarina's hand tightened around hers as the next contraction hit hard. "That's it, Sarina allow the air to flow in and out. Your baby's fine. She just seems to like being in your belly a bit too much, and we need to coax her out," she said, with a dimpled grin.

A wondrous joy quickly replaced all Sarina's pain, and eyes swamped with love looked up to Molly. "She? My baby's a she?"

Molly pivoted her gaze away from the spreading bloodstained sheets to Sarina. "Oops! Me and my big mouth. Guess I spoiled the surprise for you." Molly hoped to inject hope into the moment.

A girl! Sarina was laughing now. All the pain she'd endured the past twelve hours was forgotten. She was having a daughter. Sarina let her mind wander to imagine holding the tiny bundle in her arms, who was about to change her life forever. It was as exciting as it was scary, and still, she couldn't imagine loving anyone as much as she already loved the life in her.

The joyful moment was short-lived when Sarina braced herself on her elbows and threw her head back when the fresh wave of unspeakable pain rolled through her.

Tired, she was so tired and so weak.

"Breathe, Sarina, breathe," Molly prompted, he-heeing along with her. "Look at me. Focus on me."

Inhaling through her nose and exhaling through her mouth Sarina recalled the Lamaze teacher telling the class breathing helps to cope with the pain. Proper breathing helps to relieve the discomfort and the anxiety brought on by labor, she'd told the class, and at that moment, Sarina thought what a load of—

"Oh, sweet Jesus," Sarina cried out, followed with a string of oaths she wasn't aware she was familiar with.

Sarina was never under the illusion giving birth was going to be easy, but she never imagined it was going to be as difficult as this. Now, they were rushing her into surgery. Childbirth suddenly made the twenty-three years of her arduous life seem like a walk in the park, Sarina thought, casting her thoughts back in time.

FACE-TO-FACE WITH ONE THAT matched her own, Sarina watched her mother gasping for breath when the stabbing pain from the cancer ravaging her insides swamped her. Tears burned behind Sarina's eyes as she listened to her mama tell her she had days to live.

In a soothing voice, between hitched breaths, her mama explained that when she went to heaven, Sarina was to go live with Aunt Olga. For her mama's sake, Sarina remained composed when panic grabbed her by the throat. Sarina didn't want to live under the same roof with stony-faced Tia Olga. The thought of having to live with the religious, zealot aunt whose answer to everything was prayer, who believed in absolute damnation for a sinful soul and that no one was free of sin, made Sarina want to cry. For her mama's sake, Sarina held the tears back.

One week after their conversation, her mama died, and at the age of ten, with her grief locked deep inside her, Sarina moved into Tia Olga's home. She went from a home where music, song, and love existed to a home where happiness and emotions were a foreign notion. A home where once she became a teenager, the fear of God's wrath bearing down to cleanse her sexually craving body and sinful mind of all impurities was her reality.

Sarina wasn't sure what impurities were, but she was made to pray—always pray—to cleanse her soul from them. She was made to pray for everything she did and every sexual thought she had—and she had a lot of them.

Sarina was thrilled when she turned eighteen, and Tia Olga pawned her off as a maid to Señor Ryder. Although Tia Olga took all her wages, Sarina didn't care. Señor Ryder's home was a happy home filled with music and song as hers once was. Señor Ryder was kind and generous, and through him, Sarina discovered what love was.

When they started to share a bed, Sarina sensed Dean at forty-two—almost twice her age—was too old for her, but without anyone to talk to and never been taught the finer points of the male-female relationship, intuiting was all she had. Tia Olga had never discussed such matters with her, and when Sarina so much as looked at a boy, she'd harp about their evil ways. Stay away from boys, she'd say. Boys become men, and men are the spawn of the devil. Their only interest in women is for carnal gratification and nothing else.

Being with Dean felt good, not only when their bodies came together, but when he told her, he loved her. And when Dean showered Sarina with affection, she believed it was sincere not conjured to get carnal gratification from her. No one had ever said the beautiful things Dean said to her or been so caring and gentle. Until Dean, Sarina hadn't known what affection from a man felt like, and those feelings made her feel nice. Really nice. That couldn't be wrong, Sarina decided.

Emotions swimming into her eyes, Sarina vowed her daughter's soul would never need cleansing. Her beautiful daughter would be cherished. Her beautiful daughter would always be loved.

"BREATHE, SARINA, BREATHE," SHE HEARD MOLLY say as they wheeled her through the large steel doors that opened wide and seemed to swallow her whole.

In the operating theater, nurses crowded Sarina as they prepped her for surgery. Sarina was attached to a beeping machine with green lines. An I.V. was inserted into her vein as Molly put in a dreadful tube called a catheter into a place she didn't know could be penetrated. Sarina's eyes went saucer-wide at the needle that looked to be a foot long.

"It's an epidural. This will hurt a bit at first, but afterward, you won't feel pain." Molly explained.

As Molly stabbed her spine with the goddamn awful needle, Sarina focused her gaze past the glass window where Dr. Berkeley was getting suited with a surgical gown, mask, and gloves.

"Fetal distress. Let's get to work," Dr. Berkeley said in a matter-of-fact tone to his surgical team when he stepped into the operating theater. Although there were no alarming looks or words exchanged, Sarina felt a sinking feeling at the pit of her stomach.

"Is my baby going to be okay, Dr. Berk…?" Sarina succumbed to the anesthesia before she could finish her question.

The atmosphere was uneasy but disciplined. Vivaldi flowed through the speaker as Dr. Berkeley, with hands as steady as set cement, made the lengthy incision. The baby was nestled low in Sarina's uterus, and Dr. Berkeley's fingers moved agilely. Calling out instructions, acknowledgments were made by the attending nurses as Dr. Berkeley went about bringing Sarina's baby into the world.

"The baby's heartbeat is strong and regular," Dr. Berkeley said, to the relief and delight of everyone in the room, and minutes later, Luna was brought into the world without incident.

One of the nurses took Luna and proceeded to suction mucus from her tiny lungs. Within seconds Luna's first piercing cry filled the room with the melodic sound of life.

Eleven-forty-five p.m., October twenty-fifth of nineteen-seventy was the day Luna came into the world. October twenty-fifth of nineteen-seventy was the day Luna began to live a lie perpetrated by those closest to her.

Part I

Fate

We don't meet people by accident.
They are meant to cross our path for a reason.

—Unknown

Chapter 1

October 1984

AT FOURTEEN, LUNA Lopez was gangly and awkward. Her long black hair was stringy, her green eyes were set in a pale, thin face, and she was slender to the point of looking boyish.

Luna's life was as ordinary as she was as her friends were as her life was. She lived with her mom and dad in a tiny two-bedroom, red brick home on Sycamore Street, which verged on the prestigious enclave of Royal Hill—the dividing line between the have-all and have-not.

Royal Hill was everything Sycamore wasn't: privileged, wealthy, and overflowing with enviable excesses. Regardless of its downfalls, Sycamore Street was where children freely rode their bikes past majestic hardwoods with verdant crowns and compact Victorian homes with wooden porches and tidy front lawns.

After school and on weekends, Luna worked with Sarina and her father, Teo, at Maid For You, the janitorial business he operated from a modest, damp, low ceiling office in the basement of their home. Luna did anything and everything necessary from going out on cleaning jobs to organizing the office and cold calling to drum up business.

The have-all of Vaughan Secondary derided Luna for working as a janitor, but she rose above the petty insults.

She was happy to contribute to the small company her father had built from the ground up. Luna was exceptionally proud of the fact the elite residents of Royal Hill—whose trust didn't come easily—sought out Teo Lopez's services for his trustworthy reputation. Teo proudly boasted his roster of clients, comprised of doctors, judges, lawyers, and captains of industry, didn't allow just anyone into their homes.

Luna was Teo's pride and joy. It wasn't because Luna was his only child or because she was a well-mannered, grounded, considerate, smart girl, but because Teo had fallen in love with her, the moment Sarina set the tiny bundle in his arms. Since that day, Luna became the apple of Teo's eye.

Teo never hesitated to spoil his little girl. And why not? She's our only child and my princess, he'd say to Sarina when she chastised him for doing so.

Luna did well in school and was liked by the have-not. She never set out to become a popular girl, but in her first year at Vaughan Secondary, her winning personality and willingness to help the underdog made her one overnight.

That Luna was popular with the have-not didn't sit well with Britney Melville-Berkeley. Although she looked down on the have-not, for the past three years of high school, Britney had worked hard to cultivate her popularity. That hadn't come easy for Britney, a self-centered, narcissistic, mean-girl who repelled as strongly as a magnet attracted. Britney, however, learned early on wealth could buy anything, and dangling hers like a carrot in front of the proverbial donkey got her the popularity she craved.

A have-all from Royal Hill, Britney flaunted her lavish home with the tall columns, high ceilings, and indoor heated pool overlooking the lush ravine. When the mood struck, Britney flew those deemed worthy of her inner circle to exotic destinations in one of her grandfather's planes. At every turn, Britney was quick to inject into the conversation that her father was the renowned Dr. Berkeley, the OB/GYN who'd delivered almost every baby on Sycamore and Royal Hill, including her nemesis—Luna Lopez.

Dr. Berkeley, a kind-hearted, compassionate, dedicated professional, had one flaw. He loved the good life, liked it enough to sell his soul to the devil, or more accurately for money. It was why he'd married Tara Melville, daughter of Reince Melville, the media tycoon. Tara—pronounced Taaa-ra for the added touch of snootiness—came with a famous surname and wealth that made Dr. Berkeley's seem like pocket change. That blinded Dr. Berkeley to Tara's many character flaws, and until they came to live under the same roof, did Dr. Berkeley come to realize what a cold, heartless, arrogant woman she was. Worse, it wasn't until then he came to learn first-hand how venomous Tara's tongue was and how it never sat idle.

As much as Dr. Berkeley detested Tara and her vile tongue, he loved her money and the lifestyle it afforded him more. Wealth, like Tara's, carried a price, Dr. Berkeley reasoned, and he resigned himself to enduring her toxic personality and flapping tongue. Everyone had a cross to bear, and Tara's was Dr. Berkeley's. His only regret was that the apple hadn't fallen far from the tree, and Britney was following her mother's example.

Like her mother, Britney was a conniving, condescending snob, never shying away from flaunting her prominent name or wealth, demanding the respect, she didn't deserve. The young, flaxen-haired viper was a spoiled rich, entitled girl with a mean streak who'd do anything to get what she wanted. It was why Dr. Berkeley insisted Britney attend Vaughan Secondary with the have-not.

Tara hated the notion of her only daughter mingling with the underclass from Sycamore and often told her husband so. Dr. Berkeley, however, believed Britney needed the grounding Vaughan and its working-class students offered. A grounding Britney wasn't going to get at home from her mother, and at Dr. Berkeley's insistence, she remained enrolled at Vaughan Secondary for the duration of her high school years.

Britney's resentment for being at a school she believed was beneath her station in life fueled a bitterness that swelled into resentment, and her outlet for her pent up anger became Luna.

No one came to know Britney's malicious side better than Luna. Britney came at Luna when she could, where she could. However, she could. Britney became obsessed with Luna's undeserving popularity and her likeability, which she failed to understand. Luna lived on Sycamore Street for God's sake. Her father, a simple janitor, and her mother, a mere medical secretary, were both on her father's payroll. It stuck in Britney's craw that was it not for the Melville-Berkeley's, Luna's family wouldn't survive.

Britney's anger toward Luna intensified when she reasoned that a Melville-Berkeley was supposed to be the center of attention, not some low class deplorable from Sycamore Street.

Britney's litany of assaults on Luna began from the time she asked Lance to ask Luna out on a date, and then made sure her entourage showed up at the local pizza hangout to witness Luna being stood up.

"Hello, Luna. Are you expecting someone?" Slinking up to Luna's table, Britney said loud enough to get everyone's attention.

"Umm ... yeah. I'm, ah, waiting on my date," Luna stammered when she felt all eyes flicked to her.

"And who would the lucky guy be?" The disdain in Britney's blue eyes made Luna squirm in her seat.

"Ah, Lance." Luna followed Britney's eyes when they glanced over her shoulder.

"Lance, Luna here claims you have a date with her tonight," Britney called out over the din of the Saturday night crowd. "Give him a second to pull his tongue out of Tiffany's mouth to answer." Britney's sarcastic tone made the entourage of blonde Barbies, and everyone in the restaurant burst into laughter.

Swallowing the bitter taste of humiliation, Luna ran out of the restaurant in tears, the snickers from everyone following her out like a homing missile.

More humiliating events followed since that night until Luna decided she wasn't going to take it anymore.

"I'm not as pretty or as rich as Britney. I don't wear designer clothes or drive a Mercedes to school, but I don't deserve to be mistreated this way. Like daddy says, bullies are cowards with small brains, and you shouldn't be afraid of them. You should be outsmarting them. And that's exactly what you're going to do," Luna told her reflection in the mirror with conviction.

As of that moment, outsmarting Britney became Luna's mission.

"Luna, that's a beautiful shirt," Britney called down from the second-floor stairwell as students made their way to their next class.

Luna's eyes rolled upwards. "Thank you, Britney."

"I owned one just like it before my mother gave it to your father the day she hired him to clean out our basement." Britney's voice thundered through the thronged staircase.

"Yeah, your mother told him your raisin size titties couldn't fill the shirt as well as I could," was Luna's timely response.

The rupture of raucous laughter made Britney's eyes blaze red, and Luna basked in the wave of satisfaction.

There was the time Britney threatened every boy at the yearly Halloween bash from asking Luna to dance. After an hour of sitting in the bleachers, Luna decided to get up on the dance floor and contort her body in the craziest ways. Gapes and derision followed, but it didn't take long for everyone to see how much fun Luna was having, and every lonesome girl and boy followed suit. With her perfectly coiffed entourage in tow, Britney huffed her way past crazy Luna and out of the gymnasium.

Britney's epic mean girl prank fail came when she stuck her foot out as Luna came out of the library. With books stacked eight high in her arms, Britney tripped Luna and sent her straight into Tom Grady's arms as he came around the bend.

"I'm sorry about that, Tom. She's such a spaz." Britney sneered at Luna, sidling up to Tom with adoring eyes.

"Only because you tripped her." Tom's voice carried the elite sound of Royal Hill. "Are you all right?"

Luna lifted her eyes to meet the sultry, blue ones aimed at her. They were bluer than gossip claimed, and he was taller than she expected—six-foot by her estimation. The shock of scraggly, blonde hair made you want to rake your fingers through it. The dimpled cheeks and that cleft chin set in a finely chiseled jaw made you want to bite into him, top the good looks with a muscular, athletic body, and the entire package was very Robert Redfordish. Luna could see why every girl in school swooned over the popular quarterback.

Luna waited for a beat for the roaring in her ears and the tug-of-war playing out in the pit of her belly to ease before saying, "I'm … I'm fine, thank you," although her expression radiated nothing of the sort.

"You'll have to excuse Britney. She can't help being anything but a bitch," Tom said, captivated by the green, wide-eyed, shocked expression Luna shot Britney. "Don't worry. She knows she's a bitch."

Rattled by the way Tom eyed Luna, Britney gave him a tug of insistence. "Why are you being like this, baby? I didn't do anything to her."

"Uh-huh." Never taking his eyes off Luna, Tom batted Britney away like an annoying fly. "Shoo, Britney."

"I swear, Tom. I didn't do anything. I can't help it if these Sycamore girls have no poise. They have no clue how to femininely put one foot in front of the other." Britney snarled with a haughty tone.

"There's no such word, Britney. Now, ride off on your broom." Tom's remark garnered a snicker from Luna that got a scathing scowl from Britney.

"I have a free period now. Do you want to join me in the ravine, baby?" Britney slithered a moist tongue over her lips. "Baby, did you hear me?"

"I'm Tom Grady, by the way." He bent down to pick up Luna's books off the floor.

"I know."

"And you would be?"

"Luna Lopez," she said, taking the handed books.

Snubbing Britney's seething eyes, Tom easily fell into the conversation. "Nice to meet you, Luna Lopez. That's quite the stack."

"I ... umm ... need to read up on a few subjects. This is my first year of high school, and the sciences have me baffled."

"I may be able to help you. I'm in my fourth year and past this material," he said, eyeing the book titles. "Why don't I help you carry those to your locker, and on the way you can tell me what's tripping you."

"Umm ... you want to walk with me?"

Flashing her a dreamy dimpled smile, Tom took the stack of books from Luna's arms. "Lead the way."

"All right," Luna said, feeling a satisfying tug deep in her belly she'd never felt before.

"You get back here, Tom. Tom, I'm warning you. If you don't get back here now, you can forget about meeting me in the ravine ever again." Britney's voice trembled with rage.

"What exactly happens in the ravine?" Luna naïvely asked, unaware of how attractive her innocence made her to Tom.

"Nothing of importance."

Chapter 2

TOM'S ATTENTION FIXATED on Luna, she was now a permanent cause of tension in Britney's life. That Luna deliberately set off to aggravate her peaceful existence wasn't a surprise to Britney. She'd been an irritant to Britney for months, set on getting deep under her skin and staying there. Sure, Britney badmouthed Luna to anyone who'd listen at every turn. Sure, she circulated unfounded rumors about Luna. She was only standing up to the bitch, Britney reasoned, and Luna deserved it.

Britney never set off to steal the man Luna loved. Pfft, not that Luna would ever have a man to steal. But after months of "entertaining" Tom in the secluded enclave by the ravine, Britney felt she deserved better. The things she'd done for that man and now she couldn't get him to glance her way. Overnight Luna had moved in on her man. Tom's interest in the janitor's daughter was grating on Britney's last nerve.

Britney wouldn't let Luna get away with that. She'd devoted too much time, given so much of herself to Tom. The effort she'd put in to lure that man into her web. There was no way Britney was going to allow Tom to cast her aside for the virginal Luna.

The idea had Britney's temper igniting into a flash of fury.

Britney didn't lay blame on Tom for the turn of events. It was all on the man-stealing slut Luna. Until Miss Prissy pushed her way into Tom's life, everything was perfect between them. Britney liked the tidiness of their relationship, great sex on demand—her demands. Until Luna, Tom took care of her needs when the mood struck. All she had to do was give Tom a sly look, and he'd eagerly fulfill her needs without the complication of emotions. Britney was just fine with that, or so she'd told herself.

Bringing emotions into the equation wasn't what Tom wanted. Introducing emotions into a smoothly functioning arrangement complicated things, blurred the line, Tom told her, and Britney wholeheartedly agreed because it was what made Tom happy. And Tom was such a great lover she wouldn't dare risk losing him.

Tom, based on Britney's assessment, was more sexually skilled than Mr. Jensen or Mr. Patricelli, who she often faked orgasms while moaning their name, as they liked. You'd think men twice her age would know she was faking it, but then it wasn't a huge effort on Britney's part to put on the Emmy winning performance if it got her the As in math and biology she needed to stop her father from harping about her low grades.

Unlike many of the guys Britney bedded, who loved to talk during sex, words got in the way for Tom. But Britney didn't need words from him. He spoke to her through the cries of pleasure she roused in him. The fact Tom looked great on Britney's arm and was the desire of every girl in school was an added benefit.

Britney's mother told her a woman was always at the root of every breakup, and boy was she right, Britney thought. Everything was perfect between her and Tom until that backstabbing-slut Luna came between them.

Days after Tom and Luna's impromptu meeting, to Britney's dismay, he decided to tutor Luna. At first, Britney thought it a joke, but when the expression on Tom's face turned serious, her smile died.

"Baby, what do you know about tutoring?" Britney said, thinking, what a goddamn jock knew about chemistry or biology.

"I know enough." Tom pushed Britney away when she slithered up to him like a venomous asp.

"Let her get her tutoring from someone else." You're mine.

"I'm tutoring her," Tom said definitively. He wasn't going to pass up the opportunity to spend time with Luna, whom he felt a connection he'd never felt with Britney or any of the girls who willingly gave him anything he wanted. He needed to explore that in-depth.

"Get out," Britney shouted at her two best friends when they sashayed into the locker bay. Once they scurried away, Britney flashed Tom a sweetness he didn't believe she possessed. "Baby, I need you to help me." Rage made Britney's throat constrict when she leaned in to kiss Tom, and he turned away.

"I gotta get to class."

"Since when are you interested in getting to class?" Brittney barked.

Tom opened his mouth to answer her, closed it again, deciding she didn't deserve a response.

"But I was hoping we could, you know. I need you right now, baby." Her fist rammed the locker door when Tom turned to walk away. Huffing like a bull ready to charge her target Britney's darkened eyes followed him out the locker bay.

Britney envisioned yanking Luna's hair hard enough to snap her head back and cause a searing jab of pain sharp enough to make her eyes roll back in her head. That vision was enough to steady her.

The thought of losing Tom to Luna Lopez wasn't something Britney Melville-Berkeley was going to stand for.

BETWEEN CLASSES, FOOTBALL PRACTICE, AND THE DRAMA club—an indulgence Tom enjoyed—he spent his spare time reading up on chemistry or biology. Tom wasn't knowledgeable in either subject. He was more of a sport erudite. Luckily, his father, the neurologist, had their home library well-stocked on both subjects. It was a demanding undertaking, but Tom's mind was too full of Luna, and he'd do anything to spend time with her.

Tom was thrilled when Luna agreed to meet twice weekly in the school library for tutoring. Unlike the long stretches of silence that dragged on when he was with Britney, the two hours with Luna flew by at the speed of light. There was always so much to say, so much to talk about with her. Everything Luna said was profound and meaningful—magical.

Luna was interesting and funny, intelligent, and sensible. More intriguing to Tom was her lack of interest in him as anything other than a friend. That Luna ignored his subtle advances every time drew him to her like a bee to pollen. Tom Grady, captain of the football team and Vaughan's heartthrob, had never had a woman not fawn over him. Not Luna, though. To her, Tom was just the boy who tutored her. For reasons he couldn't understand, that intrigued him.

That Luna never saw past the friendship that had blossomed between them made Tom appreciate her more he ever did Britney. Still, that Luna didn't see beyond their friendship as he did bothered Tom. Was it because he was four years older? Was it because he was from

Royal Hill? Most girls would jump at that, but his wealth and elite status didn't impress Luna much.

Tom felt a ripple of irritation at the thought that maybe Luna's rejection of him was due to his past involvement with Britney. Because if truth be told, Tom detested Britney, always had. He'd always found Britney a shallow, capricious, cold-hearted, spiteful bitch. Tom wouldn't have spent a second with her if it wasn't for her "special talent," or the fact Britney tamed his raging teenage hormones with her talent. Britney always left him wanting more, and how could he deny her the opportunity? No man would.

It stung that Luna didn't see beyond friendship, but Tom understood she wasn't like Brittney. He didn't expect Luna to fill Britney's shoes. Luna had integrity and self-respect. Luna was the type of girl a man took care of, not the other way around. If that was what Luna expected of him, it was what he'd give her even if it meant his needs went overlooked.

Tom was willing to sacrifice his needs, everything, for as long as it took Luna to see beyond their friendship into something deeper and meaningful. Not because Tom suspected Luna was the type to save herself for that special someone or because he wanted to be that someone, or even because she'd become a challenge for him. He'd make the sacrifice because he'd stumbled into love with Luna, and that feeling wasn't going away any time soon.

When Tom opened the door to the library, the smell of pressed paper and musty carpeting painted the air. The hum of fluorescent lights filled the hushed silence. Tom's mouth curved into the smile that always came to him when he saw Luna at their usual table. He'd never seen her face doused in makeup as Britney's always was. The wholesome, natural look suited her and him just fine.

"Hi," Tom said, walking up to Luna.

Luna aimed the Jade-green eyes studying the EVERY BOOK IS A NEW ADVENTURE poster up at Tom. "What do you think?" she asked of the giant worm wearing a cowboy hat surrounded by books.

"It's the library poster you've been working on?" Tom scraped the chair back, sat.

She tipped an imaginary cowboy hat. "Yessum."

"Looks great."

"Thank yee, pardner." Luna smiled when Tom cocked a brow. "I was hoping you wouldn't show up today." When his brow lowered into a frown, she rushed to correct, "Only because I'd rather have my teeth pulled than go over the periodic table."

Lips curved again, he sunk back into the depths of his chair. "We can jump straight into biology if you like."

Crossing her eyes, she said, "And how's that any better?"

"It's not the periodic table." Her hair was damp, as it always was on Tuesdays after swim class, and the scent of chlorine and soap drove a spike of lust into his gut. Tom was sure his body temperature shot up several degrees. He'd never before felt the intimate, passionate desire he felt for Luna at that instant. He liked it. "We better get started. I have football practice in an hour."

"You know we don't have to meet twice weekly. I mean, you have football and the drama club and…"

"You have your part-time job with your dad that keeps you tied up most nights and weekends. We're both busy." Tom wanted to reach out and tuck back the wet ropes of hair that tumbled onto her face.

"I feel guilty about taking up your time." Luna lowered her voice when the librarian cocked a warning brow.

"Honestly, it's no problem, and the tutoring is helping improve your marks, isn't it?" Tom lowered his voice when a shush came from the librarian, now stocking the bookshelves.

"My teachers said they've seen a ten-fold improvement in the past weeks."

"Then it's time well spent. Let's get started." Tom flipped the textbook open to the designated page and just then, caught Britney's piercing eyes descending on Luna from the doorway.

"Well, if it isn't the studious duo." Britney sashayed toward Tom.

"Very impressive, Britney," Tom's words netted a smile from Britney. "That's quite a big word for you, and kudos to you for being able to find your way to the library."

A cold, steely glint flashed in Britney's eyes. "What are you smiling at?" Britney's hiss made Luna cower in her seat. Like Dr. Jekyll and Mr. Hyde, Britney's eyes underwent an instant transformation, and she turned a coy gaze on Tom. "I haven't seen you around much."

"I've been busy." Tom batted away the hand Britney set on his shoulder.

Britney breathed for calm. "But, baby, I haven't seen you in so long, and I've missed you," Britney said, with doleful eyes, although as recently as thirty minutes earlier, she was crying out Bart's name in the back seat of his Mustang.

"I'll leave the two of you to talk." Luna rose to her feet.

"Don't go, please." Tom reached for Luna's hand. It was the first time they'd had any form of physical contact, and he heard nothing then, but the pounding of blood in his ears. "Britney and I have nothing to talk about."

Britney's focus on the hand that had touched every part of her body wrapped around Luna's, the red rage of fury stained her cheeks. Luna was destroying her perfect life. "I'm warning you, Tom."

"Slither back to your pit, Britney. Luna and I are busy right now."

The imagined wave of snickers from everyone in the library pounding inside Britney's head, her inner bitch took over. "Look at her, Tom. How could you possibly be attracted to a deplorable like her? And you think Miss Prissy-Virgin is going to take care of you? Virgin Mary wouldn't know where to start. This is your last warning, Tom. I walk out, and you'll never see me again."

"Is that a promise?"

The blow to Britney's ego came down like a wrecking ball. "You're going to be sorry, Tom." Britney's thunderous voice trembled with rage. "Oh shut up yourself," she snapped at the librarian. I won't let you get away with this." Her expression turning from anger to determination, she marched out of the library.

Luna slid her hand from Tom's hold. "She's really upset, Tom." As much as she enjoyed Britney being humiliated, Luna couldn't help but feel sorry for her.

"Don't let her fool you. Britney has no feelings, and she's under the diluted impression she owns everyone. I have nothing to say to her," Tom said, as his mind raced. Britney would strike back at him or worse, at Luna. "Let's get back to work. We have a lot to go over for your test tomorrow," Tom said, feeling the cold shiver snaking up his spine.

Chapter 3

WINTER ROLLED INTO spring and the colorful hues of the season were popping up everywhere. A dazzling green capped trees, and tulips, daffodils, and crocus bloomed overnight—as did Luna.

Like a beautiful butterfly breaking out of its cocoon, Luna's youthful face had refined, sharpened, and taken on the edge of young womanhood. Her boyish, pencil-thin figure softened with feminine curves. Her narrow waist now tapered above gently swelling hips, and her breasts had swelled and firmed. Her long scraggly hair was now a wave of midnight-black silk that spilled like a cascading waterfall.

Suddenly, Luna was all the buzz in school. The nerd-vine labeled her a babe, and their hearts thumped wildly for her. Talk in the jock's locker room—albeit behind Tom's back— shifted from Britney to Luna. Girls both envied and despised the geeky girl who was now a beauty to behold.

Britney's entourage made every attempt to disavow her from thinking she now shadowed Luna. Behind Britney's back, though, they couldn't help but wonder about Luna's sudden transformation. Was it her new diet regimen that gave her the enviable figure, homemade products she'd concocted that gave her the porcelain-smooth complexion and silky hair?

The questions abounded, the gossip spread faster than the common cold throughout the halls of Vaughan Secondary. Regardless of what was said, all agreed Luna's beauty rivaled Britney's.

For Britney, Luna was now officially, a ginormous pus-filled boil that needed lancing, and she was keeping score. Payback, Britney told herself often enough to calm fragile nerves, was going to be a vengeful bitch, bitch.

As if Britney hadn't endured enough, Mr. Peets handed Luna the lead role in Vaughan's version of *The Sound of Music* on a silver platter. The role of Maria, Britney believed, was tailor-made for her, not a simpleton like Luna. She, not Luna, had the innocence Julie Andrews brought to the screen.

Britney reasoned the fact she couldn't sing shouldn't have factored into Mr. Peets' decision because Britney Melville-Berkeley could give an academy worthy performance. She'd done just that in the lead role of Juliet in last year's stage play of *Romeo and Juliet*. Mr. Peets critiqued her performance as different, unforgettable, and words couldn't describe. Besides, she should be the one standing on stage next to Tom, who'd landed the role of the handsome Captain von Trapp. She and Tom, not Luna, were meant to be on the stage together.

What could Miss Simpleton possibly know about acting or singing? She was a janitor. All Luna knew to do was clean toilets.

The dagger of betrayal dug deep when word reached Britney Tom was instrumental in bringing Luna to Mr. Peets' attention. The blade sunk deeper into her back when Tiffany told Britney Mr. Peets had assigned Luna the role because she could sell out the five-hundred-seat auditorium through actual sales, not intimidation—as Britney had in past years.

"What difference does it make how the seats get filled?" Britney huffed. "What do you know, Tiffany?" She pressed when her friend went silent.

"Mr. Peets said that umm... Now, these are Mr. Peets' words, Britney, not mine." Tiffany swallowed. "'Luna's eye-catching beauty will draw in every pimple-faced boy in school. And her winning personality and talent will draw everyone else.'" Tiffany braced herself for Britney's outburst. To her surprise, it never came. Britney remained strangely quiet, huffing air through flaring nostrils like a riled pit bull. "Mr. Peets is using Luna, Britt. You see that, right?"

He thinks I can't put asses in the seats. "Uh-huh."

"Mr. Peets knows you're too good to be pimped out. Imagine you being ogled by a bunch of pimple-faced nerds." Tiffany offered to calm, a fuming Britney.

"That, my addle-minded friend, is an insightful comment."

"Aww, thanks, Britney." Feeling encouraged by the compliment Tiffany shared. "Rachel told Madison who told Jennifer who told my cousin Lizzie that Mr. Peets needs to fill the auditorium and he's using Luna to do it since she has a knack for attracting the nerd element." Tiffany smacked lips together after tracing them with Red-Is-Me lipstick. "And you know Vaughan is full of those brainy, nerdy types you wouldn't be caught dead with."

The comment shot Britney with a dose of confidence. "And how does Rachel know this?" Britney tore the

Maybelline tube from Tiffany's hand, slid it across her lips.

"Rachel got caught smoking in the girl's bathroom and had to serve an hour of detention outside the principal's office. I've told her a million times to stop that nasty habit. You know it's not good for…"

"Focus, Tiffany."

"Sorry, Britt. Rachel told Madison, who told…"

"I said focus, Tiffany."

"Yes, yes. Rachel listened in on a conversation between the secretaries. She heard them say that Mr. Peets needs to fill every seat in the auditorium, twice over. If he doesn't, he stands to lose the funding for his drama department, which is supposedly on the chopping block due to cutbacks. So, there goes his job. And…" Tiffany's mind wandered when she turned her attention to the stick of gum she found in her tote.

"Jesus, Tiffany, you have the attention span of a toddler."

"Sorry. Lizzie told me Mr. Peets is counting on Luna, bringing in every loser in school. He's hoping they, in turn, will bring their loser friends, and those losers will bring their friends and those losers…"

And I can't. "I get it, Tiffany."

"Mr. Peets seems to think every nerdy boy in school is so enamored with Luna none of them will miss out on seeing her. I have to admit even though she has no sense of style she's hot looking now. She makes those old, worn, faded jeans of hers, and that baggy sweatshirt, which is probably as old as my nana, look stylish. Could you imagine if she could afford a decent wardrobe? I bet you she'd be really…"

"Shut it, Tiffany," Britney choked out with a burning rage that made Tiffany pale.

"Sorry, Britt. My cousin Lizzie told me Luna can't act as good as you."

"She can't?" Britney sang out with a pleased tone.

"Nope. That's a nice color on you."

Britney eyed her lips on her locker door mirror. "It does look perfect on my perfect, full lips. What else did Lizzie say?"

"Sure, you keep the tube," Tiffany offered when Britney threw it into her purse. "Anyway, Lizzie told me Luna's like a total spaz on stage. She can't remember her lines, where to stand, or follow cues. Imagine not remembering your lines when you're the lead. But then she could be distracted by Mr. Peets. You know he's a hunk, all that tallness, dark shaggy hair, mysterious eyes, and tight butt. How I'd like to bite down on that thick lower lip. And for an old guy, 'cause he's gotta be at least thirty, he's tight and muscular."

"Jesus, Tiffany. Stop already with your fantasy of getting into Mr. Peets' pants. Tell me more about Luna."

"Lizzie told me most times Luna's completely lost on stage." Tiffany handed Britney the tissue she dug up from her tote. "Wipe your teeth, Britt."

"Good to hear. I'm guessing she's as talentless with her singing." Britney wiped the streaks of red lipstick off her teeth.

"It's gone. Apparently, she has a set of pipes on her that surprised everyone, including Luna herself. She can rock every song in the play." Tiffany ducked to avoid the hurled tube of Maybelline. "What? You asked."

TO BRITNEY'S DISAPPOINTMENT, the five-hundred-seat auditorium sold out in days. It made no difference to Britney that pimpled-faced have-not she wouldn't give the time of the day scooped the tickets up. The fact of the matter was Luna sold-out. She sold out opening night, and the additional two nights, Mr. Peets added.

Luna was becoming a bigger and bigger irritant to Britney.

From Mr. Peets' endless boasting of his lead star to the excited whispers in the hallways of Vaughan Secondary about the upcoming play, all Britney heard was praise for Luna. Even the principal, staff, and members of the school board jumped on the praise-Luna-bandwagon, and all Britney heard was Luna, Luna, Luna, at every turn

Aggravated and consumed with debilitating jealousy, Britney's need to thwart Luna's triumph became urgent. Her quick fix came in the form of a rumor she'd circulated via Tiffany. The seed planted in Tiffany's head that Luna was a bastard child adopted after having killed her mother at birth, Britney waited for her gossipy lapdog to tell her cousin Lizzie who would telegraph it to her network of tattlers.

To Britney's disappointment, the rumor didn't get much traction once Tom cornered her in the locker bay. "If you don't stop the vicious rumor I know you started I'll have to have a chat with your mother. Imagine mommy's shock to find out her little girl is straddling her teachers for grades. You didn't think I knew," he said when her eyes rounded with shock. "I wonder how daddy and granddaddy Melville will react to the news once it starts circulating at the club."

"You wouldn't dare?" Britney hissed through clenched teeth.

"Tempt me, Britney. You fix this now, and you leave Luna alone." Tom aimed fierce blue eyes at her that told her he meant every word.

Deciding there would be plenty of other opportunities to attack Luna once Tom graduated that spring and went off to university, Britney backed down. She cut off the rumor at the root.

That night, with anger lurking behind her eyes, Britney made a quick notation in her *Get The Bitch Back* journal. For now, the written word was how Britney nursed her deep-seated hatred of Luna. In time, those notes would help plot her vengeance.

Chapter 4

FROM THE WINGS, Luna poked her head from between the heavy damask curtains. Her stomach dropped away, and clammy beads of sweat formed on her brow when she saw the packed auditorium. There wasn't an empty seat. Until then, Luna assumed Mr. Peets' animated claims of the sold-out shows as forged enthusiasm to pump her fragile ego. How could she think otherwise? Because who'd pay good money to watch her fumble on stage and forget her lines?

Luna had seen the cast rolling exasperated eyes at every botched line. On two occasions, she'd heard them threaten to quit if she remained on. Each time, Mr. Peets had stood up for her telling the cast he'd replace them before he did Luna.

They were all there to see her fall flat on her face, Luna reasoned. Britney sent out a flyer telling everyone how inept she was. That was it, Luna thought. Luna wanted to run away and hide until it was all over. She would have if her feet didn't feel like blocks of cement.

Tom's words rattled in her head: One word, talent. You're that good a singer, Luna. I knew it the moment I heard you sing. It's why Mr. Peets won't get rid of you. And I'll say it again so that it will sink into that thick skull of yours. It's not because of me the show sold out. I was the lead in *Death of a Salesman* last year, and I didn't sell out. You've sold out four shows. You and you alone, Luna, are the answer to Mr. Peets' prayers.

They did nothing to lessen the hold Luna's stage fright was taking on her twisted nerves.

The cold fear stirring inside her made Luna's stomach roll with a fresh wave of nausea when the lights dimmed, and the curtains rolled open, her cue to step out on the stage. She could feel the beads of sweat forming thick on her forehead as the spotlight shone a circle of light center stage. The hushed silence in the auditorium made Luna's breath tremble out on little hitching gasps.

The seconds ticked away like elongated hours—tic, toc, tic, toc. As the notion of Luna stepping out on stage became a remote possibility, the rhythmic click of heels on wood echoed loud in the hushed auditorium when Mr. Peets pushed her out. All eyes followed Luna as she made that interminable walk to center stage. When Luna reached her mark, a collective sigh from the audience broke the deafening silence.

Luna's unblinking eyes were saucer wide, the fright on her face clear for everyone to see when the many, eager eyes locked on her with laser-like precision. Misreading their adoring gaze for scrutiny Luna's nerves snaked tighter in her stomach. What she wanted most then was to bolt off stage and out the front school doors.

The music from the orchestra rang out. Rim rod straight, arms stiffly by her side, Luna took a deep breath and opened her mouth. Fear, a ball in her throat, made the words catch, and her voice deserted her. She closed her mouth.

For the longest time, Luna remained motionless. Although the room was quiet, in Luna's mind, tongues wagged cruelly, the titter of laughter rang loud and came at her like hurled daggers. Luna even misread her parents' look of concern as scorn, but it wasn't until she caught sight of Britney's grin spreading from ear to ear that she tried to bolt from the stage. Her legs, however, felt heavier now, and they wouldn't budge. The tears wanted to come, but she sniffled them back when Tom stepped out from behind the shadows to stand next to her.

"Close your eyes, Luna. Forget about everything, and think of the music. Let it flow into you. Let your voice soar. You can do this, Luna," Tom whispered, clamping his hand tightly around hers.

And that was what Luna did when Mr. Peets cued the band to start again. Closing her eyes, Luna forced herself to relax and let the sound of the music flow into her heart, her soul. Vulnerability cast aside, the fisted hand loosened and began to tap against her leg to the beat. Taking a deep, steadying breath, Luna felt her body like a bird in flight soar with the music and lunged into *My Favorite Things*.

To Luna's surprise, the words poured note for note in perfect harmony with the music. Her confidence growing, her fear evaporated, the tension soaked out of her neck and back, and she belted out the second verse mesmerizing the audience with her powerful voice. Until then, no one, not Mr. Peets, not her parents, not Britney, not her classmates, not even Luna herself, imagined the depth of her voice or the talent she possessed.

Tom had. He knew the talent Luna possessed the moment he'd caught her demanding respect along with Aretha as she peeled potatoes at her kitchen sink. Arched in her kitchen doorway, Tom listened to Luna match

Aretha's bluesy voice, note for note, as it flowed from the transistor radio until she sensed his presence. At that moment, Tom vowed to help Luna harness the talent she didn't know she possessed.

The auditorium went still as Luna's voice, raw and real, powerful yet tender, full of passion soared. Listening intently, her stunned audience felt her breathy voice pulse in them.

Sarina's eyes welled with tears. Teo was more restrained, but anyone could see the pride for his baby girl in the dewy eyes that never left Luna. Everyone in the auditorium in awe of the soft-spoken girl no one imagined sang like an angel, applauded, and cheered. No one was happier for Luna than Tom, who'd never doubted her talent.

Watching as everyone rose to a standing ovation, Mr. Peets brought his hands together to join in the thunder of applause. "God love this girl. You know what this means, Bobby?" Running a hand over the boy's thick, dark hair, Mr. Peets looked down from his five-eleven height to the young boy filling the role of Kurt von Trapp. When Bobby shook his head, Mr. Peets enlightened him. "She's going to have me extending the play for days. This proves to the school board that my class is far from obsolete. Those pencil-pushing bastards thought they could get rid of me. Not today, Bobby, not today." His chest swelled, and the raven-black eyes curved wide in satisfaction.

Mr. Peets extended the play for an additional five days to accommodate those who'd heard of the fourteen-year-old singing sensation he'd discovered. Luna still couldn't act, often forgot her lines, and missed her cues, but none of that mattered. Fans flocked to Vaughan's auditorium in droves to hear the angelic voice.

Luna had found her calling, and all she wanted to do was sing.

MR. PEETS CLOSED THE DOOR TO the music room. "I'd be more than happy to introduce you, Luna, but you have to want this because it's going to take dedication, hard work, and lots of time. There will be long teaching sessions and practice, lots, and lots of practice."

Luna took a seat at her desk and watched the pendulum motion of Mr. Peets' arm as he scrubbed the blackboards clean of the day's lesson. "It's what I want, Mr. Peets."

Setting the eraser down, Mr. Peets turned and aimed eyes at Luna. "It has to be what you really want. Miss Jones is the best in the business and very much in demand, and I don't want to be wasting her time, Luna. She's a good friend, and at my request will take you on as a pupil at no charge." Mr. Peets promised Tom Luna wouldn't find out he was paying for all of her classes. Spare no expense on Luna's training, Tom told Mr. Peets.

"I won't be wasting her time. I want this more than I've wanted anything in my life," Luna said with conviction.

"I'll set up the audition," Mr. Peets said, sensing Luna was headed for great things.

Chapter 5

SECONDS INTO LUNA'S audition Miss Jones concurred with Mr. Peets' assessment. Luna was the next Aretha Franklin. When Luna hit that first high note, Miss Jones felt the hair on the back of her neck stand on end. She hadn't come across a voice like Luna's in a long time.

Luna could sing anything from rhythm blues to jazz and pop. Without a second thought, Miss Jones took on the challenge of shaping Luna into the musical sensation she was meant to be.

After school four times weekly, Luna made the one-hour trip to St. Joseph's Choir School, where Miss Jones taught music by day. Miss Jones immediately set Luna on a rigorous schedule. She taught Luna vocal cord control, breathing, diction, and proper pronunciation. Luna was excited to learn how to read and write music.

Luna absorbed everything like a sponge, and as Miss Jones demanded, she devoted all of her spare time to practice, practice, and more practice. Luna's voice dramatically improved, and the following spring, Mr. Peets automatically cast her in the lead role of *Grease*. In the role of Sandy, Luna's performance rivaled that of Olivia Newton-John's. The following spring, Mr. Peets asked Luna to step in as Maria in *West Side Story*. Audiences lapped it up like a perfect sunset on a spring day.

With each play, the ten scheduled dates sold out in hours, and the school's kitty became that much fatter. Because of Luna, Vaughan's gymnasium now had a new wood floor, the lab room boasted the latest equipment, and the pool was outfitted with colorful blue tiles. Even the teacher's lounge got an update.

Tom, who'd graduated two years earlier and was enrolled at the University of Toronto, didn't stand next to Luna as her leading man. However, at every performance, from the front row, Tom's smiling blue eyes were cast on Luna.

The following year, Luna's last year of high school, Mr. Peets put on a Christmas performance of *The Night Before Christmas* with lyrics written by Luna and music by Miss Jones. The play was a huge success and catapulted Mr. Peets and Miss Jones' careers. Every school knocked on their door, begging them to bring their talent to their stage.

With the taste of song and performing, Luna dreamed, breathed, and only thought singing. Luna's three years with Miss Jones, however, was up. Having taught Luna everything she knew, Miss Jones told Luna to consider enrolling in the Juilliard music program. Juilliard, Miss Jones told Luna, would give her the additional training to take her to the next level, and help launch her career.

"Talent like yours can't be learned, Luna. It's a special gift God bestowed you. Your talent can be enriched, not taught, and I've done that to the best of my ability. I truly hope you pursue Juilliard because you, Luna, have talent, and there's a great big world waiting for you." Miss Jones told her.

That left Luna thinking. Juilliard was an excellent school, but it was also in New York and costly. Luna's mind bouncing along with the subway car, she tossed the tuition number in her head. How was she to ask her parents for money they didn't have to spare? They were already working their fingers to the bone to make ends meet. How could she possibly expect them to work longer hours and have them sacrifice everything to pay for her dream?

Her dream was dead.

Exiting the subway, Luna bundled herself into her tweed coat for the four-block walk home. Above the moon was sliced in half, its glow sharp in a dark sky. A light snowfall blanketed everything in splendid white as a January wind chilled the air and nipped at Luna's face staining her cheeks red.

At the top of Sycamore Street, Luna stood and cast her eyes down the quiet tree-lined neighborhood. Rooftops clad in white stood out against the darkened sky. Lights twinkled from windows, and from number 222, Luna heard the faint sound of young Becky butchering Chopsticks on her grandmother's old piano. Why they forced that girl to play was something Luna never understood? But it was a part of the fabric of Sycamore Street and what made it a great place to live.

At the corner of Sycamore and Maple, Luna waited for the car to drive through. When the silver Porsche got close enough, she flashed a smile at the driver.

"Nice ride." Luna poked her head through the passenger window when it slid down.

"You like it?" Tom held Luna's gaze as she slid her hood off, and let her dark hair spill, a bouncy dark contrast to her cream-colored coat.

"I do. When did you get it?"

"Just picked it up. It's a present from my parents for deciding to study medicine, neurology in particular. Hop in. I'll drive you home." Tom clicked the passenger door lock open and watched Luna slide in.

"That's wonderful. I'm happy for you. Your father must be over the moon to have his son follow in his footsteps."

"I guess he is. I mean," his eyes rolled over the car. "But it wasn't him who steered me to study medicine. It was you." He shifted the car to drive.

"Me? How did I do that?"

"Tutoring you on chemistry and biology made me realize how much I liked the sciences." Tom breathed in the tropical scent of her shampoo and instantly felt the spike of lust to his gut. If she only knew how she touched him without trying.

"I'm glad one of us did." A slow smile spread over Luna's face.

At that, Tom let out a rolling laugh. "Do you have time to grab a burger?" As she was about to turn the invitation down, Tom said, "A quick one, at Johnny's."

His blue piercing gaze on her, Luna couldn't help but give in. "That's playing dirty. You know my weakness for Johnny's Burgers." She watched him pull over to the curb. "Why are you stopping?"

"Gotta let the ambulance behind get through."

"How's school? God, you gotta love this new car smell." Luna watched the red flashing lights, heard the scream of the siren roar by.

"It is addictive, and school's..." Tom's euphoric feeling at spending an hour with Luna quickly waned into unease when he saw the ambulance come to a dead stop, its wail dying off. "Luna, I think they're stopping at your house."

Her eyes followed Tom's, and both watched the brake lights die-off in front of 522 Sycamore—her house. Swallowing a lump of panic, Luna's gaze followed the paramedics roll the gurney into the house.

Her heart in her throat, Luna jumped out of the car. Sprinting toward her house, Luna's mind raced to the worse. Her ears pulsed to the beat of the fear tearing at her stomach. Drowning out all sound, she didn't hear Tom calling after her.

With the bitter cold air cutting into her skin like razor blades, Luna ran as fast as the icy sidewalk allowed. Breathless, she sprinted up the steps and into the house as Teo, pale as the haggard features of death, was set onto the gurney.

"Daddy. Daddy, are you okay?" Luna watched in terror as Teo gasped for breath.

"Please stand back, honey." The paramedic called out a series of incomprehensible instructions to his partner and Luna watched him inject and listen to his chest with a stethoscope. "We need to get your father to the hospital," he said, while he slipped the oxygen mask on Teo's face.

"Why are you taking him in? What's happened?" What's wrong with him? Daddy, daddy," Luna called after the paramedics as they wheeled Teo wrapped in a white blanket like a newborn child out to the ambulance.

Teo held out a hand for Luna. "I'll be fine, honey. These good people just need to look after me for a bit. While I'm gone, I want you and your mother to look after each other." The labored words said from a skewed mouth. He looked as if he'd aged ten years, and something was haunting in his expression. "Promise me, Luna."

Tears streaming down her cheeks, Tom watched Luna lift a small, delicate hand to smooth Teo's hair. "I promise, Daddy. Don't worry about anything. They're going to fix you up good."

"I love you, baby, and I'm so proud of you." Teo's words made something inside Luna break, and she fell against her mother.

"I love you too, Daddy." Luna turned despairing green eyes to the paramedic whose expression told her he'd seen this scene played out far too often. "He's going to be okay, right?"

"We'll do everything we can for your father, honey."

Luna ran alongside the gurney as they wheeled Tom down the snow-covered walkway, past the once colorful impatiens now blanketed white. As Teo was loaded into the ambulance, Luna thought she heard him say forgive me, Luna.

They were the last words Teo said to his daughter.

Chapter 6

THE DOCTOR SAID it was the heart attack that followed the stroke that took Teo's life at the age of forty-one.

Luna's world turned cold and dark that day.

She'd never see her father again. She'd never talk to him or see his smiling face. Cradled in her mother's arms, Luna cried as the blinding ache ripped through her.

At her father's funeral, Luna sang *Ave Maria,* Teo's favorite hymn. The words poured out with a heartfelt passion that rolled over in sorrowful waves moving everyone to tears until there wasn't a dry eye in the church. Tom Grady, Miss Jones, and even Mr. Peets shed tears along with Luna not solely, because the occasion called for it, but because Luna's voice touched them deeply.

"WHAT'S TO BECOME OF US NOW, mom?" Luna watched her mother add diced carrots and potatoes in the pan alongside the chicken. Her mother cooked when stressed, and in the past few days, it was all she'd done.

"It's going to be all right, honey. It'll take time to get used to your father not being here, but we'll be fine." Sarina opened the oven door, set the pan on the middle rack, and turned the dial to three-fifty.

"Of course we will be," Luna said, to soothe her mother because she sensed the ache of loss when she looked over at the empty chair beside her would never go away.

"Teo would want us to get on with our lives." Sarina returned unused vegetables to the refrigerator, the salt and pepper shakers to the pantry then wiped the countertop clean. Needing more time to compose her thoughts, she ran the dishcloth under running water for longer than necessary, before wringing it dry and hanging it on the oven door handle. Taking a calming breath, Sarina turned to Luna, "I'm going to quit my job at Dr. Berkeley's and take over the company." Sarina kept her focus on her daughter's face to gauge her reaction.

"Mom, what do you know about running dad's cleaning business?"

"Nothing, but I've worked alongside your father since he started the business." Sarina raised a hand to stop Luna when she began to speak. "I know it was only part-time, and I was only a cleaner, but he shared everything he did, his every thought, with me."

Luna lifted a brow. "It's not as simple as that, and there's Jenn, Consuelo, and Stella to consider."

"The girls have been with your father forever. They know the routine, and they're trustworthy, and require little supervision." Sarina stopped for a moment. "That business is our main source of income. I want to give it a shot, honey, even though I'll be running it as your father says 'by the seat of my rear end.'" The comment netted the first smile Sarina had seen on her daughter's face in weeks. "But I need to do this. The business does well and earns more than I do with Dr. Berkeley. Grant it, it'll now be our only source of income, so we'll just be getting by, but it makes logical sense I take it over."

Luna's eyes focused picked at the crack on the Formica table for some time before looking up to her mother. "Wouldn't it be more profitable to sell the business?"

"Your father worked so hard to build it up. He put his blood, sweat, and tears into it, seven-day a week. I know it's not a thriving conglomerate, but it's his … was his…"

Luna stopped her mother there. "We'll make it work," she said, understanding this was an emotional decision, one that couldn't be swayed by logic. Juilliard would have to wait for now.

"Thank you, honey. If it doesn't work out, we'll figure something out. I'm a trained medical secretary with years of experience. I can find a job anytime." Sarina's hand curled over Luna's to give a squeeze of reassurance.

"All right, we'll give it a go. I'll help you after school and on weekends."

"No, you won't. I'll manage on my own. I want you to continue with your singing lessons."

"I only have a couple of weeks left with Miss Jones. I'm sure she won't mind ending the sessions now." She lied. "Right now, we need to stick together if we're going to make this work."

Luna was right. Still, it broke Sarina's heart to have her daughter postpone her singing lessons. "As soon as we get our lives back on track, you're going back to Miss Jones."

Shuffling to her feet, Luna leaned down to kiss her mother on the cheek. "Of course I will," she said, knowing Juilliard had just become a long lost dream.

Chapter 7

WHEN THE LAST student said her teary goodbye to Mr. Peets, he dabbed at his dewy eyes before crossing the music room to Luna. "Year after year, it gets harder to see my students move on. I can only hope I had some influence, however minor, in molding their minds, their lives." After a beat, he said, "I'm going to miss you, Luna."

"Me too," Luna said because telling him how much she was going to miss him made her an emotional wreck. She'd become very fond of Mr. Peets. How could she not? He'd helped her find herself.

"What are your plans now that you've graduated?"

Luna kept her gaze focused on the blue jay that landed on the window ledge. Majestic in his lavender-blue plumage, he eyed his surroundings, looking as lost as she felt. "I'm taking over my father's business from my mother."

Mr. Peets eased a hip onto the corner of his desk. "I'm talking after the summer break. I know Miss Jones suggested you consider enrolling at Juilliard."

"I'm taking over my father's failing business … indefinitely."

So that was what had been bothering her, he thought. In the past few weeks, he'd watched the joy in Luna's eyes replaced by a troubling sadness, which he'd attributed to her father's death. "You're sure about your decision because I can still help you secure a scholarship. I'm certain many of the schools with music programs would love to have you, Luna. I'd hate to see you throw your talent by the curbside."

Biting down on her bottom lip, she let herself dream for a moment. "I appreciate the offer, Mr. Peets, but my mother is struggling with the business. I need to take it over to try to salvage what's left of it before it gets to the point of having to declare bankruptcy. It's what I have to do. The business is our only source of income right now and…"

"You don't need to explain, Luna." Mr. Peets jumped in to ease her humiliation. "Sometimes, life forces you to take a detour. Looking after yourself and your mother is what's important right now. Once you get past this blip in your life, and you will, talk to me. My offer will be available to you when you're ready," he offered with confidence, knowing he could rely on Tom's backing. Where Luna was involved, Tom could never say no.

Luna looked up at Mr. Peets. Words couldn't express how grateful she was to him. "I … I'm so grateful to you, Mr. Peets, for everything."

"It's me who's grateful to you, Luna. You did so much for this school, and me and Mrs. Jones. You know offers are still coming in, but we're both staying put. We love our students and schools too much. It's rare to run into a student like you who makes you realize you didn't go astray for choosing teaching as your career. It's been an absolute pleasure to have you in my class, Luna. I wish you success and happiness, and I know one day I will see your name on the marquis."

"I hope so, Mr. Peets."

EARS OUTSIDE THE CLASSROOM LISTENED IN on Mr. Peets and Luna's conversation. Smiling, she congratulated herself on how well her plan had worked. Destroying Luna's life was Brittney's life mission, and for once, she was steps ahead of Luna Lopez, the man-stealing bitch.

Brittney never imagined revenge could feel this good, and she decided then, this was only the beginning.

Luna couldn't see the fury, or the threat burning in Brittney's eyes or what was to come.

Chapter 8

THE DAY AFTER graduation Luna took over Maid For You and registered for night school. She banked on the six-month business management course to help turn her failing business around. Since her mother took over the company, it went from mildly profitable to a money-losing business due to the rumor their employees were caught stealing. As much denial as her mother put out, she couldn't stop tongues from cruelly wagging or the gossip from spreading like wildfire on dry brush around Royal Hill. Within weeks, they'd lost over half their exclusive and best-paying clients.

Shortly after Luna taking over, Sarina secured a position with Dr. Henry Grady. Although it was at Tom's insistence, his father, hire Sarina as his medical secretary, Luna, and her mother would never know.

Work, night school, and what little singing Luna managed to get in with her church choir, consumed her days. It left Luna no time for a personal life. Her days were filled with whatever needed to be done for the business. Overnight she'd become manager-slash-receptionist-slash-salesperson-slash-accountant-slash-cleaner. Saturday and Sunday were spent enlisting new business, which, due to the rumor, became had become more difficult to secure.

Since laying off her staff, the nights Luna wasn't in night school, she was out on cleaning jobs until dawn.

The work was mind-numbingly dull, tiring, and physically demanding at times, but it was what she had to do to avoid bankruptcy and losing their home.

Luna's heart thudded wildly when at the end of the summer, finishing her cleaning job at *The Stags Head*, Patrick O'Malley, offered her a singing gig. Having put her singing on the backburner, Luna jumped at the offer of the forty-minute Saturday spots in exchange for a twice-weekly cleaning service. Having seen Luna's last two plays, Patrick was counting on her drawing the crowds to his pub.

Luna's performance before the drunk, rowdy, pub's crowd was a far cry from Vaughan's stage. After the second brawl, when Luna was nearly hit with a flying Smithwick's bottle, she walked off the stage and out of The Stags Head for good.

The singing gigs that followed weren't any better, and a rude awakening. Luna never expected to face so much competition for the few gigs going, but worse, she never expected to be asked to audition on her back. Outrage at the notion of demeaning herself was the catalyst for driving her fist straight into handsy Jasper Sloan—the owner of Berlin's Nightclub. The satisfaction Luna felt when Jasper reached to give her butt a suggestive squeeze, and she got that fisted punch to his stomach put a smile on her face for days.

That incident opened Luna's eyes to a world she didn't know existed or liked.

The one good constant in Luna's life was Tom. Luna could count on Tom to meet her for a quick coffee at The Brewed Bean whenever she needed to vent. Although Tom was more than happy to lend a friendly listening ear, he hoped more would come out of their encounters, but after each talk, Luna's smile was faultless in its politeness when she hugged and thanked him for being such a wonderful friend. Each time Tom watched Luna leave the cafe, he convinced himself the next time they met, he'd tell her how he felt.

That moment never came to pass.

AT THE BLINK OF AN EYE, summer faded into fall. Trees bore the vibrant gold and crimson hues of autumn, and a fall chill nipped the air as Luna made her way home. Pulling the dated, wood-paneled station wagon into her driveway, Luna caught sight of Tom perched on her porch steps.

His honey-blonde hair tumbled in the cold wind, his eyes were a brilliant blue, and the wide mouth was curved into a warm smile. In tight-fitting Armani jeans and a denim Sherpa jacket, he looked as if he was about to ride out on his stallion in a blaze of glory. For the first time since she'd known Tom, Luna couldn't help but stare.

He looked beautiful and delectably male, Luna thought. Why hadn't she seen it until now?

Seeing him for the first time as a man, not as the friend she turned to for a listening ear, Luna realized he was a head-turner. Suddenly, it dawned on her why no woman could keep her eyes off him when they were out. It wasn't because she was a Sycamorian and he a Royal hill. It was because he was gorgeous.

How blind was she not to realize this until now?

Taking a closer study of Tom, Luna saw him, as she never had before. Luna saw beyond the kind, caring, loving friend with the charming sincerity. It was why she'd grown to love Tom dearly and why he was her best friend.

"Hi," Luna called out, stepping out of the car.

"Hi, back." Tom rose to his six-foot frame, stuck his hands in his jeans pockets. It was the safest place for them when he was around Luna.

"I thought you'd be in school." Luna opened the hatch door, reached in for the grocery bags.

"Took half-day off." Tom sprang to her side and reached for the bags in her hands.

"Thank you. I'm sorry I haven't had much time to meet up for coffee these past few days."

"No need for apologies. I know you're busy."

For one tempting moment, Luna thought of explaining why she'd turned down every one of his invitations, but instead said, "Are you free to join my mother and me for dinner? It'll be a quick one, though. I have to get to Vaughan Secondary by eight. Mr. Peets managed to talk the board into taking me on for their janitorial services. At least it'll give us some time for you to catch me up on what's been going on in your life. Talking, unfortunately, is a luxury I don't have much time for these days." Luna picked up the last bag, bumped the door shut with her butt.

"Thanks for the invitation, but I was hoping to treat you to dinner." Tom followed her up the porch steps.

"As much as I'd love to join you for dinner and have someone wait on me hand-in-foot, I don't have enough time to doll myself up or have the two hours an eat-out dinner will take." Luna stabbed the key in the door lock, threw it open. "I'm sorry. I know it sounds as if I'm constantly turning you down, but I'm not. Life's just … hectic for me right now."

Long-lashed adoring eyes fixed on her. In an oversized flannel sweater and faded jeans, she looked perfect. "You look great as you are."

"It's sweet of you to say, but you and I know I look a mess. What's all this?" Luna asked when she caught sight of the dining room table set for two.

"Happy eighteenth birthday." Tom sang out.

Surprise flashed in Luna's eyes. "Jesus, I've forgotten it's my birthday today."

Tom leaned in to peck Luna on the cheek. A tug, a pull, an unabashed arousal assaulted him when the scent of her soap slid into him. "Your mother is taking your job over tonight, and she let me take over your house so I could set up for the surprise birthday dinner. Although, I'll have to confess that it was Trudy who did all this."

"Trudy?"

"This is Trudy." Tom introduce when on hearing her name the short, plump woman with the heat flushed face stepped into the dining room. "She's been our trusted cook since I was a kid. She volunteered to help me with this because she knows how useless I am in the kitchen, and because I'm crazy in love with her." He kissed Trudy on the cheek.

"It's more like you're in love with my cooking." Trudy's tone was reproving, but the smile on her face told Luna there was mutual love. "Let me take that from you, honey." Hands with thick sausage fingers reached for the shopping bag in Luna's arm. "You two settle in. Dinner will be served shortly," she said, disappearing into the kitchen before Luna could thank her.

"I don't know what to say, Tom." Luna took the chair Tom scraped back for her.

Red calla lilies spilled from the Waterford vase at the center of the table covered in white linen. Candles on matching holders burned. Silverware and Baccarat glassware complemented the Wedgewood china her mother brought out for special occasions.

"You like it. I wasn't sure how…"

Luna's unexpected peck on the cheek silenced Tom. The warmth of her breath on his skin, the feeling of her soft lips pressing against his cheek, made her nerves spark. "It's lovely. Thank you."

"You're welcome." Tom helped her back down to her seat with old-fashioned gallantry that made Luna feel special.

Trudy served a delectable meal of Cobb salad topped with a delicious dressing that tantalized Luna's taste buds. A creamy, mushroom risotto came next, and after that, they feasted on lobster and shrimp the size of Luna's hand. For dessert, Trudy brought out a flambéed, Crêpe Suzette.

Throughout the meal, they caught each other up. Tom was starting his undergraduate program. Then, he was off to medical school. He never told her he'd declined to attend Harvard and Stanford and enrolled at the University of Toronto to stay close to her.

Luna told Tom she was two months away from completing her business course. "I've learned basic accounting and business administration, which has helped to resurrect my dad's business. I didn't want to say anything, but we were days from bankruptcy when I took it over. It's why I haven't had much time to stop and smell the roses. I had to focus all my time and energy on turning the business around. If the business went under, we stood to lose everything, including this house," she confided for the first time.

"I'm sorry, Luna. I wished you would have said something." Tom's hand fisted under the table tight enough to drive nails into his palm.

Tom debated telling Luna what he knew. In the end, he decided not to tell her it was Britney who'd started the rumor her cleaners had stolen valuable jewelry from her mother. What would be the benefit in Luna knowing Britney's mother stoked the rumor by verifying her daughter's story when the calls flooded in?

Tom held back the fact he'd put a stop to the rumor by agreeing to sit through the most mind-numbingly dull dinner with Britney in exchange for her and her mother's silence. How much inane warbling about the perfect Britney or the ideal hair, shoes, and outfit could one man take? To add to Tom's nightmare, he couldn't rid himself of Britney afterward and was forced to sit through several more mindless dinners when she threatened to ignite the rumor all over again.

Only until Tom threatened to tell Britney's mother about her abortions was he able to get control of the situation. He was shocked when the concocted comment, uttered out of sheer frustration, got Britney's attention, and her unreasonable demands to be with him day-and-night came to a screeching halt. It had been a draining, soul-sucking three weeks, but he'd endured it for Luna's sake.

"I'm sorry, Luna. I wasn't aware things were so bad."

"You have nothing to be sorry about. It wasn't your fault. Anyway, even after the rumor got traction, which by the way, is false, I managed to keep the business afloat. I've even been able to rehire the employees I laid off." Luna flicked hazel eyes to Trudy, who wobbled into the dining room. "That was the best meal I've ever had. Just don't tell my mom I said that." Luna's comment netted her a smile from the buxom Trudy, who moved to clear the table. "Please, you've already done more than enough. I'll clean this up later."

"No, my darling, the birthday girl is not supposed to lift a finger on her special day. I'll take care of this. You kids take your coffee and settle in the living room. This will only take me a few minutes, and I'll be on my way."

Tom leaned down to Trudy's five-foot frame to peck a warm cheek. "Thank you. You're an angel," he said with a wink then, led Luna into the living room.

"What about your singing?" Tom asked when he settled on the sofa next to her.

"Looks like it's going to pour soon," Luna said, looking out the window as the first drops of rain pattered in a soothing drumming.

"What about your singing, Luna?" Tom repeated.

"I joined the choir at my church."

"A church choir?" Tom huffed an exasperated breath at the unfairness of life. "That's not enough, Luna. You have a gift that needs harnessing. You have the making of a great singer. I'd hate for you to let that talent go to waste."

That Luna was expected to give up on her dream because she wasn't blessed with the means to pursue it made Tom's blood boil. When he thought of how his friends selfishly threw money away on nonsensical, materialistic things, his jaw clenched. It wasn't fair.

Tom's eyes locked on hers. "Let me help you, Luna. Let me offer you the money you need for your business so you'll have more time to devote to your craft."

The unexpected offer stunned and touched her deeply. It was why she loved him. "You know you're the best friend I have, and I love you, dearly, but I can't take your money."

"Take it as a loan. I'll charge you loan shark rates if that's what it will take for you to accept. I don't want you to give up on your dream."

Luna smiled at that. "I'd never dream of letting something as ordinary as money come between our friendship. I treasure it too much." For a moment, there was only the sound of rain drumming outside the living room window. "Have you met anyone at uni?"

Knowing she meant the question as a diversion, he entertained it. "I've met lots of people."

She jabbed an elbow to his ribs. "You know what I mean. Have you met anyone ... special?"

"I've gone out on a few dates." Tom wanted to touch her. He couldn't remember not wanting to. "They didn't really go anywhere." None of those women measured up to you.

"I'm sorry."

"Don't be. They just weren't," you, "what I'm looking for."

Whether the soothing sound of the pattering rain against the window lent a romantic feel to the room or because of the way his loving eyes descended on her,

Luna thought of kissing Tom. Maybe, just maybe, the connection would stir the feelings he craved from her.

Raising her hand to his face, Tom felt Luna's thumb tracing the contours of his cheek. The simple gesture solidified something real in him, and he felt the hot punch of emotion bubble up in him. The deepening blue eyes expected so much from her, emotions she didn't feel, and it seemed wise to pull away.

Tom's hand whipped up to snag her hand. "Don't, Luna."

"I don't want to hurt you, Tom."

He trailed a finger down her cheek so tenderly, so lovingly, her heart tripped. "You never could. I lo..."

Luna rushed to press fingers to his lips to stop him from saying what she couldn't say in return. For a long silent moment, Tom held Luna's eyes. The expression in them tugged at her, and Luna leaned in to him. The anticipation had his heart pounding wildly. He'd dreamed of this moment since the day he'd set eyes on her.

When Luna's lips met his, she filled him with sensations and emotions he never imagined would feel this good. Luna reached deep into him, weakened something in him no other woman had. Her lips were soft, her breath warm, her mouth fit perfectly with his as he imagined it would.

The kiss became primal and desperate, demanding, and ardent. Both would surely remember the jolt from that staggering first kiss forever. He, because she stirred emotions, he'd been waiting to unleash for so long. She, because her first kiss was a bittersweet experience.

The urgent need in him when his tongue slid inside her mouth was a wonderful shock to her system. Tom unleashed a hunger in Luna that begged for the touch of a man, and she couldn't stop herself. Something that felt this good couldn't be wrong, she reasoned.

Luna's voice was a feline purr when Tom's unrepentant male scent slid into her and set off sparks of fire under her skin. Feeling a repressed ache to be touched, pulling deep in her, Luna crushed her mouth to his with desperate need. Her blood hummed in her head when his tongue parted her lips to search for hers. To her surprise, when their tongues came together, they moved in a fiery choreographed dance, tangling, tasting.

Lust, need, and want surged in unison in Luna. Knowing this was wrong, she damned herself, but the heat in her belly, the rawness of the kiss clouded her mind, and against her better judgment, she sunk deeper into the kiss. When she did, Tom's heart felt as if it burst from his chest, and he couldn't contain himself. Heat, want, and need taking hold of him, his hands fisted in her hair. Pulling her in, his mouth took hers in quick, to ravage.

His heated kiss was untamed, frenzied before it became tender and loving. His mouth on hers was quick, experienced, as full of energy as the bolt of lightning cutting the sky. Tom gave and gave, and took little.

The assault on her system left her gasping for breath. When Luna's moans demanded more from him, his heart beat with the rhythm of love. His fingers tangled in the thick, silky hair as soft as a butterfly's wing. Pulling her in, he filled himself with its sweet floral scent. "I've wanted you for so long."

Why, why did he have to say that?

She thought of pulling away, but the tremors of pleasure gloriously pulsing through her when he nibbled his way down the hollow of her neck made it impossible. Her breath choking back the whimpers, for one heated, reckless moment, she murmured his name. The sound of his name on her lips made love held so long in his heart bloom. Emotions he'd buried for so long rose in him, and he clung harder to her.

He'd waited so long, so very long for this. He hadn't touched another woman since she'd come into his life. He hadn't wanted anyone but her. "I love you, Luna. I have for so long," he whispered, taking her hand and laying it on his heart.

There was love true and real in the eyes swimming in emotion, Luna thought, and a guilty breath backed up in her lungs. "Tom, this is a mistake, a terrible mistake."

For one sweaty, smoldering, pleasure spearing moment, she'd been willing to put her physical needs ahead of everything and end up in bed with him. She was ready to destroy their friendship because sex without love was undoubtedly going to end up in tears—his.

Tom shook his head. "This isn't a mistake."

"You're my best friend. I can't do this to you."

Tom's eyes, calm, accepting met hers. "I have enough love for the two of us, Luna." He brushed his lips to hers to silence her. "I understand. I do. I just love you so much. I have since ... forever."

"I know, Tom. It's why I can't..."

"Be with me, Luna." Tom cupped her face with his hands when she started to turn away. "Please, Luna."

This is so wrong, she thought. It won't end up well, she told herself.

But when his mouth came down to nip on her bottom lip and trailed a lazy line of kisses down her neck, he sent the blood roaring in her brain like the thunder outside. With the fierce pull of desire striking her hard, her mind clouded, and all she could think about was quelling her needs. Taking a steadying breath, Luna got to her feet, offered her hand. When he took it, she led him upstairs.

In her tiny bedroom surrounded with the stuffed bears, the cotton candy pink-washed walls on the princess bed of her youth Luna gave herself to Tom. He was her first, and although she'd be clumsy, she knew he wouldn't be, nor would he care. Luna knew Tom would lovingly and tenderly guide her and make the experience one she'd never forget.

But for the sound of the drops of rain splatting on the rooftop, the house was asleep. His eyes on her, he slipped her sweater over her head and her jeans down her hips. Her body was golden with generous curves. The breasts thaw swelled over the white bra were firm. She wore simple white, cotton underwear, and Tom found it incredibly sexy.

"God, you're so beautiful."

"I'm not. I'm too skinny and simple and…"

He crushed his mouth to hers then, scooping her in his arms, lay her on the bed. "You're beautiful and perfect to me, and I want to love you, Luna," he said, and never leaving her eyes, undressed. His body was long, lean, athletic, so distinctly male. Straddling her, Tom looked into her eyes, "Touch me, Luna."

Slowly, she let her hands trace the muscular arms, the broad shoulders until they came to rest on his chest. "You're very, ummm, tight," she mumbled.

Smiling, he snapped her bra off, took his mouth and tongue over Luna's body, making her heart leap to her throat. As if handling a priceless work of art, Tom tenderly staked his claim over every inch of her untouched body. His mouth nibbled on Luna's neck and shoulders, and slowly, so slowly, he made his way down to her breasts. Filling his mouth with them, Tom claimed that which no other man had touched before him.

She was his. His. The thought thrilled him.

His tongue slid over the top of her breasts, laving her nipples before taking them between his teeth and detonating a healthy ripple of lust through Luna that raced straight to her loins.

Jesus! The man was talented. She screamed in her head.

When his mouth and tongue explored and skimmed the curves of her body, Tom made every nerve in her throb to a fantastic savage beat, and Luna begged for more. But it wasn't until she felt the erotic slide of his tongue over her thighs that she let her self-control slip, and she let out a long, beautiful cry of pleasure.

Something that felt that good couldn't be so wrong was the only thought rolling through her muddled brain.

"I'm going to make you soar like you never have," he whispered when he slipped his fingers under the cotton panties and into the heat.

She was wet, and he let his fingers slide until he built the pleasure that sent incredible, shocking waves through her entire body, sending her pulse racing. Her first orgasm burst like a long-dormant eruption along with the cries that filled the silence of the room.

"I'm not done yet."

"God, I hope not," she whispered, feeling him slide her panties down her hips and off her.

Wave after wave of satisfying sensations rushed at her when his tongue trailed up her thigh and into the wet heat to feast.

Her nails digging deep into his back, she bowed when the pressure coiled in her, tighter and tighter. Her eyes rolling to the back of her head, she bowed higher when the urge for release swelled quick and hard. She wanted her first time to be filled with love and shared emotions. Now, as sensations, incredible jolts of raw pleasure ruled her needy body, none of that mattered. Tom brought to light an aching loneliness she'd masked behind a rushed life, and it needed placating.

And God, he was good at placating.

Crying out his name on a choked moan, Luna bucked and soared higher as he drove orgasm after glorious orgasm in her and left her body trembling and purring in delight.

Taking her mouth into a deep kiss, he pressed his fully aroused body to hers. "I want to be inside you, Luna."

She, too, wanted him inside her. She wanted to know what it felt like to have him plunge in and out of her. She wanted him to come inside her in the throes of passion. She watched the smile on his face bloom when she opened up to him.

Forgive my selfishness.

Loving eyes never leaving hers, tenderly, lovingly, he slipped inside her. Moving slowly, careful not to hurt her, he possessed. When she rose and fell with him, his love for her surged. The euphoria he felt was one that lifted him to heights he never knew possible.

Moonlight streaming through the window, turning the room in shadows, and rain pattering mercilessly on the rooftop, Tom murmured soft, dreamy words to her. Ripe for release, the emotions he'd bottled up inside for months poured out him. Swamped with love, crying out her name, he filled her.

She was his. His.

An hour later, Luna's mind was still racing with guilt, but her sex-starved body hungered for his skilled touch, and she reached over for Tom.

Thrilled she did, Tom took her into a deep, loving kiss before moving to explore the body he now thought as his, with hands, mouth, and tongue.

As with the first time he made love with her, Tom was tender, loving, and gentle. Taking care of her needs, making her body hum under his touch, Tom prolonged his pleasure to make her body float.

He skimmed tongue and mouth over sumptuous curves. His hungry mouth explored, making her cry out with the delicious pleasure he set off in her. Pleasing her was all he wanted to do, and did just that until her body shuddered with maddening bursts of sensations.

Loving her, pleasing her as he had tonight was all he wanted to do, and only until he made her fly again and again did he thrust himself hard to fill her.

Chapter 9

LUNA MOVED BRISKLY around the offices of Wick Insurance, emptying wastebaskets, wiping desktops, but her mind was on Tom. Days after their encounter, the guilt smothered Luna like a soaked towel, and she declined to take or return any of Tom's calls. She'd used Tom to satisfy her physical needs, and she couldn't in good conscious talk to him?

Running the vacuuming over gray carpet, Luna's mind set off on a tangent of self-analysis. She was a soulless, self-centered woman. She'd led Tom on knowing damn well she could never return the emotions he desperately sought.

But oh, God, the sex was incredible. She couldn't help reliving the electrifying feeling of his hands, his mouth, and his tongue as they explored her body. The man was skilled.

Not that she knew the difference between a skilled and unskilled lover. All she knew was how amazing her body felt during and afterward—long, long afterward.

Running shoes treading over the clean carpet, Luna walked into the meeting room. She sighed at the messy remnants of what she perceived to have been a late meeting. Reaching for a black garbage bag, Luna thought that underneath the fancy education and fancy clothes, people were as common as they came. Mechanically filling the bag with paper plates, pizza boxes, empty soda cans, and beer bottles, Luna's mind wandered to thoughts of their lovemaking. She couldn't help reliving the electrifying feeling of his hands, his mouth, and his tongue as they explored her body.

She never imagined those large, manly hands could be so graceful in touch and expert on talent. Luna never dreamed his mouth was as tasty as it was or that it could do what it had and drive her to utter the throaty moans that at first, she was too shy to sound out. Was she glad when Tom encouraged her to let him know she was enjoying what he was doing to her, and she let out the piercing cries of pure animal lust bubbling inside her. Tom awakened her dormant body, and she now craved the staggering tsunami of pleasure she derived from his touch.

"How could something that felt that good, be so wrong?" Luna asked her reflection in the glass window, she wiped down with Windex when the knot in her stomach wound tighter.

Tom made love to her, true and real love, and she'd let him, although she knew she wouldn't be able to return the emotions he wanted from her. Luna hadn't known such tenderness could coexist with such detachment.

With a tug of guilt, she reached for the overflowing ashtray, dumped its contents, and wiped it clean. "How could I do this to Tom? He's my best friend. You're not supposed to hurt your friends."

She was going to hell.

And still, Luna couldn't shake thoughts of their night together. At every turn, she saw the look of love on Tom's face when he'd kissed her and touched her with such tenderness. The loving words he'd whispered to her with such deep emotion rolled in her head. She tasted his kisses, felt his touch, and the culmination of all the emotions he'd bottled up inside for years as they'd burst out when he slid inside her. Luna saw the deep-seated emotions in his eyes when he drove himself in and out of her.

Luna felt sick to her stomach at the thought of how she'd used Tom, but she couldn't stop thinking about the waves of sensation that washed through when he brought her to the fantastic heights she hadn't known existed. Luna's blood flamed at the thought of it. God, she wanted him.

She was getting that much closer to the portal of hell.

Why couldn't Tom want mindless sex? She'd be fine with that. Why did Tom need to bring emotion into it?

Everything was as complicated as Luna imagined it would become when they crossed the line from friendship into sex. Tom would inevitably expect the relationship between them to blossom, and she had no one to blame but herself.

Nothing was ever going to be the same between them, and it was her fault.

This was all on her because all she'd thought of was to satisfy her needs. She not only didn't turn Tom away, but she'd reached out to him a second and a third time. She would have turned to Tom again if her mother weren't due to come home.

Luna heard the creaking doors of hell slide open for her arrival.

Luna knew Tom was in love with her. She'd known it since months after their so-called tripped encounter. Luna knew Tom wanted more than friendship, but her heart didn't, and she'd vowed never to bring sex into their friendship. She'd never forgive herself if she lost Tom's friendship or hurt him.

Reaching for the Lysol, Luna asked herself what she was thinking when she took Tom to her bed.

Tom deserved better, she thought aimlessly pouring Lysol into the bucket of water. Tom was a good man. He deserved to be loved, she told herself wringing the mop dry. Until her body stopped craving for his touch to quell the sexual heat he'd unearthed in her, she'd avoid him. Running the Lysol scented mop across the toilet floor, she concluded it was the best option because she couldn't trust herself to be around him and not let him touch her.

It had been days since Luna had seen Tom, and God knew she'd tried to put him out of her mind. Even now, as she cleaned toilets visions of Tom's long, firm body, his sweat-dampened skin pressing against hers came at Luna. They always did at the most inopportune times, and they always made her damp.

Over the smell of bleach, Tom's scent inexplicably filtered into her. Thoughts of his naked body on top of her flashed in her mind. The sensation of heated flesh pressed to heated flesh, wildly clamoring, made the fierce pull of need come at her. When it did, Luna felt the ache of loneliness.

She could find herself another lover, but she concluded Tom's lovemaking elevated the sensation to the heightened level she'd experienced because of his feelings for her. She felt the quick churn of excitement in her gut.

She was going to hell on the proverbial handbasket, Luna thought, picking up the closest phone to her and dialing Tom's number.

Chapter 10

OUTSIDE SARINA'S FOURTH-FLOOR, office patients wheeled on gurneys whined crankily, doctors and nurses going about their daily routine scurried. Sarina was oblivious to it all as her thoughts drifted to Luna.

Her incompetence drove Teo's company into the ground and tied Luna into a situation she shouldn't be in. One year after taking over the business, her daughter was chained to it, and God knew for how long more.

Absently seesawing the pencil between her fingers, Sarina thought she should have sold the business, as Luna suggested. But she let her emotions cloud her judgment. In doing so, she drove the company close to insolvency and, in the process, depleted their small savings, Luna's modest education fund, and almost lost their home.

Now, Luna was tied to the business with little hope of any time soon being able to pursue her singing career. Sarina chastised herself for her stupidity. If it weren't for her incompetence, Luna would be enrolled in the school of her choice, honing her talent and pursuing her dream. Instead, Luna now had to settle for the odd singing request. Mediocre jobs at best: birthday parties, bat mitzvahs, anniversaries at the local legion. Once she was asked to sing at the grand opening of the local mall, and Luna happily obliged because singing was in her blood, and it was what she needed to do.

At least now, Luna had a wonderful boy by her side. Sarina still thought of Tom as a boy, although at twenty-three, he was a man. She'd always liked Tom. He was polite and well educated. Above all, he loved Luna. Sarina saw it as clear as day in the boy's eyes. The way Tom's eyes twinkled with love when he was around, Luna was inescapable.

Sarina had seen the same look in Teo's eyes all those years ago. Sarina knew the feeling wasn't going to fade from Tom any time soon.

Tom had gone as far as deciding to put his studies temporarily aside to secure a job as the stage manager at Vibe, a downtown entertainment venue that promoted professional and amateur talent. Sarina knew Tom did that for Luna after she'd told him about their business problems and having to put her singing on the backburner.

As the stage manager of Vibe, Tom was able to steer singing jobs in Luna's direction. No one, least of all Tom's father, was pleased with his decision to cast aside a secure future as a neurologist for a stage management job. Tom was at the top of his class, and medicine was in the stars for him, but the headstrong young man wouldn't change his mind. He was sacrificing his future for Luna.

It saddened Sarina she didn't see the same love in Luna's eyes for Tom. Tom had done so much for Luna. He sacrificed his future to get her back on the stage where she belonged. Tom would do anything for Luna. That was a fact. Sarina hoped Luna wasn't using the boy. She hoped she'd raised her daughter to be a better person.

Sarina was glad for Tom's help. He'd managed to get Luna appearances at Vibe she would have never had. Luna's performances were rare, and often she performed a song or two at most, but at least she was doing it in a professional venue known for headlining renowned artists.

The boy was a Godsend, Sarina thought.

On several occasions, Sarina had overheard Tom offer Luna financial help so she could focus on her singing career instead of the company. Her stubborn daughter, however, wouldn't hear it. Luna would take all the stage time Tom steered her way, but she wouldn't dream of accepting money from him. She didn't expect any less from Luna. She was her mother's daughter.

The appearances at Vibe brought Luna some attention, but Sarina knew she needed more than some attention to make it into the brighter spotlight Luna rightly deserved. What her daughter needed was professional backing. What Luna needed was to be discovered by someone in the business who could take her to the next level.

Sarina was desperate to find a way to make it happen for Luna. How she was going to do it was the million-dollar question. Sarina's salary barely covered their daily existence, and the business, although doing much better, was still playing catch up. It would be some time before Maid For You turned the type of profit required to help Luna launch her career.

Sarina was stuck in a vortex of despair, and therefore, so was Luna.

"Earth to Sarina. Halloo, darling." Sarah Platt, Dr. Grady's head nurse, sang walking into Sarina's office.

Sarina's concentration distracted, she slid the transcription headset down to her neck and looked up to the short, heavy-set woman with the cherubic face standing in front of her. "I'm sorry. My mind was elsewhere."

"I hope it was in a good place." Sarah set the file down on Sarina's TO-BE-TRANSCRIBED tray. "One more for you. It was a last-minute patient. All very cloak-and-dagger if you ask me."

Knowing that was code for ask me more, Sarina did. "Why would you think that?"

Sarah parked her rotund behind into the visitor's chair across Sarina and pulled it closer to conduct the conversation over a hushed whisper.

Sarah Platt was as smart as she was efficient. Her devotion to the department and Dr. Grady were exemplary, but everyone had their weaknesses, and Sarah's was to gossip. She did it discreetly, and there were a select few whose ears she gossiped into. Sarina was one of them.

"Well, for one, Dr. Grady scheduled him in for when most of the staff was gone for lunch and asked me, and only me," she jabbed an index finger at her chest for emphasis, "To stay behind to assist him in running a few tests for a VIP patient. Well, from the banter between Dr. Grady and Mr. VIP, I gathered he was in the music business or entertainment of some sort." Sarah's comment piqued Sarina's interest, and she leaned in.

"Really? What's his name?"

"Umm … Dino give me a second. It's a foreign name. You know how bad I am with those. I think it's Rinaldi. That's it, Dino Rinaldi." Sarina's stomach did a quick pitch and roll when she heard the name. "It's in the file." Sarah tilted her chin toward the folder, and Sarina reached into her tray.

"What did he look like?" Sarina's mind rolling, she failed to mask her shock.

"You know him?" Sarah watched Sarina cross to the gurgling coffee maker on the thigh-high filing cabinet.

"The name sounds familiar, but I can't place him." Sarina lied with a face that gave nothing away. "Double, double, right?" When Sarah nodded, Sarina added cream and sugar, stirred, and handed her the coffee cup.

"Thank you, darling. Well, let me tell you. He was a delicious crumpet I wouldn't mind taking a bite from. He looked to be in his mid-sixties, very distinguished looking with an intellectual face. The look of wealth and privilege was written all over him."

"Don't stop now." Sarina made a rolling hand gesture to speed Sarah along when she stopped to sip on her coffee.

"Aren't we the curious one?"

"Well, now you got my curiosity in full throttle."

Pleased she had, Sarah cackled in her loud, jovial manner. "He wasn't as tall as I like my men, but he had the most luscious, thick crown of silver hair. His eyes were as large as bedpans and as green as that file folder in your hand. And he was impeccably dressed in what I guessed to be expensive Italian silk. I do love a man who takes care of himself." She sipped to lubricate a drying mouth.

The image Sarah conjured told Sarina it was *him*. The shadow of worry moved into her eyes. No one came to see Dr. Grady for simple medical issues. Patients who came to see the top neurologist in the country did so for degenerative disorders.

"He sounds studly." Sarina threw out for Sarah's sake.

Nodding, Sarah tapped an index finger on the tip of her nose. "Mmm-hmm, absolutely dreamy, love. You know, he was eyeing me the entire time I was running his CT scan and MRI."

"From inside the tunnel?"

"I could feel his eyes on me, desiring this the whole time." Sarah skimmed hands down her rotund body like a model displaying her wares. That set both women off into peals of laughter until their eyes filled with tears.

"I can always count on you to put a smile on my face." Sarina dabbed a tissue to her eyes.

"You're welcome," Sarah said, taking the last of her coffee and pushing off to her feet. "Well, I gotta get back to the grind. Thanks for the coffee, love."

"Anytime," Sarina said, and waited for Sarah to waddle out the door before turning her attention back to the file.

Nervous hands inserted the tape into the transcription machine. Earphones in place, Sarina pressed the play button.

The patient's name is Dino Rinaldi, male. Sarina passed over the general information and skipped to the diagnoses. Her eyes rounded when she heard Dr. Grady's dictated notes.

I will be scheduling follow-ups every three months, and additional neurological exams in the coming weeks, but all indication is the patient is in the early stages of...

Sarina rewound the tape, played it again. She'd heard correctly. Falling back in her chair Sarina closed her eyes for a moment. Her conversation with Teo played in her mind.

"ARE YOU SURE DR. BERKELEY WON'T say anything?" Teo asked Sarina.

"No, Teo, he won't. He swore he wouldn't say anything not now, not ever, and we can't either." Sarina urged. *"He's going out on a limb for us. He understands our need for discretion."*

"I don't know, Sarina. This all seems so complicated." Teo ran nervous fingers through his hair.

"It's not, Teo. We just need to keep our stories straight and keep our mouths shut."

Teo stalked around the room. *"I don't know if I can live with this lie. And keeping the truth from Luna doesn't seem right."*

"It's the right thing to do, and it's not a lie if it's for her sake. It's what we need to do, Teo."

With a shrug, Teo gave in. *"All right, but you know a lie only remains alive until it's taken over by the truth. Sooner or later, this lie will come back to bite us in the ass."*

"IT'S LATER, TEO, AND IT'S TAKING a huge chunk off my butt. I'd hoped to face this with you. What do I do now, Teo? Do I unleash this Pandora Box of secrets that will affect so many lives—dead and alive?" Sarina let her face fall into her hands and allowed the tears of guilt, regret, and sadness to pour.

Chapter 11

TWISTING AND TURNING in front of the floor-length mirror, Luna made the necessary adjustment. Frowning, she shifted the tissue she'd stuffed in her bra to give her the lift she needed to fill the low V neckline of her red, sequined gown. When she could afford it, she'd splurge for a boob job. Until then, she'd have to settle with what little God gave her and concluded then that if the omnipotent were a man, she'd have been blessed with a C cup.

Luna was pleased she was at least curvy enough to accentuate the lines of the body-hugging dress. Eyeing the thigh-high slit of her dress in the mirror, Luna liked the way her legs looked. The five-mile runs she tried to get in at least twice weekly were paying off.

Luna adjusted the net on the red pill-hat pinned to her thick, spill of dark waves. She dabbed a light layer of silvery eye shadow and ran black liquid liner to accentuate. The exotic Cleopatra eye look in place, Luna swiped wine-red lipstick. Eyeballing herself one last time, she nodded at her reflection in approval.

Tonight, for the first time, Luna Moon—the name she'd concocted when she decided Luna Lopez didn't have the star quality sound—was headlining at Vibe. She couldn't have been more grateful to Tom for allowing her the opportunity. Because of him, she'd been performing on Vibe's stage for the past seven months.

It didn't matter to Luna the gigs were last-minute replacement for no-shows. When Luna stepped on Vibe's stage before a live audience that didn't consist of boisterous children, drunk wedding guests, or people who were focused on everything, but her music, it felt as if she'd surfaced from deep underwater for air. When Luna stepped onto the stage, her body pulsed with the need to sing. From the moment she opened her mouth, her voice flowed like the colors of a rainbow in a blue sky.

Singing was in Luna's blood. For the few months, she'd set her singing aside to focus on Maid For You, Luna thought she'd died. As usual, though, Tom came to her rescue. Wonderful, devoted, loving, Tom gave his future up to help her revive her singing again.

She was almost twenty-years-old, and although many compared her voice to Aretha Franklin and Whitney Houston's, her big break had yet to materialize. It wasn't an aversion to hard work that had held her back from attaining her dream because no one worked harder than Luna. It was for the one simple fact that in the music business, talent wasn't enough.

Luna learned along with harnessing her singing she needed connections, the right agent, a manager, a legal mind to help her maneuver through the complicated legal jargon of contracts, and that required money. Lots of money she didn't have. So, for now, all Luna could do was sing her heart out whenever, wherever she got the chance.

Luna's singing gigs at Vibe derived little income. She barely made enough money to pay for the flashy outfits she needed to wow the crowds, which meant, for now, singing was still secondary—to everything. For now, she remained stuck at Maid For You, where the money wasn't great, the stress was through the roof, and she was the sole go-to person for everything. Luna's only consolation was that the business provided steady work and a paycheck.

Luna refused Tom's offer for financial help. How could she take money from him after he'd sacrificed so much for her? How could she in good conscience take money from him when she'd been turning to him for sexual gratification and refused to defuse the situation knowing she couldn't return his love.

AT THE SOUND OF KNUCKLES AGAINST the dressing room door Luna turned from the mirror. "Come in."

Poking his head into the dressing room, Tom twitched his nose at the floating cloud of hairspray that came at him. "You're on in five, Luna. It's a full house tonight, and there's no sign of Ms. Summer. I haven't heard from her manager in the past hour. My guess is they're stuck in Vegas. Lucky for you, those gusts of wind grounded her flight. Meaning you're getting the entire hour on stage." His voice was laced with excitement.

Tom told Luna tonight there was an off chance of filling in for Donna Summer. Never in a million years did she imagine it would come to pass. Tonight Luna wouldn't be a fill-in or the opening act for a C-list performer. Tonight she was performing a complete set.

"Did you hear what I said, Luna?" Her shocked stare met Tom's eyes in the reflection coming at her in triplicate on the three-way mirror. "You're ready for this, and you're going to be great." Tom rested a hand on her shoulder, squeezed.

Luna cocked dark brows over green eyes. "I wish I had your optimism."

"It's not optimism. I know how talented you, are and I know you're going to go out there and knock them dead."

At his words, the look of panic in her eyes dissipated. "You're right. I'm ready for this."

Tom's jaw dropped wide open, and his hormones did a quick dance when she rose and turned to face him. "If you don't knock them dead, that dress will. You look stunning."

"Thank you." Luna's dimpled smile made his insides simmer. "And thank you for this, Tom. I know you could have filled the spot with a known name."

"You're as good, if not better." Tom brought a hand to her cheek. "And you're far more beautiful."

What had she done to deserve him? "Thanks, Tom, for … everything."

They were simple words, but there was warmth and appreciation in her voice, and Tom understood their deeper meaning. Tom glided lips over Luna's the way he always did before every performance. "Break a leg."

"I'll make you proud, Tom."

"You always do, Luna Moon," he said, closing the door behind him.

ON STAGE, LUNA LOOKED EXQUISITELY EXOTIC. Fire-red satin whispered against her curves when she walked on the stage. The fountain of hair as black as night, a stark contrast to her creamy skin, cascaded to bare shoulders. But for the long, gold tassels dancing in her ears, she wore no jewelry—needed none. Under the glare of the spotlights, Luna stood tall, elegant, with a staggering beauty that mesmerized. She was the envy of every woman in the room, and the desire of every man.

None of that, however, entered into Luna's thoughts as raw nerves got the best of her. The crowded room was there to see Donna Summer, a famous artist with numerous albums to her credit and as many awards, not Luna Moon, an unknown. But when the band began to play, Luna closed her eyes. Letting let the music flow in her in seconds, the words poured out of her with passion in song. Luna's voice flowed like moonlight casting a gray sheen over glass-smooth water.

The room immediately went silent. All eyes fixed on Luna, absorbed her voice, which was passionate and pulsed in you—through you.

Luna's hour-long repertoire consisting of an eclectic collection of songs from Dean Martin's Sway to Aretha Franklin's Natural Woman got her applause and cheers. It wasn't until Luna belted out The Last Dance in a powerful, bluesy voice, in honor of the artist who'd inadvertently given her her break, that the audience got to their feet and demanded an encore. Luna willingly gave it to them.

At that moment, all of Luna's struggles, Tom's sacrifices, the endless hours of practice felt well worth it. This, Luna thought, was what it was all about. This was what she was meant to do, and come hell or high water she was going to make it a reality.

"The audience loved you, Luna. You got them on their feet and had them asking for an encore. Not an easy task." Tom, who always took a joyous pride in her successes, beamed.

"I can't even begin to tell you how great it felt. Not because of the adulation, although I have to admit, that feels wonderful, but because I got to sing to people who truly appreciated my singing." Luna took Tom's offered hand as she made her way off the stage. "And I have you to thank for it all." She brushed her lips to his.

Her taste swam into him, and like a drug, he craved for more, but that would have to wait until later when he hoped she would spend the night at his place. "You have nothing to thank me for. You did it. By the way, a fan at table two wants to meet you in person," Tom told her, only because the old guy looked to be in his sixties and didn't pose a threat—to him.

Tom refused to tell Luna about the male fans who asked to meet her in person, figuring their interest went beyond a signed autograph. Tom caught the lewd gazes Luna got from the male patrons when she was on stage performing in those revealing, tight-fitting dresses, and he sure as hell wasn't going to give them access to her.

"What would you like me to tell him?"

"Make an excuse for me. I'm running late for the cleaning job I should have been at," Luna checked her watch. "Shit, twenty minutes ago. If I don't show up soon, I may lose it, and this cleaning job could turn out to become a permanent, profitable one."

"You didn't tell me you had a job tonight." Tom followed closely behind as Luna rushed, past the roar of congratulatory remarks from the band and staff, back to her dressing room.

"I got it at the last minute, and with all the excitement of tonight, I forgot to mention it." Luna threw the door to the dressing room open, and Tom followed her in closing it behind him. The scent from the dozen roses delivered while she was on stage painted the air. "They're beautiful, Tom. Thank you."

"Where's the cleaning job?" Tom tried his best to mask the disappointment in his voice. The thought of Luna, who minutes ago had put on such a memorable performance, was off to clean toilets had his blood boiling. "I'll have Quinn drive you."

"It's a mile away, at the West Enterprises building. I can run it in ten minutes." Luna's hand on his shoulder, she kicked the four-inch heels off and slipped into her running shoes. "They're looking at contracting out five floors in the building to me. I can't pass up on the offer. It's great money and easy work." She gave him her back. "Unzip me, please."

Tom let his fingers run down the length of her back. "I know there's no changing your mind once it's set. So, if you insist on working this job tonight, you're staying at my place. I'll pick you up when you're done."

She slipped out of her dress, shrugged into a T-shirt, and faded jeans. "I thought I saw Britney in the audience tonight."

"I doubt it was her. Vibe is too lowbrow for Britney."

Luna unpinned the pillbox from her hair. "Maybe you're right, about Britney, I mean. And yes, I'll stay at your place tonight because if I know you, you're not going to let me out of here."

Tom's eyes met Luna's in the lit mirror, bulbs glowing bright against her face as she wiped the makeup off. "Of course, I won't. You know the crazies are out at that time of night. You matter too much to me to leave you to wander the streets on your own that late. And Quinn is driving you."

Always protective, Luna thought. "You know, best."

"I do. When you're ready, Quinn'll meet you out back. I'll see you in a few hours." His lips tapered off to a pleased smile, although his mind was back on Britney and what the hell she was up to.

Part II

Light

And then I met you, and the sunlight poured
through the tempered clouds.

—M.L. Lexi

Chapter 12

LUNA GATHERED THE thick spill of hair and tamed it down with an elastic band. Opening the door to the supply closet, she rummaged through the shelves. The janitorial cart stocked with bottles of Windex, Pine-Sol, Pledge, garbage bags, and gloves, Luna made her way to the bank of elevators and pressed the up button.

Waiting for one of the six cars, Luna slanted a look at herself in the mirrored wall framing the elevators. Standing next to her cart, broom, and duster spearing out, Luna thought how she went from sensual and flashy to ordinary in a matter of minutes. One minute she's on stage pouring her heart out in song, watched by hundreds of admiring eyes, the next she's in jeans and a T-shirt pushing a janitorial cart. She smiled at that because nothing was going to spoil her mood tonight.

Tonight she got to perform for one hour in a real venue where accomplished artists stood. During her performance, she not only drove the audience to long stretches of applause after each song but at the end of her set, they gave her a standing ovation and demanded more. After giving them a fifteen-minute encore, they asked for more.

The ping of the elevator cut into her euphoric thoughts, and when the door slid open, she rolled the cart in and rode it to the thirty-third floor. Professional Cleaning assigned her the last three floors of the building, and Luna decided to work her way up. The job would take her three hours and just as well because she was beat. Before her singing gig tonight, she'd already put in an eight-hour day, and all Luna wanted right now was to pass out—for the next twelve hours.

Luna knew that although she and Tom were dead on their feet when they got back to his apartment, they'd end up tangling in the sheets. Tom's eyes soft and full of need would stab at her heart, and she'd willingly give in to him because she wanted to make him as happy as he did her. Then, in the darkened bedroom surrounded by the seamless windows, with a luminescent orange moon floating in a black sky sprayed with stars, Tom would make love with her, while whispering tender words in her ears. Afterward, he'd chain strong, warm arms around her, and watch her fall asleep before he closed his own.

Many were the nights, Luna desperately tried to reciprocate Tom's feelings, but no matter how hard she tried, her stubborn heart wouldn't cooperate. There were times when after Tom made love to her, she'd shed tears, and Tom would assuage her guilt.

"I don't make any demands of you, Luna. Just know that no matter what, I love you. I always have and always will. And come what may I will always be there for you when you need me."

Luna had no reason not to believe Tom. Still, she felt as if she was betraying him because, in time, she stood to break his heart. Luna's heart ached for Tom, and her eyes were full of sorrow, but she didn't know how to fix it, and now she was in too deep.

Luna put the thought plaguing her day in, day out, away when the elevator doors opened on the thirty-third floor and turned her focus on cleaning. She'd worked the building a few times, but each time she had, it was with two of her girls. Tonight she was flying solo, but she was familiar with the floor layout well enough. She'd get through the lines of cubicles and offices by the time Tom finished up at Vibe.

Now, on the west side of the thirty-third floor, Luna took one last look. Satisfied with what she saw, she ran a quick scan of her cart. Deciding she had enough supplies, Luna made her way to the next floor.

With light-speed efficiency, she cleaned, wiped, emptied wastebaskets, and cleaned the bathrooms in under forty minutes. Once Luna restocked her cart, she headed for the bank of elevators. Muscling her cart onto the first elevator to ping, Luna rode it to the thirty-fifth floor.

In the same systematic method she used on the previous two floors, Luna dusted, wiped, and vacuumed. The thirty-fifth floor housed the top executives of West Enterprises, and doing a thorough job was imperative to locking in the contract.

At J.R. West's office, Luna keyed the security code on the door pad. Throwing tall mahogany doors open, she set the stopper in place and wheeled in her cart. No matter how many times she'd been in that room, it never failed to wow her.

Unblinded floor-to-ceiling windows looked out to a panoramic view of downtown Toronto lit for the night, and Lake Ontario plunged in black. A mahogany bookcase behind the large Cocobolo desk stocked an eclectic collection of books and artifacts from around the world: Ming and Victorian vases, Tang horses, delicate ceramics, and porcelains. Two long, buttery-soft, leather sofas and a round table with six chairs filled one-half of the office. Walls washed in warm olive green the perfect contrast to the thick cream-colored carpet that flowed right up to your ankles and was as soft as marshmallows. It screamed power and privilege.

"Let me know if I'm in your way." The unexpected man's voice startled Luna, and she dropped the bottle of Windex in her hand.

"Shit! Look what you made me do," she said, falling to her knees to wipe the blue stain quickly seeping into the carpet and spreading like a Rorschach inkblot.

"I'm sorry. I didn't mean to frighten you." He circled the high backed chair to face her, but all he got was a view of the compact rear-end swaying back and forth as she rubbed away.

"I would dab, not rub," he said, never taking his eyes off the tight butt straining against faded denim.

"I know what I'm doing." She growled.

"Hmm, doesn't seem like it. You've spread it wider."

"Could you please shut up? Better yet, get out so I can get my work done. This was my last office to clean, and I was close to done. Now I'll have to run the steam cleaner, which is going to add more time to an already long day."

He walked over to where she knelt. "I'm sorry for the added aggravation. You don't have to bother with the steaming. Leave it as is."

"That's a brilliant solution. I'm counting on getting this cleaning job on a permanent basis, and leaving a blue stain on a cream-colored carpet for J.R. West to find tomorrow morning ain't going to bode well for me." Luna sprayed Resolve on the spot and sat back on her heels to wait on the five-minute soak. It was then her eyes fell to the brown Magli shoes, and continued their scan up the black pants with the knife-edged pleats, to the white silk shirt clinging to broad shoulders. Wide eyes continued up to the long-lashed blue eyes eyeing her.

Luna had seen pictures of James Robert West in The Economist and Forbes, and now face to face with him, she thought they didn't do him justice. J.R. West was the embodiment of tall, dark, and handsome. Rich chocolate-brown hair fell in waves around an intensely manly, handsome face with a sharp jaw that even at that late hour boasted a fashionably trimmed stubble.

And it wasn't just handsome good looks James Robert West had going for him. The man was loaded. Forbes valued the West dynasty in the billions. Although his mother, Poppy West, was the majority stakeholder since inheriting the business after his father's death two decades ago, James Robert West was the brains behind the operation.

In his mid-thirties, J.R. West had been at the helm of the family dynasty for the past ten years, taking over the CEO role after graduating from Harvard. Luna remembered the article in Forbes, saying the young West, although born and bred to take over the family dynasty, had big shoes to fill.

J.R.'s father, James West Sr. was an entrepreneurial wizard who, after returning home at the end of WWII, a decorated Captain rose from poverty to own the multi-faceted company. West Enterprises was comprised of print media, broadcast, and entertainment media. They owned venues such as the Vibe nightclub. Their portfolio also boasted valuable real estate holdings in Toronto, Vancouver, New York, Los Angeles, and throughout

Europe. More importantly, West Enterprises owned and operated WE Productions, one of the largest recording studio in North America.

"Jesus! I'm…" The air clogged Luna's lungs, and her cheeks flushed red. "I'm very sorry for the intrusion, Mr. West. I assumed it wasn't you. I mean, it's almost one in the morning."

"No worries." Smiling warmly, he offered her his hand.

"Thank you." Wiping her hands on her jeans, Luna nervously took the offered hand.

Rising to her height, she eyed him more closely. He was taller than she anticipated six-one by her estimation. Her eyes roved over the tone arms and firm chest against white silk. She'd bet all the Pledge in the world he was solid, nothing but lean muscle.

Sweet baby Jesus, he was gorgeous and tall and gorgeous. Her mind shut off when the staggeringly blue eyes met hers. "I … umm … sorry about the…"

"Carpet?" He finished when her mind turned to mush.

God, even his voice was sensual, Luna thought. "Yeah, about that."

"Don't worry about it. I'll get it taken care of," J.R. said, his eyes never leaving hers.

"All right, sir." Luna reached up to tousle her hair back until she realized it was pulled back into a ponytail.

"Sir is too formal. My friends call me J.R."

"Sure. Okay, all right. I'll, umm, get out of your way and umm… I need to get to the bathroom. To clean it. Would it be too much to ask, not to mention this to Professional Cleaning? They want to contract this job out to me and… I need this job."

She was breath-stealing, beautiful, J.R. thought. "Mum's the word."

"I appreciate that, thank you. I'm going to head in there now," Luna said, pivoting toward his private bathroom and giving J.R. her back.

He'd never tire of appreciating the fit of those tight jeans. "You're Luna Moon, aren't you?" J.R. called out when belated recognition flashed in his eyes. Halfway across the room, Luna stopped, propelled around to face him, the jolt of shock clear on her face as she nodded. "I thought you looked familiar. Our head producer, who's also my uncle, and I were at Vibe earlier this evening to see you perform." J.R. walked to the bar cart, poured two fingers of scotch, raised the bottle in offer.

Luna waved it down. "You were there to see me?"

J.R. rested a hip on the corner of his desk. "My uncle is a big fan of yours. He saw you perform at Vibe a few weeks ago, and he's become such a fan he's been to see everyone one of your performances since. He steered my music producer and me in your direction. That's why we were there tonight to see you open for Donna, and I'll tell you after seeing your performance, I've become a fan. You were exceptional. When you belted out that Aretha Franklin tune, you had my uncle in tears. And that's saying a lot. I've never seen him cry." J.R tossed back part of his drink.

"Uncle Dean wanted to meet you in person and asked the manager to invite you to our table, but we were told you'd already left. He was very disappointed." J.R. watched her over the rim of his glass. Without a trace of makeup, in a practical T-shirt, and faded jeans, she looked as beautiful as she had in the sensual, red dress, which now he couldn't get off his mind.

"I had to rush here to get this cleaning job done."

When Tom told her, a fan wanted to meet her, Luna assumed it was an old-timer. They were the only fans to pass Tom's overprotective screening. Luna knew for her protection Tom kept the younger, handsy, male fans at bay. Had she known it was J.R. West, owner of WE Productions, one of the top recording studios, who wanted to meet her, she would have trampled fans to get to his table.

"There's no need to apologize. I admire a conscientious work ethic," he said, trying to come to terms with the fact the woman with the angelic voice who'd mesmerized him was cleaning his office. "We, my uncle, my music producer, and I wanted to have a chat with you."

Her pulse already fast, went racing. "A chat, Mr. West?"

"J.R. and yes." He couldn't help but drown in the large, unblinking green eyes. "Seeing as it's almost one in the morning, why don't you leave me your number and I'll have my assistant call you to schedule a more fitting time for us to meet." J.R. handed her a pen and paper. He hadn't expected the stunned arousal that snaked through him when their hands briefly touched.

Luna handed him the inked telephone number and caught a glimpse of the time on her wristwatch. Tom would be by soon to pick her up. "If you don't mind, I need to get on with my work."

"Of course, don't let me hold you up." When she turned her back to walk away, J.R. called out after her. "Miss Moon?"

"It's Lopez, Luna Lopez. Luna Moon is my stage name." she clarified.

"I like it. Luna means moon in Spanish. It was nice meeting, you Miss Lopez."

Twenty minutes later, when Luna stepped back into J.R.'s office, he was gone. The unexpected pang of regret that washed over her at the sight of the empty room surprised her.

Chapter 13

DEAN RYDER STROLLED into J.R.'s office with a whistle on his lips and a smile in his eyes.

J.R. looked up from the blueprints spread out on his desk to scan his Patek Philippe. "Gracing us with your presence before noontime. It must be something important if you've managed to rouse yourself out of bed at this early hour." J.R. eased himself into his buttery-soft leather chair.

"Always the smartass." Dean's tone was terse, but his lips curled into a smile for the boy he loved as his own. "Hot off the press." Dean dropped the handwritten music sheet on J.R.'s desk before crossing to the bar cart.

J.R.'s blue gaze followed the man who embraced him as his own twenty-five years ago when on his return from a fishing trip James West Sr. lost control of his Cessna. The plane plunged into a densely wooded area and burst into flames on impact, killing James and his three passengers.

Without a second thought, Dean Ryder, James's best friend, and longtime business partner stepped in as a surrogate father to a seven-year-old during the most traumatic time of his life. Dean embraced J.R. like a son, loved him as his own, and had done so since that time. Since then, J.R. leaned on Dean for guidance and direction in his personal and professional life. There were times when J.R. dared to turn to his philandering uncle for matters of the heart, although Dean never married and told him he never would.

"What's this?" J.R. reached for the sheet music.

"It's a new song I hammered out in the past forty-eight hours." Dean waved the bottle of scotch at J.R. I offer.

"No, thanks." J.R. was tempted to mention it was only nine in the morning but thought better of it.

"I started working on it right after we left the club. The song came to me on a flash of inspiration." Dean filled the Waterford tumbler generously.

J.R.'s lips creased into a smile. His uncle was thirty years his senior, but he recognized the glint in his eyes. This all came down to a woman, and he suspected he knew exactly who. "You wrote this for Luna Moon, didn't you?"

"I did."

"She sure has gotten deep under your skin."

Unable to deny that singular fact, Dean nodded. "I won't deny she has, my boy."

J.R. watched his uncle fall into the guest chair and lift the glass to his lips for a long, satisfying drink. "You know that even by your standards, she's way too young for you."

Dean waved a finger. "It's not like that, my boy. I simply had an inspiration. Grant it, she was the reason for it, but it's not what you're thinking. So get that testosterone-driven mind of yours out of the gutter. The girl is young enough to be my..."

"I believe the word you're searching for is daughter." J.R. finished.

Dean's appreciation for younger women was well known. J.R. had always admired his uncle's ability to seduce women half his age into his bed. It wasn't solely because Dean Ryder could launch their singing career to stardom as the tabloids claimed that they willingly did. It was because they enjoyed his company, his sense of humor, and exciting energy.

Over the years, J.R. watched the parade of women traipse in and out of his uncle's life. Although more out than in—not by their choice—they were all beautiful, desirable, exotic models, starlets, and singing artists who swooned at the mere sight of the man.

Twice J.R. ventured to ask Dean why he'd never settled down, each time he dismissed the question telling J.R. he liked the unencumbered bachelor life. J.R., however, suspected there was more to the story, and he was still waiting for the day when the truth prevailed.

"Don't be such a smartass. Just because you're behind that desk in this huge office, doesn't give you immunity from being disrespectful to your elders. Not to mention the fact I'm a major stakeholder of this company and should be treated with respect. Oh, and there's also the fact I've generated millions of dollars in revenue. Money, which I presume is going into your trust fund." There was nothing in Dean's eyes to indicate J.R. should take his comment seriously.

"Tsk, tsk, the hold women can have on us is certainly far-reaching. I mean, to stir your passionate side to the point of making your creative juices flow so fluidly that you produce a Grammy award-winning song like this one in just a couple of days, speaks volume of Ms. Moon's effect on you."

"It is Grammy worthy, isn't it?" Pleased with himself, Dean stretched luxuriously, crossing his legs at the ankles.

"You look tired, Uncle Dean. I think we need to get some caffeine in you."

"I should look this way. I've been up two days straight writing that masterpiece. And it's too early for coffee."

"It's nine in the morning." J.R. steered Dean's eyes out the unblinded window to a clear blue skyline drenched in sunshine.

"This is all I need," Dean said, taking a generous sip of his scotch.

"How you've lived this long with the way you abuse yourself is a mystery to me, but that's a discussion for another day." J.R. pressed the intercom button. "Belinda, can you please bring in two black coffees." J.R. turned to Dean. "Now, about this song. It's definitely award-winning material, and you wrote it for her, didn't you?"

"What would you say if I did?"

"I'd say it's—" J.R. broke off at the knock on the door, waved Belinda in. Walking the cups to his desk, she brought with her the aroma of freshly brewed coffee. "It's perfect for her. She has the perfect bluesy voice meant for this song."

Dean smiled at J.R.'s perceptive comment. There was no doubt the boy inherited his father's gift for sizing up talent. J.R. could spot talent a mile away and knew exactly how to harness it.

Although over the years, West Enterprises diversified to encompass a wide array of businesses, Dean and James had built the company through their interest in music. James' eye for scouting talent and Dean's flair for writing lyrics and music was perfect synergy. It had been a long, tough road for both of them when they'd first started the business, but in time, their tiresome search for the right artist to put them on the map came through in Tommy King.

After months of endless hours in smoked filled nightclubs and bars, listening to what some called music, but which leaned more into clatter, they came across Tommy King. Busking on the streets for nickels and dimes, Tommy not only had the perfect stage name and presence, but he had a perfect voice, one that needed to be recorded for mass consumption.

Dean and James immediately signed Tommy King, a complete unknown, and set off to make him a star. Overnight, they transformed Tommy King into a teen idol. With Dean writing the lyrics and music to suit Tommy King's baritone voice, he was introduced to the world. It didn't take long for the youthful and handsome Tommy with the dreamy voice and the seductive dance moves to become a source of steady revenue for Dean and James. But it wasn't until Tommy was invited to perform on American Bandstand that he became a money printing machine for West Enterprises.

"I'm glad you think that because I did write this song just for Luna. And yes, it's perfectly suited for her style of singing. I believe she also has the right look for it if you know what I mean." Dean waved away the cup of coffee Belinda offered. "Scotch and coffee aren't a good mix, darling. It'll kill the buzz I've been working on all morning." His comment got a flirtatious giggle out of the young brunette and an incredulous gaze from J.R.

The girl was twenty-years-old, and Dean had her bones liquefying. If he could only bottle the charismatic essence Dean Ryder exuded that made women melt, no man would spend another lonely night, J.R. thought.

"Leave it there, Belinda. I'll force it down his throat if I have to."

When Belinda shot Dean a lost look from under dark lashes, Dean took the cup from her. "We both better do what the boss says, darling," he said, with a dimpled smile that had Belinda flipping Dean a sidelong flick of lashes out the door.

"If you're done flirting with my secretary, who by the way is young enough to be your granddaughter, I'll let you in on my secret,"

"What's with all the familial references this morning? And I'll have you know it never hurts to flatter a woman. No matter their age, they appreciate it."

"For one, she's a member of my staff. And two," J.R. stopped abruptly, wondering why he was entertaining the ridiculous conversation. "Can we please forget about Belinda and focus?"

"Your problem, my boy is you're too uptight. Just saying." Before J.R. could shoot out a surly remark, Dean said, "Fine. You have my undivided attention."

"I met her that night." J.R. picked up his coffee, sipped, and encouraged Dean to do the same.

"Who?" Dean winced when the dark liquid assaulted his scotch-laced taste buds.

"Luna Moon." With a cocky grin, J.R. leaned back in his chair, clasped hands behind his head, and propped his feet on the desk.

"How? She didn't come to the table."

"She was right here in my office." J.R. flicked eyes to where a blue stain spread a couple of days ago. "I tried to get a hold of you to let you know, but you didn't return my calls."

Dean bolted up, giving J.R. his full attention. "Why didn't you press Mrs. Bertinelli to disturb me? You know she lives for disturbing me."

"She's even more stunning close-up," J.R. said when the vision of the large, green eyes and the top-heavy mouth popped into his head and went on to tell Dean about their brief encounter and conversation.

Heat flashed in Dean's pale green eyes. "Imagine talent like hers wasted on cleaning your toilet."

"Hey, don't get pissed at me. I had nothing to do with that."

Dean drew in air, exhaled. "I know. It just doesn't seem right that someone as gifted as her can't pursue her dream because of her circumstances. She didn't ask to be born into the situation she's in." The anger pulsating in Dean's tone confused J.R.

J.R. didn't need a magnifying glass to recognize Dean's fascination with Luna Moon. Her reach went deeper than mere infatuation, J.R. reasoned. "This woman has gotten to you. Are you going to tell me why, Uncle Dean?"

"There's nothing to tell, my boy. I just hate people's talents going to waste. And this girl has stardom quality." Was Dean's response, but J.R. suspected there was more to this story than his uncle cared to admit, and knowing Dean Ryder as well as he did, it was bound to be a complicated novella.

"If you say so. Are you still heading out to Palm Beach Thursday?"

"I am. I plan to spend a few days on the Seas the Day. Me, the seagulls and nothing but blue ocean."

"And the crew."

"Well, you can't very well expect me to work on my vacation." Dean tilted back the tumbler for a long sip of scotch.

"What was I thinking? Mind if I tag along?"

"You're taking a holiday?" Dean's tone sounded as dubious as the idea seemed.

"I am. I'll fly out Saturday at dawn and head straight from the airport to the Yacht club. Can you get her ready to sail then?"

"I can. What do you have in mind, my boy?

"You'll see."

Chapter 14

THE LOUD, SHRILL woke Luna out of a sound sleep.

"Shut up. Shut up, shut up," she moaned as her hand slapped the snooze button on her clock radio and fell facedown into her pillow.

Seconds later there it was again. Her hand came down like a wrecking ball on the annoying contraption. She'd banked four hours of sleep since her last job, and she wasn't in the mood.

The irritating shrill continued to scream in Luna's ears. This time, the tangle of dark hair rose, and she listened more carefully. It took fifteen seconds for her to realize it was the telephone ringing. Turning heavy-lidded eyes to the clock radio, Luna's eyes hardened. What kind of nut called at that ungodly time of seven in the morning?

With a colorful string of words her mother wouldn't be happy to hear her only daughter spout, Luna snatched the telephone. "This better be goddamn important. I've only had four hours of sleep and..."

Luna's tone of irritation was cut off when the man's voice said, "Luna Lopez?"

"Who the hell wants to know this early in the morning?" Luna barked.

"It's J.R. West."

"Yeah, right, and I'm the queen of England." Luna hung up before the caller got another word in.

Twenty seconds passed when the telephone rang again, and Luna answered with an abrupt, "Stop calling. It's way too early in the day for this bull…"

"This is J.R. West, Miss Lopez," he said, before she had the chance to hang up again, then quickly injected as a means of verification, "We met last Friday night at my office while you were trying to scrub off the Windex stain on my white carpet."

Shock rushing into her head in a flood, Luna bolted up in bed in one quick jolt causing her to roll off and drop to the floor. A thump and a curse followed with a distant, "A moment, please." Although she spoke under her breath, J.R. could hear the long stream of curses as she reached for the dropped telephone and scrambled to her feet. "I'm sorry. I just…" she started to say, but quickly decided it wasn't necessary to enlighten him on her clumsiness.

"I'm sorry if I woke you, Miss Lopez." J.R.'s grin came through in his voice.

"You didn't. You just caught me… What can I do for you, Mr. West?" Luna caught her reflection in the dresser mirror and was grateful he couldn't see the knotted hair.

"J.R., remember? I know this is short notice, but I wondered if you would do me the favor of performing for a group of ten people this weekend."

Surprise filled Luna's eyes. "I'm sorry, what?"

"I'd like you to perform this Saturday for a small party I'm putting together."

Shock came first then, a slow, easy smile. "Can you hold for just a moment?" Muffling the receiver, Luna proceeded with a silent, but vigorous interpretation of the Flashdance-maniac dance.

The excitement flushed out of her system, Luna composed herself and turned back to the telephone. "It is very last minute. I mean today is already Wednesday, and well, I have commitments, J.R."

He liked the sound of the sultry voice now pouring through the receiver. "Yes, of course. I would have called you sooner, but the time got away from me. Uncle Dean is your biggest fan, and I'd like to surprise him with a performance from you."

"So, this is for your uncle." Luna softened at what was clearly a gesture of love.

"It is."

"Then, how can I decline."

"Thank you, Miss Moon."

"Luna, please."

"Well, Luna, the venue is in Palm Beach. We fly out on the corporate jet at sunrise Saturday morning. We'll be staying at West Enterprises' Playa Azul resort. All expenses paid, of course."

"Sounds very … tropical." Luna laid back down on the bed and studied her hands mid-air. They were looking dry, she concluded. She made a mental note to soak them later in that special solution Maxine gave her. "You know I'll have to cancel a couple of cleaning jobs."

She was pulling out all the stops, and J.R. could only smile. "You will be well compensated for your trouble."

"And all expenses paid." Luna sprang out of bed, crossed to the window and tugged on the blind. A prism of light cut through the impeccably clean glass pane. Her mother's doing, Luna thought. The woman was a compulsive cleaner.

"Of course, and as an added benefit, let me throw in that it's going to be eighty-seven degrees in Palm Beach this weekend, and the resort is beachfront with two pools." An unexpected heat hit him like a punch to the pit of his stomach when he envisioned her long, lean body in a tiny, white bikini.

"Sounds great, but I don't even own a bathing suit." That was a fact. She'd never needed one since she barely knew how to float, let alone swim.

"That's not a problem. There's a boutique at the resort. You can pick up whatever you need, on my tab, of course."

Luna slid the window open and breathed in air filled with the scents of the morning, lilac, and mowed grass. "Offering a broke girl a blank shopping cheque, you do like living on the edge."

If J.R. didn't know better, their conversation was now verging on the flirtatious, and he was enjoying it— immensely. "I do like the taste of adventure, but I doubt you'll give me a reason to worry."

"I hope that's not code for unadventurous or worse predictable." Luna shot out defensively.

"That's not at all what I meant."

"I can assure you I may be many things, Mr. West, but ordinary is not one of them."

"I'd never presumed you to be an ordinary woman."

"I mean it." She spat out.

"No one said you didn't." The picture of the moss-green eyes lit up in anger flashed in his mind, and he smiled. She was a firecracker.

"All right then."

"All right then." Met with silence, J.R. assumed they'd exhausted the ridiculous exchange and proceeded to give her the instructions. "We fly out Saturday at six in the morning and sail at ten, which is when you'll perform. If you give me your address, I'll send a car for you."

A quick panic surged in Luna. "Wait... Sail? We're going to be on water? As in ocean." The mere thought had her stomach churning.

"Yes, is that a problem? I never assumed you'd be scared of anything, especially something as mundane as water."

The wave of nausea sweeping through Luna at the thought of being on a bobbing object, on water, one she couldn't save herself from if it went down, had her overlooking the subtle jab. "I've never performed on a ship..."

"Boat," he corrected.

"Whatever. I don't know..." how to swim, and I sure as hell don't want to die by drowning, "about this."

When J.R. thought she was reconsidering, he said, "I'd hate to disappoint an old man. He'd be so thrilled to see you perform." J.R. negotiated million-dollar deals daily. None of them presented as much of a challenge as she was, and he reconsidered telling her she'd be performing a song she'd never seen before, written for her by a man, who, in his opinion, was obsessed with her. And he certainly wasn't about to mention the fact she'd be singing it to his music producer and her team. "I'd hate to disappoint him, Luna." J.R. appealed to her conscience, the last card he had left to play.

After some consideration, Luna hesitantly agreed. "All right, but I have to warn you I may be umm..." blowing chunks were the words that came to mind, but she opted for the more polite, "sick for most of the trip."

There was a smile at the end of the line. "A Gravol should take care of that."

Luna thought it doubtful as she nervously curled a strand of hair around her finger. "If you say so."

"I appreciate this, Luna. Uncle Dean will be forever grateful, as am I. I'll see you then." J.R. surprised himself by how much he was looking forward to seeing her.

When the line cut off, massaging the bridge of her nose between her thumb and forefingers, Luna wondered what she'd gotten herself into.

Chapter 15

SEAS THE DAY was a two-hundred-foot yacht of pure luxury. The four-deck boat was as long as it was stunning. Polished teak and Oregon fir gleamed. The upper deck housed a piano bar. Below, a sweeping line of long angled windows allowed sunlight to pour into an oversized salon and the six cabins, which included a master suite and a fully equipped office. A helipad on top of the wheelhouse accommodated a small helicopter.

In addition to a captain, there were three deckhands and a Michelin star accredited chef. Today, two liveried servers handed out Cristal in Baccarat flutes, and hors d'oeuvre. Any other time Luna would have been awed by the luxury around her. No today. Today, her heart was doing a fast roll in her chest and centered her focus on avoiding sinking to the depths of the Atlantic Ocean.

Setting sail, Luna braced her legs against the pitch of the boat as knuckle-white hands gripped on the rail. Twenty minutes out, to Luna's surprise, it felt as if they were gliding on ice, and she didn't feel the nauseating effects she'd imagined. Still, she wasn't taking chances and passed on the offer of food and drink for fear of the outcome. As an added precaution, Luna slipped on a bright yellow life vest.

Tilting her face up to a sun streaming gold, Luna followed the screams of gulls high in a staggeringly blue sky. A warm breeze whistled past her as the boat picked up speed, and the sound of lapping water soothed. Calmer now, Luna settled in to watch the beautiful vista awash in the tropical colors of blue and green rolling past.

The Seas the Day cruised along the Intracoastal Waterway to merge onto Atlantic waters. Luna watched the line of coastal homes, arched windows reflecting sunshine. Each one swanked with a perfect roll of green lawn that sloped to the curve of white sand beach dotted with tall palms heavy with coconuts. Many of the homes had piers with moored boats as extraordinary as the Seas the Day.

To keep her mind occupied, Luna did a mental review of her upcoming performance. She didn't know what J.R. wanted from her. On the flight down, J.R. locked himself in his office, and they'd spoken few words. Without much information to go on, Luna was glad she'd pre-planned a repertoire of her own. She hadn't seen musical instruments or a band on board and guessed J.R. wanted her to go acapella. She could do that, but not for the entire hour.

Luna's heart began to pound. What had she gotten herself into, and what if she bombed? She was performing for J.R. West, hoping to get her foot in the door of WE Productions.

Her muscles bunched up.

And she still had to meet the elusive Uncle Dean. Grant it, she hadn't moved from the spot since boarding for fear of everything water-related. Still, she was starting to wonder if she hadn't thought this through. She was on a boat she didn't want to be on, waiting to sing to a man that might not exist. Luna then wondered if it had been a good idea to lie to Tom.

The moment she'd accepted the gig with J.R., her mind began to work fast on the excuse she'd give Tom for bowing out of spending the weekend with him. She hated lying, but she wouldn't distress Tom and let his imagination run wild all weekend by telling him she was off to perform on J.R.'s yacht in Florida. She could still see the angst on Tom's face when she'd told him about her encounter with J.R. and that she'd given him her telephone number. Tom went strangely silent, and the guilt smothered her. Luna wouldn't put either of them through that again. This was a well-paying gig and an excellent opportunity she sensed Tom would have her pass on.

Tom had nothing to worry about. At least that's what she told herself.

"Are you all right?" J.R.'s voice made Luna spin around, and she lost hold of the rail.

Luna's eyes turning dark with fear, she tried to regain her footing, but her knees buckled. With the choked scream strangling in her throat, and her arms flailing in the air, Luna fell back and into the arms that reached out to break her fall.

For a moment, J.R. held Luna as if suspended in air. Their faces inches apart, blue eyes on sparkling green eyes, an unexpected punch of lust struck his male sensibilities. His mouth a whisper from hers, he leaned in closer. Eye to eye, mouth to mouth, J.R. could feel the heat of her breath on his face. She could feel his. It was a solid punch to both their guts, one either Luna or J.R. was prepared for.

As fast as his mind reeled, so did Luna's, when the hot punch of emotion either had felt before struck them. She wanted to bite on the thick bottom lip, and he wanted him to bite down on hers. The thought of J.R.'s mouth taking hers, his tongue dancing with hers stirred emotions Tom never had. Luna wanted J.R., and not in the same way she wanted Tom. She didn't want J.R. just to satisfy a sexual itch, as Tom did.

Those wishful thoughts swiftly collided with guilt. As much as Luna tried to shake Tom from her thoughts, guilt bit down hard, and she pulled away. "I don't have my sea legs yet."

"You will." Reluctantly, J.R. took a quick step in retreat, scanned her face. Seeing the confused look in her eyes, the nervous tension in her, J.R. concluded he hadn't misread the signs. She'd wanted to lock lips as much as he did. "There's no chop today, and I've given instructions to remain in protected water."

"Yeah, I have no idea what any of that means."

J.R.'s amused eyes held steady on Luna as he watched her tightly wrap small, delicate hands around the rail. "It means it should be smooth sailing for most of our trip. Just give it a few more minutes to acclimatize yourself."

Luna steered her gaze away from the brilliant blue eyes descending on her. "Thank you."

"This looks very stylish," he said, tugging the waist strap of her life jacket with a seemingly intimate gesture that caught her off guard.

"Stylish or not, it's going to keep me from drowning."

"You're not going to drown. I wouldn't let that happen."

There it was again. An intriguingly touching indicator, Luna thought, and softening said, "I'm sorry I sounded so bitchy, but I don't know how to ... swim. There I said it. I don't know how to swim. Yes, a grown woman doesn't know how to swim. Not that I ever had reason to learn. The last time I was near water was, yeah, never, and…" She prattled on, and he let her.

How could he not? Those fiery green eyes, which were deepening in color, for no apparent reason, were too enticing to tame. She was a firecracker, he thought. "I don't know how to swim either," J.R. said when she finally stopped talking. When her brow arched in disbelief, he added, "All right, I'm a gold medal swimmer, but it was in high school." Now, she raised a dramatic brow. "Okay, it was on the Harvard swim team, but I only did well because I was long-limbed."

That made her smile. "Well, at least you won't drown if we sink."

"We are not going to sink. This is a state of the art boat."

"So was the Titanic." She reached for the rail.

J.R. laughed at that. "You got me there. I'm sorry I didn't get a chance to talk to you on the flight. My work is never done." He put distance between them when the sweet scent of her perfume nagged at him, and something began to stir inside him.

"There you are." Dean's voice came at them. "I'm sorry, am I interrupting?" he asked when J.R.'s eyes spit annoyance his way.

"As usual, you have perfect timing." On a hiss of breath, J.R. bit back irritation when Dean shot him a grinning look.

The boy is smitten, Dean thought eyeing J.R. from over the rim of his scotch-filled glass. An unexpected turn of events he hadn't counted on. "Well, son, are you going to introduce me to this beautiful, young lady?"

"It would be my pleasure." J.R. shot Dean a sarcastic smile. "Luna Moon, my uncle, Dean Ryder, who has a knack of making his entrance at just the right time."

"Miss Moon, it's a pleasure to finally meet you." Dean studied Luna with piercing scrutiny. She was taller than he'd anticipated, and up close, she was more beautiful than he'd envisioned. Her eyes were sharp, intelligent, and wise beyond her youthful years, Dean thought.

"It's nice to meet you, Mr. Ryder." Luna locked hands with Dean's, but her eyes remained on J.R.

The smitten bug had bitten her too, Dean thought. An unforeseen situation, he'd have to do something about. "I caught your last performance at Vibe, and I thought you were nothing short of fabulous."

"That's kind of you to say, Mr. Ryder." At the flow of his name on her tongue, Luna's eyes rounded wide, and she turned to Dean. "Wait. Dean Ryder? As in, Dean Ryder, the renowned songwriter, and producer?" Disbelieving eyes darted from J.R. to Dean and back. "*The* Dean Ryder, is your uncle?" She waved a dismissive hand in J.R.'s face when he started to speak and turned mooneyes on Dean. "You're Dean Ryder."

Dean's lips ripe with a smile of satisfaction, he nodded. Luna's knees buckled. She was standing before Dean Ryder. The most respected and admired man in music. The man had launched hundreds of voices to stardom, written countless award-winning songs. A single critique from Dean Ryder could make or break an artist. Dean Ryder didn't come to you, you went to him—on your hands and knees—and the chance of him seeing you, let alone getting within inches of him as Luna was now, was as remote as lightning striking.

Luna forgot all manner and decorum when she turned to J.R. "Why didn't you tell me your uncle was *the* Dean Ryder?" Luna flung out with anger, and Dean couldn't help but admire her moxie. Few dared speak to J.R. as brazenly. "This is *the* Dean Ryder for God's sake."

"Yes, the fantabulous Dean Ryder is before us." J.R.'s clipped voice was laced with jealousy.

"Aww, that's so nice of you to say, son. You're making my ego swell." Dean swilled scotch with a smirk.

"Like it can get any bigger," J.R. muttered between clenched teeth, then turned to Luna. "I'm sorry I didn't mention it to you sooner."

"It would have been nice for you to mention that detail." Luna's eyes glowed with anger, and J.R. thought she was nothing short of magnificent. "This is *the* Dean Ryder." Luna gave each word separate weight.

"So, you've said enough times already." Irritation edged into J.R.'s voice. "I didn't say anything because I thought it would make you nervous, and you'd back out from performing today."

"I'll give you that, but still, you should have said something." Luna spat, her eyes were hot, and her face flushed scarlet in anger.

God, she was splendid, J.R. thought staring. "I know, and I'm sorry."

Trading anger for sweetness, Luna turned her attention away from J.R. to Dean. He was shorter than Luna imagined but younger than the tabloid shots gave him credit. His face was strikingly handsome, and he had a charismatic presence. A thick shock of silver hair billowed in the wind, and the eyes that stared back at her were green, kind, and warm in their gaze. In tan chino pants and a canary-yellow shirt, he didn't look like the womanizer portrayed in the glossy magazines.

"It's a real pleasure to meet you, Mr. Ryder. I've been a big fan of yours since ... well, forever. I think everything you write is amazing. And I'm sorry I didn't come out to meet you when you sent for me at the club." Luna's hair tumbled in waves over her shoulders. In the willowy, white, summer dress with red brushstrokes, Luna looked so much like her, Dean thought, and the memories came fast.

Dean's mind cast to the past. The vision of her beautiful face and the smile that lit up any room bright flashed in his mind as clear as if she was standing before him. It was as if Marina's shadow walked beside him just then. The pain in his heart and the ache of loss that slapped him was excruciating. God, he missed her.

Drawing a long, cleansing breath, Dean returned to the moment. "There's no need for apologies, my dear. I hope my nephew at least mentioned how big a fan of yours I am, Miss Moon?"

"Please call me Luna, Mr. Ryder." Luna's gentle, sparkling voice reminded Dean of his Marina.

Everything about Luna was so much like his Marina, Dean thought. He had to take a breath to steady himself. "Did my nephew mention why we wanted you to perform for us today, Luna?"

"Your nephew wasn't forthcoming with information." Luna flicked hot eyes at J.R.

"Forgive him, Luna. Sometimes he doesn't think straight." Dean leveled a look at J.R., whose infatuation with Luna made him deaf to the conversation.

Dean couldn't imagine how this had come to pass. Luna wasn't the type of woman J.R. sought out or was accustomed to drape on his arm. She was from the opposite side of the tracks, far from the elite circles of wealth—inherited or nouveau-riche. And knowing women, as well as Dean did, Luna wasn't the type to fawn over a man or idly stand by devoting her time and energy to planning the perfect dinner party or attending the fitting charitable event. Luna was an ambitious, goal-oriented, strong-minded woman, out of J.R.'s league and one Poppy Barclay-West—J.R.'s mother—wouldn't see fit to stand by J.R.'s side.

"Why don't we head down to the cabin to discuss our proposition in more detail?" Dean felt the choking at his throat when Luna moved to bite on her bottom lip in the same way Marina used to when nervous. "Is there a problem, Luna?"

"Well, umm…"

"She's afraid of drowning." J.R. injected with a sardonic tone, eliciting a scowl from Luna.

"Nonsense, my girl, this is a state of the art boat. She's not going under anytime soon."

"That's what I told her." J.R. met Luna's look sneer for sneer.

"The information carries more weight when it comes from a wise man." Luna arrowed the comment at J.R.'s smug ego, and Dean couldn't help but curve lips into a pleased smile.

"She's not just beautiful, but smart." Dean slapped a hand on J.R.'s back. "Escort the lady down to the salon, my boy. You don't mind do you, Luna? I need to grab my sheet music."

"No, I don't mind in the least, Mr. Ryder."

"No, I don't mind in the least, Mr. Ryder," J.R. mimicked under his breath.

"You know, you really should stop being so jealous of him. It's not becoming."

"Jealous? Where do you get off saying that?" Was J.R.'s retort with a bitter laugh, although even to himself, he sounded like a jealous little boy. This was all on Dean, J.R. thought. How was he supposed to react when his eminence showed up at the most inopportune time, then proceeded to draw her attention away from him?

"It's written all over your face." Luna shot back.

"Don't be absurd. He's my uncle." Temper bubbled under his skin. "Are you coming?"

"I'll walk it on my own." She'd set her hands on her hips for effect if she could let go of the rail.

"Pfft, I'd like to see that," he said, under his breath.

To prove a point, Luna loosened her grip on the rail, but her legs gave way easily enough, and she reached for the brass rail again. "I'm just going to wait here a few more minutes, and by the way…"

J.R. jumped in when he sensed the rant coming on. "No more of your blather."

Heat flashed in the moss-green eyes. "I don't blather. I was going to say you may only think of him as your uncle, but he's a man who makes careers." And as easily ends them because if Dean Ryder didn't believe you had the talent necessary to make it in the music business, you'd be hard-pressed to find any other producer to take you on. "Oh, God! I'm going to be singing for *the* Dean Ryder." Luna pressed a hand to her stomach as it did a long, slow turn.

"Please stop referring to him as *the* Dean Ryder?" He's just a randy old man with an inexplicable talent to charm the pants off any woman, even you. J.R. was ready to pull the trigger on that retort from his arsenal until he realized nerves was what had her attacking him, and what she needed was reassurance not egging on. "You'll do fine."

"You think so?"

"I know so. I'm going to love you, and he will too. We all are."" J.R. brushed away a strand of hair that had fallen in front of her eyes and was happy when she let him. "Now, let me walk you below deck."

The deliberate intimate gesture, coupled with the tender words tugged at Luna's heart, and she linked her arm with J.R.'s.

Chapter 16

THE SALON WAS spacious with large panoramic windows that looked out to a calm, blue ocean and bathed the space in natural light. Walls were paneled in glossy rosewood. There were two ivory leather couches, and between them sat a Kazan coffee table. A mahogany table in the formal dining area sat twelve. There was a U-shaped bar stocked with bottles of what Luna deduced to be expensive spirits. The carpet at their feet was royal blue, thick and soft as clouds and yellow daisies speared from vases.

"Can I get you something to drink?" J.R. released Luna's hand once she'd settled into the couch.

Nodding, Luna's eyes followed him to the bar appreciating the fit of his jeans the entire way. The smooth contours of the white Polo shirt against the rippling muscles sent an unexpected punch of want to her stomach—again.

"It's cognac. Drink up. It'll make you feel better."

Luna took a long swig. It was stronger than she expected, but it had the right amount of kick she needed to quell the uneasiness J.R. roused in her when he draped his left arm over the couch behind her. "This is a beautiful, umm, boat?"

"It's one of Uncle Dean's toys." J.R.'s blue eyes steady on green unnerved her.

"I've never been off land." Luna nervously stammered.

"So, you've mentioned." Small talk, he thought disappointed because what he wanted to do was glide his lips over hers. But the yearning he'd seen earlier in her eyes had faded since *the* Dean Ryder injected himself between them.

"Sorry for the delay, but Jean stopped me. She's wondering when Luna's going to perform." Dean came at Luna and J.R. out of nowhere, and both pivoted in his direction. "You all right, son?" Dean asked an irate J.R.

"Dandy." Eyes narrowed, J.R. smiled, just the faintest curve of lips.

"Glad to hear. Now, Luna, take a look at this." Dean handed her the music sheet.

When Luna finished scanning over the song, Dean named Treasured Memory, a tear spilled down her cheek. "This is beautiful, Mr. Ryder, just beautiful. I'd have to hear it played out, but I can already tell it's been written from the heart, meant to stir emotion you can only feel for that special someone. I love it." Dean's throat constricted when he watched Luna run her fingers over the pages as if connecting with it. "But why are you showing it to me?" Luna tilted her head up to Dean, but J.R. answered her when his uncle remained surprisingly silent.

"Uncle Dean wrote it for you. It's your song, Luna."

"My song?" The eyes registering shock looked over at a nodding Dean. "I don't know what to say, Mr. Ryder."

"I want you to make it yours, Luna. This song will make you the star that you're meant to be. This song will launch you to stardom."

Dean's words sent a shiver up Luna's spine. "What are you talking about?"

"J.R. and I have discussed it, and we'd like to help you launch your career."

"That's right. Uncle Dean sees huge potential in you. He's rarely wrong when it comes to scouting talent, and he and I are willing to do whatever's necessary to help you launch your career. We want to make you a star, Luna." J.R.'s eyes held to her unblinking, stunned gaze.

"That's right, love. J.R. and I are more than willing to financially back your career."

In shocked silence, Luna considered the enormity of their words. The two men before her, with a generous gesture, meant to change her life in unimaginable ways.

She thought of the endless hours of practice, of all her struggles. She rolled over in her mind the sacrifices she'd made. Cleaning anything that came her way to save what little money she could, most days, she ran on little sleep. She couldn't remember the last time she'd slept a full six-hour night. All to lead her into hopelessness that more often than not grabbed her by the throat and choked her until she felt as if she couldn't breathe.

She thought of Teo. He was the reason she never gave up. He was the reason she'd been determined to make something of herself, to have something for herself and her mother. "I ... don't know what to say." Her eyes welled up, and J.R. thought he saw a tear in Dean's eyes.

J.R. handed Luna a tissue. "You don't need to say anything. What you need to do is sing this song for Jean, our music producer, and her team, the people you met on the flight. They're as anxious as Uncle Dean, and I are to hear you."

"J.R.'s right, and if my hunch is right, we're going to want you in the recording studio right away," Dean said.

"I don't know what to say." Luna's voice was a soft, shaky whisper.

"Say you'll sing for us now because I know for a fact Uncle Dean won't let up until you do." J.R. refreshed their drinks with Rémy Martin.

"But I'm not familiar with the song. I haven't even had a chance to rehearse." Luna took the offered glass from J.R. and took a quick gulp, although she knew it wasn't going to agree with her empty stomach, but the buzz she was getting from it was calming.

"You'll be fine, Luna. If uncle Dean says you're ready, you are." J.R. handed Dean his glass.

"I think you both have far more confidence in me than I do." Luna's saucer-round eyes added that final spark of animation for Dean, and he smiled.

"I know deep down, you know you can do this. You're good, Luna, really good. You're meant for great things. And if it's the last thing I do, I'm going to make this happen for you, not for money or glamour or stardom, but because a gift like yours is meant to be shared." There was an undisputable genuineness in Dean's tone.

The same misty shade of gold-flecked green as Dean's held his gaze. Luna felt the tug of affection, a special bond, a connection with the man she'd only met minutes ago. "All right, Mr. Ryder."

WITH DEAN AT THE PIANO, SURROUNDED by Jean and her team, and J.R. watching on, Luna closed her eyes and let the music flow like the billowing wind around her. In a few short seconds, her water phobia and nervous fear dissolved, and the words to Treasured Memory poured out as fluid as the blue waters around her.

I was running scared and feeling lost
Always searching, always on the run,
Feeling as brittle as butterfly's wings
But I no longer am because today
You came into my life
And everything fell in place

Like a soaring white dove in bright blue skies
You filled me with a beautiful peace
and perfect love
You touched my heart
and took away my lonesome blues
But above all, you made my dream come true

The world is a good place
and it's better with you in it
You changed my life in every way

And Darling now, after the light fades
And I'm led to that lonely place
I will no longer feel alone
Because even in darkness
You will always be
My treasured memory

My darling, I wish you love for all eternity
I wish you happiness to infinity
And always know that I love you

Because you will always be my treasured memory

With the sun at Luna's back, and the wind teasing her hair like gentle fingers, the warm liquid sound of her voice poured with a passion that came from deep within her. Emotions raw and real burst from Luna like a shooting star streaking light into blackness. Her words effortlessly flowed in tune to the music. As Dean expected she would, Luna embraced the song. It became a part of her. As Luna launched into the second chorus, there was no doubt Treasured Memory was her song.

As Dean ran his fingers over the keys, and the melody swelled, his eyes misted. Luna's voice stirred emotions long dormant in him. Her voice, silky as air, was like Marina's. All at once, the memories, his love for her, the regret, the guilt rushed at him.

Luna's voice, just as Marina's was powerful yet graceful, soothing but fiery, comforting, and provocative. It pulsed under your skin and sent shivers of sheer pleasure down your spine.

Dean let himself be consumed by the voice that spoke to his soul, pulled at his heart. He let Luna's voice, the song, and the memories of Sarina drift around him like a feather in the wind.

This was Luna's song, J.R. thought. He'd never felt the thrash of passion deep in him as he did then. Luna stirred something in J.R. he found gratifying. It made him want more from Luna than the flash of the moment.

Captivated by her beauty, mesmerized by her voice, J.R. drank her all in. He was drowning in the .sea green eyes brimming with tears as the swell of power rose in her throat. When Luna's passionate eyes fell on J.R., it made his body throb and shot a wave of torrid heat through him. Want, need, longing, desire, swamped him all at once. For the second time today, Luna set his emotions in turmoil, made him feel fragile, and moved him in unimaginable ways.

Luna could have gone on singing forever. She felt a pang of regret when it was over, but when her audience rose to their feet clapping, unreservedly, Luna's lips curved into a huge smile.

"Thank you." Luna turned to Dean, who, with a wide grin along with J.R. rose to his feet and clapped enthusiastically.

"It's your song, love." Dean mouthed.

"You were wonderful." Pure delight glowed in J.R.'s blue eyes.

It was an audience of eight, but they were all that mattered. Because of them, Luna's life was about to take a one-eighty turn and be presented with changes she never in her wildest dreams imagined possible.

Chapter 17

THE WEEKS THAT followed Luna's performance on the Seas the Day took on a strange cast. It gave a new definition to the word insanity. The rigors of training to get to world stage performing level, which was where Dean and J.R. aimed for Luna, were far more demanding than she imagined. Luna, however, didn't mind it in the least. She was willing to work twenty-four-seven if that was what it took.

There were marketing meetings and photoshoot sessions that took hours to take the flawless photograph for the promotional campaign to break once Luna hit the recording studio. There were voice lessons, much more specialized than Miss Jones', which helped develop her vocal range. Luna learned the finer points of monitoring the power of her tone and how to support the vocal cords to avoid strain. The more Luna learned, the more she realized there was to learn to perform on a professional level.

The hours of training turned into long, demanding days, which meant less time with Tom. To Luna's surprise, as disappointed as Tom was, he was nothing but the perfect, encouraging, and supportive friend. Although Luna imagined Tom wouldn't be as supportive if he knew of J.R.'s involvement in her career.

There were questions, discussions about J.R. brought on by Tom's overprotective, probing mind. Each time,

Luna eased his wild imaginings by assuring him her days were spent with Dean Ryder at his home. It wasn't as if she was lying. Dean had offered to take her under his wing to teach her everything he knew.

"Do you believe it, Mom? Dean Ryder offering to work with me one-on-one to teach me everything he knows." Luna watched her mother fish cups from the cupboard as the last drops of coffee spurted into the carafe.

"He sounds like a wonderful man." Sarina flipped the button off on the coffee maker, poured steaming coffee into two cups.

"He is, Mom." Luna reached into the refrigerator for the milk carton. "Do you know what this means?"

Sarina knew precisely what it meant for Dean Ryder to be in her daughter's life, but said, "No, I don't," not to dim Luna's excitement.

"It means I get to learn everything from the best in the business." Luna set the sugar and spoons on the table. "I don't know if he does this for all his up-and-coming artists, and honestly, I don't care. I'm just so grateful he's willing to spend so much time with me to make me, in his words, 'a household name.' Me, a household name, do you believe it?" She rested her chin on her knees and let her thoughts drifted to daydreams.

"I do. You're very talented." Sarina watched her daughter through the rising steam from her cup. "I'm so happy for you, honey, and grateful to Mr. Ryder."

"I want you to meet him, Mom. You'll like him."

"I already do. We'll meet when the time is right. You know me. I'd rather stay in the shadows. Besides, I want the focus solely on you. This is your time, baby, enjoy it."

"I am, Mom. I love working with Mr. Ryder. He understands me so well. It's as if we have a spiritual connection from another life." Does that sound weird?"

Sarina shook her head. "You're both like-minded."

"We are that, but it goes beyond our love of music. We're both so ... attuned with one another."

"I'm glad you're enjoying the time you're spending with him. It puts my mind at ease, knowing I don't need to worry about you."

"Mr. Ryder's a perfect gentleman and a great mentor. Besides, he's old enough to be my grandfather." Luna rose, kissed Sarina on the cheek. "So, you don't need to worry about anything. I'm craving a piece of your cheesecake with my coffee. Any left?"

"Bottom shelf in the refrigerator," Sarina watched her daughter happily float to the refrigerator as she had since meeting Dean, and she couldn't be more grateful to him—or terrified by his presence in her life.

It was now a matter of time before the truth came out.

DEAN'S HOME, A PEACEFUL OASIS WITH acres of green fields north of the city, became Luna's training base. In the elegant music room, Dean referred to as his sanctuary, and where he escaped to let his emotions flow into the music when thoughts of Marina filled his head, was where Luna spent most of her days holed up with him.

Except for the lack of framed photographs of family one often found in a cozy room like Dean's music room, the music room looked as it had when Marina last set foot there. Dean made sure of that. Walls were banana-yellow, the color Marina had chosen for its coziness and warmth.

Mahogany bookshelves behind the glossy, black Steinway piano burst at the seams with the books Marina had loved to read. In front of the black, marble fireplace, a cheery floral sofa with matching chairs Marina picked during their week in Rome, sat atop the chocolate-brown Persian rug she'd chosen for its thick pile. Dean's many platinum awards, Oscars and Emmys, were displayed on what Marina had labeled Dean's-Accomplishment-Wall. A magnificent crystal chandelier glittered under the late morning sunlight streaming through bowed windows.

It was Marina's room, and now it was Luna's.

Luna felt the passion abound in the room every time she stepped in. It was as if the room spoke to her. Whether because it was where the great Dean Ryder created his music she revered or whether because of the romantic notion it was where he was shaping her career, was up for debate.

"You look tired. Let's take a break." Dean offered, seeing the exhaustion on Luna's face. "You need to relax your mind and body along with your voice, Luna. Have you been getting enough sleep?"

Luna nodded, and when Dean pinned her a look with raised brows, she broke down. "Okay. I haven't for some time."

"Luna, you need your rest to be at your best." Dean walked over to the bar, picked up the scotch bottle, and poured three fingers into a snifter. "Have you finalized the sale of Maid For You yet?"

"It will be final this week. I can't thank you enough for finding me a buyer. J.R. assured me DR Enterprises is a reputable company and will take good care of my employees." Luna watched Dean fall into the couch across from her.

"He's not wrong about that." Dean tossed back part of his drink.

"Between you and me, DR Enterprises paid me a considerable sum for my company. More so than I thought it was worth." Luna watched the three blue Jays perched outside the window, pecking at the seeds Dean set out for them every morning.

"Mazel tov. So, once the deal is signed and sealed, I want your complete focus on your singing."

"It will be, Mr. Ryder. Between the money from the sale and the generous salary, you insisted WE Productions set me up with my financial concerns will be nonexistent. I'll be honest with you. Our money problems were draining me. Now my mom and I, for the first time, can rest easy." Luna smiled awkwardly when she realized she divulged too much, but Dean made her feel as if she could tell him anything.

"There's no shame in that, love. We've all been there," Dean said, with a glow of empathy.

Luna's eyes on the blue Jays now staring in as if window-shopping said, "Well, with money worries taken care of, I can concentrate solely on my singing."

"Good because that's what I want you to do." Dean made a move to get up but remained seated when she rose to her feet and took the snifter from his hand to refill.

"If truth be told, sing and sing some more is all I want to do, especially now that the vocal coach made my voice that much better. Miss Jones was a fantastic teacher, but she had her limitations." Luna refilled Dean's glass and walked it back to him. "You know she wanted me to go to

Juilliard, but I couldn't afford it. That was also around the time my dad passed away, and leaving mom wasn't an option."

"I'm sorry, Luna. You've certainly had a lot to contend with at such a young age." Dean could see the sadness in her eyes and wished he could take it for himself.

"We all do. It's what makes us survivors." Luna stretched a hand full of seeds out, watched the blue jays come to her. "My dad used to say that."

"He wasn't wrong."

"Anyway, I certainly wouldn't have been able to afford a top-notch singing trainer like Sondra. She's taught me so much, and her training has made a huge difference. Don't you think, Mr. Ryder?" Luna didn't wait for a response and launched into excitable prattle about her training, her singing, and the songs they were working on. It pleased Dean to see her happy. Sipping scotch from his refreshed glass, he cheerfully listened.

"It's nice to see you excited and motivated. Shows me you want this. Believe it or not, there's a lot of talent out there, but once we bring them in and they find out the hard work involved, many give up," Dean put in when she finally went silent.

"Why would anyone give up on their once-in-a-lifetime opportunity to do what they love?" Turning to Dean, the sunlight streaming through the window at her back made Luna's hair glow blue, and for a brief moment, Dean mistook her for Marina.

"They didn't have a true passion for the music, a respect for their God-given talent. If they had, they wouldn't be blinded by the hype of stardom and would have been more interested in harnessing their talent. Stardom doesn't land at your feet because you have talent. It takes discipline, one that many people, when push comes to shove, don't possess. You hungry?"

"Now that you mention it, I could eat something more…"

"Substantial than coffee? How many times do I have to tell you, young lady coffee is not a food group?" His tone was that of a concerned father. "I'll get Mrs. Bertinelli to whip us up a chicken Caesar salad. Her Caesar dressing should be bottled," Dean said, leading her out of the music room, across the length of the white and black tiled hallway to the kitchen where Mrs. Bertinelli was setting a freshly baked angel food cake on the rack to cool.

The kitchen, like the woman who ruled it, was efficient and breathed family. Walls were eggshell white, and dark mahogany cabinets wrapped it. Appliances were state of the art, and floors matched the mahogany on the walls. On the window ledge, a collection of fresh herbs speared from small clay pots.

"That smells fantastic." Dean filled his lungs with the freshly baked aroma lingering in the kitchen and bent down to peck the cherubic woman with the salt and pepper hair wrapped into a neat bun on the cheek. "Have I told you lately how much I love you?"

"You mean how much you love my cooking." Mrs. Bertinelli banged the colander against the edge of the sink to shake excess water off the strawberries.

"If I were fifteen years younger, I'd marry you." Dean's dimpled smile made the matronly, septuagenarian woman smirk. "She only has eyes for younger men."

Mrs. Bertinelli slapped the back of Dean's hand when he reached for a strawberry. "He has this crazy notion I'd be romantically interested in him," she told Luna, waving the knife like a conductor's baton before proceeding to slice the stems off the strawberries with expert precision. "Pfft, artists, they think the world revolves around them."

Knowing their banter was all in good fun, Luna smiled. As Dean's cook for the past twenty-five years, Mrs. Bertinelli considered him—her words—her illegitimate son.

"Would you like something to drink, Luna?" Dean offered, poking his head into the refrigerator.

"I'll take an ice tea if you have one."

Dean grabbed a beer for himself and an iced tea for Luna. Twisting the cap off the Snapple bottle, he handed it to her before turning to Mrs. Bertinelli with his instructions for lunch.

"He thinks I'm his servant now." Mrs. Bertinelli covered the bowl of sliced strawberries with plastic wrap and set it the refrigerator.

"I can help you, Mrs. Bertinelli," Luna said automatically.

Alarmed eyes turned to Luna. "No. No, no, my dear. You're not touching my kitchen."

"But I'd be happy to…" Luna started to say but went silent when she saw the cautioning look in Dean's eyes.

"It's a nice day. Let's have lunch on the terrace." Dean steered Luna out the sliding door leaving a gap wide enough to ease his head in. "We're three for lunch, Mrs. Bertinelli," he said, shutting the door before Mrs. Bertinelli could say anything. "The woman terrifies me."

"Then why keep her on all these years?" Luna's eyes flicked to the gardens surrounding the pool and Jacuzzi. Shades of deep purple, rust, blue, and gold from chrysanthemums, asters, and blue mist shrubs poured stunningly vibrant.

"Because of her cooking, of course. The woman cooks like a Michelin starred chef." Dean wound the cheerful striped umbrella open and angled it to shade them from the burning sun. "Haven't you ever heard the saying the way to a man's heart is through his stomach? And I am but a simple man with a demanding stomach."

Luna snorted a giggle. "I'll agree with you there. She's a better cook than my mother, although I'd never admit it to anyone but you." She brought her knees up and circled them with her arms.

"Mum's the word." Dean reached for his beer and swilled before resting it on the armchair. "I haven't heard you mention your mother before today." He watched the beads of sweat trickle down the side of the bottle to his hand.

"She's a wonderful, loving, hard-working woman who has devoted her life to me and my father. That is until he died. Daddy was a wonderful father, kind, sweet, loving. I miss him so much." Luna confided, and Dean felt a distinct pang of envy at the thought of what he'd missed family, children, the love of a woman.

"He sounds like a great man, and your mother sounds like a wonderful woman."

"I'd love you for you to meet her." Luna watched Dean pick at the label on his bottle with his fingernail.

"I'd love to meet her." Dean and Luna turned at the whoosh of the opening sliding door.

"Am I interrupting?" J.R.'s voice flowed through the opened door when the two pair of eyes came down on him. "I was in the area and thought I'd pop in."

"Not at all, my boy." Dean motioned J.R. to the chair next to Luna. "You have time for lunch?"

"Mrs. Bertinelli already talked me into it."

"Good. How about a beer?"

"Mrs. Bertinelli is getting it for me." Anchoring his sunglasses on his head, J.R. eased his tall frame into the offered chair.

"She is, is she? I couldn't get her to fetch me the antidote for a lethal snake bite if my life depended on it."

"I can't help it if she likes me better than you." J.R.'s smirk was more teasing than prodding.

"Sometimes, I wonder who that woman works for."

"I work for you, but I like him better." Mrs. Bertinelli belted out, stepping onto the terrace. "You forget, I hear everything. Here you go, my darling." Affectionately, she handed J.R. the bottle then turned to Dean. "Now, you get in there and help me bring the tray of food out."

Without argument, Dean rose to his feet. As Luna was about to do so, J.R. shot her the same warning look Dean gave her earlier. "You do what Mrs. Bertinelli says, especially when it comes to her kitchen. You don't offer help unless she asks for it. Besides, she enjoys bossing him around. She has him on a short leash, and if he wants her to continue cooking for him, he does what he's told. He reasons it as the cost of doing business."

Luna let out a snort of laughter. "Small sacrifices, I guess."

J.R. took a long pull of his beer. "Uncle Dean tells me your training is coming along well."

"It is." Luna watched J.R. remove his jacket and drape it on the back of his chair. When he loosened his tie and unbuttoned the top buttons, she felt the fierce pull of desire he always set off in her.

"Are you enjoying yourself, Luna?" J.R. studied her. Her hair tied back in a ponytail made those irresistible green eyes jump out at him.

"I'm loving every minute, and Mr. Ryder has been wonderful. I mean to devote so much of his valuable time to mentor me."

"Yes, he is a saint." The sarcasm rang clear.

She let the comment pass. "I'll forever be grateful to him, and you, Jimmy." Luna absently called him by the name that swirled in her head when thoughts of him filled her, which was constant lately. "I'm sorry. I should process things in my brain before I say them aloud. I meant no disrespect," she clarified when she misread the crease between his brows for disapproval.

"My father was the only person who called me Jimmy." J.R. picked the label on his bottle in the same way Dean had, and she realized how similar they both were, although they were related by circumstance.

"I'm sorry I stirred such a painful memory."

"You didn't. I liked you calling me Jimmy. It felt nice," he said quietly.

When Luna's lips curved, as he liked, he pictured, pressing his lips against them as he'd thought of doing so often. His uncle had told him women controlled the tide of life, but this woman was steering his life into a wild emotional ride.

"So, are you pumped about performing at the JWAC next month? Uncle Dean thinks you'll be more than ready to step out into the limelight by then."

With a jolt, she sat upright in her seat. "JWAC? What are you talking about?"

"Didn't Uncle Dean tell you we've booked you to perform at the James West Arts Center for my mother's yearly Cancer Society fundraiser?"

Luna could only hear the blood buzzing in her ears. "He didn't mention anything. I'd remember that. It's a five-thousand seat venue, isn't it?"

"It is. You know my mother is Poppy Barclay-West, and she's on almost every fundraising board. She's been organizing the Cancer Society fundraiser at that venue for the past ten years. It's a big event."

Because her mouth was dry now, Luna picked up her Snapple, drained it.

"I'm sorry I sprang it on you like this." J.R. absently reached for her hand. The sensation of her skin against his left him tingling. It left him feeling awed and thrilled even after she pulled away when Dean stepped onto the terrace with the tray of food.

"Lunch is served," Dean announced.

Always popping in at the most inopportune time, J.R. thought. "You never mentioned to Luna about performing at mom's fundraiser." The piping song of birds filled the ensuing silence. "You never told her she'd be performing Treasured Memory. And I'm guessing he also didn't mention about the recording session we've scheduled in six weeks or the tour we're working on." J.R. finished in a clipped tone when it became clear Dean hadn't mentioned any of those things. "I thought we discussed how we'd leave it up to you to keep Luna updated."

Dean calmly set a plate of salad in front of Luna and J.R., and taking the last one for himself, fell into his chair. "No. I didn't mention any of it to Luna."

"Don't you think it would have been a good idea to do so?" J.R. watched Dean as he casually pulled out a fork and a knife from between the rolled napkin. "Say something."

"I was eventually going to tell you, Luna. I just haven't because ... well, I didn't want to derail your focus from your training. You're doing so well, and I figured there was no sense in distracting you. Thank you very much, Mr. Big Mouth." Dean stabbed at his salad.

J.R.'s brows lifted. "You're angry with me? I think she deserves to know what we're planning."

Dean dropped his fork on the edge of his plate with a thud. "Not when it's going to derail what we're trying to accomplish in the next few weeks."

Sensing she was now in the middle of a testosterone-fueled moment, Luna plunked palms on the table, making J.R. and Dean go silent. Turning their gaze to her, they saw the eyes blazing with anger. There was a fire in them both men hadn't seen before.

"Mr. Ryder is right. Knowing would have rattled me as it's doing right now." When Dean shot a cocky smirk at J.R., Luna pivoted a fiery gaze at him. "But J.R. is correct in that I need to be told what's coming down the pike so I can mentally prepare myself. Springing it on me at the last minute wouldn't have garnered better results."

J.R. gave Dean an I-told-you-so look, leading Luna to conclude she was sitting between two boys rather than the two of the most influential men in her life right then.

"Now, I want you to tell me all about the recording session and the tour that's being planned. And I want to discuss the possibility of singing more than just the one song at your mother's fundraiser. Mr. Ryder and I have written a few songs, which I think would be perfect for the event. And..."

Silently, both men followed Luna with their eyes as she stalked the terrace, excitedly chirping on.

Chapter 18

AT FIFTY-SIX, Poppy Barclay-West was a formidable woman. She was tall and willowy with a sleek cap of warm chestnut hair and piercing blue eyes. As the many generations of Barclay women were bred to do, from the moment Poppy uttered her first word, she carried herself with grace and dignity. Poppy attended the best all-girl schools, and in her spare time, etiquette training was her focus. In her circles, confidence and poise in social situations was a skill expected from the men whose side the Barclay women eventually graced. Maintaining the highest level of decorum was conducive to your husband's flourishing career.

Following in the footsteps of the Barclay women, Poppy dedicated her life to philanthropic work. She generously contributed her time and her name to raise millions of dollars for fashionable charities. For optics sakes, Poppy would throw in a couple of lesser-known charities catering to the indigent—destitute or needy were such unmusical words. As an extension to her charity work, Poppy was instrumental in raising millions of dollars for political allies because you never knew when you needed a political favor.

It wasn't out of a moral responsibility that Poppy did it. She did it because it garnered her positions of influence. Her name appeared on the roster of several hospital boards and museum committees. As a bonus, the living room wall decorated with the numerous awards recognizing her selfless contribution gained her the praise and admiration she thrived on.

Separating donors from their money came easily to Poppy, but then all she had to do was flash the Barclay-West name and donations poured in. The Barclay surname was an institution that could be traced to Edward, Duke of Kent, whereas the West surname was inconsequential. In Poppy's circles, the West name was considered vulgar. It hadn't gained its prominence through old money as the Barclay's had. Old money wasn't nouveau riche. It had its own smell, its own class and came with its own privilege. But the West name was worth billions, and it never failed to draw the who's who of old and new money.

Unlike the women of her circles, Poppy didn't believe in their elitist ways. She'd never refuse to marry new money because her family bore a respected name attained through inherited wealth. In fact, she'd gone as far as marry James when he was broke.

She'd been shunned for marrying James, but how she'd proved them wrong. Barclay-West's combined assets now put them fifth on Forbes richest list. Moreover, her once despised hyphenated name, now secured millions of dollars for her charities and bolstered Poppy's reputation to where organizations clamored to attach her name to their events, and tonight's fundraiser was no exception. Tonight, the James West Arts Center brimmed to capacity with supporters who willingly paid fifty-thousand dollars per table for the Cancer Society event. No easy feat, but one Poppy made happen with a few telephone calls.

In her element, Poppy did what she did best—take charge. Imperiously barking instructions to the wait staff like a general charging into battle, Poppy inspected every meal sent out to the annoyance of the head chef who, in his French tongue, vowed many times over never to work with the controlling bitch again. Poppy inspected the sound system, the stage set up, not that she understood the machinations of it, but she had to ensure everything was in perfect working order for Dean. It was what he'd asked of her and what Poppy aimed to give Dean. Keeping Dean happy, looking out for him had always been her priority.

Poppy was anxious to meet his current protégé, a woman by the name of Luna Moon, whom Dean was spending an inexplicable amount of time with. Poppy wondered whether their relationship went beyond mentor and protégé. If anyone knew Dean Ryder's penchant for younger women, it was Poppy, and there was no doubt in her mind, Dean was obsessed with Luna. She hoped Dean would come to his senses and in the fullness of time and deem the twenty-year-old Luna Moon too young—even by his standards.

Poppy long ago learned to turn a blind eye to Dean's philandering ways, deciding it was part of his DNA. Still, there were times when seeing him with women half her age tied Poppy's stomach in knots. In the end, though, she forgave Dean. As always, she protected him from the tarts who, in her opinion, seduced him for a shot at stardom. Because she loved Dean with all her heart, and that was what you did for the man you loved.

Dean was her soulmate, the man she was meant to marry and spend her life with, but they'd met too late. When Dean came into her life, she was married to James, and a Barclay didn't divorce. She'd married James at the young age of seventeen not out of love, but because they were perfectly suited to fill each other's role, she was stuck for life.

Rebellious by nature, Poppy chose twenty-seven-year-old James because he filled the requirements to defy her overbearing, controlling parents who'd dictated her life for long enough. Knowing her parents would blacklist James as a possible suitor Poppy purposely sought him out and offered him what he needed—money in exchange for marriage.

Although James West had come from a long line of wealth, he went into the marriage penniless. The West family, having lost their entire hard-earned fortune during the Great Depression, crossed the line into destitution. Worse than that, they were stripped of their dignity and their standing in society.

A substantial trust fund at her disposal, Poppy presented James with an opportunity for redemption. Poppy offered James financial help in return for marriage. James not only agreed to marry Poppy, but he promised to elevate himself to a level she'd be proud of. A Barclay is born and bred for minks and diamonds, not wool and rhinestones James told Poppy, and she never doubted him.

True to his word, a few years after their marriage, James and his partner, Dean Ryder, struck gold with a singer by the name of Tommy King. Tommy became the first in a long line of successes that brought James and Dean a level of financial realization that exceeded Poppy's expectations.

Poppy now had everything anyone could ask for. Not that it was anything new to her after all she'd been born in the lap of luxury. Now, however, there was a greater sense of satisfaction for Poppy because what she had was hers. It wasn't her father or her mother's. It was hers—all hers.

Poppy had homes in exotic destinations, staff in each one to cater to her every need. There were private jets at Poppy's disposal to whisk her off at a moment's notice. There were days Poppy flew to Paris just because she fancied a walk down the Champs-Élysées. Poppy spent weekends on the beaches of Bora Bora or Sardinia. She'd fly off to Milan to lunch with Giorgio then go on a crazy shopping spree at his store, spending hundreds of thousands of dollars.

With all that going for her, Poppy felt hollow. She didn't have the one thing she craved—the one thing her obscene wealth couldn't buy, Dean's love.

Poppy fell in love with Dean the moment James introduced them. She wasn't sure why or how it happened; it just did. Maybe it was Dean's handsome good looks or his smoldering sexuality and sexual prowess, which the women in his life bragged about to any tabloid that would listen, that drew Poppy to him. Whatever the reason, all Poppy knew for certain was James never made her feel the way she imagined Dean could, and she longed for the day when he would.

Poppy blamed James for feeling about Dean as she did. If James were more like Dean in bed, maybe she wouldn't be so drawn to the man. James was a decent lover, she supposed, but then he'd been her one and only. She wanted the type of sexual encounters Dean's women bragged about. Poppy wanted the steamy toe-curling roll in the sheets his women boasted about. Poppy wanted more than looking up at James' face as it contorted into satisfaction at their lovemaking sessions. Poppy wanted from James the cry-at-the-top-of-your-lungs experience as Dean's women described their encounters with him.

At James' death, Poppy was a youthful thirty with sexual and emotional needs, but as a Barclay, mourning protocols had to be met. She set two years as the appropriate mourning period before pursuing her next relationship. More to the point, the long-awaited loving relationship and sexual encounter with Dean, she'd fantasized her thirteen years of her married life.

Eighteen months had gone by, and Poppy now began to mark the remainder of her mourning days off on the secret calendar locked away in the top drawer of her desk away from the staff's curious eyes.

The countdown was nerve-racking slow. Five months away, the anticipation was making Poppy lose sleep. At four months, Poppy flew to Paris, and spent thousands of dollars on silk negligées and lingerie, at Sabbia Rosa on Rue des Saints-Peres.

Poppy's loins ached for the moment she'd get to experience tangling in her newly purchased ivory silk sheets with the man she'd fantasized of for years. The anticipation had her ready for the moment Dean plunged himself inside her, until they were joined together like magnets. Poppy imagined him rising and falling on top of her as he slid in and out of her. She could feel the flood of liquid heat coursing through her and making her entire body spasm with waves of mind-numbing pleasure. Poppy fantasized about the words of love they'd whisper to one another as the orgasm like a long-dormant volcano, burned in her until it violently burst along with her cries.

Swimming in emotions and anticipation, when the six months were up, plans months in the making, were set in motion. There was lobster flown in from Maine and cheeses from Italy. There was a case of Romanee-Conti wine at the cost of eight-hundred dollars per bottle, brought in from France for the special dinner.

Poppy called Dean and invited him to dinner at her estate. The time was set for seven on Saturday. Ten hours before the long-awaited moment, Poppy spent hours at the salon. Seven hours to go, a manicure and pedicure followed. Six hours and counting, she moved on to the leg and underarm wax, and for the first time, Poppy set her mind on a Brazilian wax, the most God awful, painful experience of her life. But Dean was worth it.

Three hours before the long-expected dinner, the table was set, the lights dimmed, and the room delicately scented with two huge rose bouquets spearing from Waterford vases. The music was carefully selected for the perfect sensual ambiance. With the room and table setting passing her inspection, Poppy slid the doors to the dining room closed and headed upstairs to get ready.

Wrapped in a white towel, Poppy stepped out of the bathroom and made her way to the bed where the red lace bra and matching thong along with a very short, strapless, red dress she picked out were spread. With an impish smile, she slipped on the bra and thong she knew Dean was bound to appreciate. Zipping into the body-hugging silk dress, she caught the blinking light on her answering machine. She pressed the play button, and her smile quickly deflated when Dean's voice flowed with an apology.

Curled in a fetal position on her bed, holding the answering machine like a newborn baby, Poppy replayed the message over and over. Tears stained with black mascara rolled down her cheeks onto the unused silk bedsheets.

Poppy cried until she had no tears left in her.

Later that week, Poppy read in the tabloids that Dean had spent the weekend frolicking on the beaches of Menorca, with an exotic Latin beauty half his age by the name of Marina Banderas. It was a bitter pill for Poppy to swallow, but Dean was a man, she reasoned. It wasn't his fault that Latin floozy seduced him.

She wouldn't forget Marina Banderas any time soon.

Poppy's future attempts to seduce Dean into her bed and steal his heart were as unsuccessful. Dean had fallen head over heels for the Latin tart who was now always by his side. To soothe her pain, Poppy rationalized her failure to persuade Dean into a more intimate relationship was all due to timing.

Dean, she talked herself into believing, was too loyal to James to delve into a relationship with her so soon after his death. Poppy concluded, she reminded Dean of James, and two years wasn't enough time to put the loss of his best friend, and partner, behind him.

She'd give Dean the time he needed. After all, she'd waited all these years for him a few more months wasn't going to kill her. They would be together soon enough, she told herself often enough to the point of believing it.

In the meantime, as a virile, youthful widow, Poppy's answer to her demanding hormones was to take on several lovers, reasoning they would fulfill a temporary void while serving to make Dean jealous. She wanted to make him feel as miserable as she felt when she saw him parading that tart in her face.

To Poppy's annoyance, Dean's eyes were full of Marina, and her meaningless sexual encounters had no effect on him. Her young lovers, however, were very adventurous, and in the end, led Poppy to a sexual awakening.

Antonio, her first lover, was her twenty-year-old gardener. From her patio sipping martinis, Poppy watched him rove the grounds trimming and shearing, bare-chested, his long, dark waves flowing in the wind. One week later, Antonio was in her bed, making her experience the multiple orgasms she'd never had before.

Her sexual needs awakened, Poppy couldn't get enough of young Antonio or the orgasms that left her shuddering and spent. Often he drove her over the edge for no less than five successive orgasms, a phenomenon she thought was a myth experienced only by the characters in her romance novels. James had brought her to ecstasy during most of their encounters, but in many instances, he hadn't, and she'd dismissed it as par for the course.

After Antonio came Daniel, her twenty-two-year-old tennis instructor. Daniel was a tall, muscular flaxen-haired Adonis who taught Poppy less about tennis and more that the mouth could be a sexual tool. Although it took, some getting used to—a Barclay with unimpeachable breeding didn't indulge in such primal acts—in the end, she found it perversely erotic.

Timothy, her masseuse, followed Daniel. Timothy had fiery red hair and the greenest eyes she'd ever seen. During one of her leg massages, he let oily fingers cruise up her thighs. When Poppy didn't stop him, he slipped fingers further along. Finding her hot and wet, his fingers proceeded to do things that made her eyes roll back in her head. While begging him not to stop, Poppy pondered how she, a Barclay, could allow a stranger to touch her as he was. At the end of the session, drained and utterly satisfied, Poppy decided, damned be the Barclay protocols, and penciled him in for a massage three times weekly.

Poppy's session with Daniel took place on the massage table until he decided to show Poppy that his oily fingers could bring her gratification anywhere at any time. He made Poppy moan his name at the local park with a baseball game going on feet away. There was the time Daniel unexpectedly slipped those long, agile fingers under white lace at Chez Phillipe while the waiter poured their wine, and afterward in the car while driving her home. To this day, her lips curved into a wide smile whenever she heard Silhouette drift from her car radio. Once he gave her multiple orgasms in the fifth row of the Humber Cinema as Honey Ryder emerged from the sea.

As good as Daniel was, Christian, her Cary Grant looking golf instructor taught Poppy the most when he introduced her to the Kama Sutra. One scan of the book and Poppy was determined to experience every page with him.

As much fun as Poppy was having she felt incomplete and rootless. Aimlessly drifting from lover to lover, she imagined how wonderful her newly acquired lovemaking skills would feel when shared with the man she loved. To share her bed and share her sexual knowledge with the man she loved was what Poppy craved.

It was now over a quarter-century of waiting for Dean, but hope was an eternal spring in Poppy. Catering to him, pleasing him until the day he took her to his bed was why at the last minute, she bumped Céline Dion from performing at her Cancer Society fundraiser and scheduled Luna Moon—a complete unknown.

It was a huge request Dean made of Poppy. The promotional campaign lauding Céline as the performer for the event was set in motion months ago, and every ticket sold out within an hour. People paid big money to see an A-list performer, not Luna Moon, a complete unknown, but for Dean, Poppy willingly made the concession. Poppy had gone as far as allowing Dean to do the introduction after he insisted he should be the one to introduce Luna.

Poppy kept adoring eyes on Dean when he stepped onto the stage and sauntered with confidence to center stage. At sixty-five, he looked as striking as the first day they'd met, and set her heart pounding as forcefully in her chest. Silver hair framed the handsome, tanned face, and the firm, generous mouth was curved into a smile. He wore black Italian silk against a white shirt and a black bow tie with sophisticated elegance.

A pained expression came over her face when she saw the pride that sparkled in the ocean-green eyes as he introduced Luna to a restless crowd. Gushing about his protégé, giving Luna praise and compliments as Poppy never heard Dean do for any of his other discoveries had nails digging deep into her palms as intense anger snaked through her. When Dean waved Luna onto the stage, Poppy's eyes never left his. There was more than admiration in them as he watched Luna sashay from left stage to his side. After handing Luna the microphone, Dean kissed her on the cheek and stepped off the stage.

There was love in his eyes, Poppy thought, a deep, meaningful love.

Poppy studied Luna carefully. She was a stunning beauty. Jet-black hair tied into an elegant updo with dark tendrils cascading around a porcelain face studded with Jade-green eyes and wine-red painted lips. A waterfall of diamonds—undoubtedly, a gift from Dean, Poppy thought—dangled from either side of her face. Her skin was bronze against the white strapless gown that showed off generous curves and fell sensually low to ripe breasts.

Luna, Poppy decided, was the type of woman that stirred envy in every woman, and set men's minds fantasizing. She was Dean's type of woman, young and beautiful with trusting guileless eyes full of hope, and Poppy felt the sharp claws of resentment tearing at her stomach. This woman was another in the long line of women half Dean's age she'd fought for his attention.

The more Poppy studied Luna, the more she felt a sense of familiarity. Something about her left Poppy digging deep into the recesses of her mind looking for answers. None came just then.

When the lights dimmed, and the spotlight fell on Luna, she closed her eyes and breathed a silent prayer willing the fear of failure churning at the pit of her stomach away. She couldn't let Dean or J.R. down. They'd invested so much in her in the past few months, but more importantly, she couldn't let herself down. This was what she'd been working toward all her life.

Taking a deep breath, Luna focused on the wail of brass, the moan of a Sax, the sweet strumming from the acoustic guitar, stirring from the orchestra. She absorbed the bluesy sound of the music. Let it flow in her. The music pounding in her, Luna's sultry voice let the words to Treasured Memory flow passionately, seductively, for the first time in public. The instant the words were out, a hush fell in the room.

The audience of five thousand was entranced by the voice that rolled over them in powerful waves. As the audience watched the emotions pour from misty-lake colored eyes, Luna made their pulses pound. Mesmerized by the unexplained throb of emotions, men reached for their partner's hand, and women easily fell back into their arms. Everyone in the room had their eyes fixed on no one but Luna as they swayed like wildflowers in the wind.

Poppy watched Luna shine like the diamonds at her ears. There was something so familiar about her, but Poppy's memory wouldn't cooperate.

In the wings, Dean watched Luna, the pride in his eyes inescapable as right before him, she blossomed into the star he knew her to be. Her voice was smooth, soothing, yet powerful. Tonight, the audience of five thousand witnessed, before them the birth of a star. Luna Moon would not be forgotten, Dean thought, and soon enough, he'd make sure she reached the four corners of the earth.

At the end of the song, the cheers rose and fell in intensity, but never faded. Everyone in the room was on their feet and remained standing until she dove into her next song. When Luna segued into her third song the low, husky voice that poured from her like a bomb detonating, it hit Poppy straight on, and with perfect clarity, saw what she hadn't before. She paled and the fist that plowed into her stomach when recognition hit her with such force was sharp. Her legs weakening, Poppy dropped into the first chair she found.

It couldn't be. It just couldn't be.

Fighting off the sickness in her stomach, Poppy forced herself to her feet and made her way through gowned women and tuxedoed men swaying to the sensual music, to the front of the stage. Up close, Poppy studied Luna, her eyes, the way her lips curved into that sultry smile, the manner she lifted a delicate hand to tuck the loose strand of hair behind her ear. The resemblance was uncanny. How had she not see it until now? There was no doubt in Poppy's mind why Dean was so drawn to Luna. Luna was the spitting image of Marina.

The affectionate look in Dean's eyes as they rested on Luna confirmed for Poppy Dean saw what she saw. Poppy felt the lurch in her stomach, and the sickening sensation overtook her.

FROM HER FRONT ROW SEAT, SARINA'S eyes filled with pride as the soothing sound of Luna's dulcet tone fanned out in the room.

A wave of memory hit her and tears flowed from her eyes.

Sarina followed Luna's eyes, when after singing her last song she turned to Dean for validation. Dean's prideful gaze didn't falter, and as the roar of applause filled the room, and the crowd demanded more, Dean's lips puckered into a smile that stretched from ear to ear.

Sarina saw Dean mouth, "You did it, my girl. You're on your way."

It was then Sarina felt the slice of pain through her heart. "I've lost her, Teo," she murmured, and melding into the crowd, faded from sight.

Chapter 19

LUNA SWEPT A green gaze over J.R. when the last of her fans left.

"I thought you could use a drink. It's champagne. I think you'll like it," J.R. said, hearing the awkwardness in his tone. No woman had ever visited that awkward sensation in him that left him stammering as she did. She'd gotten inside his head, and was turning his world upside down.

"That's very thoughtful of you."

"I wanted to congratulate you on your performance and tell you how great you were," and how stunning you look.

"Did you really like my performance?" She sipped on champagne, felt the bubbles tickle her throat. "This is lovely."

J.R. watched her shyly tuck the errant tendril behind her ear and found the gesture wildly alluring. "Yes, I very much enjoyed your performance. I thought you were magnificent."

Luna grinned pleased to hear the compliment, which tonight she'd heard many times over, but coming from him meant so that much more. "I'm so happy to hear because I didn't want to disappoint you or Mr. Ryder."

"That was a wonderful performance, Miss Moon. Your voice moved me, stirred so many emotions. We're great fans of yours now. Aren't we, baby?" The petite blonde eyed her husband with enamored eyes.

"I'm definitely a fan. Come on, baby, we're checking into the Sheraton next door for the night," her husband chimed, and wrapping an arm around his wife's tiny waist led her away, but not before turning to give Luna a thumbs up.

J.R. cocked a brow. "I'd say he's a satisfied fan."

Luna gave a soft laugh. "I was heading to my dressing room to change."

Why couldn't he ever think when he was around her? He ran a billion-dollar company, negotiated complex deals, spoke to audiences of thousands at the annual meeting, and he couldn't think what to say to her. J.R. asked himself what Dean would say.

"Can I escort you?" J.R. cringed when the words were out. Who said, escort you? J.R. couldn't understand how Luna unhinged him to the point of brain freeze. "I'm sorry that sounds…"

"Lovely, of course, you can escort me." Luna's dimpled smile arrowed into J.R.'s heart.

"How did it feel up on stage?" J.R. opened the door to her dressing room. The air that rushed at them was laced with the scent of orchids.

"Thank you for the flowers," she said, reading the card. "I'm not sure how you and Mr. Ryder knew that pink calla lilies are my favorite, but I love them."

What would Dean say? J.R. combed through his head and came up with an exotic flower for an exotically beautiful woman, or its striking beauty made me think of you. In the end, he decided he couldn't pull either line off and said, "A girl can never have too many flowers." J.R.

made a mental note to thank Dean for sending them. The man thought of everything. It was why the man had women lining up at his doorstep.

"True, and in response to your earlier question, it felt exhilarating to be up on stage." Luna set her champagne glass on the dressing table and began to pull pins out, letting her hair tumble into a cascade of black around her face and over creamy shoulders.

"You sounded great, and you looked every bit the professional."

"Thank you, but the credit goes to Mr. Ryder. The songs he wrote for me, including those we collaborated on, felt right. It's... as if he knows me. As if he knows my innermost soul. He poured his heart into every song he wrote, but Treasured Memory was the one that clinched it. It was the song that built the bond between me and the audience." Luna swilled champagne to calm nerves when J.R. stepped closer.

He'd never felt to such an overpowering degree the burning sensation of need and want she kindled in him. J.R. liked it. "From my perspective, it was you who bonded with your audience. They connected with you. They fell in love with you."

Sensing J.R. wasn't talking about the audience, Luna said in return, "And I fell in love with them."

He felt the flash of pleasure sing through him at the words he understood were meant for him. Dean, not he, mixed business with pleasure, but at that moment, J.R. stopped thinking with his brain, and let his heart lead him. Logic tossed aside, in one swift move, J.R. wrapped his hands around her waist, pulled her tightly to him. In one instant, his mouth was on hers. Mouths pressed together,

J.R. felt a sense of wondrous discovery as if he'd come across the Holy Grail. In Luna's eyes, in her touch, J.R. saw and felt the echo of his feelings.

He tasted the sweet taste of champagne on her lips. J.R.'s molded his mouth to hers. Fervently his tongue parted her lips and tangled with hers, probing deep, he filled himself with her taste. Luna's soft moans were a feline purr that made J.R.'s head spin, his pulse race.

His heart pounding, J.R. kissed her passionately, as he'd never kissed another woman, but then no woman had reached so deeply into his soul as Luna did. His kiss was loving, and it touched Luna in a way Tom never had. Tom had never stopped her heart then set it off pounding faster than the pistons of a racecar speeding down the track.

He'd waited months to be able to share in a kiss like this with her. Many nights alone in bed, J.R. wondered if he ever would, and now as his mouth crushed down on Luna's, the moment held all the passion, the excitement, the fire he dreamed of.

Breathless, J.R. lowered his mouth to trail a lazy line of kisses down her neck. "You taste as wonderful as I thought you would."

The warmth of his lips, feeling the hardness of his body against her, made Luna shiver. "Do I?"

"Do you know how long I've dreamed of kissing you?" Gliding lips over his shoulders, J.R. made her heart pound like a jackhammer. Tom never did that to her.

"For as long as I've wanted you to do it, Jimmy," she murmured, softly, tenderly.

"Say my name again, just like that."

When she whispered his name like a song, J.R. struggled to keep his emotions tamed. He wanted their next kiss to be slow and sweet, but the sound of his name on her lips, the taste of her hot and powerful pumped through his blood. His mouth came down hard against hers with recklessness abandon.

J.R. reached up to stroke a fingertip over her cheek as if checking to see that she was real. "Since the night I watched you wipe the stain off my carpet, you've been on my mind. You've been in my every thought and my dreams. I want than to be with you, Luna. I want to make love with you all night. I want to whisper in your ear how I feel about you."

Luna drew back far enough to look into his eyes. "And what would you say, Jimmy?"

"That I love you as I've never loved anyone before, that my love for you is like a beautiful love song, profound and everlasting. I'd tell you how much meaning you've brought into my life since coming into it. I'd tell you you've brought so much meaning into my life. That I think of you with every love song I hear. I'd tell you that when you walk into a room, it feels as if you fill it with oxygen."

Luna responded by brushing her lips to his, sweetly, tenderly. "I love you too, Jimmy."

J.R. rested his forehead against her. "I want to be with you, Luna. Let me love you."

"I'd like that, Jimmy."

The smile on J.R.'s lips bloomed. "My limo is right outside."

"Can you have him drive to the back entrance so we can sneak out without having anyone follow us out?"

"Already dodging your fans?"

"Something like that. Give me a few minutes to change."

J.R. ran a hand down the sleep trail of hair. "I'll wait for you in the car."

The rap on the door followed with the words, "Can I come in, Luna?" cut into the moment.

"Don't answer it." J.R.'s thumb traced the contours of her hand, and Luna let her mind wonder what it would feel like to have them touch her body. It took every ounce of willpower for her to pull away from his embrace.

"I'm sorry, Jimmy, but I have to. I want you to meet, Tom."

The spell was broken. "Tom? Who's Tom?"

"My new road manager." Luna ran a hand to smooth her hair and dress.

"When did you hire a road manager?"

"Come in, Tom," Luna called out.

J.R.'s eyes bearing down on Tom with distrust Tom remained standing at the doorway. "I'm sorry if I'm interrupting. I thought you were alone."

"No, you're not. I'd like you to meet J.R. West, our boss. This is Tom Grady, my new road manager." Luna watched J.R.'s suspicious eyes dissect Tom.

"Pleasure to meet you, Mr. West." From the corner of his eyes, Tom caught sight of J.R.'s bouquets dwarfing his.

"I wasn't aware you'd hired a road manager." There was a sick ball forming at the pit of J.R.'s stomach.

"Jean suggested it, for when I go out on tour, and I immediately thought of Tom. Tom was the stage manager at Vibe, and he and I go way back. We've known each other since high school."

J.R. felt the sucker punch to the stomach come quick and swift. "I see," was all he managed to say, doing his best to mask his irritation. The thought of Luna traveling city to city with a man who, from the look in his eyes, had more than a working interest, had his muscles bunching up.

"Don't you worry, Mr. West, I'll take good care of Luna." Tom's words meant to jar J.R.

From the moment he set foot in the room, Tom saw the look of yearning for Luna in J.R.'s eyes. A man could read another man's intentions, and he'd be damned if he was going to let rich boy hone in on the woman he loved. "We need to get going, Luna. You have an early start tomorrow. We have to be at the recording studio by seven. While you change, I'll bring the car around. Pleasure meeting you, Mr. West, and I want to assure you again that I'll take good care of Luna." Tom's words were laced with enough sarcasm to get J.R.'s back up.

"I don't trust him," J.R. said the minute Tom closed the door behind him.

"He's a good friend." Luna squeezed J.R.'s arm, and feeling the tension in him added, "Just a good friend, Jimmy."

"How good of a friend?" J.R. grumbled, fisted hands seeking the depths of his pants pockets.

"I trust Tom with my life." Luna called out from behind the bathroom door.

J.R. raked fingers through his hair in a gesture of pure frustration. "That's what I'm afraid of. I wasn't aware you're scheduled to start recording tomorrow."

"Mr. Ryder and I finished the last song last week, and he and Jean thought I should get into the recording studio right away." Luna emerged from the bathroom in a T-shirt and jeans, her hair tied back into a ponytail. "Mr. Ryder wants to label the album Treasured Time. I like it. What do you think?"

"Yeah, sure, sounds fine." J.R. rubbed his hands to his temples as if massaging the brewing headache away.

"I'm sorry about tonight, Jimmy."

She'd washed off all traces of makeup, and all J.R. could do was stare. He never ceased to be struck by her natural beauty. "So am I."

"I'm leaving on tour as soon as I finish recording the album."

"I know, but..."

"I'm just saying, Jimmy." She traced the curve of his cheek with her finger. "I know you're a very busy man."

J.R. pulled her into his arms. "Come with me to London, Luna. I'll set all the time I can aside to spend it with you. You can take the company jet back first thing Monday and be in Toronto by late morning."

"As lovely as that sounds, I'm sorry I can't. They've already booked studio time for this weekend." She pulled away and scurried around the room, gathering her clothes and makeup to toss into her carry on.

"It's my studio, Luna. I can sure as hell have them reschedule the booking with one phone call." J.R.'s voice quaked with frustration.

Luna's smile was soft. "I know you can, but you know these things work as a chain reaction. I delay the recording and the entire schedule, the release of the album, the launch of the tour, the press releases, and the appearance on the various talk shows will be set into absolute chaos."

"Two days is not going to derail your schedule."

"There are too many people depending on me right now, and I can't let them down. I can't let Mr. Ryder down. I can't let you down. You've invested so much in me."

Of course, she was right, but the tour taking her across Canada and to every major city in the United States was going to take her away for the better part of eight months. It was time she'd be spending with Tom whose interest went beyond managing Luna's tour. A man knew.

"You know I'm going to be traveling for the next four weeks, and when I get back, you'll be far too busy to spare any time for me. The month before any tour is a hectic one. This should be simple. But it doesn't seem to be." J.R. wondered when did his life became so complicated.

"I know." Luna brushed her lips to his. "I'm sorry, Jimmy, but I have to go."

J.R. eased her in, locked her in his arms. His heart hurting with want, his loins hungry for her, he crushed his mouth to hers and ravished. All he wanted to do was absorb the taste of her. To carry it with him until the next time he saw her.

"I'll see you soon. I promise," J.R. vowed, and Luna nodded, believing him.

Her hand slowly slipping out of his he watched her as she started away.

ALL NIGHT POPPY FOLLOWED DEAN'S EVERY move. She watched him hug Luna. Although the hug on Luna's part was one of innocence, the sentiment in Dean's eyes was anything but. Poppy could see Dean's eyes were full of Luna and Poppy's stomach pitched, threatening to expel her lunch.

Poppy had also seen the look in J.R.'s eyes when he'd sidled up to Luna. It took a woman's eye to know her son was smitten with the girl and that Luna had him wrapped around her little finger. Then, how could she expect any different? J.R. was a man, and men did their thinking with the only functioning organ to operate when a woman so much as fluttered their lashes in their direction. Men were so idiotically predictable, Poppy thought. She'd have to reign this in before it got out of hand.

No one could have imagined what was to come.

Chapter 20

LONELINESS WAS A crippling feeling; it marred your spirit and tarnished your soul. No one knew that better than Tom.

Since setting off on tour, although he and Luna were often together, he'd never felt more alone. Luna was immersed in her singing before, but since the tour bus hit the road, she'd become obsessed. Luna spent an excessive amount of time rehearsing, claiming that a seamless performance was vital to her performance and the success of her Treasured Moments tour.

In between rehearsals and the nightly performances, Luna got Tom to book her into random appearances. She visited hospitals, singing the songs of her youth to the children in the acute care ward. Luna performed at charity events. Her days became long, her nights short, and her social life nonexistent. Most nights, exhausted from the day's hectic schedule, Luna headed to her hotel room, showered, and passed out until it was time to get up and do it all over again.

Performing was Luna's lifeblood; all she cared about.

In a short few months, Luna achieved a level of success no one, not Dean, not Tom, not Jean, not even Luna herself, anticipated. Luna was becoming famous beyond her wildest dreams. There were forty-foot billboards throughout the cities she was scheduled to perform depicting her smiling face. Luna saw herself in the sequin gown seductively splayed on a settee, spread across the side of buses and taxi toppers. Articles praising her performances popped up in notable publications. Weeks into her tour, Luna was already being recognized and stopped for autographs. As much as Luna relished in her newfound success, she felt a void inside her that left her feeling empty and incomplete.

I'll see you soon. I promise, J.R. vowed, but it had been five long months since he'd said the words Luna believed to be true. Five months since he'd told her he loved her and shared the kiss, she'd hoped it led to something more. Since then, J.R.'s shadow walked beside her. Luna saw him everywhere, only to become a figment of her imagination when she cast smiling eyes his way. When she came off her sets, she hoped to see him backstage waiting for her. She expected to find him in her dressing or hotel room when she opened the door. J.R. was never there.

Luna's heart ached, and distracting her mind was what she needed to do. Sinking herself into her work, took her thoughts off J.R. and led to Luna's rise to stardom. Luna's tortured heart fed her performances. It made her voice swell with a passion that poured out into her music and straight into her audience's hearts. The tears Luna shed on stage when she sang were not for optics sakes, but came from a broken heart. Her audiences lapped up her outpour of emotions, which, in their eyes, made her one of them. Many nights women in the audience cried along with her, and Luna suspected they were women whose hearts were as shattered as hers was.

Except for Dean, Luna didn't think anyone suspected her dolor was caused by J.R.'s marriage to Britney. Some supposed her outpour of emotions was her brand. Some thought it was par-for-the-course for someone who sang the type of love ballads she did. Regardless, it led to sold-out shows and exceptional record sales. Luna's album skyrocketed up the charts, and Treasured Memory was ranking in the top ten on the singles charts. Dean predicted it was a matter of weeks before it reached number one.

Demand for Luna saw her tour extended by three months. One of those months was for sixteen performances at Caesars Palace's Copa Room, which, thanks to Tom's negotiation skills, made Luna the highest-paid up-and-coming artist in Las Vegas history. When Tom told her the news, Luna sounded excited for his benefit.

Luna and Tom were together day and night, yet he'd never felt as distant as they were now. It had been months since they'd spent time alone, in or out of bed. It scraped Tom raw inside at not being able to kiss or touch her, as he desperately wanted to.

When Luna suggested they stay in separate rooms to avoid salacious gossip that would feed the tabloids, Tom readily agreed. He never expected Luna would maintain the ruse even when he'd booked connecting rooms. It had been months since they'd spent a night together, and Tom missed her.

Many nights Tom lay in his bed in darkness, thinking of Luna, reminiscing on memories of their time together and persuading himself he hadn't lost her. He'd tell himself, maintaining his distance was a sacrifice he had to make for Luna's career. Still, Tom couldn't dismiss the feeling Luna no longer wanted him in her bed because of J.R. Optics had nothing to do with anything. J.R. did.

He'd interrupted more than a conversation between Luna and J.R. the night he walked into her dressing room. He was sure he'd seen love for Luna in J.R.'s eyes. It had clawed his confidence and eaten at him for days afterward because losing Luna wasn't an option. Luna was his, always would be. He'd staked prior claim to her.

"You were fantastic tonight, Luna. You brought in a full house for the dinner benefit. The chair of the American Cancer Society of New York and Mrs. Barclay-West couldn't have been more pleased. And they were very grateful when I told them you were donating the performance fee." Tom followed Luna into the living room of her corner suite.

At Dean's insistence, Tom spared no expense on Luna's accommodations, and for the next three days, they were staying at the Ritz-Carlton. For reasons Tom had yet to figure out, the old man wanted only the best for Luna, insisted on it.

"It's only money and time, and it's the least I could do for Mrs. Barclay-West. She's been so supportive. You know she has yet to miss one of my concerts." Luna rested a hand on the back of the couch and toed her four-inch heels off.

"Now that you mention her, she asked me to apologize for not being able to have dinner with you tonight. She claims something came up, and she wasn't able to make it."

"As much as I enjoy my dinners with Mrs. Barclay-West, I'm relieved she didn't make it. I'm beat, and besides, I don't know how much more I can tell her about myself. She's so keen on getting to know my family and me. She's made every attempt to meet my mother, but you know mom is not the type for one-on-one dinners, and she's turned her down every time. Luckily, Mrs. Barclay-West has been very understanding and patient with mom." Luna crossed to the window when Tom slid the curtains open to a view of Central Park and the city. "Isn't that stunning?

She was stunning, Tom thought watching Luna's reflection on the windowpane as she stared out to the sea of green and New York in its lit splendor. Standing next to him, as tired as she felt, in the slinky, gold gown, her hair tied up and a low draped cowl accentuating the milky white shoulders, she stole his breath.

"Are you sure you're all right, Luna? I'm starting to think Mr. Ryder's right. You've been working yourself ragged and heading for burnout." Tom picked up the bottle of brandy, poured into two glasses.

Removing the gold columns dancing at her ears, Luna tossed them on the table. "I'm fine. Really I am," she said, deciding it was easier to lie than admit how exhausted she felt.

Knowing a discussion about her overworking herself would only fall on deaf ears, Tom didn't pursue the conversation. "This will help you wind down." Luna took the offered glass of zinfandel. "Do you want to go over your schedule for tomorrow now?" God, he hated the predictable triteness of their conversation.

Sipping on the drink she'd become dependent on for calm, Luna absently nodded. "But first, let me shower the day off and slip into something more comfortable."

"While you do that, I'll order dinner. Hamburger with a side order of salad?"

"Sounds good." Luna turned her back to Tom for him to unzip her. Tom's fingers lingered for as long as possible, letting the heat of her skin penetrate them. An electrifying shudder snaked down his spine, and the punch to the pit of his stomach came quickly.

"There you go," he said, putting distance between them when he felt himself go hard.

"I'll be out in a few minutes." Luna started toward the bathroom, and Tom watched her lose her updo and let her hair fall and brush against smooth shoulders. Then she was gone.

Tom's thoughts ran wild. He wished he could join her and make love to her under the spray of hot water as he had so many times before. His mind filled with thoughts of his hands and mouth roaming over her wet body to secret places that made her sing his name. Thunder boomed loud then and broke the thoughts crowding Tom's mind. His eyes out the window he watched the rain come like a flood of tears to beat against glass.

"That's exactly how I feel," Tom murmured, picking up the telephone and dialing room service.

Dinner ordered, Tom crossed to the connecting door and walked into his room. Shedding his clothes, he stepped into the shower to wash his despair down the drain. Minutes later, in jeans and a powder-blue polo shirt, he walked into Luna's room, bringing with him the scent of clean man. He was freshly shaven, and his honey-blonde hair was still damp from the shower. He was such a staggering sight, Luna thought, following him with her eyes to the seat next to her.

"Dinner just got here. I thought we could go over tomorrow's schedule while we eat." In a pair of old Levi's and a T-shirt, her face washed clean of all makeup and her hair tied back into a smooth ponytail Luna looked comfortable and relaxed. She'd set the radio to an oldies station, and between the rumble of thunder, Tom heard the Four Tops assuring they would be there to give all the love needed.

"All right." Tom sank back into the soft cushions of the sofa, facing out onto Central Park. The April sky was thick with rain, and from time to time, lightning lanced it bright, lending a dreamy feel to the night. "It's coming down now." He took the handed plate and glass of wine from Luna, watched her reach for hers.

With the rain outside coming down like a thick, velvet curtain, they ate as Tom went over Luna's schedule. "And then at four, you're back at the hotel for a bit of R&R before the eight o'clock show." Tom waved a hand to silence the oncoming protest. "You need rest, Luna, and I'm going to make sure you get it. It's no use to anyone, least of all for you, if you burn out before the end of the tour. The Bottom Line, where you're performing tomorrow night, is a small, but popular venue where you can stray from your usual repertoire because sometimes you need a break from the routine." Tom took a forkful of chocolate cake as Luna cut into it at the opposite end.

"It sounds perfect. A break from the larger venues is exactly what I need for a couple of days. Thank you," Luna said, thinking how perfectly well he knew her.

"And Mr. Ryder is flying in to meet up with us tomorrow. His flight is scheduled to arrive at..." Tom scanned his notes, "seven."

"That's wonderful news." She took another bite of cake and pushed it away. "You finish it. I can't eat another bite."

"I thought you'd like that," Tom said, happy to see the excitement flicker in the emerald eyes. "It's been weeks since he last joined us. He's anxious to see you." Tom closed the portfolio and set it down on the coffee table before reaching for the cake plate. "He's become quite smitten with you." Toom much if you ask me.

"And I with him. Although he never fails to call me every night, I look forward to our time together."

"You've grown attached to him." Tom set down the empty cake plate.

"I have. I adore him. He's like the grandfather I never had. I love talking with him. We have so much in common, you know, and I feel such a close bond with him I wished I could see him more often."

"Well then, you'll be pleased to know when we hit Vegas he'll be staying over for the entire month since we'll be set in the one location for the duration. Why don't you have your mom come out then?" Tom offered, hoping to infuse some normalcy into Luna's overly hectic life.

"I've already tried to get her to visit, but she won't come. She says my hectic schedule is too much for her to handle." Luna took a sip of wine and watched the rain whipping sideways by a gale wind coming off the Atlantic.

"Isn't that funny? Neither your mom or dad was the type for the limelight, which makes me wonder where you got it from because you're built for it."

Luna had wondered that herself. She wasn't sure where her love of music or talent came from since her father and mother couldn't string a note together, and music ran in her blood. "It must skip a generation."

A smile played across Tom's face. "Anyway, I booked Mr. Ryder into the penthouse suite and arranged for the limo to pick him up at the airport. The driver will take him directly to The Bottom Line. After the show, I booked the two of you at Delmonico's for a late dinner." More trite conversation, Tom thought.

"Why don't you join us?" Luna lifted her glass, sipped, felt the wine warm her.

Surprise flew into Tom's eyes. "I'd like that. Thank you, Luna."

"I know I've been distant these past few months, and I'm sorry."

"You're under an enormous amount of pressure right now." Needing something stronger than wine, he got to his feet and crossed to the small refrigerator. Reaching in, he helped himself to two small bottles of bourbon. "I understand that now more than ever, it's essential you keep your mind focused on your career."

Everything washed over Luna at once: guilt, remorse, regret. Why did he have to be so understanding when she'd been cold and alienating all these months? When her thoughts were with J.R., and all she did was pine for him. Here was this wonderful man ready to love her and her thoughts were on a man who hadn't thought to pick up the telephone to call her.

God, she was messed up. What was wrong with her?

Devoted, unconditionally loving Tom was there with her. Tom, the man who took care of her without demands or expectations, yet Luna couldn't stop thinking of the man who thought nothing of making promises only to break them.

"I am sorry, Tom. I haven't been fair to you," she said, watching him pour bourbon over ice.

Tom calmly met her eyes. "You've been perfectly fair, Luna. You're on the fast track now. Your focus is on your career. This is what you've been dreaming of, and I wouldn't dare stand in your way."

"Stop making excuses for me, Tom." There was anger in her voice, but it was aimed at herself. "I haven't been good to you, and I'm sorry."

"Apology accepted." Tom reached for her hand, brought it to his lips. Every inch of him ached for her. "I've missed you, Luna."

She felt the sharp pinch in her heart. "You deserve so much better than me."

"You're all I want."

Luna felt his thumb tracing slow circles over her hand. "I don't deserve you."

"You do." He traced the curve of her cheek with his finger. "Now, you should get to bed. You have an early start tomorrow."

"I should," she said, and to her surprise and his held out a hand for his.

His heart rising to the base of his throat, Tom gave her his hand and let her lead him into the bedroom.

Tom wanted to move slowly, but emotions bottled up inside for months poured out in violent need, and he tugged her T-shirt up and away, snapped open her jeans. Tom sucked in his breath on the sharp pull of desire that rushed at him at the sight of her naked body. He skimmed his hand over her shoulders, down her arms to her hands. Wrapping his hand around hers led her to the bed.

Her pulse rapid and thick thrilled him. She'd missed his touch, Tom thought.

Being with her, kissing her, touching the body he'd craved for months made the swell of need in him erupt like the dormant bubbling core of a volcano. Tom's hands and mouth ran desperate over her. Her body throbbed gleefully under his expert touch. It pleased him.

She'd missed him, he thought.

It had been months since she'd felt his hands on her body, and the intense power of his touch left her craving for more, and she arched her hips in demand. Everything blurred when his frenzied mouth and tongue found the center of her being to taste and ignite the dormant geyser. The first wave of heat rolled through her, wildly and savagely, and she begged him not to stop.

Her whole body shuddered when he made her ride the thrill for what felt like hours until the pleasure careened through her like a tidal wave of blissful sensations again and again, and she moaned with unbearable joy.

When he plunged inside her, her nails dug deep into the slope of his soaked back. Joined, she fell into step with him. Her body flowed with him, and together they danced to the rhythm of old lovers. His mouth fused to hers, she swallowed the greedy sounds he made when his feral and powerful release ripped through and filled her.

Tom's body slaked, his heart full of Luna he folded her into his arms and together they watched lightning split the sky over the rise, lancing it white like fireworks on the Fourth of July. Luna's mind, however, was on thoughts of

J.R.'s betrayal, and her heart was breaking into a million pieces.

Chapter 21

THE SCENT FROM pink calla lilies sent by Dean mingled with the sweet fragrance of Luna's perfume and hit Tom when he stepped into her dressing room. As was always the case with Luna, the dressing room looked as if a tornado had swept through. Shoes were scattered on the floor. Hangers strewed around the room. An Azzedine Alaïa strapless dress and a Gaultier gown, along with a black off the shoulder, knee-length Chanel was carelessly draped on the back of the sofa and chair.

Tom smiled at that. No one would guess Luna Moon, once the owner of a cleaning service, wasn't one for order when it came to her own space. He found that out the first time, she'd spent the night at his place and turned his bedroom from an orderly one into a chaotic mess.

"Luna, you're on in ten. Oh, hello, Mrs. Barclay-West." At the sight of Poppy pecking Luna on the cheek, Tom stopped short of entering the changing room.

"Hello, Tom. I just stopped in to wish Luna luck tonight," Poppy looked the essence of wealth. Diamonds and rubies hung from her ears, neck, and fingers, and although it was April, she was swathed in a blonde mink. "Is Dean making it in tonight?"

"He didn't say." Tom's expression, Luna noted, turned awkward. She'd never understood why Tom always felt intimidated by Poppy.

Poppy turned to Luna. "I'm sure Dean will be here. The Gardens is a huge deal for you. I can't imagine him missing the biggest night of your life. I best get to my seat. Break a leg, Luna."

"Thank you, Mrs. Barclay-West, for being here tonight. It means a lot."

"I wouldn't miss it, darling. Tom, I'd like to see you when you have a chance," Poppy said, to a stoic Tom as she walked past him.

Tom nodded and waited until Poppy closed the door behind her to cross to Luna. "She's not wrong about Madison Square Garden being a big deal. It's your biggest venue yet. How are you feeling?"

Luna lifted her hand to cover the one on her shoulder. "I'm pumped and ready for it."

Tom met her eyes in the mirror. "And they're ready for you. Listen to that, Luna. Listen to the buzz of excitement from a crowd waiting to hear you perform. It's an exciting, electrifying feeling, isn't it?" In Tom's eyes, tonight, Luna reached stardom. This was New York, and she'd sold out The Garden in one afternoon. He heard scalpers were lurking in the shadows selling tickets to the show at three times their value.

Luna met Tom's smile. "It certainly is an electrifying feeling. And it thrills me to know Mr. Peets and Miss Jones, who by the way are now a couple, accepted my invitation and are right there front row center with Mrs. Barclay-West, and I know Mr. Ryder will be there. And you're taping this for mom, right."

"They're ready to roll when you are."

Everyone was there, but J.R. Going on six months now, she hadn't heard from him, not a call, not a note, nothing. She never imagined he'd miss the biggest night of her life. Before the hurt descended on her, Luna pushed her thoughts of J.R. out of her head. She wouldn't allow him to highjack her emotional state tonight. Tonight was her night.

Getting to her feet, Luna took one last look at herself in the mirror. "Let's do this."

"Before you go out there, I got you something." Tom pulled the box from his jacket pocket, handed it to her. When Luna eyed the signature Valentine's wrapping paper, he said, "I've been waiting for the right time to give it to you. You..." became so distant these past few months it never seemed the right time, "got so busy and... Go ahead, open it."

"It's lovely, Tom," she said of the heart-shaped pendant with the embedded diamond. "Help me put it on." Luna gave him her back.

"You don't have to put it on now."

"I want to." The necklace clasped around her neck, Luna stole a look at herself in the mirror.

"It looks great on you." Tom's arms wrapped around her, his eyes fell on their reflection in the mirror. They looked perfect together. "I've had a wonderful time these last couple of nights with you. I love being with you. I love waking up next to you. I love you, Luna."

"I've loved being with you too, Tom."

Although his heart filled with an unspeakable sorrow at Luna's inability to say the words back to him, it didn't register on Tom's face. "They're getting restless. Let's get out there." Tom jumped in to say before she set off on the all too familiar apology.

HIS EYES FOLLOWED LUNA'S EVERY STEP as poised and brimming with confidence she stepped onto the stage. She looked stunning in the metallic satin gown with the thigh-high slit that rode up a long, toned leg. Her hair floated in shining waves around her face. Diamonds sparkled at her ears and neck. For a long moment, he drank her in.

He watched her close her eyes seconds before the music flowed, and the words poured out from her with the emotion and power that made the audience of twenty thousand go silent. As it always did, her voice entranced him. At that instance, he felt as if she was singing to him. She made his heart thud and sent his pulse pounding as only she could. He let the sensation wash over him.

As she looked over the sea of faces focused on her, he thought she met his gaze, and for a long moment, in the cavernous space of Madison Square Garden, amid the thousands of fans, he felt as if it was just the two of them. There was a desperate crushing need in him to be close to her, touch her, take a tasty bite of that thick bottom lip, and whisper in her ear how much he loved her.

During Luna's performance, his eyes never left her, and he thought hers never left his.

AT THE SOUND OF THE DRESSING room door opening, with breathless anticipation, Luna spun in her chair. She thought she'd seen J.R. in the sea of faces, and as much anger and hurt in her there was in her for his neglect, she hoped he'd make his way to her dressing room. When she saw it was Dean standing at the door,

Luna convinced herself that what she'd seen was but another hopeful figment of her imagination.

"Hello, love. That was… I'm sorry. Did I come at a bad time?" Dean asked when he saw the disappointment roll on her face.

Shelving her thoughts of J.R., Luna waved Dean in. "No, you surprised me. I thought you'd head back to the hotel to rest up before our late dinner." Luna leaned in for a hug. "When did you get in?"

"A few minutes before you walked out on stage. You don't think I'd miss seeing you perform at Madison Square Garden, did you?"

He looked handsome in the black suit and the contrasting thick mast of silver hair stylishly combed back, Luna thought. "I'm glad you're here. How did I do? And I want your honest critique."

Dean followed Luna to the couch, watched her push clothes, hangers, shoes, and a towel to one side. The girl wasn't one for neatness. Green eyes smiled at that. She was so much like Marina, he mused.

"You were wonderful tonight. Magnificent. You looked like you were having a grand old time up there. Are you enjoying yourself, or is it an act you've been putting on for the crowd?" Dean took the seat next to Luna when she gestured him down.

"That's where that went." Luna set the brush Dean dug out from between the sofa cushions on the side table. "To answer your question, I'm enjoying every minute. Tonight, when I stepped out on stage, I had butterflies doing somersaults in my stomach, but once I began to sing, and the audience joined in, I was blown away, and the butterflies flew right out of me. They knew every word to Treasured Memory, to all of my songs. They love your music, Mr. Ryder."

"They love *you*, Luna."

"But without your music, I'm nothing."

"And I'm nothing without your voice, charm, and beauty. Need I go on? Besides, you forget some of those songs we wrote together." Dean watched her cheeks flush red, and felt charmingly entranced by her. "You Luna are the one who's drawing the crowds, and I'm glad you're having fun in the process."

"I am, Mr. Ryder."

And there it was. The pain-stricken look Dean had seen too often on her face in the past months. The more famous Luna got, the more in demand she became, the more records she sold, the unhappier she became. None of her successes seemed to wash the gloom away.

"I have something I need you to do for me, Luna."

"Sounds ominous." Luna circled the room looking for her makeup bag and finally found it on the dressing table under a towel. "I'll just touch up my face, and we can discuss it over dinner. Tom's booked us at—"

Dean stopped her. "We're not having dinner together tonight, love."

"Is something wrong? I was looking forward to having dinner with you."

"Nothing's wrong. Tom and I are having dinner together. I have some tour issues to go over with him. You're staying put here."

A crown of confusion creased Luna's face. "Why, what's going on, Mr. Ryder? What kind of tour issues?"

"Minor details I want to review with him, nothing to concern yourself with. We'll have lunch tomorrow. Come up to my room at one."

"All right. Are you sure everything's all right?"

Dean nodded. "You wait right here. And, promise me, Luna, to keep an open mind."

"What do you mean?"

"Sometimes things don't appear to be what they are. Promise me, love, you'll keep an open mind."

When Dean's eyes pressed for a response, she said, "I promise," then watched him walk to the door and pause with his hand on the knob.

"You've accomplished so much in such a short time, and I'm very proud of you, Luna," he said, before closing the dressing room door behind him.

Left baffled by the cryptic conversation, Luna fell into a contemplative silence. After several minutes of mulling it in her head and getting no answers, she rose and crossed to the dressing-table mirror. Looking at herself, she decided a makeup refresh was needed.

Lately, cameras tended to flash at the most inopportune time, and the need to be perfectly made up was becoming an occupational nuisance. Dressing in a tracksuit without an ounce of makeup-free, as Luna preferred, was no longer an option. Not when her face was being splashed across the television, in the tabloids, newspapers, and magazine articles.

Luna brushed a light dusting of rouge over her cheeks, touched-up the slate-grey above her eyes, and ran a fresh layer of wine-red color over her lips. She finger-combed her hair and neatly tucked the silk blouse into skinny jeans. She should be wearing something more camera-friendly than black ballet flats, but her feet ached from the four-inch stilettos.

Walking out of the bathroom, Luna immediately sensed his presence. Their eyes locked on one another, and for a long time, neither spoke. This time, he wasn't a figment of her imagination. It was J.R. standing before her, his blue eyes dripping love and contrition.

Her familiar scent, one he'd carried with him since their last encounter, floated around him. The glossy mink-colored hair that haloed her face was longer than he remembered, and she looked more womanly. He thought that was the best word.

A rush of emotions assaulted him.

"Hi," he said when the silence lingered.

As happy as she was to see J.R., the pain she felt was greater. For six months, she hadn't heard from J.R., not a card, not a telephone call. He'd hurt her, hurt her pride, but more than that, he broke her heart.

The humiliation on top of the pain was more than Luna could stand, and the anger bubbled in her. "What are you doing here?" She heard herself snap.

No more Jimmy, he noticed. "I've come to talk to you."

"We have nothing to talk about. There's nothing you could say I'd be interested in hearing." Eyes blazing, she began to gather her things, tossing them in her bag without the finesse designer garments required.

J.R. reached for her arm. "There's a lot I need to say to you, Luna. There's a lot I need to explain."

His touch made her heart do a quick gallop. Shaking her head free of the emotions taking over her head, the fury consuming Luna took over again, and she pulled away. "There's nothing to explain, Mr. West. You're my boss, and I'm one of your many employees. It's as simple as that. We have a working relationship and nothing more."

"I hope you don't mean that. I haven't been able to get you out of my head."

"Really? You could have fooled me. It's been six months, and you couldn't be bothered to pick up the phone or come to see me. Not even a note." Luna debated tossing the brush in her hand at him or into her bag. She threw it at him and followed it with a fiery glare.

J.R. managed to duck the brush. God, he'd missed her. "I haven't forgotten what happened between us."

"Nothing happened between us. You have me mistaken for one of your many conquests."

"Don't say that, Luna. You're certainly not that." He moved to his left to avoid the four-inch pump with the deadly pointed toe.

"Too bad, I missed it would have impaled you. And you're right about me not being one of your conquests. You said all the right things that night to get me into bed, and you came that close." Luna held a forefinger and thumb close together. "But I was smarter than that, and instead of letting you bed me that night, I took Tom to my bed." The painful expression that spread over J.R.'s face told Luna the lie she aimed at his ego hit the bull's eye. "He's a fantastic lover." That was said with conviction because it was true.

Clenching his jaw for control, J.R. brushed the comment he hoped was said out of anger aside. "My intention wasn't, as you call it, 'bed you.' I meant every word I said."

Luna fell back into the couch, covered her face with her hands. "That's why it's taken you months to come around. Whatever happened that night was a … mistake, Mr. West." She couldn't bear the waves of humiliation washing over her when she thought of that night and how she'd believed everything he'd said to her. *My love for you is like a beautiful love song, profound and everlasting.* She'd believed those words. "I trusted you, but it was foolish to do so or think it meant anything to someone of your stature." Luna's words came out slowly, each one, a drop of pain, and his heart tripped at the thought he'd caused her to feel this way.

J.R. rushed to Luna's side, sank to his knees. "It meant everything to me, and I meant every word I said, Luna."

She bolted to her feet to put distance between them. "You promised, Jimmy. You promised," she said softly, fighting the flow of tears.

"I'm sorry, Luna. I never meant to hurt you. There was… A lot has happened since I last saw you. There are things I need to tell you. I do love you, Luna." He reached for her hand, but she tore free from his hold.

"You don't know what love is. You rich types are so used to getting everything your way you blur the line between true and bought emotions. You may be financing my career, Mr. West, but you can't buy me. Get out of my dressing room." The cold, steely glint in the green eyes that tilted up to him was meant to send a chill down his spine, but he only saw the pain and tears that swam in them. It was pain he caused.

"Luna, please just give me the chance to explain. Please." Why did he only manage to bring pain to her life when he carried nothing but love for her in him?

Luna wiped her cheeks dry. She'd allowed him to play with her emotions for too long, but not anymore. "I have to go." Luna reached for her bag and started for the door.

"I was scared to see you. I was scared of … your rejection." J.R. blurted out, feeling a strange sense of relief at saying the words.

Luna stopped short of opening the door. "That's rich?"

"It's the truth, Luna. You're deep in me, and I can't get you out of my head. I've never felt for anyone the way I feel about you. When you turned me down that night, and introduce me to Tom, I saw deep feelings in his eyes for you. I figured there was more than friendship between the two of you, and my mind set off racing. When I put it all together, I figured you were just…"

When he trailed off, Luna turned and looked straight into his eyes. "Using you for your money, for your influence? Really, J.R., you think I'm that shallow and so morally bankrupt that I would do such a thing."

A flush of regret stained his cheeks. "I'm sorry, but I've found this love thing does crazy things to you. It consumes you with jealousy and makes you vulnerable. And I don't know how to manage either. I've never had to before." He always found himself saying and sharing feelings with her, he'd never discuss with anyone else. "Uncle Dean had a long chat with me and ultimately gave me the push I needed to come to see you tonight. He thought I should talk to you."

Promise me to keep an open mind, Luna heard Dean say.

"Will you join me for dinner?" When the silence lengthened, J.R. pleaded. "I have things to explain."

Calmer, she turned back to him. "I'm only saying yes because I promised Mr. Ryder I would keep an open mind," she said when J.R.'s lips curved into a soft smile.

"There you are. I've been looking all over for you." In a short, skin-tight, red dress that left little to the imagination, Britney strolled into the dressing room stunning Luna and leaving J.R. seething with anger.

"What are you doing here, Britney?" J.R. fired back.

"Your office told me your flight schedule, and I thought I'd surprise you and Luna, this being her big night and all." Britney's voice sent razor-sharp cuts into J.R.'s ears. "Hello, Luna. It's been a long time. Last time I saw you, you were cleaning toilets, but look at you now. Haven't we come a long way?" Britney wrapped her hand around J.R.'s arm, ensuring a full view of her engagement ring for Luna's consumption.

The glinting ring on Britney's left hand doused Luna with a cold splash of reality. It was a knife to the heart, and as much as she didn't want to, the shock had her transfixed on it.

At the devastated look on Luna's face, heat flashed in J.R.'s eyes. "That's enough, Britney." He let raw temper carry him out.

"Didn't you know? J.R. and I are engaged to be married." Britney's blue gaze flashed a malicious smile. "Isn't it stunning? J.R. picked it out himself."

The dagger of betrayal sank deep into her heart. Everything he'd said to her, then and now, was nothing but a lie, and she'd fallen for it again. The wave of humiliation washed over Luna like a cold arctic wind. The room began to close in on Luna. It was suffocating her.

Feeling the need to regain her dignity, Luna bit back the tears fighting to burst, "I guess congratulations are in order."

As if marking her territory, Britney tightened her grip on J.R.'s arm. "Thank you. Baby, did you know Luna and I go way back? We even dated the same man. Well, she did after me, of course. As I understand, Tom's now your road manager. Is he around? I'd love to say hello," Britney said, with the innocence of a viper.

The pain, hideous pain, was choking Luna, and the tears burned hot behind her eyes. "Tom's having dinner with Mr. Ryder." Luna wanted to run, far, far away, but her lead-heavy feet wouldn't allow it.

"Are the two of you still an item, Luna? Not that I blame you I mean Tom was very … skilled," Britney said in the cloaked manner that came so easily to women of her ilk. "No, not better than you, baby. You are a stallion. Anyway, have you told Luna?"

Fury bubbled over in J.R., and he barked, "Now is not the time, Britney."

"Now's the perfect time, baby." Britney flashed J.R., a contrived smile that left him, narrowing his eyes to thin slits.

A terrible overwhelming sadness washed over J.R. when the reality of his life assailed him. He was marrying this conniving, manipulative bitch, out of a sense of duty, and his and Luna's love would never be.

Although nothing would change, before Britney walking in, J.R. was about to tell Luna about his engagement to her. He was about to explain their impending marriage was nothing but a business deal, hashed by his mother. His marriage to Britney was to secure the merger between West Enterprises and Melville Media. Fusing the two companies as Poppy sought to do to fulfill James' dream stood to make West Enterprises one of the largest entertainment-media companies in the world and carry on his father's legacy for generations to come. How could J.R. say not to that?

"J.R.'s and I want you to sing at our wedding. Don't we, baby?"

Luna felt something inside her break.

Although Luna said nothing, J.R. recognized the pained look on her face, the wounded look in her eyes. On a surge of fury at what this was doing to Luna, he barked, "Let's go, Britney."

"But, darling. We haven't given Luna the details of our wedding. It's going to be lavish, huge, and wonderful. About five hundred guests, and don't even get me started on our honeymoon. Two glorious weeks on a private island in Bali where we'll you know ... get to know each other better. Isn't that right, baby?" She salted the wound with such pleasure she could savor it.

"Stop talking, Britney." J.R.'s tone quivered with rage.

My, my, wasn't he her knight in shining armor, Britney mused rushing to protect his little Luna, the love of his life. And the devastated look in Luna's eyes told Britney she was as head over heels in love with J.R. as he was with her. A blind person could see how they felt for one another. But guess what bitch? J.R. is mine now, and he's going to stay mine, Britney decided because it was what a backstabbing, man-stealing bitch deserved.

Tom would have loved her if Luna hadn't come between them. Britney was certain of that. If Luna hadn't been so willing to jump into bed with Tom, she and he would be married by now. She and Tom were meant to be together, but Luna played the poor-little-girl-whose-father-died card and drawn him into her lair as a spider did its prey.

She didn't blame Tom for running to Luna. He was as weak as the next man around a woman, thinking with the one organ they loved more than themselves. That Luna's act was a ploy to seduce Tom and steal him from her was clear to Britney. Since then, she'd nursed her hatred for Luna and plotted her revenge.

Britney had to admit Poppy Barclay-West's call came at the most opportune time. Two days before Poppy placed the call to her mother, she'd read the monthly report on Tom and Luna from Detective Nelson, whom she'd hired to follow their every move. The report, which stated Luna was planning to hire Tom as her road manager, had Britney panicking. With Tom traveling, she'd no longer be able to plan the coincidental run-ins at The Brewed Bean or Vibe or any of the venues Tom frequented.

Tom accused Britney of stalking Luna, but that wasn't the case. Britney told him as much, but Tom refused to believe her, but then she omitted to tell Tom he was the one she was following. The fact Luna was around whenever Britney showed up was an irritant she'd had to endure, but she had because not seeing Tom wasn't an option.

When Britney listened in on her mother's conversation on the extension—as she often did—and heard Poppy proposing the union between her and J.R., she was thrilled. Britney's elation didn't come from wanting to marry J.R. because, in her eyes, Tom was ten times the man he was. And it wasn't because she would play a part in bringing West Enterprises and Melville Media together. That was in her grandfather's and Poppy's interest. She wanted to marry J.R., but for the simple reason, Luna was in love with him.

From the moment Britney read in the detective's report of Luna and J.R.'s tender encounter in her changing room after the Cancer Society performance, she set in motion her plan to slink into J.R.'s life.

Sharing the same tennis instructor as Poppy, Britney traded a roll in the sheets with Daniel in exchange for a game. The connection made, Britney spent weeks with the annoying woman cultivating a relationship, ingratiating herself, listening to Poppy babble on about nuisance she had no interest. Britney went as far as feigning interest in Poppy's life. When the time was right, Britney planted the seed in Poppy's head how a union between her and J.R. would benefit West Enterprises.

The pièce de résistance came when Britney arranged a timely run-in between Poppy and her grandfather at their country club. The moment Reince Melville sat down with Poppy, a merger was born, and the marriage between Britney and J.R. became the conduit.

Who could have anticipated her plan would work so perfectly? No one took what was Britney's, and she would now take what Luna wanted—JR.

"Anyway, we want you to perform at our wedding. I thought you could sing Treasured Memory as I'm walking down the aisle to marry this gorgeous man. J.R. and I also want you to perform at our reception for the entire night. Only the best for our guests, right, baby?"

"I'm booked solid with the tour." There were tears in Luna's eyes and voice that played on J.R.'s guilt. He hated himself for it, for hurting the only person he'd ever felt been able to love fully.

"Well, luckily now that I'm about to become Mrs. J.R. West, I never get tired of hearing that name, I own your contract. One call from me, and I will make it, so your schedule is cleared, so you're able to sing at our wedding. I wouldn't dream of not having the great Luna Moon perform for us. Pencil, April twentieth into your calendar, Luna." Britney salted the wound with such pleasure she could savor it.

Seeing the injured expression in Luna's eyes, the storm of feelings tearing her up, J.R.'s hands curled around Britney's wrist tightly. "It's time to go."

"But I haven't finished, baby. Luna, I want…"

"Yes, you have." J.R.'s eyes were hard and cold on Britney as he hauled her out of the dressing room.

Behind her back, Britney heard Luna shedding the tears she'd been fighting back the entire time. The sense of satisfaction as Luna watched J.R. walk out of her life—forever—was priceless. Revenge, Britney mused, was a sweet bitch. She could now cross out DESTROY LUNA'S RELATIONSHIP WITH J.R. from her Get-Luna-Back list and move on to the next bullet point.

Chapter 22

STRETCHED OUT ON the couch, her eyes cast out the window to a sky as black as her heart felt was where Luna had been the for past two hours, dried eyed. She refused to shed any tears for J.R. No one had made her feel as betrayed or humiliated as J.R. had. No one had made her feel the stabbing pain she felt then.

No, J.R. didn't deserve her tears, and she would shed none for him.

But Luna couldn't stop her mind from floating to the fact J.R was marrying Britney in April. To the fact, he'd picked out her ring. The wedding date was set; the plans were already in the works. This was months in the making, and in that time, J.R. had been sharing her bed. The sonofabitch was probably already sharing it when he tried to get her into it.

Luna picked up her glass, drained it.

How stupid was she to think he'd meant what he said. How he must have laughed behind her back when she'd told him she loved him. She bared her soul to him. She'd said the words Tom wanted to hear from her for so long to a man, who had no interest in hearing them.

She hadn't known a hurt like the one she felt then.

The guilt and remorse were like two vicious, heavy blows to her gut when the thought this was the hurt Tom felt when she didn't return his, I love yous crossed her mind. Hoping to ease the queasiness in her stomach, Luna refilled her glass and tossed it back. As she hoped it would, the brandy burned straight down to the sickness in her belly.

"Are you all right, Luna?" Tom said when he saw the bottle of brandy on the coffee table and the tall glass in her hand.

Startled by his voice, Luna turned a dazed look at him. "Yes, I'm fine, just tired."

Knowing she was deflecting, Tom didn't pursue it further. "It's no wonder. You put on a spectacular show tonight."

When Tom leaned forward to touch his lips to hers, Luna smothered the quick pang of guilt. "Thank you. How did the meeting with Mr. Ryder go?"

"I'm not sure that it was a meeting. He tells me one minute he wants to go over our schedule and review the budget for the upcoming tour months. So I'm thinking I've been spending too much booking five-star hotels, which by the way, is what he requested. 'Only the best for Luna,' he tells me. So I prepared myself for a beating, but from the beginning, he goes off on..." He stopped to think."

"To tell you the truth, I'm not sure what he went off on because, for the first fifteen minutes of our dinner, I didn't understand a thing he was saying. Then he touches on trivial matters, which we could have discussed over the telephone. When dessert comes, he steers the conversation to hotels and your wardrobe, and I figure here comes the beating. But he reiterates what he's been telling me all along that I should spare no expense on your accommodations or wardrobe or anything else you need. To sum it up, he makes me promise to take care of you. When he knows damn well, I do. The entire night was an absolute waste of time." Tom reached into the mini-fridge for a bottle of Perrier.

"Don't be upset with him. He's getting up in age, and his memory is not what it used to be." Luna offered in Dean's defense.

"It wasn't more apparent than tonight. A couple of times during our conversation, he became incoherent. Maybe it was me who couldn't understand him. You know the man can drink like a fish and every time he ordered a round, he asked me to join him. I unwisely tried to keep up, but by the fourth drink, my mind became muddled. The man has decades on me, and I can't keep up with him." Tom uncapped the Perrier bottle, swilled three-quarters in to drench his dehydrated throat. "God, I needed that. I thought I'd find you in bed, passed out," he said, sinking next to Luna and gesturing her to rest her feet on his lap.

"Couldn't sleep. I needed to wind down. It's been a ... taxing day." Luna tilted the glass back to drink.

"I assumed tonight would be. It must have been nerve-racking up there. I don't know how you do it, Luna. How you stand up before so many people, their faces staring up at you demanding flawless entertained." With the right amount of pressure, he ran his thumbs up and down her sole. "And you were seamless tonight. This is what you're meant to do." Tom hoped to make her mind drift from whatever was bothering her.

"I do love it. Something overcomes me when I'm out on stage. When the music starts and I sink into the song, it's as if there's no one up there but me. It's ... transcendent."

"Well, I'm sure the reviews are going to be exceptional. And this is New York, Luna, and as Frank says, 'if you can make it here, you can make it anywhere.' I'm very proud of you. This, tonight, is what you've worked your butt off for, and you did it." Tom studied her when she remained stoic, unwilling to share in his enthusiasm. "Are you sure you're okay, Luna?"

"Yes, I'm fine." Luna kept her eyes on the face that radiated so much love for her. She felt both pleasure and sympathy in it. Pleasure because it always felt good to know she was loved, and sympathy because she couldn't return that love.

Why couldn't J.R. love her as Tom did? Why couldn't J.R. love her back as she did him? Why would he lie to her and build her hopes up like the crescendo of a song for months only to show up with his fiancé to tell her he was getting married?

She'd dismissed Tom when he pointed out J.R. was born with a silver spoon in his mouth, with all the luxuries at his fingertips, and that men like him only took and used as a jealous rant. But Tom had been right all along. Money did cloud reality to the point of isolating a person from feeling real emotions.

J.R. was an emotional assailant, Luna concluded. He'd done a fantastic job of taking her dignity and manipulating her emotions. The anger clawed at Luna's chest.

Tom had never lied to her. Tom would never hurt or take her for granted. Yet, she cast him aside to pine for a man who only thought to lie and hurt her. How could she have been so callous, so stupid? So blind.

Luna tossed brandy back, savoring the burn in her throat, and in an unexpected move, she grabbed Tom, pulled him in, and crushed her mouth to his. Her mouth moved restlessly and hungrily over his. The kiss became ardent, full of need. The fire in it told him she wanted him. Every emotion in him burst like an overflowing dam. His head reeled, his heart pounded so violently Tom thought it would burst from his chest. Fingers diving into her hair, he pulled her closer so that his fevered mouth could move over hers, claiming.

Nibbling her way up to his ear, she purred, "I want to be with you tonight, Tom. I want you to make love with me all night long. I want you to tell me how much you love me while I feel you inside me, while you come in me."

The glimmer in Tom's eyes could have lit up the night sky. The words she'd never said before made his heart burst like a flash of thunder in his chest. With eyes full of love and renewed optimism, Tom swept Luna into his arms and carried her into the bedroom.

LUNA'S GREEN EYES LOCKED ON TOM'S as he moved in and out of her in long, slow strokes. Her breathy agreements, ones Tom never heard before, as he told her he loved her, made pure joy burst inside of him. She was finally following her heart, and it led to him.

Luna had finally crossed into love with him as he knew she one day would. His dream was finally becoming the reality he'd waited for so long, and he felt as if he was floating.

The pressure in him building to a crescendo, she wrapped tighter around him, took him deeper. It felt glorious. He knew then what it felt to be loved by her. With all those wonderful feelings crowding inside of him, riding on the thrill, Tom cried out her name and filled her, as she wanted him to.

Luna was finally his wholly and utterly—finally.

Tonight, Tom thought, was the most memorable night of his life.

Tonight, Luna thought, was the saddest day of her life.

Chapter 23

DEAN'S FORKFUL OF salad stopped mid-air. "Engaged? When did this happen?"

"Last night." She reached for the cigarette pack, pulled one out.

Dean wanted to point out the perils of smoking to her voice, but seeing trembling hands fumbled with the match, he thought best to let it pass for now. "Tom never mentioned during our dinner, he was planning to propose marriage."

Luna inhaled smoke; let it out in a quick stream. "That's because I proposed to him."

"Why, why would you?" Dean didn't bother to conceal the shock on his face.

"It's what I want, Mr. Ryder," Luna said before Dean could chime in with his protest. "I know you're not particularly fond of Tom, and I hope this doesn't affect our working relationship." Drawing in smoke, Luna expelled it with a coughing fit.

"Are you sure that's what you want to be doing?" Dean watched Luna crush out the cigarette and rise to pace the room with nervous energy. "I don't dislike Tom. He's a fine young man who I trust to take good care of you. And of course, this will not affect our relationship. I've just become very fond of you, Luna."

"And I'm very fond of you." Luna walked to the mini bar, picked up a small bottle of brandy, tossed it back wincing as the liquid washed down her throat. "Tom's been in love with me since high school."

"I know he's in love with you. It's written all over his face. Just as the fact you're not is written over yours." Dean studied her sad eyes. "It's your life, Luna. I just want to make sure this is what you want. You're still young and... Are you sure this is what you want, honey?"

Luna picked up a second bottle, took a healthy swallow. "Since the day I met Tom, he's been nothing but caring and supportive and wonderful to me. He would never dream of hurting me."

And there it was Dean thought. Her proposal to Tom came out of hurt, anger, and spite for J.R. As indifferent as Dean was toward Tom, he didn't believe he deserved to be used as Luna was now. "I know you're hurting right now, love, but J.R. has a perfect explanation for..."

Luna whirled, green eyes blazing. "J.R. has nothing to do with this, and I don't know where you're getting that I'm hurting because I'm not. I just think it's time to solidify things. Tom has been by my side, helping me with my career, and supporting me ever since I can remember. He doesn't think I know, but he paid for my singing lessons with Miss Jones. He gave up medical school to help launch my career. Because of him, I found my love for singing. He's been my one true friend and given so much to me. It's time I gave back." She tilted back the brandy bottle, drained it.

"He sounds like a wonderful man, but you don't jump into marriage to as you put it, give back." Dean blamed Poppy for J.R. and Luna's predicament. If only she thought of someone other than herself and that goddamn company, the two most important people in his life wouldn't be heading into a life of loneliness and misery with people they didn't love. "You don't love him, Luna."

"I will, in time." Luna turned her eyes away from Dean's piercing eyes out the window to a sky misted in a haze of blue. Her gaze seemingly lost in it, Luna thought of how she could never love Tom, as he deserved to be loved, but they'd been lovers for years now. He was her first and only, and in that time, Luna learned that the bonding of two bodies didn't necessarily require the emotion of love.

"I don't want to intrude in your life, love."

"Then don't," she shot out with unusual sharpness, immediately regretted it.

When remorseful eyes whirled to Dean, he saw regret, sadness, pain, and his heart ached for her. "All I want is for you to be happy, and Tom deserves as much."

"I know," she said low-voiced.

"He deserves someone who will love him."

Luna whirled eyes back to the window. "I know," she said, watching the two colorful kites rising from the trees to glide in the wind, tails swaying in an S motion. She wished her emotions could sway from man to man as easily, then she could love Tom, as he deserved to be loved.

Luna walked to Dean, who'd settled into the living room chair with his coffee and sat across from him. "Tom does deserve to be loved. He's such a good man." The tears welled in her eyes.

"Then why marry him, Luna? There's only one life you'll live, and you and Tom deserve to live it full of love."

Luna's thoughts drifted to J.R., wondering why he'd marry Britney, a woman she was sure, didn't love him. "Do any of us ever live the life we want or one full of the love we deserve, Mr. Ryder? Nobody gets it all. It all comes in bits and pieces. Life is full of complications, and the best we can do is settle for the next best thing. So, to answer your question, no, I don't love Tom to the depth a woman should the man she's going to marry, but he knows that. He's known all along, and still, he's willing to marry me. I'm his next best thing, and he's mine."

It pained Dean to see so much sadness in Luna's eyes. He knew too well what settling meant, and he didn't want that for her, for J.R., or even Tom. "But, love…"

She held a hand up to silence Dean. "There's nothing more to say. Tom and I will marry."

THE SALES CLERK BEHIND THE TIFFANY counter gave Tom a dazzling smile when she reached for his credit card. "Your fiancée is going to be in absolute awe, Mr. Grady," she said of the princess two-karat diamond ring Tom bought for Luna.

"I hope you're right because she deserves the best." Tom reached for the blue, velvet box and eyeing the ring one last time, slid it into his jacket pocket.

"That's so sweet." The sales clerk returned his credit card. "And she is getting the best," the clerk said, as Tom turned to leave and was sure he understood the double entendre.

Stepping outside the store, Tom breathed in April air and started back to the hotel. Wending through the crowded sidewalk, he dismissed the loud din of people and traffic, the ceaseless beeping of car horns, the gunning engines, the car fumes, the scent of hot dogs and coffee of everything that was New York.

Tom thought of the engagement announcement he'd seen in People along with the photographs of a beaming Britney cozying up to J.R., who wore an expression of doom on his face.

There had been reports of their celebrated nuptials on the television tabloids, in the many magazines. Tom surmised Luna had also seen them, and it was likely the reason for her unexpected proposal. It made no difference to Tom what had led to it. What mattered was that she had proposed, and in a few months, they'd be husband and wife—for all eternity. His life would no longer be an endless stream of disappointment.

For one heart-stopping moment, Tom rolled the words husband and wife in his head. He loved the sound of it. It had been a long wait. There were times when Tom thought he'd lost her, first to her music and then to J.R. But now she was finally his. His.

Tom made a detour to pick up a bottle of Cristal. They would toast their engagement after he slipped the ring on her finger, which he would do as soon as she got back from her lunch with Dean.

Luna would almost certainly wear the ring on her right hand to keep the prying press and paparazzi off her heels, but Tom didn't mind. She'd already told him she wanted to keep the engagement between them and family, and he'd agreed because making her happy was all that mattered to Tom. Besides, Luna had already committed to marrying him, and soon enough, they would become husband and wife. He felt ecstatic at the notion.

They'd been lovers for a long time, and he considered them a couple since the night she gave herself to him, but that wasn't enough. Tom was a traditionalist at heart, and until they vowed before God to join in holy matrimony, Tom didn't feel that solid commitment between them. Until death do us part, Tom thought because he planned to be with Luna all his life.

Although Tom never expected Luna to give up her career, he was certain she wanted to have children. Tom's smile was ripe with happiness, knowing they would be his children.

They'd buy a house in the country somewhere away from prying eyes where they'd spend their time when she wasn't touring. They'd have horses and land, lots of land for their children to roam freely.

Even after marriage, Tom wouldn't leave Luna's side when she was on the road. Luna was a star, and he'd be the doting husband that took care of her. Tom didn't mind being Mr. Luna Moon or living in her shadow.

They would take the children on tour with them, especially on those long drawn out tours, he decided. It would be hard on the children, but they were better off with them than raised by nannies. Tom knew what that was like. As much as he loved Trudy, he vowed never to subject a child of his to growing up in the absence of his parents.

It was going to be a fantastic journey.

Tom loved Luna as he'd never loved any woman before. He loved her naiveté, her childlike sense of wonder, her sense of humor. He admired her work ethic and dedication, but most of all, Tom loved her purity. He was her first and only, and he wanted it always to be that way.

Chapter 24

IT WAS SIX a.m., and the world was hushed with dawn. The sky was lightening up with as an October sun rose out of the darkness. The air smelled of the ocean that stretched far and beyond. In an oversized T-shirt, her feet bare, Luna stepped onto the hotel balcony, drank in the view. The blue waters, the sound from the roll of waves, filled Luna with a soothing calm.

Tom was right Santa Monica was a perfect vacation spot to recharge.

Unlike her crew, who were looking forward to the well-deserved R&R after the tour's end, Luna wasn't. To them the tour was a haze of bus rides, hotels, venues, and fast food restaurants, but to her it was an exhilarating ride. Luna already missed the frenzied schedule, the city hopping, and the bright lights. She loved meeting people, being surrounded by fans. She even loved the camera clicking and the hovering reporters.

Odd, Luna thought. Only months ago, she'd lived in a bubble of work, home, and school, and overnight, her life turned into a whirlwind adventure. Never did Luna imagine her life would take the one-eighty turn it had. She certainly never imagined wrapping up her tour at the Hollywood Bowl in Los Angeles, where the iconic Elvis Costello, Frank Sinatra, and the Beatles had performed.

At her closing show, Mrs. Barclay-West was front row and Dean at right stage. Before taking her final bow, Luna announced her temporary hiatus from touring to work on her next album and promised it would be more epic than Treasured Time.

Luna's elbows propped on the balcony rail, she watched Mr. Takanawa dive into the hotel pool for his daily swim. Swimmer's arms cut through the water with strong, steady strokes, leaving small rippling waves behind him. Luna had yet to make it to the pool, preferring to lie on the white sand beach to tan her pale body, but it was on her to-do list, as was getting back to her morning runs. For now, she'd enjoy doing nothing.

The past eleven months had been filled to bursting with the demands she'd put on herself, and she'd worked herself to exhaustion. Luna only came to realize how mentally and physically drained she was when she woke up the day after the end of her tour, and with nowhere to go and nothing to do, she remained in bed. She slept for eighteen straight hours, and her tired body and mind were grateful she had. That was five days ago, and although it took as long to decompress and succumb to the foreign concept of being idle, Luna was now at the stage where she relished her me-time.

As Luna often did when she was alone, she let her thoughts drift to J.R. Even with Tom in her life, Luna hadn't been able to escape the ache of loss for J.R.

In a way, she had J.R. to thank for her success. Bittersweet Luna thought that her broken heart had propelled her successes. It catapulted Treasured Memory into the number one spot for a record thirty weeks. Her album, Treasured Time, boasted sales numbers in the millions now, and demand had seen her appearing on every top-rated television talk show.

Luna's life had surpassed her dreams. She had everything, money, success, the career she'd fantasized about, a man who loved her, yet happiness seemed as distant as the bright rising sun.

The sound of the sliding door opening had Luna turning to Tom, stepping out onto the balcony. His flaxen hair sun-bleached lighter was still wet from his shower. Barefoot, in jeans that hugged his hips and a cotton shirt tight enough to hug muscular arms and broad shoulders, Tom fit right into the California beach scene.

"Freshly brewed." The smile flashing across Tom's tanned face turned into concern when a frown creased Luna's brow. "What's wrong?"

"I..." Luna hesitated reconsidering whether to tell Tom she thought she saw Britney.

The last few times she'd told Tom she thought she'd seen Britney lurking in the shadows, Tom dismissed the sighting as the illusions of a tired mind. Luna was certain the sightings were real, but without proof or a motive for Britney's random appearances, Luna couldn't justify them

"Nothing's wrong, just that you read my mind on the coffee." Luna accepted the handed cup.

"Don't I always." He kissed her forehead. "Is everything okay? "I've ordered breakfast."

"I'm not hungry." Luna caught sight of the lone jogger in the distance, focused on the runner as she followed the curve of the beach. There was too much distance between them and all she could make out were the running shoe impressions pressing into the wet sand that trailed her.

"It's a light breakfast of croissants and fruit salad, and you're eating one or the other." Tom brought his coffee cup to his lips.

"You're a bossy one, but you know you're off manager duty, at least for the time we're on vacation." Luna crossed with him to the wicker chairs.

"The man who loves you, not your manager, is asking you to eat something. I love your figure as is, but you could use a few extra pounds. So you're eating." He waved a finger to silence her. "You're eating something."

"All right, I will."

Tom stretched his legs out, crossed his feet at the ankles. "You must be thrilled we're going home Monday. I know I am. We can start working on our wedding plans."

Luna set her mug on the table and turned to him. "I wanted to talk to you about that."

The expression on her face worried him and set the flutter of familiar nerves in his stomach. He wondered if there would ever come a time when he would master the confidence that didn't make him doubt their relationship. That Luna kept him on pins and needles was an understatement. Even when he made love to her, when he was deep inside her, he didn't feel the tight bond he wanted.

"What's on your mind?" Tom asked hesitantly.

"I thought we'd take a couple of additional weeks to relax and regroup, and then... Well, I'm itching to get back on stage."

"But you just came off a long, grueling tour, Luna. You need more than a couple of weeks of R&R to regenerate." She was dodging, pushing the likelihood of a wedding to the backburner, Tom thought.

"I can't sit idle for so long, and I think I need to take advantage of this energy I have in me."

"But..." Tom paused when Luna waved a hand to silence the oncoming protest.

"Hear me out. I spoke to Mr. Ryder last night, and he's already written a few songs he wants me to look at. I have a few lyrics I've written during the past months, which need Mr. Ryder's musical touch. Between us, soon enough, we should have enough for an album. I want to keep the momentum with my fans going."

"But..."

I don't want to go home to sit around watching the television and reading newspaper articles on J.R.'s upcoming wedding assaulting me at every turn, Luna wanted to scream, but cut Tom off with, "Think as my manager. You know what I'm saying makes perfect sense. The interest in my music is high right now. I'm a new artist, a new face, a new voice, and I need to tap into that now." She stood in one swift, fluid motion and sat on his lap. "Please, this is something I want to do," she said, brushing her lips to his.

She made perfect sense, but for a few weeks, Tom wanted her all to himself. He wanted time with her away from the fans and the paparazzi, away from the ogling male eyes she inspired with the fantasies that made them drool and do whatever else. Tom wanted to set a date and plan their wedding. For a few short weeks, Tom wanted not to have to share Luna with the world. He wanted her to himself.

Drowning in the pleading green eyes staring at him, Tom couldn't help but succumb. "All right, if that's what you want."

"It is."

The gleam in Luna's eyes stirred him. Nothing made him happier than to see her happy. "How about I put a European tour together? It makes perfect sense to hit that market next. I know Mr. Ryder will agree with me and won't hesitate to approve the financing for the tour."

"Europe sounds exciting." Luna's voice came out a happy squeak.

"I'll get to work on it right away." His fingertips traced lightly over her face. "I want to make you happy, and if this is what you want, it's what I'll give you."

"It makes me ecstatic. Thank you." Luna turned her face into his palm.

"I'll make it as memorable as your Canada-U.S. tour."

"I know you will. Thank you for being so understanding and for always looking after me."

"I want to make you happy, Luna. Always." Tom buried his face in her throat, breathed in her familiar scent, one he couldn't live without.

"I know you do." Luna rested her hands on his chest. "Tom?"

"Hmm?" He twined the loose curl of her hair on her face around his finger.

"You're going to be busy for some time planning the tour."

"I will be. Why?"

She toyed with his shirt buttons. His skin pulsed at her touch. "I was thinking of spending some time with my mom. Although we talk most nights, I haven't seen her since we set off on tour. Maybe I could fly out ahead of you, spend one month with her, and then you can fly out to join us."

"But I wanted to spend time with you, Luna. Just you and me." Tom's tone sounded wounded.

"We're practically living together now. We sleep together. We eat together. We're together day and night." The hurt expression on his face had Luna skimming her lips over his to soothe. "I thought she and I could spend time taking in the sights, doing girl stuff, and shopping for my wedding dress."

Tom's heart tripped. Luna had put off setting their wedding date every time he brought it up, but the tide, it seemed, was finally turning in his direction. It was a drugging feeling. For years, he'd been dangling by a thread, not knowing where they stood. The mere thought she wanted to go shopping for her wedding dress, made their union feel that much closer.

Tom took Luna's hand and brought her palm to his lips. "It sounds like a good plan. I'll make the arrangements. How does Italy sound?"

"My mother and I have always wanted to go to Italy." She squealed with excitement.

"I know. I'll start working on your itineraries right away. Until then, I have you all to myself, and I have a surprise for you."

"What is it?" she asked, unable to hide her grin.

"I rented a yacht. It's a belated birthday present for my fiancée and me to cruise over blue water with nothing but calm and the sound of gulls squawking. We sail at noon. The car service will pick us up a half-hour before."

"Sounds divine. I can't wait."

"Me too." Tom's mouth lowered to Luna's, and she joined in the kiss. "Make sure to pack that white bikini I love to see you in."

"All right," she hummed when his tongue probed deeper, and the kiss became steamy.

Tom trailed a lazy line of kisses down her neck as his hand slid under her T-shirt. She was delightfully feminine, curvy, soft, he thought as his fingers skimmed over her lace bra until he found the clasp. With a flick of his fingers, he bared her breasts and yanking her T-shirt off, filled his mouth with them. A hot gush of lust had her body quaking from the staggering pulsing shocks of pleasure, sparking every nerve ending.

"God, that feels amazing." She drove her breasts deeper into his mouth.

Feeling her body pulse under his touch, Tom's hot mouth crushed down on hers to swallow the moans he knew would burst when he slid his hand between her legs.

Her nails dug into his shoulders when she felt his fingers snaking under the lace panties. He found her wonderfully hot, deliciously wet. His fingers slithering in the wet, heat shot a long liquid wave of absolute delight, and she buried her face into his throat to temper her moans.

He knew her well, knew exactly how to stir her blood hot. He knew where to touch her, how to touch her the way she liked. And God, did he know how to touch her with those long, creative fingers, Luna thought when her blood pumped like hot magma. But then, they knew each other well as lovers and knew how to please one another.

"Does that feel good?" His fingers skimmed lightly, teasing her.

The staggering waves of pleasure pulsing in her a long hum, a murmur, and a sigh was all she managed to say.

"I love touching you, Luna."

"I love you touching me," she said, imploring him not to stop.

Deliberately Tom's fingers roamed and teased, drugged her body with the sensations that made her tremble, and her breaths come fast.

"Now, now," she pleaded in his ear when the pressing need to release the layer upon layer of delirious pressure he built up in her became immediate.

"Not yet, Luna. I want to touch you a while longer. I want you to relish in it," he whispered, letting his fingers sink deeper.

He loved to hear the humming sound she made when his touch made the liquid warmth spread through her and cloud her mind.

With stunned arousal in her eyes, her breathing deepened, her fingers latched onto his shoulders. She held on for as long as she could, delighting in what his clever fingers did to her as they slid, stroked, caressed driving wave after wave of blinding pleasure through her.

"I have to now, now, please," she mumbled and arching her body back until her eyes could see the sky, came, in a flurry of torrid fire that erupted from her and snaked through her entire body.

She wanted him right then, and she rushed to unhook his jeans and pull them down. He was ready for her. "I want you inside me. Now."

Her words sent his heart hammering so fast in his chest it felt as if it was going to rupture. Lifting her with the lightness of a feather, he set her down on top of him. His breath unsteady, with a soft moan, he scrambled frantically to plunge inside her. Deep and deeper, he sunk into the sweet, moist heat until she swallowed him whole.

Clamping him like a wet vice, he felt her hips begin to pump as she rocked and rode him like a stallion.

Watching each other, with the sound of white waves lapping the shore and birds chirping in song, they moved together in long, concerted strokes. It wasn't long before his eyes went dark, and she heard his strangled gasps mingled with her murmured name as his climax rolled and shocked his body. Her body trembling with his, she arched back and plunged over the edge with him.

"THE CAR SERVICE IS HERE TO take us to the marina, Luna. Don't forget your carryon." Tom called out when he heard the knock at the door. "Mr. Ryder, what are you doing here?" Tom said, painting a feigned smile over his annoyance when he opened the door to Dean instead of the chauffeur.

"I'm here to see Luna, of course." Dean walked in when Tom stepped aside.

"Yes, of course, but I meant I thought you'd flown back to Toronto after Luna's last performance." Too often, Tom thought the old man's obsession with Luna went beyond that of a mentor, as she innocently put it.

"I did. I have a meeting in Las Vegas that came up at the last minute, and I thought I'd fly out a day early to spend it with Luna. I came straight from the airport." Dean scanned the room. White shutters framed large picture windows looking out to a breathtaking beachfront view. Walls done in olive-green were accented with colorful abstracts and a perfect contrast to the Terracotta tiles. A long, cream sectional and chair with blue and white striped cushions filled the living room. The sliding door to the balcony was wide open, and Dean could see the ocean as a backdrop, smell brine and beach. "Nice room."

"Only the best for Luna," Tom reiterated Dean's words.

"That's right, my boy." Dean's lips curved into a smile when Luna opened the bedroom door and stepped into the living room, lighting it bright. It was as if she brought the sunshine with her wherever she went, Dean thought just as Marina had.

"Mr. Ryder, what a wonderful surprise." Luna rushed to throw her arms around him. "Tom didn't tell me you were flying in."

The same misty shade of gold-flecked green eyes held Luna's gaze. "That's because Tom didn't know about this trip." No one knew about it. Dean wanted to spend time with Luna without Poppy encroaching into the moment. Lately, the woman was everywhere he was, and he suspected, whether knowingly or not, Tom was keeping her abreast of his comings and goings. "It came up on a whim." Dean pecked Luna on the cheek. Not an ounce of makeup on her face, in simple blue shorts, a white flowing shirt, and her hair tied back, she looked the picture of beauty, Dean thought. The picture of Marina.

"Would you like something to drink? Tom, would you get Mr. Ryder, and me, a Perrier." Luna walked Dean to the couch.

"How long are you staying? I'm sure I can find you a room nearby." Tom handed Dean and Luna the uncapped bottle of Perrier and took the seat across them.

"There's no need for that. J.R. and I are staying not far from here, at his house in Malibu."

Luna felt her heart leap out of my chest. Needing to shake off the momentary shock to her system, Luna rose and crossed to the bar to pour scotch into a tumbler.

"J.R.'s with you, here, now?" Tom's voice sounded edgy and annoyed at seeing the distressed look on Luna's face.

"Why would he be?" Dean took a pull of Perrier, winced. "Darling, can I have one of those?"

"I'll get it." Tom rose. "You just said you're both staying at J.R.'s place."

"Sorry, my boy, what I meant to say is that I'm staying at J.R.'s home." Dean corrected dismissing the curt tone and reaching for the offered glass of scotch. "Have you had lunch yet, love?"

Luna shook her head and caught the scowl on Tom's face when she failed to mention their plans.

"You don't mind if I steal her away, do you, Tom? Since I'm here, I thought Luna and I could go over the compilation of songs I've written for her."

"We were planning to spend the afternoon and tonight sailing on the Dolce Vita." Tom's voice dropped thirty degrees.

"I'm sorry. I didn't mean to intrude on your plans."

"I'm sure you didn't," Tom murmured under his breath.

"You're not, Mr. Ryder. Tom can postpone our sailing trip to tomorrow afternoon." Luna turned to Tom, who looked up at her with deep lines carved between his brows and mouth. "Please," she mouthed.

"Sure, I can." Tom conceded when he realized he wasn't going to get his way. Nothing ever went his way when the great Dean Ryder was around.

"That settles it. I'm all yours," Luna said, eliciting a wide smile from Dean.

"Good. We'll have a nice lunch and spend the rest of the day going over music and lyrics."

Luna beamed. "I can't wait to hear them, Mr. Ryder. From what you've told me, they sound perfect for my next album."

"They are, honey. I've been working hard at coming up with just the right sound for the lyrics you wrote, but enough talking." Dean picked up his drink, took it in in one swallow. "Let's get to work. Tom, will you arrange for the car service to pick us up and take us to," Dean rattled off the address. "You know we'll probably be at it all afternoon and night. Why don't you plan to stay over, Luna? There's plenty of space, and I'm sure Tom won't mind if I sequester you for the rest of the day."

Luna turned to Tom. "You won't, will you?"

Biting annoyance back, Tom answered with an abrupt, "No."

Staring out their fourth-floor hotel window, Tom sipped on whiskey and watched Luna and Dean get into the Town Car. His eyes followed it until it turned the corner and disappeared. Tom's mind raced to wonder what the old man was up to. Showing up unannounced, mentioning J.R. was with him, then taking it back, luring Luna away for the night, added up to something. What Tom wasn't sure.

Taking the drink in one gulp, he slammed the glass on the counter and reached for the telephone. "Dean just whisked Luna away, and I have a feeling he has more than just dinner in mind... Yeah, she's staying the night at J.R.'s Malibu house... He claims they'll be working until late, and he talked her into spending the night... I don't like it either... I did have plans with her, but she brushed them and me off when... I know I'm her fiancé, but she's a grown woman with a mind of her own... Yeah, this is not getting us anywhere... Okay, I'll come over now to talk face to face... I'll see you in twenty minutes, Poppy," Tom said, reaching for his keys.

Chapter 25

OVER A DELICIOUS meal of poached sea bass paired with a savory bottle of Cabernet Sauvignon and the most decadent chocolate-ricotta tart Luna told Dean of her plans to get back on stage as soon as possible.

"Tom suggested a European tour." Luna sipped on the after-dinner espresso.

"And he would be right, love, but are you sure you want to get back into the rigorous routine of a tour so soon? I mean, you have several television appearances coming up that will have you performing."

"I'm positive. I'm itching to get back on stage." Luna assured, but Dean suspected there was more to it.

"Well, I want you to relax for a few weeks." He waved a finger to silence her. "By relax I mean your vocal cords. You have your public relations campaign Tom, and the WE team has put together for you. Tom will go over it with you soon enough, but I'll give you the highlights. You have appearances on the late-night and daytime television talk shows as well as a few nightclubs Tom is working with the team on booking. Those will fill up most of November. For early next year, I've managed to get you a spot on the American Music Awards, and the Grammy's, and you'll have an appearance in a couple of months on the Motown tribute they're filming right here in L.A."

"That sounds great. I wonder why Tom hasn't mentioned it."

"Because I told him to let you rest up for now." Dean sipped on the scotch Consuelo served him in place of coffee. "Performing takes a toll on your vocal cords. Combine that with the hectic work pace, you tend to embrace, and it's enough to physically and mentally drain you. Right now, what you need is time to recharge. Let's finish our drinks in the living room."

Dean led the way to a grand room with white Italian marble floors, high beam ceilings, and classy, but masculine dark, wood furniture. Walls washed in warm brown were covered with colorful Picasso's, Schifano's, and Doris McCarthy's. African artifacts were on display on pedestals and shelves. In one corner, a Steinway shiny and white stood. The room breathed male elegance.

"The truth is that I love the frenetic energy of being on stage. I thrive on the rush I feel before a show. And when I get out there, in front of hundreds of people, they ignite a fire in me that makes me want to sing and sing some more. Is that wrong of me?"

"Of course not, it's that drive that's made you successful so quickly." Dean tilted back the snifter for a long sip.

"Well, I'll have enough relaxation. Three weeks I'm spending here with Tom hiding away from the cameras and paparazzi. Then, in December, I'm planning an Italian holiday with my mom. She's always dreamed of visiting Italy, but could never afford it. I thought a month with her should do it. Although I know she'll love Italy and spending time together, mom is very much a homebody, and she'll be itching to get back home after a few weeks." Luna sank into the butter-soft cushions of the sectional with a view of pool's still blue waters. The gardens beyond it burst with pinks and purples, flaming yellow and reds.

"That sounds like fun, and the timing works with the planned P.R. campaign. I'll arrange for the company plane to fly you and your mom to Italy."

"Thank you for the offer, but that won't be necessary. This is something I'd like to do for mom."

"All right, and I think now you can swing for first-class tickets and a five-star hotel." A teasing smile tugged at his lips.

Soon enough, she'd be able to afford her own private jet, and it was all because of this wonderful, caring man who'd believed in her enough to finance and support her dream. How she'd ever repay him for such kindness was a mystery to her?

"You still have to meet each other, don't you?" she said, eyes widening with the sudden realization.

"We do. She's a very elusive woman." Dean put his feet up on the lacquered coffee table inches from the Baccarat crystal vase filled with roses and linked hands behind his head.

"She's a homebody, hates the spotlight. She couldn't deal with the chaos around me. I'll have to arrange for the two of you to meet."

Dean let his gaze casually slide to Luna. "How about I meet you both toward the end of your Italian trip?"

Luna smiled at the suggestion. This was why she'd come to adore this man. "You'd do that? You'd fly across an ocean to meet us?"

"You don't think I'd let you lose on your own around those lecherous Italian men."

Luna laughed that girlish laugh that sounded so much like Marina and tugged at Dean. "That sounds perfect, Mr. Ryder."

"Why don't we keep this to ourselves, make it a surprise? It sounds to me as if your mother likes to avoid being the center of attention."

"You're right about that. If she found out we were planning this, she'd never go for it," she said and made a mental note to tell Tom to set them up in adjoining rooms. "This is going to be so much fun."

"It will love."

"Then, we're set." Luna toed shoes off and tucked her legs under her.

They settled into comfortable banter, and Luna went on to tell Dean how she'd come into singing. He laughed when she told him how she'd frozen with fear the first time she stepped on the stage, and how Tom was there in the wings to talk the stage fright away. Reflecting on the moment, she told him how once she began to sing and the audience looked as if they were mesmerized by something she was doing, it was then she decided singing was what she wanted to do.

Through it all, Dean listened intently, hanging on her every word, as he always did hoping his memory would retain every detail, every word, every story she recounted.

"Would you like more coffee?" Dean asked when Luna was talked out. Her eyes drawn to the beams of colorful spotlights flicking on in the garden, she shook her head. "Then let's take a look at those songs now, Marina."

Jet lag was setting in, she thought. "What do you say to you getting a nap in before we do?"

Dean glanced up to her with a distant, tired gaze. "I'd say that's a good idea."

Luna took the glass from Dean's hand and linking her arm with his walked him up the curved staircase, down the long tiled hallway.

"You rest for as long as you like," she said, helping him to bed.

"You'll be here afterward?"

"You can count on it." Luna kissed Dean on the cheek.

With concern in her eyes, she made her way back to the living room. Dean's shaky grip on the wrought iron railing, the vacant, confused look in his eyes worried Luna. He'd given Tom the wrong home address and had to correct it when the limo wound its way through unfamiliar streets. Tonight Dean didn't seem like the same energetic, vibrant man she'd come to know.

Luna's mind on Dean when she wandered back into the living room, she didn't see him at the bar, pouring himself a drink. J.R., however, immediately sensed her presence, and he lifted his gaze to her. Her hair flowed thick and dark around the beautiful unpainted face he dreamed of every night. She wore a cheery, floral sundress, and her skin was tanned to a dark caramel.

"Hi."

At the sound of J.R.'s voice, Luna's stomach twisted. The wrenching pain slammed into her, and Luna turned to flee.

"Please don't go." J.R.'s words arrowed into her clouding her brain, and against her better judgment, she stopped, hung back at the doorway.

"It's just me," J.R. said when he saw her green eyes subtly scanning the room.

"I didn't ask, nor do I care." Luna turned to leave.

"Don't go, Luna. Please, I don't want you to go." J.R. poured a second drink and made his way to the couch. "Will you join me?"

"I'm fine right here." Luna's tone sent a chill through the room.

"Please, Luna, come sit with me. There's so much I need to say to you."

Her eyes narrowed. "Nothing that would interest me."

"I know it's not much, but I am sorry for everything. I didn't want to hurt you. I didn't want any of this to happen. You have to know I don't want to marry Britney, and I sure as hell don't love her. I need you to know that. It's you I love." Luna said nothing as tangles of emotions passed across her face, and for a moment, the only sound in the room was the chorus of lovesick cicadas singing out in the garden. "It's you I love, Luna," he repeated, thinking she hadn't heard him the first time.

"Stop talking, J.R." Her heart picked up when he began to walk toward her. He wore a white linen shirt under an olive-green leather jacket, jeans, and tan loafers. His shock of glossy black hair was sexily tousled. Why did he have to look so good? "I'm happy for you and Britney, and I wish you both a long and happy life. Don't come any closer." As much as she wanted to run away, her legs felt led heavy, and she couldn't move.

J.R. took a few more steps closing the gap between them. "I love you, Luna."

She set hard, unwavering eyes on J.R. How could he claim to love her and hurt her as he had, then show up months later with a feeble apology? She wouldn't allow him to break her heart again. Not this time.

"I feel nothing for you. I'm engaged to Tom." She flashed him her ringed hand. "We're going to be married soon. He loves me. He, J.R., knows what love is. He would never dream of hurting me." The words meant to scar, from the pained expression on his face, had.

J.R stopped dead in his tracks and sunk hands deep into his pockets. "Do you love him, Luna?" Her silence told him all he needed to know. "You don't do you? You love me."

"You're so full of yourself, J.R." Luna's voice trembled before she steadied it to a chilled fury. "You think that arrogant charm of yours is going to work on me? I'm not one of your bought floozies. I have to go. Tom's probably waiting up for me. He doesn't like to go to bed without me by his side."

The comment came at him like bullets aimed straight for the heart. Understanding it stemmed from the pain he'd caused her, he shrugged them off. "It's you I want to spend the rest of my life with. It's you I want to marry."

Luna opened her mouth to say something. Before she could say anything, J.R. wrapped his hands around her waist. Pulling her in, he covered her mouth with his. His arms chained around her tighter when she attempted to wrench away, and he sank deeper into the kiss. Emotions poured out of him into her, making every bone in her body go limp. When he finally pulled away, he left her gulping for air, and she couldn't help but melt into his arms.

"I hate you." Her brain felt hazy.

"I love you." J.R. feathered kisses over her face.

"You hurt me." His lips were impossibly tender. "It's the second time you've hurt me, and I won't let you do that to me again, Jimmy." They soothed every ache.

It seemed they were back to Jimmy, for the moment. "I'm sorry. I never wanted to hurt you." Before Luna could say anything, J.R.'s hungry mouth latched onto hers. His kiss was passionate, desperate, full of need.

In marked opposition to J.R.'s emotions pouring from him like a breached levee, Luna's temper flared hot. "Don't," she said, pulling away, but his tight hold overpowered her, and he pulled her back in.

Ignoring the hands pounding on his chest, J.R. pressed his mouth to hers again. His lips were hot, his tongue quick, his emotions flowed more passionately into the kiss, reaching deep into her heart. J.R. set off feelings in her Tom never could, and she felt herself come alive.

A storm brewed inside Luna raged war against her better judgment. She couldn't allow him to hurt her. Not again. If she gave into him, she wouldn't be able to tear herself away, and J.R. would go on to hurt her again.

As much as her brain told her, walking away was the right thing to do, anger rolled into need, need rolled into want. Luna couldn't pry herself free from J.R.'s hold because she didn't want to. He was in her bones, in every fiber of her being. In her, and she let her tongue part his lips and find its way to his.

Something unexpectedly shifted inside Luna, and she turned. "Let go of me. I can't do this," she said, pushing him away.

When Luna started to walk away, J.R.'s hand gripped her wrist and spun her around so fast her body plowed into him. "I want to love you tonight, Luna. Let me love you."

"You're persistent. I'll give you that. You don't get me in bed on your first attempt, and you don't give up."

J.R. could hear the hurt in her voice; see the tears welling in her eyes. "Please don't cry. It's not like that at all. I'd never do anything to hurt you, Luna. You have to believe me. It's just that I ... have responsibilities. So many people are dependent on me. Can you understand that?"

Lost in the eyes that stared at her, Luna buried her face in his chest. "What do you want from me, Jimmy?"

"You. I want to whisk you away at this very moment to a beautiful tropical island, overflowing with palm trees surrounded by a turquoise ocean where just the two of us will spend our life together for all eternity. It's you I love, Luna. It's you I want." J.R. brushed dark curls from her face. "I wish it was all different. I wish my life weren't the complicated mess it is. I'd give up everything to be with you, Luna. Marrying Britney is a duty one I have to fulfill for my mother and father, nothing more. You believe me, don't you? I need you to..."

Luna raised a finger to his lips. "I do."

With her fame came the added pressure of being accountable to her crew for their living, to the growing number of people who became associated with each performance, and the demands of filling stadiums to generate profits. Luna could only imagine the demands and pressures on J.R.'s shoulders in running the West dynasty.

J.R. rested his forehead against hers. "Stay with me tonight."

Luna gazed at him for a long moment. She could have easily step away, but she didn't want to. Feelings crowding inside her, she held her hand out for his. The room filled full of oxygen then, and taking her hand, J.R. brought it to his lips. If only for tonight, he'd love her, and she'd love him back.

With ribbons of light from an orange moon lending a silver wash to the room and the sound of the ocean whooshing outside the bedroom window, J.R. took Luna in his arms and kissed her.

Slowly, tenderly, he traced butterfly kisses across Luna's face, down the curve of her neck, leaving a wonderful tingling feeling and letting the taste of her flood him. "I want to breathe you in. I want to touch you. I want to taste you. I want to carry the memory of us together with me because it's the only thing that will make my life bearable."

"Me too, Jimmy."

"I can't imagine ever loving anyone as I do you, Luna."

"Me too, Jimmy." Luna traced a finger over her ring before removing it and tucking it into her dress pocket. "I want to carry the memory of your kisses, your touch, your scent, your taste with me. Make tonight the memory I will carry in my heart forever." She let her dress fall to the floor.

"You're more beautiful than I envisioned you in my dreams."

She lifted a hand to his cheek. "You've dreamt of me, Jimmy?"

"Every day since meeting you, you've been in my thoughts. In my dreams, I've made love to you thousands of times. Right now, all I want to do is touch you and make love with you."

J.R. ran fingertips over her arms, took them down to the swells of her breast, skimmed his thumbs over the nipples straining against lace. When her nipped became hard, expert fingers flicked her bra off. She shuddered, and his name escaped her lips in a throaty whisper when his mouth streaked over her breasts.

It was like music to his ears. "Have you thought of me?"

"Every day, Jimmy."

"Have you, Luna?"

"Mmm-hmm." Her skin hummed as he played his mouth over her milky-pale skin. Dozens of nerve endings exploded in unison when his fingers roamed over curves, to places she wanted him to touch.

"I've dreamed of loving you like this from the moment I watched that cute butt of yours swaying back and forth as you wiped Windex from my rug."

She flung her head back in laughter. "Show me how much, Jimmy."

Her body was a miracle, one of a kind, J.R. thought as he tasted, ravaged, loved. The sensation of his touch on her was explosive. Hearing her moans of cried pleasure, his name on her lips as his fingers dug deep, as his mouth and tongue sought places he'd dreamed of possessing, was magical.

Luna never wanted it to end. She wanted him to love her forever.

"Let me enjoy you longer, Luna," he said when he heard her breaths coming quick and short.

She held out for as long as she could, but when the final intoxicating flash thundered in her, her self-control snapped. His name burst from her lips when the orgasm bulleted through her.

Fusing his mouth to hers, he swallowed her last cries. In between kisses, he told her how much he loved her. When she opened up to him, in an instant, he was on top of her, inside her, one with her.

At that very moment, they became a part of something bigger. They were part of the stars, the earth, and the moon casting shadows over the city.

This was love, she thought—a need more basic than air and food.

She clamped herself around him, and together, they began to move. When the glorious burst of pressure careened through him, with her name on his lips, he floated in a loving euphoria and filled her.

Both knew that moment was going to mark their lives forever.

Afterward, holding her, J.R. said the words he wanted her to take with her on her journey through life. "The world is a good place, and it's better with you in it. I love you, Luna. I always will. You're the best thing that's ever happened to me, and I will forever carry you in my heart and memories. Tell me you will too."

Luna heard raw emotion in J.R.'s voice. The fist wrapped around her heart squeezed tight, and her eyes filled with tears. "I will. I love you, Jimmy. It's always been you."

This wasn't the way it was supposed to be. Love was supposed to be forever, for always. They were the words she sang out in her songs, yet she and J.R. would never be forever, would never be for always.

In J.R.'s arms, she didn't cuddle, she clung to him as if never wanting to let go and cried silent tears. J.R.'s heart clenching with every tear rolling down her cheeks, he willed the thought they'd soon reach the end of their time together away. When she cried herself out and slipped into sleep, J.R. watched Luna for a long time wishing life wasn't so unfair. He'd give up everything to be with her, but that wasn't an option—not with his mother in the picture.

The thought of Luna marrying Tom made J.R.'s heart break, but he didn't want her to be lonely. He wanted only happiness to fill her life. J.R. wanted her to be loved, and he knew Tom would. He'd seen the depth of Tom's love for Luna in his eyes the first time they met. There was no doubt in J.R.'s mind Tom would take care of her, love her as he would.

With Luna nestled in his arms, in darkness, J.R. cried his first tears since the death of his father.

Chapter 26

TOM AND LUNA lazed the afternoon away on the Dolce Vita, a seventy-eight-foot yacht with a mahogany deck varnished to a deep shine. Drifting away from boats skimming on the surface of calm, blue water, the Dolce Vita sailed around Catalina Island. The scent of the ocean and cocoa butter mingling in the air, Tom and Luna soaked the sun while sipping on mimosas.

When the Dolce Vita dropped anchor, under sparkling diamonds of sunlight dancing over glass-smooth waters, Tom and Luna dove in and swam together for a long while.

When Tom tired out, he jutted out of the water. "I'm going aboard. You coming?"

Loving the solitude and the expanse of blueness around her, Luna called back, "You go ahead. I want to swim for a bit longer."

"I can stay with you," Tom offered, although he was confident he'd taught her to swim well enough for her to wade through the deep, brackish water.

"I'm fine. I want to start getting more exercise into my day." She called back, although what she wanted was to work J.R. out off her mind, wash away the ache of loss from her heart, and the guilt from her soul.

Luna dove in. Like a mermaid in her natural surroundings, she glided through the water. She swam past a school of mackerel, eyes round and wide, rushing past her like flashes of silver. With nothing but the ocean and the soft diffused glow of sunlight, J.R.'s words inked on the note he left on his pillow crowded her mind.

> *My sweet Luna,*
>
> *When you wake, I will be miles from you, and I'm sorry about that, but I couldn't bear to say goodbye to you. I want my last memory to be of us making love, of me holding you in my arms, and watching you in sleep as the moon and stars outside our bedroom window burned bright.*
>
> *I will carry our night together and the words we shared in my heart forever.*
>
> *Promise me you won't shed any tears for me, Luna. I don't want to be the cause of your sadness, the cause of your pain. I want only joy and happiness to fill your life, but above all, I want love to fill your heart.*
>
> *You turned my world upside down in the best way possible. I will never forget you, for wherever I am, I will envision your face with every ballad and melody I hear. I hope you will see me in them too and only think of our night together with fond memories.*
>
> *My heart is yours, always and forever.*
> *Jimmy*

Tears blurred Luna's vision.

In the depths of the sapphire-blue waters, she saw J.R. A Love, true and pure washed over Luna, and touched her to her core. She'd never felt anything as powerful and as real as she felt last night with J.R. with Tom.

Tom made love to her, but J.R. possessed her. J.R. had given her the gift of love and the feeling of belonging.

Would they never be able to share that again? Would they never love one another as they had last night? The heavy ache that boundless love wouldn't fill her life stabbed at her, as did the guilt when thoughts of Tom came at her. But even as the guilt and shame balled in the pit of her belly at her betrayal, Luna didn't regret spending the night with J.R. She knew now J.R. loved her. Truly loved her, and there was some comfort in knowing he did.

Beneath the surface of the ocean, Luna wept for a lost love that would never be.

When Luna surfaced for air, Tom's eyes were on her. He watched her arms cutting through the water with swift strokes to swim in the opposite direction as if racing to escape. Tom gave instructions to the captain to follow Luna as she swam until, physically exhausted and mentally drained, she had no choice, but to take Tom's hand and climb back on-board.

"You certainly got your workout." Tom draped a towel over her shoulders. Her skin was a golden-brown against the tiny white bikini.

"It feels great, but as much as I enjoy swimming, I think I'll get back into my running routine. Running helps clear my head." Luna toweled her face dry, squeezed the excess water from the ropes of dark hair.

Her gaze focused on some distant point Tom asked, "Is something bothering you, Luna?"

Everything. I cheated on you last night with a man I love in a way I'll never love you. How could she possibly tell him of her emotional and physical betrayal? How could she break his heart by telling him she'd spent the night in bed with J.R.? How could she tell him she'd shared her love, one her heart wouldn't allow to give him, with J.R.? Tom didn't deserve this, Luna thought. All she wanted to do was to shut down.

Luna wanted to forget everything. She wanted to forget nothing.

"Nothing's bothering me," Luna lied with a face that gave nothing away even as the war inside her raged at the knowledge she'd lost the man she loved forever and cheated on the man she vowed to marry.

Tom watched Luna busy herself, spreading the towel on the reclining chair before she stretched her long body across it. "Did something happen last night at Mr. Ryder's?"

"Nothing happened. What would make you say that?" Guilt disguised in irritation edged into her voice.

Tom's narrowed eyes studied Luna, wishing he could read her mind and get at the truth. "I just wondered if he said anything to you. You know you can talk to me about anything."

"I know I can." Guilt made her eyes dart away.

The concern began to inch up into his chest. "You sure you're all right, Luna? Tom perched himself at the edge of her chair, and she felt crowded by him.

"For the last time, I'm fine." Luna tossed her head back and aimed her face to the sun watching the gulls above them, wings spread, in full flight circling in search of their next meal. "Is there anything stronger to drink on this boat than mimosas?"

Tom rose to give her the space her eyes demanded. "I'll make you a martini, but you really should get some food in you. You've had too much sun, too many drinks. After all the swimming, you need food in your stomach."

The wistful expression on his face had Luna holding back a barked response, and forming an apologetic smile. "Food sounds good, and I'm sorry I lashed out at you. I'm … worried about Mr. Ryder." She tossed out, hoping to steer the conversation away from her.

"Why, what's wrong with him?" Tom filled the shaker with ice cubes, gin, vermouth, shook.

"He seemed distant and unfocused. He gave you the wrong address and called me Marina a couple of times. I don't know who Marina is. He quickly corrected his error, but he just seemed … confused."

"Maybe it was jet lag." Tom poured martini from the shaker into two glasses.

"That's what he said, but my gut tells me it's more than that. I didn't want to leave him."

Now that Tom thought about it, he'd seen the same confused look on Dean's face. He'd dismissed it as part of an aging mind, but maybe Luna was right, the old man might be going loopy, Tom thought.

He regretted now calling Poppy. Her reaction when Tom told her about Dean's unexpected visit to Luna was extreme. Since signing on with WE Productions, Poppy had demanded Tom report to her every exchanged word between Dean and Luna. Although Tom often told Poppy nothing of consequence was ever said, her ongoing threats to terminate Luna's contract had him telling her everything and doing precisely what she asked of him.

Now, last night's incident was proving to be nothing but a reaction of his overactive, jealous imagination. If he'd temper his suspicions, the old man was trying to get J.R. and Luna together he'd have realized that Dean giving him the wrong address wasn't an orchestrated ruse. He'd triggered Poppy's anger by telling her his suspicions and setting her off on a tear. The woman was one scary bitch when her temper bubbled hot.

Tom was panicking. He had to right this before it took root, and Poppy made good on her threats to hurt Luna. He'd arrange to meet the bitch in the next couple of days to set things straight.

"The flight from Toronto to L.A. is a long one for anyone, Luna, let alone a man his age." Tom tried to put Luna's mind at ease.

"You think so?" Luna took the martini glass from Tom, fished the skewered olive out.

"I know so." Tom's confidence made Luna's lips curve into a smile for the first time that day. "You're worrying for nothing."

"Maybe you're right. He did seem better when I dropped him off at the airport this morning."

"There you go. All he needed was a good night's rest." Seeing the turmoil behind her green eyes ease somewhat, his own did as well.

BELOW DECK, WITH A VIEW OF a falling sun painting the sky shades of yellow and red, the chef spread a meal of grilled perch with wild rice and an arugula salad dressed in an orange vinaigrette. A decadent chocolate torte followed for dessert. Luna ate everything on her plate.

"You enjoyed the meal." Tom sat back to watch Luna. The coral sundress she wore brought out her dusky skin. She'd left her hair loose, and he liked the way it spilled over bare shoulders. Her face had a rosy, sunburned tinge, and her lips were glossed pink. She looked stunning and sultry.

"I did. I didn't realize how hungry I was." Luna's eyes didn't bear the irritation Tom had seen earlier in the day, and her tone was relaxed.

"It's a warm night. Why don't we finish our drinks on the main deck?"

"All right." Luna followed Tom up the short flight of stairs.

Blue skies had given way to night, and the ocean was plunged in black. The air smelled of salt riding on the spray from the sea, and the steady roll of frothing waves.

"It's so beautiful and serene," Luna said, listening to the night, the calm, and hearing the ocean whisper to her.

"The captain suggested we anchor here, and I can see why." Tom's gaze was on the flickering lights from seaside homes, and the rising green peaks behind them cast in shadows.

"Thank you for today, Tom." Luna tipped her face up to meet his lips. It was the first intimate gesture she'd made to him all day.

"I'm glad you enjoyed it. You know I only want to make you happy."

"I know." She let her gaze skim over him. His sun-streaked hair fanned around a tanned face with a fashionable stubble and sparkling blue eyes. With the moon casting a grey sheen on the ocean at his back, he looked like a fine painting. He was a beautiful man inside and out, she thought. "I don't deserve you."

"It's me who doesn't deserve you." Tom ran his fingers down her arm until their hands linked. "By the way, I spoke to the WE travel team before dinner, and they came back to me with a recommended itinerary for you and your mother."

Luna's eyes lit up. "Well, don't keep me in suspense."

"You fly into Florence, spend a few nights there. From there, a guide will drive you to Pisa, then travel along the eastern coastline, stopping at many of the cities along the way until you reach Rome. West Enterprises owns a hotel there, The Cesare Hotel. And it just so happens they have a recording studio close by if you wanted to get to work on your next album."

"That sounds perfect, Tom. Mom will love it."

"I'll book it tomorrow. I should be able to join you three weeks into your trip."

"All right." Her gaze tilted to the blinking red and green lights from the small Cessna as it buzzed overhead, and she caught sight of the stars and the moon that seared the sky, and the memory of J.R. flooded her. My heart is yours, always and forever—each word brought with it a stab of pain.

Was this the way it would always be? Would J.R. forever be in her head?

Was she to always drift into thoughts that reinforced what could never be?

Life was corrosive, eating away at the spirit, at your soul, she concluded. Spurred by the searing pain biting down on her heart and spitting it out, without thought, she blurted out, "Let's get married in Rome, Tom."

The unexpected comment rocked him on his heels. "All right," he said, with love rippling through him.

"Nothing big, nothing fancy. I don't want reporters, paparazzi, or flashing cameras cutting into our moment. We could have the church wedding my mom's always wanted. Just you, me, my mom," she pressed lips together when the words Mr. Ryder almost escaped. That would be a surprise. "We can invite Jean and the We Productions team. My mom will help me buy a nice dress, and..."

Tom pulled her in. "That sounds wonderful. All of it. Rome sounds like the perfect place for a wedding. I'll start making the arrangements right away." Tom drew Luna closer and slowly traced his fingers across her face. "I will love you, take care of you, and make you happy, Luna." He kissed her, and she kissed him back with the sensation of loss swelling in her.

Chapter 27

LUNA AND SARINA fell in love with Italy. Florence offered wonders of art and architecture that left them awed. In Pisa, they visited the Leaning Tower of Pisa, historic churches, and medieval palaces dating as far back as the twelfth century. Their travels progressed along the Italian coast, to cities straddling the gleaming waters of the Tyrrhenian Sea until they arrived at their destination.

The Cesare Hotel in Rome was an opulent five-star hotel set in a nineteenth-century villa. Their room was spacious and provided a comfort that awed Sarina. Walls were oyster white, and the thick, plush carpet made Sarina kick her shoes and relish in its thick pile. There were two queen beds in the bedroom, a separate living room, and a dining room with a balcony overlooking Via Piacenza.

In the days that followed, after a breakfast of decadent pastries and cappuccino, Luna and Sarina set off on foot with a planned agenda. The cooler December temperatures lured fewer tourists to the city, and getting around was a relaxing experience.

The eternal city was more spectacular than Luna or Sarina imagined. Its monuments were breathtaking, its fountains were pure romance, and cobbled streets transported you to its historical past. With Christmas in the air, roads and piazzas were domed with strings of colorful lights and silver garland. Markets were thronged with shoppers and vendors filled with the spirit of the season.

Luna and Sarina visited the Colosseum, the Pantheon, and the Roman Forum. They tossed coins into the Trevi fountain after making wishes. Luna and Sarina toured St. Peter's Basilica, the Vatican and the Sistine Chapel spending hours admiring the Renaissance artwork by Botticelli, Pinturicchio, and Cosimo Roselli. They were in awe when they took in Michelangelo's The Creation of Adam splayed on the chapel's ceiling.

Luna treated Sarina to a shopping spree along the fashionable Via Condotti, where the fashion icons Gucci, Valentino, and Armani lined the fashionable street. At Salvatore Ferragamo, they bought white stilettos for Luna's upcoming wedding with matching purses. Luna scanned her credit card at Dolce & Gabbana, Dior, Furla, and Damiani, where she placed an order for her wedding bands.

By early afternoon, their feet begging for respite, Luna, and Sarina stopped at the Caffè Greco—the oldest coffee shop in Rome. The din of conversation buzzed in the café with high ceilings and walls awash in colorful oils of Italian landmarks. With the exquisite aroma of brewing coffee painting the air, they enjoyed espressos along with their famous pistachio cake.

"I'm having a great time, Luna, thank you for this. I'm loving Rome." Sarina let her taste buds savor the luxurious taste of the rich espresso.

Luna smiled, pleased to have fulfilled one of her mother's many dreams. "I am too, Mom, and I'm having a great time. And you know I'm not one to enjoy shopping, but I enjoyed our spree today."

"Spending money is usually good for the soul, but you may have gone overboard, honey. I mean, do we each need five pairs of shoes with matching purses?"

"Haven't you ever heard that a girl could never have too many shoes or purses?" Luna forked the last of her pistachio cake and gave some thought to ordering a second slice.

"I know, honey, but…"

"Mom, we both deserve this and besides as Mr. Ryder says, 'money is meant to be spent.'" Luna waved the waiter down and ordered a second piece of cake and another espresso for her mother.

"I thought when he said that he was referring to business."

"Potato, potahto. We deserve this, mom. You deserve this." Luna watched the lively group of young women step into the café, in animated conversation, eyes filled with youthful excitement.

The petite woman with the flaming red hair reached for the camera strapped around her neck to snap a shot of her friends posing in front of the display case flaunting a selection of Italian delicacies when she caught sight of Luna through the camera lens.

Red lowered her camera and rushed to Luna's table. "Excuse me. Aren't you Luna Moon?"

It was the first time since arriving in Italy, Luna was recognized, and the question stunned her. "I … yes, I am."

"Oh my God, you guys. It's Luna Moon. It's Luna Moon. It's really her." Red called out, and within seconds, the women swarmed Luna's table. "We're from New York, and we, all of us, saw your show at the

Garden. I dragged my boyfriend to it as well. And he was like 'I'm not going to that chick concert,' but by the end of it, well, let's just say boyfriend was thrilled because I couldn't wait to get him back to our apartment." Red's wink was one of pure mischief. "It was the same with Gabby, wasn't it?" She elbowed the wide-eyed brunette staring at Luna.

"Yeah, my boyfriend was the same, but after listening to you for two hours, I was like, let's check into a hotel now, babe." She whispered the last words through a cupped mouth, and the little light that lit her hazel eyes told Luna she was reflecting on the memory.

Each of the women had similar stories to tell, and Luna couldn't get over the fact she'd had such an impact in their lives. That her music had brought people together to share their love was a surprise to her.

"I'm glad I could be of service, ladies." Luna gave them a wink, setting the women off in giggles.

"Your voice is so," Gabby gnawed on the side of her cheek, "Sweet and moving. It's as if it reaches into your soul and evokes such emotion. You can't help but want to reach out and be close to the person you love. Can I get your autograph, Miss Moon?" Gabby asked in unison with Red.

"Luna, and of course." Luna took the offered pen, and napkin Red turned over. "Who do I make it out to?"

"I'm Roxie, and you know Gabby. This is Marcie, Tanya, Toni, and Lisa. Did I mention that the next day we had to go out to buy your album?"

"Thank you so much for your support and your kind words, ladies." Luna flashed a warm smile, handed each of the women a signed napkin, and treated them to lunch.

Several more people who recognized Luna gathered around her table, and it was then Sarina realized the level of stardom her daughter had attained. Along with the gratification came a frisson of panic.

It was a matter of time now before someone dug up Luna's past. Sarina needed to tell her daughter the truth— sooner than later.

THROUGH THE WINDOW OF THEIR HOTEL room, the light from a late afternoon sun haloed Sarina. "The view is so beautiful." Sarina's introspective eyes turned to Luna when she felt her daughter's probing eyes at her back. "I love you, honey, and everything I do is for you."

The haunted expression on Sarina's face made Luna's stomach tighten. "What's wrong, mom? Are you all right?"

Her mind weary and her body tired, Sarina decided to leave the conversation she had to have with her daughter for later when she had the strength to delve into it head-on. "I'm fine. It's been an exciting day." Her eyes flicked to the ivory, silk dress spread out on Luna's bed.

The thoughtful expression on Sarina's face told Luna her mother's thoughts were elsewhere. She'd let her tell her what was on her mind on her own time. Sarina Lopez wasn't one to be rushed. "You don't mind that it's not a full-out wedding gown, do you, mom?"

Knowing Luna wasn't for traditional norms, Sarina sent her daughter an understanding smile. "No, darling, the short Fendi was a good choice."

"I hope you mean it. I mean, this dress is elegant and stylish, and I can wear it again. I'd never be able to do that with a wedding gown." Luna held the flowing satin off the shoulder dress to her body and eyed herself in the dresser mirror. "And it's as close to white as I'll wear."

Sarina didn't bother to mention Luna no longer had to wear her clothes until they became threadbare. "Tom's going to be awestruck when he sees you walking down the aisle in it."

The thought it wasn't J.R. watching her walk down the aisle or that he wasn't the one she'd meet at the end of it had tangles of emotions crossing Luna's face.

"You're thinking about J.R., aren't you?"

"I can't stop."

"You need to forget J.R., honey."

"I'm trying, but it's hard," Luna said, even as thoughts of J.R. turned in her mind.

"I know it's hard, but…"

"It's harder than you think, mom. I…" Luna paused.

"Saw him recently?" Sarina watched her daughter catching her bottom lip between her teeth in obvious admission of guilt. "I hope Tom can't read you as well as I can."

Luna fell into the closest chair. "It's worse that that. I spent the night with him a few days before his wedding."

Sarina picked up Luna's wedding dress off the bed, threaded it on a hanger. "I see."

"That's all you're going to say?" Luna watched her mother walk the dress to the closet.

"What would you like me to say?"

"That I'm a horrible person, a cold-hearted, uncaring bitch, a homewrecker." The silence was smothering, and Luna blurted out, "He told me he loved me, Mom. He told me it was me he wanted to marry. He said so many things, beautiful and wonderful things, and I said them back without hesitation. Say something, Mom."

"Safe to say Tom doesn't know."

Luna didn't see the disappointment she expected on her mother's face but thought she heard it in her voice. "No."

Sarina walked to the mini-fridge and pulled out two bottles of water, handed one to Luna. "You shouldn't have let him into your bed."

Luna cringed. "Jesus, Mom."

"I'm not as much of a prude as you think me to be, Luna. Don't you think I've known you've been sleeping with Tom since the night of your birthday? The day after, it was as clear as day on your face you had. Why do you think I insisted you see Dr. Berkeley? I'm the one who told him to put you on the pill." Sarina sipped on water to allow the time for the comment to sink into her flushed-faced daughter. "Anyway, the reason I say you shouldn't have let J.R. into your bed has more to do with emotions than sex. Being with J.R. and knowing how it feels to share your love with him will now forever be in your heart and mind, and prevent you from loving Tom as he deserves."

Why did her mother always have to be right?

"J.R.'s married now, honey. He's moved on. You need to as well."

"I know." Luna's mind flashed to the magazine and newspaper articles her mother tried to keep from her on the flight.

But Luna had already seen the numerous articles chronicling J.R. and Britney's life from birth to date. She'd seen the photographs of the lavish wedding and honeymoon. She'd already shed her tears over them. Weeks later, the articles and pictures still hunted Luna's thoughts. Her only consolation was that in every photo, J.R. looked as miserable as she felt.

"Marriage is a beautiful, worthwhile experience, Luna, but it won't be if you're not in love with the man you're planning to share your life with. The lack of love in a marriage can be corrosive," Sarina said, reflecting on her life with Teo and the many difficult challenges they'd endured, which they were able to weather only because of the deep love and devotion they shared for each other. Without loving one another as they had, they would have never survived their eighteen-year marriage. No marriage could.

"I do love Tom."

"Not in the way he loves you."

Luna walked to the balcony door. "I've never lied to him about how I feel." Leaning on the doorjamb, she wistfully looked to the horizon where a setting sun had begun to streak the sky with a glowing red shimmer.

"That may be so, but he loves you so much, has since you were kids that it blinds him to your faults. He knows you don't love him, but deep down, he hopes you one day will. And maybe you will, but that's a gamble where the stakes are slanted against him, and he deserves his love returned, Luna."

The same thought had haunted Luna from the moment they became lovers, Giving in to a physical relationship with Tom had been a mistake. That Tom had been the man she'd turned to for sexual gratification was the worst decision she'd ever made. She played with his emotions, and she now felt indebted to him. Now it was too late. The damage was done.

"It's exactly why I have to marry him. He's cared for me, been there through thick and thin and... God! When I think of the things, Tom's done for me." You could always repay a debt, but you could never pay off a favor, her father told her. "And he's waited for me for so long, Mom. I can't in good conscience, not marry him."

Marina could all but feel the pain she saw in her daughter's eyes. Her heart ached for Luna.

"Life's not fair, is it? I can't marry the man I love, and I cannot not marry the man I don't. I can't hurt Tom. He's with me because I allowed our closeness to flourish. I, me, turned to him when I needed comfort when Jimmy hurt me." Luna's eyes welled up in tears. "Jimmy's the man I love, and I think to some extent, Tom realizes that and understands."

"But, honey..."

"I will love Tom as best I can."

"Love is precious, and when it doesn't flow both ways in a relationship, it... "

"I will do my best to make Tom happy." Luna's gaze was earnest when she met her mother's eyes. "Please understand that I need to do this—for Tom."

Staring at Luna with a mixture of regret and sorrow, Sarina gave her a subtle nod. When the silence fell between them, Sarina sensed they'd exhausted the conversation, and she suddenly felt tired.

"Why don't you take a long soak in the tub and turn in early? I'll go downstairs to grab a bite to eat. I need some time on my own. We'll have breakfast together in the morning," she added when her mother began to speak.

Kissing her mother on the cheek, Luna grabbed her purse and walked out of the room, leaving Sarina deep in thought.

Chapter 28

DEAN WALKED INTO his room at The Cesare Hotel one day ahead of schedule. It was time he'd use to mentally prepare to meet Sarina Lopez. Tipping the porter, Dean headed straight for the requested eighteen-year-old bottle of scotch he spotted on the coffee table the moment he walked in. The flight had taken a toll on him, and what he needed was a shower, sleep, and food, but by his reasoning, the infusion of alcohol took precedence over everything else.

Dean enjoyed the hot burn of Chivas Regal on his throat so much he chased it with the remaining liquid in his glass and poured a refill. Walking to the window, he sipped, watching a lit up Rome. The sky was bright with stars and the glow from a three-quarter moon. Streetlamps blazed, and color flickered from Christmas lights dangling above cobbled streets. In the distance, the Colosseum looked like a gleaming jewel under a darkened sky.

With the second glass of scotch in his system, Dean kicked his shoes off and shrugged out of his jacket. Loosening his tie, he undid the top two buttons of his silk shirt and stretched out on the velvety cushions of the living room couch.

His mind drifting to Luna, fatherly pride shone on his face. He'd come to love her more than he knew possible. The young woman with the beautiful, green eyes and the voice of an angel defined him. Luna gave him a sense of purpose that until her he hadn't realized was missing from his life. He wished she'd come into it sooner. He was turning sixty-eight, and that wouldn't give her nearly enough time to get to know her better. The gnawing in Dean's stomach grew sharp at the thought his time with Luna was numbered.

Dean sipped scotch to smooth over the disappointment.

At least he was finally meeting the elusive Sarina Lopez, whom he suspected was the author of the anonymous letter, which led him to Luna. Sarina Lopez, Dean, was sure, held the answers to his many questions.

Sarina Lopez, Dean, imagined was his Marina.

When he opened the letter urging him to help a young singer by the name of Luna Moon to fulfill her dreams, he quickly dismissed it. Over the years, he'd received thousands of similar letters from parents praising their children for a talent that didn't exist. Dean quickly qualified the letter as one for the trash-bin until his gut kicked in, and he retrieved it and ventured to read on.

His first reaction was one of shock, followed by denial. He had to reread the letter two more times before reality sunk in. When it finally did, Dean decided to follow through on the writer's request to watch Luna perform at the Vibe nightclub.

The moment Luna stepped onto the stage, he saw her. Dean saw Marina in Luna's walk, in her eyes, in her face, but it wasn't until Luna launched into Aretha Franklin's A Natural Woman that he was brought to tears. Her voice was as smooth, as soulful, and as powerful as Marina's was. It reached deep into him and stirred memories long buried.

It was as if his Marina was standing before him.

Dean's thoughts drifted back to the petite, pencil-thin eighteen-year-old girl with the thick, dark mane and large, shy eyes in threadbare jeans and wrinkled T-shirt standing on his doorstep all those years ago.

"THIS IS MY NIECE. SHE needs a job. You can afford to hire her." The rotund four-foot woman with peppered hair tightly knit into a bun and hard eyes snapped.

"What makes you think I can?" Arched in the doorway, Dean sipped from the glass in his hand.

"Anyone who lives in a house this grand can." Her eyes rolled across the impeccably tended grounds with a circular driveway and the façade of the sizeable home guarded by an iron fence to drive the point. "She can cook and clean, do laundry, mow the grass, wash your car."

"Good resume." From over the rim of his glass, Dean looked down to the petite girl, shoulders hunched, the thick unkempt hair spilling over a pallid face and bony shoulders.

The woman babbled something in Spanish to the girl, and Dean watched her straighten up and brush the uncombed hair away from her face. "She can sing, which I understand is something you're interested in."

"I've been known to be." Dean leaned on the doorjamb, stirred his drink with his finger to the old woman's disgust.

"She sings only spiritual music, none of that devil-worshipping rock and roll."

"Good to know."

"She's been singing with the St. Boniface church choir since she was ten. The last two years as the lead singer."

"I've been known to appreciate a good hymn." Dean looked to the girl who restlessly caught her chapped, bottom lip between her teeth and couldn't ignore the pleading eyes begging to be rescued from her rabid-looking aunt.

"Good, then she'll start to work for you now. Her name is Marina Banderas."

Dean straightened. "But…"

"She starts now," rabid woman said with finality.

"Well, I guess you start now," Dean said simply his mind turning over the lashing he was in for from Mrs. Bertinelli. There was no way his long time housekeeper-slash-cook-slash-mother-slash-everything was going to allow another woman to infiltrate what she claimed to be her home.

"She's all yours." The rabid woman tossed out a number. "That will be her salary, and it gets paid directly to me. I manage the girl's money."

Dean opened his mouth to refute but swallowed the remark when the girl quietly said, "That's fine, Tia Olga. I'll make sure the money gets to you."

"Good. Now, you're going to live here with this man, so you be sure to remember everything I taught you." Rabid woman cited the rules counting them off on sausage-thick fingers as she did.

Dean cleared his throat. "Excuse me. Who said anything about living here?"

"It's a live-in job she needs. She will not travel back and forth. There's evil lurking out on these streets for a young, naïve girl like her. She's living here." Rabid

woman handed the girl the paper bag containing her belongings. "Your bible is in there. You pray every night as we have. And you remember that sinners all burn in the scorching fires of hell," she added complete with preachy voice and a judgmental shaking finger before turning to leave.

"I think I better get myself a good fire extinguisher." Dean's comment prompted a shy grin to play across the girl's face. "I guess you better come in out of the cold, love."

It wasn't until months later that Dean managed to gain young Marina's trust and got her to tell him her story. Finding Marina's story strangely sad, Dean decided she would never go back to rabid woman's home. He made sure Marina felt valued, safe, and loved in his home. Dean ensured Marina never felt afraid again or be caged in as she had been for the past eight years. She was free to do, as she wanted, to eat what she liked, and hear music again as she had when her mother was alive.

Dean never imagined his kindness would, in time, lead to finding Marina standing at the foot of his bed one night with a wanton smile on her face. She was twenty then, and he forty-two, and although women her age rolled in and out of his bed as often as the sun rose, he couldn't bring himself to tangle in the sheets with her.

"I want to be with you. Like the couples in the movies." Big, adventurous eyes no longer shadowed by the fear he'd once seen in them gazed at him.

She was no longer the scrawny girl that once stood at his front door. She was a beautiful woman. Her skin had a healthy glow, and the once brittle hair now spilled thick and shiny as silk over a glowing face. Through the thin cotton nightgown, Dean could see the sensual curves and ripe breasts, nipples straining against the fabric.

Feeling the unabashed arousal assault him, absently, Dean brought the bedsheet up to his bare chest like a shield. "That's not a good idea, Marina."

"Is it because I'm… inexperienced? I know I've never been with a man, but I've been watching television. I've learned a lot. I'll know how to please you."

Jesus Christ! He thought he felt his heart stop. The Last time he'd met a virgin was—he rolled the thought in his head—never. He didn't think they existed. The mere thought she was, and that she wanted him made his male ego, and everything male flare up with heat and want.

Machismo blurring his moral compass, and Dean wanted her more than he'd ever wanted any other woman. "You're beautiful, Marina, and great for my ego, but I … can't."

"Are you sure?" Marina's eyes flicked to the bulge under the bedsheet.

She sent his heart drumming in his chest as relentlessly as the rain pelting on his bedroom window. "Jesus, Marina, no, I'm not sure, maybe, it's why you need to leave right now."

She didn't move. Instead, she pushed her hair back, slowly, provocatively just as she'd seen the women do in the movies. The gesture was intensely erotic, and the heat hit him like a punch to the stomach. Eyes never leaving Dean, Marina slid the nightgown over her head to expose voluptuous curves, taut breasts. They were small, but firm and her nipples were diamond hard.

"Oh, Jesus!" The second wave of heat to strike Dean was as intense as the bolt of lightning that shocked the sky *white, and his quickened breaths became stunned gasps. "Please, please put your nightgown back on."*

Pleased she could have that effect on him, Marina's lips curved into a delighted smile. "I want to be with you. Don't you want to be with me?" She didn't think her heart could bear hearing him say no, but she had to ask.

Dean's mind warring between desire and want, honor, and integrity, he remained silent. The sound of the whistling wind and rain drumming against the window swelled in the silent bedroom.

With apprehension in his eyes, Dean watched Marina sashay her way from the foot of the bed to stand by his side. A streak of lightning flashed the room bright, and he caught sight of the triangle of dark hair against the creamy skin. His breath caught in his lungs and the clammy beads of sweat formed on his brow

"Oh, sweet and sour, Jesus." Dean pressed a hand to his speeding heart. She was going to kill him.

Wavering between reluctance and want, the refuting words caught in his throat. He wasn't sure how to run away from the tension she roused in him, maybe because he didn't want to.

"I love you, Mr. Ryder. Not in the way, I loved my mom, but in a way, that makes me think about you all the time. When I do, all I want is to be near you, to be held and kissed. I want to breathe you in." She'd heard that said in moments of passion on the television. "I hoped you'd feel the same way. I hoped you'd love me in that way. Don't you love me, Mr. Ryder?"

"I think the formality ship's sailed, love. Call me, Dean."

"I love you, Dean. Don't you love me?" The emotions swimming in Marina's dark eyes clutched Dean's heart. All at once, the tension nagging at him, the doubt, dissolved into pure love. It flooded him. Hell, it drowned him. He did want to love her. He did want to touch her, to take her in his arms and kiss her.

When did that happen? How did it happen?

Was it when she curled up on the couch in the music room to keep him company all the nights he worked late? Was it when she'd encouraged him when frustration set in at a failed melody? Was it when she'd comforted him when he found out about James' death? Was it during the soothing words she offered the months he'd grieved his friend's death? Whatever the reason, at that moment, he realized he was in love with her.

"I do, love you, but…"

"I'm not a child anymore, Dean. I'm a woman who loves you and wants you to love her back." She moved closer to him, her lips hovering so close to tasting it may his head spin.

"It's because I love you that I can't sleep with you. I don't want to just have sex with you, Marina. I don't want it just to be that between us," Dean uttered the words he never imagined he would. Jesus, what was this woman doing to him?

"Who says it's going to be just sex. I want you to be my first and my forever." The glint in Marina's eyes sent his nerves jangling.

"I can't possibly be your forever. You're young, beautiful, smart, and loving. There will be lots of men lining up at your doorstep."

"I don't want other men. I want you. And you will be my first and my forever," she said, slipping into bed next to him.

With the sound of rain drumming against the window and lightning lancing a dark sky, white Dean loved Luna tenderly, passionately, lovingly, ensuring she felt nothing but the shock of unimagined pleasure through her body. Expert hands touched her in ways she would forever reflect on with warm memories.

Patiently Dean guided her hands over his body to discover. He showed her how her mouth and tongue could please her and him. Never once did he make her feel conscious of her innocence.

Dean whispered love in her ear when he thought she was finally ready to receive him. When for a moment she winced in pain, his mouth took hers to soothe, and only when she told him not to stop did he fill her.

He moved in her so gently, so tenderly. When her hips instinctively arched up, he plunged deeper into her, reaching to her core. Trembling above Marina, Dean struggled to focus. He waited until she cried out, trembling beneath him. When she did, his control snapped, and he cried out her name like a beautiful song before filling her.

Marina laid a hand over his heart. "You are my first, and I want to be your forever. Will you be my forever?"

His hands brushed away the glossy mink hair that haloed the beautiful, flushed face to look into the slumberous eyes. She was a woman, one who had just filled him with life, swamped him with a love he didn't know existed.

His lips met hers with tenderness. "I will."

From that night, Dean dedicated his life to no one but Marina, and she to him.

The press wasn't kind to Dean. DEAN RYDER CRADLE ROBBER, KEEP YOUR DAUGHTERS LOCKED UP, DEAN RYDER'S IN TOWN, headlined the tabloids. Although Dean and Marina paid no attention to the persistent, offensive headlines when he told her he could make her a singing star, famous beyond her wildest dreams, she told him she didn't want the attention stardom, or fame brought. All she wanted was him.

Dean not only gave Sarina his love but everything he could. He lavished her with gifts, clothes, and jewelry. He showed her the world. Traveled to places, he'd been, but which until her had no meaning. They spent time in Aspen, where Dean taught Marina to ski then, made love to her before a crackling fire in their chalet. They snorkeled in the marine oasis of Raja Ampat. Kissed her deeply and passionately on the golden sands of the Maldives and vowed his love for her. They frolicked on the beaches of Menorca, Spain, like young teenagers in love.

Life was as perfect as it could be. Dean had never been happier and never wanting to lose the euphoric feeling he proposed marriage to the woman he wanted to be his forever for all eternity. The day Dean rushed home with the five-karat ring ready to get down on one knee Marina was gone.

Three years after they became lovers, Marina disappeared from his life. Taking only the clothes she walked into his house with, she vanished like smoke in the wind without reason or explanation.

Marina was supposed to be his forever.

For months, Dean searched for Marina. Wherever he was, he scanned his surroundings, hoping to see her in the crowd, hoping that when he did, she would jump into his arms and tell him it was all a mistake. But that never happened. Marina was gone forever.

Since that day, he'd felt alone and empty, and his heart never mended.

THE CRISP SOUND OF THE HEATING system turning over in the room sliced into Dean's thoughts. In the background, the television he'd turned on and left muted flashed the weather report. Dean propped a pillow behind his head and let his eyes float beyond the tall window to a moon that reached its apex in the sky. He thought that just as he'd once promised to give Marina that moon if Luna asked him for it, he'd do that for the girl who reminded him so much of her. But the moon wasn't what Luna wanted. As grateful as she was, neither was the stardom and fame he'd made a reality for her. What Luna wanted, he couldn't give her, and it tore him inside.

That Luna was in love with J.R., and he, with her, was a simple deduction. The look Dean saw on their faces for one another was the once he and Marina once shared. Dean tried his best to bring them together, but Poppy's hold on J.R. was a formidable one. Poppy's manipulative control of J.R. denied him the happiness he rightly deserved. Dean knew Poppy to be a scheming bitch who wanted control over everyone's life, but he never imagined she would go as far as denying her only son the woman he loved.

Poppy was devoid of emotion. That was clear when after James' death she turned the boy over to his nanny to raise while she indulged in numerous affairs. J.R. was a child then, impressionable, hurting from the loss of a father he'd only known for seven years of his life. If that wasn't bad enough, years later, when she trickled back into J.R.'s life, it was to mark the direction of his life when she capriciously pushed the boy to take over the management of West Enterprises at a young age. It was difficult for J.R. to dismiss her when all she did was continually burden him with guilt and chip away at his pride—and his dreams.

Dean knew well it was because of Poppy J.R. walked away from Luna and broke her heart. He didn't excuse the boy for handling the situation as poorly as he had, but he knew J.R. never meant to hurt Luna. J.R. wouldn't. He loved her.

J.R. tried to set things right after Britney made her unexpected appearance, but Luna's stubborn pride hadn't allowed him to do so. She refused to take his calls, and returned every one of his letters unopened, with the name Luna Moon crossed out and replaced with Mrs. Tom Grady to drive a stake through his heart as he had done to her.

She was so much like Marina, stubborn as a mule and full of pride.

Dean didn't fault J.R. or Luna. It all came down to Poppy. Had the selfish bitch not guilted J.R. into marrying the carbon copy of herself with the excuse of fulfilling James' dream to merge the West and Melville dynasties, Luna and J.R. would be together.

That the merger was what James wanted was utter bullshit. Dean knew that to be a fact because James would never use J.R. to advance his interests. James loved J.R.

too much to use him as a pawn for profit as Poppy had. All the woman cared about was the goddamn business. Well, Poppy was in for a rude awakening. Dean owned a thirty percent stake of West Enterprises, and he'd taken the necessary legal measures. Dean only wished he were around to see Poppy's face when the announcement was made.

Chapter 29

LUNA WAS DETAINED at the hotel bar for longer than she'd anticipated when fans who recognized her surrounded her table. With a graceful smile, she spent time exchanging small talk and signing autographs. In the end, she ordered a round of drinks for the group and made her graceful exit.

Hoping to elude further recognition, Luna tucked her hair into the red cloche hat, and shaded her green eyes behind the black-rimmed glasses she'd bought in the gift shop. Raising her coat collar to conceal her face, Luna set off for the three-block walk to Il Bocconcino, her favorite trattoria.

Sidewalks were thronged with people making their way to cafés and restaurants for dinner. Cars zipped along the streets. The crisp early evening wind on her face, Luna gave thought to get the security detail Tom suggested when her album hit platinum. It was difficult to give up her privacy, but with the upcoming European release of her album, she didn't think she had much choice anymore. As much as she loved her fans, being approached at every turn was becoming an unsafe experience.

Gianni flicked a quick smile at Luna the moment she walked into the restaurant. "Table for two, *Signorina* Moon?" he whispered, not to draw attention to her.

Candles flickered on white tableclothes. The conversation was animated, punctuated with laughter. The air was ripe with the rich scents of fried garlic and wood oven pizza.

"For one tonight, Gianni. My mother is relaxing at the hotel."

Gianni's thick, dark eyebrows knitted in concern. "I hope she okay."

Luna followed Gianni to her usual secluded table by the back wall. "She's fine, just tired. We went on a shopping spree today."

"Did you visit Ferragamo and Fendi like a say." He scraped the chair out for her, set the menu down.

"I did, and thanks to you, I'm deep in debt and now own shoes I don't need." Her tone was stern, but her smile playful.

"Ah, then a good shopping day. *Prego*, or how you say?" He searched for the words. "You are welcome."

Luna's jaunty laugh caught the attention of the man walking past her table. "Luna?"

When the faintest trace of impatience flickered in her eyes, Gianni said, "You no worry, I get rid of him."

When her green eyes met the ice blue ones gazing down, she said, "No, it's all right, Gianni."

Gianni shot a cautionary look at the man staring on. "You are sure, *signorina*?"

Luna debated for a moment, but in the end, nodded. "Yes, I'm sure. Could you please bring me a bottle of Cavallotto Barolo and two glasses, Gianni?"

"*Subito, signorina*. I be right back." Gianni's brows tilted at the man in warning before pivoting toward the bar.

"Does that mean I'm joining you?" J.R. asked.

"Do I have a choice?"

"You do."

"But you're not leaving," she said when he made no effort to move.

"I'm not unless you say so."

"Well, then." She gestured him to the chair next to her.

"He's very protective of you. This is one of my favorite restaurants in Rome. I've known Gianni for years. In all that time, not once has he given me such a cold, steely look. I think he was ready to punch my lights out for you."

"He's smitten with my mom, who's here with me, and by extension, feels the need to protect me."

"Never hurts to have a protective man around." J.R. caught a whiff of her lavender shampoo. It took him back to their night together.

"What are you doing here? I thought you were supposed to be on your..." Luna stopped short at honeymoon. "In St. Tropez."

"She changed her mind at the last minute. Insisted we come to Rome, and here we are."

"I suppose you're staying at The Cesare."

They went silent when Gianni walked up to their table with the wine and proceeded to pour a sample for Luna. When she nodded approvingly, he filled two glasses, then set the bottle on ice.

Only when Gianni moved on to the couple at the entrance waiting to be seated did J.R. say, "I'm sorry. Had I known you were here, I wouldn't have agreed to come. This trip is for optics sakes, and nothing more."

"My mom and I will find alternate accommodations." Luna calmly sipped on wine, although her stomach was tangled in the nerves set off by J.R. the from moment she saw him.

"I own a condo a few blocks from here. My dad bought it before he acquired The Cesare. It's sitting empty. You're welcome to use it for as long as you like." When her face weaved into an expression of confusion, he said, "At the hotel, Britney and I have separate rooms, separate beds, and we never have reason to bump into each other."

Luna remained silent for a moment. "I'll talk to my mom." Luna followed J.R.'s eyes when they darted to her ringed finger. "We're getting married this weekend. There will be a press release coming out soon."

He left his fingers to run up and down on the stem of his glass. "So, you're still going through with it."

She shot him a look of real pain. "You did."

"I'm sorry. I shouldn't have said that." A measured silence hung between them.

"More wine?"

"Sure."

"Would you like to order an appetizer?"

The knots twisting tighter in her stomach food was the last thing she needed. "I'm good with the wine for now, but you go ahead."

"The food here is very good."

"It is." The restaurant was filling up, and the din of conversation was getting louder. The aroma of tomato and fried garlic-scented the air. "I particularly like the chicken marsala."

"Me too." The banality of their conversation was driving J.R. insane.

"The gnocchi is…"

"Do you want to get out of here? My friend owns a place, what he calls his man cave that no one knows about," J.R. proposed not wanting to risk running into Britney at his apartment. He never knew what the bitch was up to half of the time. "We can have privacy there."

"That's not a good idea, Jimmy. You're married, and I soon will be."

"We're going to talk."

"You know that if we're alone together, we'll end up in bed."

"Is that so wrong?" J.R. started to reach for her hand, but she pulled it away.

"We're both committed to other people."

"I'm not. I told you I only married her to fulfill a responsibility. She and I have never shared a bed, Luna. I haven't touched Britney. I never will."

Luna fell into silence listening to the laughter of patrons, the whoosh of the kitchen doors as Gianni and the waiters walked through them with dishes in hand. A few tables from theirs, a couple touched glasses to toast their tenth wedding anniversary.

"Tom…"

"Don't say anything else, Luna," J.R. cut in. He didn't want his mood blackened by hearing Tom's name on her lips. "I want to be with you." J.R. laid a hand over hers, and when she started to wrench it away, held it tighter.

"Don't, Jimmy. I can't have you coming into my life and then leaving me and my heart broken."

J.R. skimmed his fingers over Luna's cheek, pleased that she didn't pull away. "It kills me too, Luna. Being with you and then having to leave you tears me apart, but when I'm with you, the world's a perfect place. Even if for just a few minutes, will you share in that perfect world with me?"

"Maybe you can compartmentalize our time together afterward, but I can't. It stays with me twisting my stomach into knots and hurting. And it's not fair to…"

"Don't say his name, Luna. It kills me to think he's the one lying next to you, not me. It tears me apart to know you let him." There was so much pain in him. She saw it in his eyes, heard it in his voice. "We're both here now, Luna. Give me, if only for a few minutes, of that perfect world I want for us."

LUNA GAVE J.R. TWO HOURS OF the sweet love that transported him to the perfect world he never wanted to fade away.

His lips met hers with tenderness. "Don't think about anything right now," J.R. told Luna when her eyes held a faraway expression.

"I wished we could stay like this forever." Luna tangled her legs with his.

"You know I love you." J.R. breathed her in. She smelled of Chanel and him.

"I wouldn't be here if I thought otherwise. But committed or not, you're married, Jimmy, and I soon will be."

Not wanting to darken the moment, J.R. dismissed the thought of not seeing her again. "Tell me you love me."

"I love you, Jimmy. I love you so much."

The words sounded like a sweet song to J.R.'s ears. "No matter where life takes us, I want you to believe in us. I want you to know that I love you and always will."

Luna swallowed the whispered words. "Always and Forever."

"Always and forever."

She let her head rest on his chest. "I think I'll go see your apartment on the way back to the hotel. I need to sell my mom on the idea of moving, and it will be easier with a visual in my head. I want to move in tomorrow if I could. How many bedrooms does it have?" Her mind was calculating to move Dean and Tom in.

"Four bedrooms and you can move in anytime. There's a key tucked under the planter next to the doorway." J.R. casually wound a curl of her hair around his finger. "Can I see you tomorrow?" He released it and watched it bounce back in place.

"Mr. Ryder is flying in tomorrow, late evening." She went on to tell him about Dean meeting her mother while his fingers slid silkily over her breasts.

"Sneaky bugger never told me anything."

"As I said, it's a surprise. I couldn't see any other way of bringing them together. Every time I bring his name up, my mother dismisses the conversation. It's as if she wants to avoid him."

"He is an intimidating man to some." J.R. nibbled on her ear, trailed a lazy line of kisses down her neck and over her shoulders.

"Maybe." Luna slid out of bed and walked around the room, gathering her clothes.

Following Luna with his eyes, J.R. rolled his naked body over in bed to face her. "Don't go yet. Come back to bed."

"I need to check on my mother. She was a bit off when I left her." Slipping into her jeans, she looked over at him. His dark, sexily tousled hair spilled around his face, and the long toned body glistened under a layer of sweat from their lovemaking. He was male and sensually beautiful, she thought.

"Can I see you again?"

"I don't know, Jimmy." Luna tucked her hair under her hat, slid her glasses on.

J.R. pushed his naked body off the bed and walking to her, kissed her with a tenderness she'd carry in her heart. "I'd like to see you again. I'm here for another week. I'm staying in the presidential suite. You can reach me there." He moved fast, snagged her wrist hauling her against him when she backed away. "You're in my system, and I want to be with you. Please, Luna."

She rested her hand on the one he lifted to her cheek. "I can't make you any promises, Jimmy," she said before drawing away and walking out.

Part III

Truth

For the truth is a terrible thing.

—Robert Penn Warren

Chapter 30

FROM THE SECOND floor of J.R.'s apartment, Tom looked on as Luna, back against the wall, slid down to the floor. Luna's arms wrapped around folded legs, she rested her head on her knees and rocked herself as Britney went on with her rant. Tom wanted to step out of the shadows and bolt down the stairs to comfort Luna, but that wasn't a possibility.

Anger pulsed inside Tom's chest when Britney announced her pregnancy for the world to hear. "All I want to do is to talk. This is your baby. Open this door now."

Tom could have strangled the stupid bitch for showing up at the apartment and airing her dirty laundry without consideration for who was listening. Britney had always been a brainless, empty-headed bimbo. All she'd ever been good for was a good blowjob and a quick fuck. Now Tom would have to take care of this. As if he didn't have enough on his plate already.

He had no one to blame but himself. Tom was kicking himself for telling the stupid whore he was flying in a few days ahead of schedule or taken her up on the offer to use J.R.'s apartment. Tom should have known better and taken Britney seriously when she'd told him she'd see him there. But how was he to know J.R. would agree to cancel their honeymoon trip to St. Tropez and fly out to Rome?

It burned Tom to the gut Britney was upsetting Luna. Although why Luna was reacting as she was to Britney's announcement distressed him. It was clear that although they were to be married in a few days, Luna was still pining over J.R.

Tom's jaw set tight. Hadn't he done enough for her? He'd given up his studies, his career, worked at a thankless stage manager job at Vibe for pennies to get her a spot on stage. As much as Luna went on about the old coot making her career, Tom was the one who'd steered her in the direction that led to where she was today—a platinum artist.

He'd degraded himself after his father all but disowned him when he dropped out of medical school and cut off his trust fund. On hands and knees, Tom had begged his father to buy him the downtown apartment, so Luna could be close to Vibe and have somewhere nice to live.

For months, Tom patiently waited for Luna to realize J.R. wasn't going to show up after he told her he would. Once or twice, Tom almost let out J.R. wasn't going to show up anytime soon. He'd made it so that rich-boy wouldn't get anywhere near her, but Tom bit his tongue and waited on the sidelines, as he always did, as he always had.

It almost destroyed Tom when night after night, Luna turned him away from her bed. To distract his broken heart, he turned to Britney, and she filled in nicely all those months. Tom could easily manipulate that blonde, bimbo, into doing anything he wanted. All it took was one phone call from Tom for Britney to agree to follow him from city to city, lurking in the shadows, waiting until he showed up at the motels he booked her into. Crying out, I love you, Britney, when he filled her, kept her coming back and under his hold and if it got her to do what he wanted, Tom had no problem saying the words with a dash of emotion and an Emmy worthy delivery.

Tom regretted sleeping with Britney, but a man had needs. Besides, Britney meant nothing to him. He loved Luna. She was his virgin. He'd staked his claim to her by being her first, and he'd always be her only. No one was going to have Luna. Least of all, J.R. Tom vowed to make sure of that.

He'd never forget the night they came together. Luna was so naïve, so inexperienced. He had to guide and show her how to pleasure him. Luna was awed by his expertise, by him, by his manliness. Tom would never forget how Luna's breathless shock when he peeled his jeans and showed her he was ready for her. No one reacted as Luna did, and he'd been with a lot of women—all whores, until her.

Luna had been so responsive, so vocal, so fulfilled by him. Until her, no woman made him feel so overwhelmingly manly. It was an extraordinary feeling, but not more so than when after making love to her, Luna rushed to the bathroom, and Tom saw her virginity in full display. It did something to him, and the need to make her his came at him like rams charging at one another to claim their mate.

Now that fucking idiot Britney was set on destroying Tom's relationship with the perfect woman, days before, he was to put the ring on her finger and make her his forever.

Tom was sure the bitch set him up. Britney told him she was on the pill. He shouldn't have trusted her. He should have used his own protection, but should-haves weren't going to change the fact Britney was claiming she was pregnant with his child.

Tom had to take care of Britney before it got out of hand.

In the ribbons of silver light casting the apartment in shadows, Tom watched Luna get to her feet and press her ear to the door when Britney went silent. When the receding footsteps, then the swoosh of the elevator doors closing sounded, Tom watched Luna open the door and cautiously peer down the hall. Determining the coast was clear, Tom watched Luna dart out of the apartment.

Tom waited for the click on the front door lock before turning and heading back into the bedroom.

"Is she gone?" She watched Tom shed his jeans. Under the glow of candlelight, his muscular body looked good enough to eat. She was looking forward to doing so. She lifted the bedsheet for him to slide his naked body next to her. It was lusciously warm.

"Yeah, she's gone," Tom said, of Britney because he'd never tell her Luna was also there.

"Whose baby is it?"

Tom's body stiffening at the question he snatched the glass of wine from her hands, drank deeply. "I don't know."

She slid her hand under the bedsheet, wrapped long, smooth fingers around him. A pleased smile played across her face when he clasped his hands behind his head, set his eyes toward the ceiling as she stroked the tension away. "I think you do."

"Well, I don't." Tom glanced over to her with a firm gaze.

"Relax, baby, enjoy my touch." Her smile spread when she felt him go steel hard. He was wonderfully huge. "It can't be J.R.'s. She claims to anyone who will listen that he hasn't touched her. You need to take care of this."

"I will." Tom eyed the large, flawless breasts when she began to play with her nipples. They never ceased to amaze him. That they were lusciously round and pleasingly firm was a credit to modern science. Science aside, she was a magnificent woman, shapely, fit and lithe—so very lithe. Too bad, she was such a callous, cold-hearted bitch.

"Play with them," she commanded. He did. "You like them?"

"I do. They're perfect."

She dipped her fingers into the wine. "Brazilian plastic surgeons are so talented." She let red liquid drip over her breasts. The contrast of the rosy tinge over the creamy-smooth skin was seductive. "Suckle them." She watched him eagerly take her left breast in one breath, running his tongue over her nipples to lap up the dripping wine. She broke into a smile of wicked pleasure when his hungry mouth moved to her other breast to devour. "Just like that, baby. You're enjoying them?"

"Mmm-hmm," Tom hummed, suckling loudly.

"Oh, that feels good, baby." She let out a long, satisfying groan when he bit down on her nipples then, lapped his warm, wet tongue over them. "She's bound to come back here, and next time she may find the key under the planter. I'll have to move out. You should have never told her you were flying in early."

"I'm sorry. It slipped out."

She moaned with pleasure when he sunk long, thick fingers inside her. "Am I wet?"

"Mmm-hmm and hot."

"You do that to me, baby." She let out a squealing moan when he slid his fingers through the moist heat, as she liked. "No need to bullshit me. I know you have to keep Britney distracted until the deal goes through. God, you have magical fingers," she murmured when the wave of heat rolled through her. "Don't stop, baby, please don't stop." He liked it when she pleaded. It was the only time he felt manly around her. "After the deal is finalized, you can do what you want with her. Until then, you need to keep your end of the bargain or…"

"I am keeping my end of the bargain. I'm here now, aren't I? I dropped everything the moment you called and flew out here with you. I've done everything you've asked of me. So don't go threatening me again." Tom knew she was close to orgasm, but rage had him pulling his fingers out of her, and bolting to his feet.

There would have been fire in her eyes if her body weren't urging to drive the burning pressure backing up in her to completion, and instead of demanding he get back in bed to finish what he'd started, her fingers took his place. "You like watching me pleasing myself?" She knew he did. She knew it would make him want to plunge himself into her like a rabid dog after making herself come.

"I do." Tom watched her body arch and shudder as she brought herself to orgasm.

"He seems pleased with my performance," she said in a breathless whisper.

"He is." Elemental male pride had him proudly displaying himself for her to admire.

"Does he want to please me again?" Collagen plumped lips curved into a sultry dare.

The woman was insatiable. They'd been tangling between the sheets for the past eighteen hours, and although what he needed was sleep, she'd made him steel-hard and seconds from release. "He does." Tom straddled her.

"Good because I want him inside me. I want to watch you come in me." She pressed the palms of her hand against his chest when he moved closer. "I don't care whether the baby is yours or not. You're going to have to take care of this."

No one could heap guilt on top of pressure on top of demand as she could, he thought. "I always take care of things, just as I'm going to take care of you now," he said because, perversely enough, he wanted to. She certainly knew how to get a man's blood humming. She did things no other woman was willing to do, shown him things that had him hooked on her like a drug.

"Make sure you do. Mmm, oh," she hummed when he kneed her legs open, and plunged into her with a feral thrust, hard and deep, to shut her gob. He'd had enough of her talking already, and this was the only way he knew to shut her up. "That's it, baby." She'd never tire of the slapping sound of hot flesh on hot flesh. There was something unspeakably erotic about it. "Harder, you know I like it rough."

"I know exactly how you like it," Tom said, pounding Poppy like a jackhammer. No emotion, words, or kissing, all gasps, moans, and mechanics—just as she liked it.

Chapter 31

LUNA DIDN'T KNOW where she was running to, but run away she did. The cold night air seeping into her bones, bringing color back into her pallid face, Luna ran as fast as she could to put distance between her and J.R.'s apartment, always scanning for Britney, praying she wouldn't run into her.

Feeling at a safe distance, Luna scanned her watch, surprised it was only eight-thirty. It felt as if a century had circled around her life in the past couple of hours. Right now, all she wanted was to shut her brain off. A hot shower, a glass of brandy, and sleep would help with that. With that thought in mind, Luna hailed a taxi, and giving the driver the address to The Cesare, told him to press foot to the pedal.

AT THE SIGHT OF LUNA WALKING out of J.R.'s apartment building, the shock that ran down Britney's spine was ice cold.

Fuck! Fuck, fuck. She must have heard everything, Britney thought. Tom wasn't going to be pleased with her. Had she mentioned Tom's name in her rant? She closed her eyes and went deep into her brain, but she couldn't remember. Her brain was frozen. Britney hoped Luna assumed it was J.R.'s.

Fuck! Fuck, fuck, what if she didn't?

It was Tom's fault, Britney reasoned, but he wouldn't see it that way, he'd blame her. He blamed her for everything. She'd have to make it up to him, smooth things over because she wouldn't lose Tom to Luna— again.

Britney conceded she should have never agreed to marry J.R. when Tom asked her to do so. Although she'd set the plan to befriend Poppy in motion, it was never her intention to marry J.R. Britney only wanted to slip into J.R.'s bed and keep him coming back to make Luna feel the sense of loss she'd felt when she'd stolen the man she loved. Britney only agreed to marry J.R. when Tom promised he'd marry her once the merger between West Enterprises and Melville Media was finalized.

You'll get a divorce from J.R. and walk out with a tidy sum for us to live on. We'll buy an island far away from everyone where you and I will live together forever. Those were Tom's words to Britney, and she believed him.

Everything was going according to plan, but then Tom went and got engaged to Luna. He did it to stop J.R. from pursuing Luna, or so he said. J.R. was in love with Luna and wanted to marry her, and by him getting engaged to her, he'd prevent it from happening. It was a sacrifice Tom was willing to make for their plan to succeed.

Britney believed Tom. She believed every word until she got pregnant and he refused to accept the baby was his. His rejection punched like a fist.

Britney would never let J.R. touch her. Not that J.R. wanted to. Once they were married, Britney thought J.R. would demand she fulfill her wifely duties in the bedroom. To Britney's relief J.R. never even wanted to be in the same room with her, let alone in the same bed. That was fine with Britney because her heart was Tom's.

When she insisted it was his baby, Tom told her to abort it. He referred to their baby as it. Britney died twice that day. She was no longer the promiscuous high school girl, Tom knew. Britney was devoted to him. She was a one-man woman now and what Britney wanted more than anything was to be Tom's wife and to have his children.

How could Tom tell her one minute he loved her and the next to abort their baby? Every time they made love, Tom told her he loved her. Britney loved hearing him cry the words out as he came inside her. If that wasn't true love, what was?

Britney needed to talk to Tom. She had to tell him how much she loved him and wanted to have this baby— his baby. She needed to tell Tom how much she wanted to make them a family. She needed to apologize for her outburst.

Looking up to the darkened penthouse apartment, Britney wondered where Tom was. He should have landed in Rome hours ago. At the café across the street from J.R.'s apartment building, Britney waited for Tom. She'd wait all night to tell him how she felt.

THE KNOCK AT THE DOOR WOKE Dean from his nap.

A crown of confusion creased his face when he heard the wail of a police siren or possibly an ambulance. Rubbing the sleep from his eyes, Dean sat up on the couch and caught sight of the flashing images of the car chase on the television. He shut the tv off.

The knocking persisted, and Dean followed it to the connecting door. He remembered the note. Luna must have picked up the note he left at the front desk, telling her he'd checked in. A fresh smile creased his face at the thought of seeing her.

"Hello, love," Dean said, opening the door. The moment his eyes landed on her, the staggering shock made his breath back up in his Lungs. Dean's face turned bone-white as disbelief snaked through his system,

"Dino Rinaldi?" Sarina's stomach pitching and rolling, she fought to keep her tone calm and even.

Dean's eyes turbulent with emotions, the name rose in his throat. "Marina?" His hand reached out to stroke her face. "It's you. It's really you. You've come back to me after all these years."

"I'm sorry, Dino. I'm not Marina."

"You're the only one that called me by my given name." The past loomed over him as the memories flooded his mind.

It had been two decades since he last saw her, but it was Marina standing before him. She was more beautiful than he remembered. Her hair, just as dark and thick, spilled around the angelic face he loved waking up to a lifetime ago. The big coal-black eyes held experience and a few lines around them, but he could tell she'd had a good life.

"I'm sorry, Dino. I'm not Marina."

No, his mind wasn't playing tricks. It was his Marina, and he felt the tears begin to form in his eyes. "Where have you been all these years, Marina?"

"The front desk gave me the message you left for Luna telling her you'd checked in to me by mistake." She held the note for him to see. "May I come in, Dino?"

"Yes, of course." Stunned eyes never leaving her, Dean stepped aside.

"Thank you. We need to talk, Dino."

"Yes, yes, talk. Please have a seat." Dean gestured Sarina to the couch.

The way her hair bounced on her shoulders, the graceful sway in her walk, was Marina's. His mind crowded with memories. So many memories. "Where have you been all these years, Marina? Why did you leave me? Why, Marina? I looked for you for months." Dean wanted to reach out to touch her but didn't for fear of scaring her off. "I brought home a ring for you the night you left. I was going to ask you to marry me." His voice trembled with emotion when he reached for the chain around his neck. "See, I still carry it with me just in case I ran into you again."

When he held it out to her, the guilt balled in Sarina, and she shut her eyes for a moment. Forcing herself to think straight, she said, "I'm sorry, Dino. She didn't know. If she'd known, she would have never…"

"Stop talking as if you're not here, as if you're not her. I know it's you, Marina."

"Have a seat, Dino. I'll get you a drink." Sarina offered when she noticed his trembling hands.

"Scotch. On the counter."

"How about water?"

Water sure as hell wasn't going to cut it right then, and he insisted. "Scotch. On the rocks."

"Here you go." Sarina took a beside Dean and watched him take a healthy swallow, the ice rattling in his glass as he drained it. "Dino, I'm not Marina. I'm her twin sister. Her identical twin sister. My name is Sarina Lopez, and there's a lot I need to tell you."

Chapter 32

WORKING ON HER third double espresso, Britney anxiously tapped red painted nails on the table as she kept watch on J.R.'s building. The aroma of coffee in the café was becoming overwhelming, making her nauseous. When Britney thought she was going to retch her dinner, Britney pushed to her feet and started for the bathroom. It was then she caught sight of Tom stepping out through the front doors of the building.

Eyes sprang wide open, and her blood drained from her face, at the scene playing out before her. Britney squeezed her eyes shut, opened them, but there it was still. Tom's lips locked with Poppy's and not in a friendly way, but a long, fervent kiss.

Wide eyes went to slits when Britney saw Poppy caressing Tom's face, then lean in to whisper something in his ears that made him smile before she ducked into the taxi. The woman was old enough to be his mother.

Britney's eyes went hard, and her stomach rolled with the anger she felt. How could he? Why would he when he had her? He was doing it again. After he committed himself to her, Tom was pollinating the western hemisphere.

"What are you looking at?" She snapped when she plunked palms on the table, and all eyes in the café turned to her.

The cool night air felt cold on Britney's wet cheeks as she cut across the cobbled street, ignoring the blast of horns from swerving cars. With speed, Britney crossed the marble-floored lobby to the elevators. Swiping tears from her cheeks, she impatiently pressed the up-button watching the elevator numbers reach the top floor and then begin its descent. Before the doors fully opened, Britney jumped into the elevator and continuously pressed the close-door button.

"Open up now." Britney banged on the door with hands wound into fists. "I know you're in there. I just saw you locking lips with Pop…"

"Get in here." Tom hauled her inside.

"You're hurting me, Tom."

Tom loosened his grip on her arm and, without uttering a word, pivoted toward the bar.

"Were you fucking her all night?" Britney's heated eyes watched Tom pour himself a whiskey, swill it, and refill the glass. "You're fucking her, aren't you?" In silent contemplation of the clusterfuck he'd created, Tom sipped, taking a moment to settle his nerves. "Isn't it enough I have to put up with you being engaged to Luna? Why do you need to fuck Poppy too?" Tears spilling down her cheeks, Britney watched Tom's gaze cut straight into her, and she put the couch between them to shield herself. "Who else are you fucking aside from Poppy, Luna, and me?"

Closing the distance between them, Tom said nothing.

"I wonder how Luna would feel knowing her precious fiancé is sleeping with at least two other women."

"Shut up, Britney." Tom's voice was steel sharp.

"And that one of them is pregnant with your baby."

The scorching gaze Tom aimed at Britney could turn her into ashes. "I told you to shut the fuck up." Falling back on the couch, he raked his fingers through his mussed hair. It was a mess, a giant clusterfuck of his doing, and he had to fix it.

"You told me you loved me, and I believed you." Britney sank to her knees beside Tom when he refused to look at her. "I love you, and I want to have this baby, your baby, for us."

The words wrapped around Tom's neck like a noose tightened until he couldn't breathe. The stupid bitch was going to wreck all his plans. Temper leaped into his throat, what he wanted was to throttle Britney, but he thought it wiser to contain his anger.

After taking a long, deep breath, Tom said, "Forgive me, baby." He touched her cheeks with a loving hand. "It was never my intention to hurt you. I should have told you about Poppy."

Britney's face flushed with blazing fury. "So you have been sleeping with her. Why, Tom, why?" Tears blurred her vision.

Tom cupped Britney's chin, brought her face up to meet his eyes. "It's all part of my plan, baby. To get us that tidy sum of money so we can buy that island for us."

"Did you have to sleep with her?"

"You have to know I would never have slept with that relic unless I had to. It's part of my plan. I did it for us, for you and me. For our baby."

The words delivered with emotion and tinged with remorse sliced a piece of Britney's doubt and anger, and she fell into his arms. "I do, I do believe you, baby, but I've told you we could live off my trust fund."

"I know, baby, but you know I've been cut off from mine, and I want to give you only the best. It's what you deserve, and West money will allow me to do that for you and our baby. Don't you see? It's why I had to sleep with Poppy. It was for us. Forgive me, but all I want is the best for you?" Tom had to swallow when the words left a sick, vile taste in the back of his throat.

"I believe you, and I forgive you. I don't care if you slept with her. I want you to promise me you won't anymore. I want us to be a family."

"I promise I won't, and soon we will be a family. We just need to play this through to the end." Tom took her mouth into a long, passionate kiss to cut off the oncoming spew of tender bullshit from her. "I love you, Britney, and I love our baby."

Britney wept with joy. "I love you too, Tom. I love you so much."

"Let's get out of here. I don't want to stay one more minute in this apartment. I'll book us," Tom lowered his hand to her belly, "into the Hilton by the airport away from everyone. Would you like that?"

"Yes, yes, that sounds wonderful."

"I want to make love with you all night long. Is it okay to say that around the baby?"

Britney's eyes lit with a bright smile. "It is when it's mommy and daddy talking."

LUNA RODE THE ELEVATOR TO THE fifth floor and opened the door to her hotel room. She toed her flats off and tossing her hat, glasses, and jacket on a chair flicked a quick gaze to the bedroom. The door was ajar, and she could see the room bathed in darkness. Quietly, so as not to wake her mother, Luna walked to the mini-fridge for the drink she'd been thinking about the entire taxi ride to the hotel. Reaching into the refrigerator, she fished out a small bottle of brandy, uncapped, and drank. Flopping her weary body down on the couch, she closed her eyes.

Her mind calmer, Luna thought back on Britney's words and reasoned the baby couldn't be J.R.'s. She believed him when he told her he hadn't shared Britney's bed once. He detested the woman, of that, Luna was certain. She wondered whose baby it was, but soon enough gave up. With Britney, the possibilities were endless.

Luna sipped brandy, appreciating the warmth on her throat, its calming effect on her nerves.

She didn't believe Britney told J.R. about the pregnancy. Merger or not, J.R. wouldn't have married a pregnant Britney. Luna was sure of that too. She thought of calling J.R. to share what she knew but decided against it. It was going on ten p.m., and her mother was in the bedroom within earshot. Besides, this type of news had to be delivered in person, on a clear head. Luna would call J.R. at first opportunity, although when that would be was anyone's guess.

Dean was arriving tomorrow, and Luna needed to be there when the awkward meeting between him and her mother took place. Tom was due in the following day, and the wedding was to take place the day after. That thought made Luna's stomach jittery, and she swilled the last of her brandy.

A second bottle necessary, Luna pushed to her feet and made her way to the mini-fridge. The muffled sound of voices caught her attention, and Luna followed it to the connecting door. Peeking in through the half-closed door, Luna saw Dean and Sarina on the couch deep in conversation. She watched Dean's saucer-wide, stunned eyes staring at her mother. It wasn't hard to sense the tension between them.

Luna was about to walk in when she heard Dean say, "Marina told me she had a twin sister, but she never told me you both look so much alike."

Mom had a twin sister she never mentioned. Luna mulled that in her tangled thoughts.

"Our mother couldn't tell us apart."

"Where is she? Why did she leave me and disappear? She gave me no reason, no explanation. Picked up and left. I love Marina. I wanted to marry her." Dean's words came out slowly, each one a drop of pain.

Mr. Ryder wanted to marry mom's twin sister? He never mentioned it to me? Why wouldn't he? Luna pressed her fingers to her tired eyes.

"I'm sorry, Dino, like I said, Marina didn't know. She would never have left you had she known you wanted to marry her." Sarina assured.

Why is Mom calling Mr. Ryder, Dino? Luna moved closer to the door.

"How could she not know? I worshipped her. I've missed her so much, thought of her every day of my life." Silent tears slipped from between Dean's closed eyes and Sarina's heart clenched. "Luna reminds me so much of Marina."

"She should, Dino." Sarina reached for his hand, wrapped it in hers. "Luna's your daughter."

Luna's face drained of color. Her heart was stampeding in her chest. *What's Mom talking about? Me,*

Mr. Ryder's daughter, that's not possible. Why would Mom blatantly lie?

Luna reflected on her past, her childhood, her teen years. She thought of Teo and Sarina. Nothing. Nothing led her to believe he wasn't her father or that Sarina wasn't her mother.

"But I think you know that," Sarina said.

Dean nodded. "I knew Luna was my and Marina's child the moment I saw her. Luna's the spitting image of Marina. Her sultry voice, the thick, dark hair, the introspective eyes, her beauty, it all came from Marina. The green eyes, her mannerism, her temperament, that's mine."

"Would you like a refill?" Sarina offered when he brought the empty glass to his lips.

Dean nodded. "But I better not. I need a focused mind right now. This is a lot to absorb."

"I know. I'm sorry to be piling this on you all at once."

"The math tells me Marina was pregnant when she left me."

"Yes, she was."

"Then why would she leave me? I would have been thrilled to know she was pregnant with our child, my daughter." A storm of emotions swam into Dean's moist eyes.

Sarina considered her next words carefully. "Marina loved you, Dino. She was so happy when she found out she was pregnant with your child, but Poppy told her you wouldn't be."

"Poppy? What's she got to do with this?"

"Poppy found out Marina was pregnant and told her you wouldn't be happy about it. She told her you had no desire for children. Said there was no room for a child in Dino Rinaldi's flamboyant lifestyle, and you'd never embrace a child who'd disrupt it."

The name Dino Rinaldi tugged at Luna. She dug deep into her confused mind. Her eyes rounded when it came to her. Dino Rinaldi was the name on the Purchase of Business Agreement. Dino Rinaldi owned DR Enterprises, the company that paid her a great sum for her company.

J.R. told me DR Enterprises was a reputable company, and it would take good care of my employees. J.R. knew DR Enterprises belonged to Dean Ryder or Dino Rinaldi or whoever he is. J.R. knew, and he never told me anything.

"Marina believed Poppy, Dino? Poppy led Marina to believe you'd have asked her to abort the baby." Sarina saw Dean's green eyes tilt up to her in disbelief. "As much as Marina loved you, and she did love you, she would never have chosen you over Luna."

Suspended in a bubble of shock, Luna slid down to the floor, rested her throbbing head on her knees. She was deep in sleep. Had to be. She closed her eyes, opened them. It wasn't a dream, and the voices continued coming at her with the fantastic tale.

"I would never have asked her to abort. Why, why would Marina believe Poppy?" Dean's voice shook, broke.

"Marina was young, naïve. We'd both led a very sheltered life. Poppy played on that naïveté. She sympathized with Marina, drew her into her confidence, and, I believe now, manipulated her into thinking you would never accept her pregnancy. Poppy talked her into leaving your home, or as she called it, 'escape to save her child.' She gave Marina enough money to help her get established with her baby far away from you."

Luna's world lurched into darkness. None of this could be real, none of it could be right, Luna told herself. If it was, her entire life had been a lie. Teo, the father she'd known all of her life, wasn't. Neither was the mother she loved and trusted.

Luna let her face fall into her hands. Everyone had lied to her. The people she trusted lied, the people she loved most had been lying to her all her life.

Nothing was, as it seemed.

J.R.'s mother blatantly manipulated a young, innocent girl, and tried to do as much to Luna. She realized that now. Expressing an interest in Luna and her family was only a ruse to ensure—what?—that her secret didn't get back to Dean.

In all the months they were together, Dean never mentioned he thought he was Luna's father.

Did J.R. know, Luna wondered? Had he too deceived her as everyone else she loved had?

The treachery and betrayal from everyone in her life rolled in unrelenting, painful waves.

"When Marina left your home, she moved in with Teo and me, and we made her disappear. She assumed my name, my identity. The two of us became one. You wouldn't be able to track Sarina Lopez, and I was married, so no one questioned the pregnancy. We were careful. No one, but for her doctor knew there were two of us. We played out the charade for her entire pregnancy."

"God, this is just too surreal for words." Nerves bouncing, Dean rose to pace. "Where is she now? I want to see her. I need to see her."

"I'm sorry, Dino, but Marina…" There was a beat of silence. "Marina died during childbirth. I'm so sorry, Dino."

The news knocked the breath out of Dean and Luna, and the tears sprang to their eyes. Hugging themselves, Dean and Luna rocked, trying to shake the pain, the surreal moment away.

"Teo and I took Luna as our own. It gets complicated and even illegal from there. After some doing, Teo and I talked Dr. Berkeley into documenting Marina's actual name on her death certificate for me to slide in as Luna's mother. Sarina Lopez and Teo Lopez, my husband, are the parents on Luna's birth certificate. I'm sorry, Dino, but it was what we thought we had to do for Luna's sake. We're all complicit in deceiving you and Luna. I'm the first to admit it, but none of this would have happened if Poppy hadn't preyed on a young, scared, pregnant girl."

The pain was drumming in steady rhythm at Dean and Luna's temples now.

After a long moment of reflection, Dean raked frustrated fingers through his silver mane. "You did what you had to, for Luna's benefit. It's that fucking, conniving bitch's fault. She destroyed my life. She took from me the only woman I ever loved, the daughter I would have welcomed with open arms."

"I know that now, and I'm so very sorry for keeping Luna from you. It's why I wrote you the letter." Sarina watched Dean walk to the window and set stormy eyes up to a black sky.

"I always suspected it was you who sent the anonymous letter urging me to go see Luna perform at Vibe, and consider helping her launch her career." Dean's eyes followed the blinking lights of a plane as it traversed the sky.

"It wasn't so much to help her career as much as bring the two of you together."

"She's very talented. She's going to become a worldwide star. She's that good. She gets that from Marina."

"And you, Dino. You did have some input." Sarina added. That put a smile on Dean's face. "Thank you for making her dream a reality. I could have never done what you did for her."

"I've loved every minute of it. I've loved spending time with her. You raised a fine woman." Hands deep into his pants pockets, Dean turned to Sarina. "Not that I'm not grateful for bringing us together, because I am, but why now? Why, after all these many years?"

"I'm Dr. Grady's medical secretary," Sarina said simply.

Dean met her eyes calmly. "So, you know about my Alzheimer's diagnosis."

Alzheimer? Luna tossed the word around in her crowded head. Her heart sank deep in her chest when it finally came to her. His memory was fading. He'd soon forget everything, everyone. Luna felt herself go numb. She wanted the nightmare to end. She wanted to run away from all of it, but there was nowhere to run, and she did the only thing she could. Luna buried her face in her hands and let the tears flow.

"As soon as I found out about your condition, I felt an obligation to bring you and Luna together. Even if it meant her hating Teo and me for lying to her all these years."

Dean cocked his head, swept a green gaze over Sarina. "That took courage. Thank you. These past few months with Luna have been very special to me." His stores of energy depleted, Dean sank into the couch next to Sarina. "I wrote Treasured Memory just for Luna. I wanted it to be our song, so that when I'm... So it would remind her of how much I love her."

Sarina nodded. "I know. I picked up on the songs meaning the moment I heard it."

Luna mopped her tear-stained cheeks and rolled the lyrics in her mind.

> *And Darling now, after the light fades*
> *And I'm led to that lonely place*
> *I will no longer feel alone*
> *Because even in darkness*
> *You will always be*
> *My treasured memory*
>
> *My darling, I wish you love for all eternity*
> *I wish you happiness to infinity*
> *And always know that I love you*
> *Because you will always be my treasured*
> *memory*

The words were his story. Luna's chest squeezed her heart with an unforgiving force, and she felt the sadness choking her throat.

"I wish I could have more time with her. Just as I'm getting to know her, I'm going to forget her. I'm going to forget the joy she's brought into my life. I'm going to forget how much I ... love her." Dean squeezed his eyes shut, drew in a breath, let it out slowly. "Damn this brain of mine. It made my career, took me from poverty to prosperity, and now at the most crucial time in my life, it's deserting me."

"You still have some time with her, Dino." Sarina reminded.

Luna watched Sarina stroking Dean's head as he cried in her arms, and her heart hurt. It hurt so much. The anger, the confusion, the hate in her shook loose like boulders rolling downhill during a landslide. There was no hate or anger in her for Sarina, Teo, J.R., or Dean for lying to her. There was only forgiveness and love in Luna's heart.

Luna couldn't muster anger for people who'd risked so much, given so much of themselves to her. She couldn't hate the people who'd given her the wonderful life she had for filling her life with love and helped her fulfill her dream. How could you hate anyone for that?

Getting to her feet, Luna set aside the headache expanding inside his skull. Wiping her face dry, she turned on her heels and walked into Dean's room. Dean and Sarina turned to her with a quick intake of shocked breath.

"Hi, honey. When did you get in?" Sarina asked although Luna's swollen eyes gave her the answer.

"Forty-five minutes ago."

Distress came into Sarina's eyes. "You heard…"

"Everything," Luna said.

The realization was crushing. "I'm sorry. You shouldn't have heard what you did in that way," Sarina said as Dean silently watched on.

"No, I shouldn't have. You and Daddy should have told me the truth." Luna's voice was soft but firm.

"We should have, and I'm sorry." Sarina's thin shoulders hunched over.

"I'm not angry. I'm disappointed. You should have trusted me to understand. You made me the person I am today. Didn't you and daddy trust me to understand?"

"Of course we did. But…"

"I do understand why you did what you did." Luna cut Sarina off.

"Do you, Luna? Do you really understand?"

"I do, Mom. Sometimes we do things, right or wrong because we believe them to be the right decision for those we love." Luna thought of Tom and J.R., the decisions she'd made because of circumstances. They may not have been the right decisions, but they were the ones called for.

"I want you to understand it wasn't because Teo and I wanted to keep this from you or even because of something as noble as loving you as deeply as we do. It was because I didn't want your life to become as jaded as Marina's, and mine was. Life becomes a difficult journey when your youth is stained with resentment, anger, and pain. Then as time wore on, we just couldn't find the courage to tell you—me more so than Teo. In retrospect, I think it was the fear of losing you that made me hold Teo back from telling you the truth. Don't blame Teo, Luna.

He loved you as his own. Please forgive me, and if you can't, at least forgive Teo. I know he went to his grave heavy with guilt for not telling you the truth."

The words burned straight down to the sickness in Luna's belly, and fresh tears welled up in her eyes. "Oh, Daddy, of course, I forgive you, and I forgive you, Mom." Luna fell into Sarina's arms, and she held her while she cried out her shock.

The sight of Luna crying broke Dean's heart, but he remained silent.

"Luna, honey." Sarina wiped tears from her daughter's cheeks. "I want you to meet your biological father."

Luna turned to Dean, looked at him with warm affection. "I always felt a special connection with you."

"Me too. From the moment I set eyes on you, I sensed the special bond between us. You're so much like your mother." Dean's voice was warm and rich.

Luna smiled through teary eyes. "I am?"

"You are. You got your zest for life, your compassion, and your beauty from her."

"I want you to tell me all about her," Luna said to Dean, then turned to Sarina, "You too, Mom."

The word arrowed into Sarina's heart; she was still mom. "Of course, honey."

"How ... much time do we have?" Luna hesitantly asked Dean.

"Months, a year."

Luna felt something crumble inside her. The father who'd just come into her life was leaving her as quickly as he came into it. The realization was crushing. How did you get to know someone's life, decades of it, in a few months? How could she get to know a man who was a poet, a romantic, a dreamer well in a short time? How could she get to know the man who'd given so much to the world, touched so many lives with his music, in such a limited time?

Even as the immense sadness washed over Luna, she gave no indication of it. "Well, then, we'll have to spend every minute together. Right after the wedding, I'm flying back to Toronto with you, and you and I are going to spend the days talking, reminiscing, and sharing."

"But you wanted to work on your next album here in Rome. There's a European tour in the works. Then there's your honeymoon." Dean reminded.

"All that can wait. Right now, what I want is to spend time getting to know you, Dad."

For all of Dean's accomplishments, all the awards adorning his shelves, all his success, nothing surpassed the extraordinary feeling he felt when Luna called him dad.

Chapter 33

IT WAS NEARING midnight, and except for having to maneuver around light traffic and night haulers, the drive to the Hilton by the Fiumicino airport was an easy one. It was a long drive, but the farther away, Tom kept Britney from Poppy and Luna, the easier he'd be able to breathe. He'd check Britney in and leave her at the Hilton to wait for him—as she always did. Although how he was going to manage a sexually demanding Poppy, Britney, and his upcoming wedding was enough to drive a man to drink.

Tom looked over to a sleeping Britney in the passenger seat. In sleep, blonde hair spilling around her face, she looked angelic. She was anything but. She was as conniving and manipulative as Poppy was. She'd purposely gotten herself pregnant to tie herself to him. As much as he recognized it was his doing, the last thing Tom wanted was to be tied down to her or her spawn.

The mere thought made the bile rise in Tom's throat

He'd had to sleep with Britney before leaving the apartment when after he spewed all that love-you shit she'd wanted to hear she asked him to prove how much. Although he enjoyed plunging into her and watching her bounce on top of him like a seasoned jockey, he'd done it to shut her up.

He could smell her on him. It was a vile, revolting smell, nothing like Luna's sweet, powdery scent. He would have hopped into the shower before leaving the apartment but thought better when he imagined Britney would want to join him.

Had his life reached the point of no return? He'd made promises, he'd done his best to keep them, but even his best effort wasn't working to his advantage anymore. Everything was catching up to him, unraveling faster than a run on a silk stocking. Tom didn't know how long he'd be able to continue the charade.

Tom was tempted to drive the car off the road and end his torture there and then. Pure cowardice stopped him.

He should have never told Britney he'd marry her if she went along with his plan for her to marry J.R., but it was part of the chain of events started after his meeting with Poppy. He should have never agreed to the meeting with Poppy when she'd called him the day following Luna's performance at the Cancer Society and told him she wanted to discuss Luna's contract, he had no choice but agree.

Over an excellent dinner and good wine, Tom and Poppy discussed Luna's contract. Tom wasn't sure why they needed to when Dean and J.R. had finalized it months earlier, but he was an employee of the West's and felt obligated to entertain her conversation.

It wasn't until the innocent after-dinner stroll Poppy insisted they take around the pool of her massive estate that the night took an unexpected turn. That short walk set off the hell Tom had been living for the past few months.

"YOU LIKE WHAT YOU SEE," POPPY said, and when Tom turned her silk dress slid down her body to pool around her feet. Before Tom knew, hot, naked bodies

rolled on the floor of the cabana, and she was demanding, he thrust harder and faster.

The woman was insatiable, skilled, and so very willing to do just about anything. Tom tried walking away after their first encounter, but Poppy pulled him back into her lair. Next thing he knew, they'd moved from the cabana and into Poppy's bedroom, where she introduced him to her collection of whips, handcuffs, and everything in between.

They spent two days in her bedroom sleeping little and exploring sadomasochism, a new phenomenon for Tom, but one that piqued his interest. When he'd finally had enough, wanting to get back to Luna, Tom gathered his clothes off the floor and started to dress.

"And where do you think you're going, my darling?" Poppy's lustful eyes drank in the long, slim lines of his naked body. "You know you have a beautiful body. I hope Luna appreciates it."

"I really need to get back. I have work to do."

"Darling, I'm not done with you yet. Come sit by me." Poppy patted the edge of her bed and Tom reluctantly sat. "I enjoyed being with you so much that I want you to come back—often." She moved her hands up his thigh in slow circles.

"I can't come ... often." Tom jumped to his feet when she found him, and her hand took hold of him.

Poppy caught the panicked look in Tom's eyes and found it amusing. "Haven't you enjoyed the past couple of days with me?"

"I have, but Mrs. Barclay-West I can't do ... often."

"Darling, what's with Mrs. Barclay-West? You've been fucking me for two days, and now you get polite on

me?" Her eyes laughed at him. "Call me, Poppy, darling. And you can, and you will be back often because I like being with you, and if you don't do as I say, I'll tell Luna about us."

The muscle in his jaw twitched as he ground his teeth. "Go ahead. See if I care."

"Oh, darling, but I think you do. I know you wouldn't want Luna to know about our time together. I'm not going to tell her. As long as you work for me, and from time to time," Poppy ran a finger up his thigh, "you take care of my needs. For a young man your age, you're very—how should I put it?—capable."

"Work for you?"

"Yes, darling, work. You'll, of course, be well compensated for your trouble, but more importantly, Luna's contract will remain intact as long as you do keep me happy." Poppy sprinted out of bed, wrapped her naked body in a pink, satin kimono. "J.R.'s in love with Luna as I believe you are." She looked to Tom for confirmation, but his eyes gave nothing away. "As her manager, you'll be around Luna a lot. I want you to help me keep Luna away from J.R."

Tom was beginning to like the conversation. "I can do that."

"I thought you'd be agreeable. I don't want you to allow any communication of any form. No calls, letters, or visits. I want you to report all contact between my son and Luna to me."

He and Poppy were working for a common goal. Tom could get behind that. "Can do."

"Good. I'm not done, darling." Poppy sat at the mirrored dresser, ran a brush through her hair then *dabbed perfume on herself. "I want you to keep tabs on Dean too." She rifled through her lingerie drawer, held up a virgin-white lace bra and thong that left little to the imagination for Tom to see. "You like?" When Tom nodded, Poppy closed the drawer. "I want you to keep tabs on everything Dean does with Luna, when he plans to visit with her."*

"Yes, ma'am, I can do that too."

"I'm going to get angry with you, darling. Someone who has tasted every inch of my body should feel at ease calling me Poppy."

"Sorry, yes, Poppy." Tom watched as she neatly lay the lingerie on the bed.

"Better. I'll put those on for you after my shower so you can tear them off me when you handcuff me to the bedpost."

"I really should get going."

"Not yet, darling, I'm not done talking to you. Now, I also understand that you're a good friend of Britney Melville-Berkeley."

"I wouldn't say a good friend."

"I want you to do whatever necessary to steer Britney in J.R.'s direction. I need to talk her into agreeing to marry J.R."

"I can do that." Tom was really enjoying the conversation.

"My gut told me you could. You've proven to be a very creative young man." Poppy walked to him and slid fingers under his chin, pinching as she turned his face toward her. "But to make it clear, if you don't do as I ask, Luna's contract goes up in smoke. I know you don't want that to happen to the woman you love. My sources tell me

you've worked all your life to get her here. It's quite very admirable you didn't do it for the money." Poppy offered Tom a drink from her champagne flute, but he waved it away. "One has to wonder what Luna offers you that no other woman has, which drives you to give so much of yourself to her?"

"Leave Luna out of this, don't you ever dare touch her." Raw anger flared and mingled with posturing. When she arched a thin, dark brow, Tom said, "Sorry, I'll do what you want. Just leave her be."

"I mean her no harm, darling." Poppy slid her kimono off. "Now, why don't you join me in the shower my virile Greek sheepherder and turn me into your naughty black sheep."

THE HEADLIGHTS THAT FLASHED BRIGHT IN Tom's eyes, along with the loud blast from a horn, brought him out of his daze. Eyes flew wide, and a rush of adrenaline infused his system. Instinctively, Tom gripped the steering wheel with a firm hold. His foot slammed on the breaks, shifted the clutch to a lower gear hoping to slow the car down. Tires over pavement screamed, smoked as Tom tried to evade and maneuver the car away from the oncoming gasoline tanker back into his lane. They were only a couple of car lengths from each other, and at eighty miles per hour, the correction didn't come quickly enough.

Tom's lungs expanded when he inhaled his last breath before steel hit steel. The taste of blood filled Tom's mouth when the dreadful screech of rending metal mingled with the sound of shattering glass and the crunch of bones. Bono's rich tone declaring Sunday bloody

Sunday flowed into Tom's ears. He thought of Luna. He saw her face that first time she fell into his arms, the first time he made love to her. Images of them holding hands and walking on the beach in Santa Monica flashed in his mind. He saw himself on one knee when he slid the ring on her finger.

Tom whispered, "I'm sorry, Luna. I love you." before everything went dark.

The blast, as loud as the roar of thunder boomed and pierced Tom's ears. He saw the sky light bright. Tom felt the intense heat, smelled the rank smell of gas fumes. Black, billowing smoke filled the car and his lungs. Then everything went dark.

Chapter 34

LUNA'S MIND WAS tired, her eyes were under the weight of shadows, and her body craved rest. In the past twenty-four hours, she had little food and downed too many drinks on an empty stomach. After being presented with the facts of an inconceivable past, she knew nothing about she couldn't shut her mind down, and sleep hadn't come.

It was more than any person could handle in a lifetime, and now, she was in the waiting room of the San Michele Hospital waiting for Tom's body to be made presentable for her to see. The doctor and nurses suggested Luna not see Tom, explaining that ninety percent of his body had suffered third-degree burns, and he wasn't recognizable, but she demanded it.

Luna needed to see for herself because they were mistaken. They had to be. There was no way the man who was involved in the head-on collision with the gasoline tanker that exploded and lit the night sky white was Tom. It couldn't be. Tom wasn't scheduled to arrive in Rome for another twelve hours.

Reading the grief in her eyes, Sarina framed Luna's face with her hands as Dean helplessly watched on. "Honey, I just spoke to the doctor. There's nothing but a charred... Please, Luna, listen to them when they tell you it's not a good idea to see Tom this way. Seeing him like this will mar every memory you have of him, of the two of you. You don't want to remember him like this."

"Mom, it's not him. It can't be. He's…"

"Luna, listen to me." Sarina turned her daughter's face until they were eye to eye. "I'm sorry, honey, but it is Tom."

It felt as if a fist plowed into her stomach. Luna's knees buckle, and she fell into her mother's arms. Luna forced herself to breathe when the tears chocked her. "He didn't deserve this, Mom. He didn't deserve such a horrible death."

Sarina looked into her daughter's tired, teary eyes. "No, he didn't."

The universal hospital smell of despair and illness seeped into Luna. "He didn't deserve to die alone."

Sarina debated, considered whether to tell Luna. In the end, she turned to Dean, and it was he who said, "He wasn't alone, honey."

Blinking the moisture from her eyes, Luna turned to Dean. "What are you talking about?"

Dean's eyes darted out the waiting room door to avoid Luna's piercing stare. An old woman moaning the Lord's Prayer was wheeled by on a gurney while the young woman by her side held her hand. The expression on the orderly's face pushing the gurney watched the two women with indifference in his eyes. "There was someone in the car with him."

"Who? Who was in the car with Tom?"

"Britney was with him, in the passenger seat. She was brought in with Tom. She's in the ICU in critical condition. Along with several other injuries, she has a head concussion and fades in and out. Somehow, she survived the accident. The police think she was pulled out of the car," Dean told Luna straight on, deciding she needed to hear the truth.

"Britney? Why would Britney be in the car with Tom? Why was he with her? Why were they heading toward the airport and at such a late hour?" Luna took a much-needed deep breath.

"I don't have the answers to any of your questions, but Britney may. She's asked to speak to you."

TUBES AND WIRES STEMMED FROM BRITNEY'S body. There was equipment beeping, flashing numbers, giving readings of her blood pressure, her heart, and her lungs. An IV dripped clear liquid into Britney's hand. Like a spider at the center of her intricate network, Britney lay motionless in her bed. Her honey-blonde hair was a tangled mess around a heavily bruised face. Her eyes were sunken, and her cheeks stained black and blue. Her hands were bandaged in white gauze. Other parts of her body may also have been, but the blue bedsheet covering her shielded her body.

"Come in." Britney's strained voice startled Luna.

"I'm sorry. I didn't mean to wake you."

"You didn't. I was resting my eyes. Water." Her groggy voice was barely audible.

Luna picked up the cup of water on the side table, brought the straw to Britney's dry lips, and watched her take a few strained sips.

"Thank you." Britney went silent for a moment, surveying Luna's face.

Although Luna looked tired, and her eyes were puffed from crying, Britney could see the beauty she'd been threatened by. It touched a nerve as it always did.

"More water?" Luna set the cup down when Britney shook her head.

"Tom's dead, isn't he?"

"Yes."

"I was with him."

"So I'm told."

"Aren't you curious to know why I was with him?" Britney signaled for more water, and Luna obliged.

"Yes." Luna waited.

"His last words were, 'I'm sorry, Luna. I love you.'" Britney watched the tears swim into Luna's eyes. When Luna brought her hands to wipe wet cheeks, the glint from her engagement ring smothered Britney in resentment. "It's why I killed him."

"You didn't, Britney. It was a terrible accident." Luna corrected, attributing the wild statement to the pain medication.

The despairing, cynical laugh Britney broke into set her off into a coughing bout, and Luna brought the straw to her lips. "That's enough." Britney exhaled the words after a few sips of water. "Christ Luna, you've always been so nice, so proper, so goddamn naïve. Tom was sleeping with Poppy right under your nose. Right under my nose. He was in bed with me every time you were up on stage. Then he'd rush back to the hotel to slip into your bed."

Britney's flat and detached tone had a chill arrowing down Luna's spine. "What are you talking about?"

"He told me he wasn't, sleeping with you, but I knew better. I didn't care, though, because he promised he was eventually going to marry me, and I believed him. To be with Tom is all I've wanted."

Despite the chill in her bones, Luna felt her hands go clammy. "What are you saying?"

"I've loved Tom from the moment I set eyes on him, and he loved me, but you had to come between us, steal him away. You couldn't keep your hands off him." Britney paused to take a breath when she felt another coughing fit coming on. "I'm pregnant with Tom's baby. I'm four months along."

Luna's face went paler, and she could hardly breathe. "You're lying."

"You don't believe me ask the doctor or nurses." Britney wheezed, tried to take in air to lungs scarred by smoke and heat before she went on to tell Luna her story. "I thought he meant every word when he told me he loved me. *Me*, not you, but when he whispered 'I love you, Luna,' with me sitting next to him, I lost it. He was pledging his love to you even after I'd told him I was carrying his child. I knew then he'd never be mine."

Britney broke into a wheezing cough, and a pounding headache began to drill in her head with unrelenting force, but she was determined to finish her story. "I reached for the steering wheel and aimed the car straight for the tanker truck. He pulled my hands off, but I gripped it even tighter. It wasn't until he landed a backhand to my face that I let go. We were going at a high rate of speed, and the tanker truck closed in on us quickly. Tom tried to evade, maneuver the car back into our lane. It all happened so fast."

Shock flew into Luna's eyes as the tears blurred her vision. "You're making all this up."

"Little gullible Luna. Tom had us all fooled, you, me, maybe even that domineering bitch Poppy," Britney said and in between ragged breaths told Luna everything. "So you see, I had to kill him. Yes, Luna, I killed him, and I'm glad I did. I just wished I'd gone with him, but that idiot driver from the tanker truck decides to play hero and pull me out of the burning car after he jumped out of his cab. They'll probably award him some stupid medal for what he did, but to me, he's just an interloper. I wanted to die with Tom." Britney began to cough uncontrollably, and as she desperately tried to take in air into her lungs, Luna stood by in complete shock watching on.

The machines beeped faster and louder. From the corner of her eye, Luna thought she saw the green line on the heart monitor flat line, but her mind was too hazed to piece anything together. Nurses and doctors rushed into the room, and someone's hands wrapped around a numb Luna and escorted her out of the room.

Chapter 35

LUNA SHIFTED HER gaze out the window. At forty-thousand feet in the sky, the sun streamed gold out of a clear sky. Cotton-soft white clouds drifted past at a dreamlike pace. Nothing in the past few days felt as safe and peaceful, Luna thought. Her eyes fixed on the expanse of blue sky she thought of how glad she was that in one hour they'd be landing in Toronto. Home, she thought.

Luna hadn't been home in too long. She was looking forward to sleeping in her bed and waking up to the sound of frying eggs, sizzling bacon, and the scent of freshly brewed coffee the flowing from her mother's kitchen. Luna couldn't wait to turn on the screaming, grumbling shower, which took forever to spout hot water. She couldn't wait to set her feet down on the cold, creaking hardwood in her bedroom. Waking up to some form of normalcy, was what she craved most right now.

There was a lot to be said for ordinary, Luna thought.

Tossing her head back on the plane's seat, Luna closed her eyes and reflected on her conversation with Britney. One week later, it still felt dreamlike. There were still moments when she had to remind herself of the horrible events she had trouble coming to terms with happened.

She hadn't mentioned one word of the vile exchange with Britney to her mother or Dean, and neither pressed her. They wouldn't. They'd leave her to digest Tom and Britney's death and everything in between. Luna knew her mother and Dean would wait for as long as necessary for her to open up. What they didn't know is that day wouldn't come because Luna decided that sharing Britney's fantastic story served no purpose. It would remain locked in her mind.

Implicating Britney as Tom's murderer after her death benefited no one and dragged Luna into months of questioning, supposition, investigations, and God knew what else when the media got a hold of the story. Reliving the worst day of her life over and over wasn't in the cards. Luna just wanted the whole thing over with, and right now, Dean needed her.

The moment Tom's body was wheeled off Dean's plane Luna turned him over to his parents. She'd attend his funeral not solely for optic's sake or because— regardless of what Britney claimed Tom did—she had an emotional attachment to Tom, but because she believed her soul was as blackened as Tom's, Britney's, and Poppy's. Luna believed she too had lapsed in judgment and committed sins that required absolving and forgiving was simpler than carrying anger, resentment, and hate.

Those emotions had consumed Britney and led her to love Tom to death.

There was no way Luna could find her way back to the innocence that once reigned her life, and she needed to move on, had to for Dean's sake.

After Tom's funeral, Dean invited Luna to move into his home, and father and daughter spent their days talking and getting to know one another. Dean told her all about

Marina, and it was clear to Luna from the pained look in his eyes he loved her deeply.

As much as Luna enjoyed their long talks, she loved the time she and Dean spent in the music room writing lyrics and music for her next album. Dean's love for his newfound daughter gave rise to his best work yet. It was his gift to Luna for all the lost years and his way of keeping himself alive in Luna's memory long after he entered into darkness. Together doing what they both loved, father and daughter compiled what became Luna's upcoming album labeled *Con Amor*.

"With Love. It's the perfect title," Dean said with tears behind the green eyes.

January gave way to June, and out in the terrace sipping her early morning coffee, Luna felt the warm summer wind on her face. The sun painted the sky a golden yellow, and the air smelled of fresh-cut grass and rich wet earth from the overnight rain. The garden was infused with the vibrant colors from tulips, hydrangeas, rhododendrons, and bleeding hearts. Lilac blossoms scented a warm wind and a deep green carpeted the estate. It was hard to believe just months ago betrayal, death, grief, and a broken heart loomed over Luna. Time did heal most wounds, Luna thought.

It had taken Luna weeks to shut her mind down, compartmentalize the unwanted memories, and ease herself off the guilt, which in her mind had led Tom to his death. Had she pushed Tom away long ago, his life might have gone in a different direction, and he'd still be alive, Luna reasoned. Maybe Britney did love Tom as Luna never could, and perhaps her love would have changed the course of Tom's life. The would've, could've, should've, endlessly crowding Luna's head were all jockeying for positions.

Although they were both unattached now, since arriving home, Luna hadn't wanted to see or talk to J.R. She avoided him at all costs, refused to take his calls. Luna disappeared from sight when J.R. popped into the house unannounced or when she met with Jean and her team at the WE Productions office. Blocking J.R. out of her life meant Luna didn't have to rehash Britney's conversation and all the awfulness that came with it or feel obligated to tell him what she knew.

Seeing J.R. meant telling him his wife was pregnant with another man's baby, and that her plan all along was to drain him of whatever money she could. Worse, she'd have to tell him he was married to a confessed murderer. Luna would have to tell him about his mother being a manipulative bitch who was sleeping with a man half her age to bring about his marriage to Britney. No, that wasn't a conversation Luna wanted to have.

"Jean thinks the new album is platinum worthy," Dean said, stepping onto the terrace with Maestro, the white-spotted Basset Hound Luna gave him for his birthday, lumbering at his heels. The floppy-eared dog with the goofy face had evolved into Dean's loyal companion, always by his side. Exactly what Luna hoped for since Dean's memory lapses, were becoming more prevalent.

Dean now had difficulty concentrating, struggling with his words, and finding his memory became a daily undertaking. He was forgetful at times, confused at others. When the episodes hit him, it broke Luna a little more inside, but she made no mention of it. Dean hadn't either, but Luna sensed he was feeling the effects of his steady deterioration, and pride had him pushing it out of his mind.

Luna began leaving subtle notes around the house, claiming they were for her, to keep things straight. Luna was glad when Dean didn't make a fuss about them. It was a temporary fix, but it offered momentary respite without the loss of dignity.

"And what does Jean think about the quality of our home-studio recorded album?" Luna watched Dean stretch out on the chaise lounge, a recent addition Mrs. Bertinelli insisted Dean have. In a white polo shirt and tan chinos, he looked rested and better than he had in days.

"She thinks it's as good as any the WE Productions has produced." Dean's hand lowered to rub Maestro perched on his back, his tongue lolling out of one side of his mouth.

"Good because it's your best work yet. It's a beautiful collection of love ballads."

"Our best work and Jean loved the album's title. She thought *Con Amor* was perfect."

Luna reached for Dean's hand, squeezed. "With much love."

"With much love," he said back and slipped into a short silence w gathering his next thought. It was something he had to do often now. "Jean told me you want to postpone your next tour."

"For a few months. No big deal. I don't want you to worry about it." Luna watched Maestro flip to all fours and toddle to the edge of the terrace when he spotted two squirrels making a mad dash up a tree. He barked a few times to announce his presence, then deciding he had no interest in joining in squirrel games and slumped where he stood to enjoy the show.

"He's a lover, not a chaser."

Luna nodded. "Clearly."

"You know you need to get out there again to keep the…" Dean paused, forced the calm to flow through him when the word escaped him. "Momentum going, and the sooner you do it, the better. Treasured Memory has already landed on the European top ten, and I predict it's a matter of time before the album also does. Jean told me sales are better than anticipated." Dean watched Maestro with raised hopes he would venture down to the grassy knoll for some exercise when he started to get up.

Luna's face dimpled when Maestro turned to trudge back to Dean. "Yeah, he's not chasing after any squirrels."

"Don't change the subject, Luna."

"I know I need to get out there, but right now, there are more important things than music or performing on my mind."

This, Dean thought, from the girl who once said, she loved the frenetic energy of being on stage, thrived on the rush of it. "I don't want you to postpone your career because of me." Dean urged the dog to jump onto his lap. "You are a lazy one. You're lucky I've taken a liking to you."

Luna watched Maestro lovingly lick Dean's face before settling in on his lap. "I think he just said, 'right back at you.' Anyway, I want to spend time with you. We still have so much to talk about. I'll pick up my singing again when the time is right."

"You leave it too long it may not be there. You know this business is a fickle one. One minute you're in and the next you're out. And you have a completed album to..."

"Being with you is my priority right now. End of discussion." Luna held up a hand to stop Dean from adding to the conversation.

Having had enough women traipse in and out of his life, Dean knew better than to argue with a woman holding a defiant hand up to his face, and he said nothing.

Chapter 36

LUNA OUT FOR her run and Mrs. Bertinelli off for the day, Sarina busied herself in the kitchen, making lasagna for lunch. She was adding the last layer of mozzarella when Luna walked into the kitchen, her body glowing under a layer of sweat.

Reaching into the refrigerator, Luna fished a bottle of water, uncapped, and drank deep before flopping onto a chair at the table. "Is he asleep?"

"Yes, he went down shortly after you left. I talked him into going upstairs to his bedroom. It's more comfortable there." Sarina closed the oven door.

"Maestro, go with him?" Luna wiped her face dry with a paper towel.

"You know they're inseparable." Sarina busied herself stacking dirty dishes and utensils into the dishwasher, added dishwashing liquid, and turned it on.

"And I'm so glad they are. Maestro's good for him." Swilling the last of the bottled water, Luna's eyes focused out the window to the expanse of green in the woods, on the hills. A light fall rain drizzled, and the grass deepened in color.

"What's wrong, honey?" Sarina set another bottle of water in front of Luna.

"If it weren't for that goofy dog, I wouldn't have known where he'd gotten to yesterday." Luna wrapped hands around the bottle.

"What are you talking about?"

"When I came down from my shower, Dad was gone. I couldn't find him anywhere. That silly dog came looking for me. After I figured out he wanted me to follow him, Maestro led me to the creek. Dad was just standing by the bank, dazed. For a long while, he didn't know who I was."

"Where was Mrs. Bertinelli?" Sarina watched Luna nervously uncap and cap the water bottle.

"Where she usually is at that time of day, in the kitchen making breakfast. She didn't see him go out because he slipped out through the living room doors. He wasn't wearing a jacket, just a cotton shirt, and pants. It was forty degrees out. He could have caught pneumonia, and it would have been my fault if he had." Luna sank her face into her hands and sobbed.

"Oh, honey, I'm so sorry." Sarina moved to hold her daughter. "He's progressing into the next stage rather quickly."

"It's tearing me apart to watch such a loving, wonderful, accomplished man slip into darkness. What am I going to do, mom? I can't expect Mrs. Bertinelli to care for him. Aside from the fact she's getting up in age, Dad's my responsibility." Luna lifted eyes glistening with moisture to her mother. "As much as I want to, I can't do this by myself."

Sarina pulled back, set dark, unyielding eyes on her daughter. "Don't do this, Luna. Don't blame yourself. Dino's situation is more than one person can handle. It's the nature of the disease. This has nothing to do with you not being capable or you being uncaring because that's not what this is. This is about you needing help."

Luna knuckled tears out of her eyes. "But I promised him I'd take care of him."

"Well, honey, you need help, and the person who's going to help you is me. I'm moving in. I've become very fond of Dino, and I'd like to help you take care of him."

"I can't ask you to do that."

"You're not asking. I'm offering it. I have some medical knowledge. I don't think it's enough for what we're dealing with, but let's start there and see how things work out."

"I don't want to foist this on you? Dad's my responsibility."

"What's family for if not for imposing and you, Dino, and I are family. You and I will trudge along, see how it works out," Sarina said, hoping to give Luna the additional time she needed to resign herself into enlisting the professional help she refused to bring on.

Chapter 37

"THERE'S NOTHING YOU can do about it, Poppy," Sean Conway said, delighting in the apparent frisson of uneasiness his words shot through her.

Poppy's temper spiked and eyes shooting daggers, she restlessly paced the office furnished with antiques, Tiffany lamps, and built-in bookcases displaying every law book ever published. It was a room designed for a powerful, influential man such as Sean Conway, Dean's lawyer of forty years.

"The hell I can't. I'll fight this. I'll fight Dean, you, and you know I'm not the type to easily give up. I'm not allowing some common entertainer to take thirty percent of the company because Dean's eyes are full of her. He can easily find another twenty-something to plunge himself into."

Understanding the comment was meant to unhinge, expressionless, dark eyes behind thick glasses gazed up at Poppy. "You always have had a way with words."

"Tell me you'll talk some sense into Dean, Sean." Poppy's voice went from vinegar to the sugar sweetness that always managed to get men to do her bidding.

"I represent Dean, not you, Poppy."

"Well, here." Poppy dug into her purse and slapped a one hundred dollar bill on the desk. "I'm hiring you now."

I'd rather be waterboarded than take you on as a client. "That's generous of you, but I'm not taking on new clients."

Poppy let out a cynical laugh. "Don't give me that bullshit. I have yet to meet a lawyer who'll turn down billable hours." When Sean remained silent, she walked up to him and drilled a finger into his chest. "Listen to me. Whether you or one of your blood-sucking associates does this for me, it will get done. That woman will not get thirty percent of my company. My money got this company off the ground. It's my company, and I'm not about to sit back and allow that ... that Luna Moon to snub it from under me," Poppy's anger becoming more resilient she was quivering.

"Her name is Luna Banderas-Lopez," Sean said, sounding particularly lawyerly.

If Poppy recognized the name, she gave no indication of it. "I don't give a rat's ass if her name is Jacqueline Onassis. She's not getting my company."

"For one, Poppy, the company is not entirely yours. You are the majority shareholder with forty percent, but Dean owns thirty percent. What does J.R. say about this?"

"Leave J.R. out of this. He has nothing to do with it." Poppy snapped with the viciousness of a pit bull.

"Well, that's not entirely true since J.R. now owns thirty percent of the company. When he married Britney, the stock in trust, which belonged to James, was turned over to him."

"She's dead now."

"Irrespective of her status, J.R. did marry, and the moment he did, that stock was turned over to him. It was what was stipulated in James' will." Sean let out a smirk of satisfaction knowing James had put the clause in place to protect his son's interest from her once he found out who Poppy Barclay really was once J.R. was born.

"A stipulation you kept concealed from me."

"Don't play ignorance, Poppy. It undermines your intelligence. You knew the terms of James' will well enough. It's why you married J.R. off to Britney. The fact she came with a merger was the icing on the cake. Well played on that front by the way for making that happen." Sean sunk deeper into his chair and brought steepled fingers to his lips.

"There was no play as you crudely put it. J.R. was in love, and it just came together. I had nothing to do with the merger."

He cocked a brow. "Mmm-hmm, of course, you didn't, and I'm certain J.R. was in love with Britney."

Poppy took the guest chair facing Sean, dug into her purse for a tissue, and let the waterworks run. "We've known each other for a long time, Sean. You know me better than that." When she realized her crocodile tears didn't have the impact she hoped, heat flashed in Poppy's blue eyes. "Don't believe everything, Dean tells you."

"Don't insult my intelligence, Poppy. I haven't built my reputation and this firm by pandering to gossip. It's because, as you say, 'we've known each other for a long time' I can guess your every move. Correct me if I'm wrong, but this is how I've pieced together this scheme of yours to play out." Sean ignored her hissed breath and pressed on. "Your objective was to talk J.R. into eventually turning his shares over to you, and with the majority of the voting rights in your hands, you'd oust

Dean from the company before dean succumbed to his illness."

The burning edge of her rage banked down to frustration, and she balled the tissue and tossed it into her purse. "I'd be careful not to make any inflammatory remarks. Isn't that what you vultures refer to as defamation?"

"That you were out to screw, non-legal term, Dean and your son all along is as obvious as your botoxed face, Poppy."

Poppy pressed a hand to her chest in indignation. "How dare you."

"When Luna came into the picture that put a kink in your plan. You figured once Dean found out Luna was the biological daughter you separated him from years ago out of sheer spite he'd turn his shares over to her instead of J.R. as you imagined he'd do all along. And when Luna and J.R. fell in love, you had to stop them from coming together because there was a strong possibility the two of them would end up owning sixty percent of the company. Luna and J.R. would become majority shareholders, and you would no longer be in control. You couldn't have that happen."

Poppy's patience straining, temper bubbling beneath the panic, she slammed the palms of her hands on his desk. "I am going to sue you for slander, defamation of character, and everything in between."

"How can it be slander when you're the only person in the room, Poppy and when I speak the truth?" A smile creased one corner of his mouth. "Anyway, that's when you concocted the plan for J.R. to marry Britney. Luckily, there's a force called Karma, and it's come back full circle on you."

Poppy's lips tightened. "How dare you. Do you know who you're talking to?"

"I certainly do. It's why your plan to discredit Dean or Luna will not go forth. This will ensure it doesn't." Sean slid the letter across polished mahogany to Poppy.

"What is it?"

"Go on, read it." Sean's tone was insistent.

Poppy slid a perfectly manicured nail across the seal like a razor-sharp knife and drew out the typed document. At the first paragraph, her heart gave on hard thud against her ribs, and her stomach did a free fall summersault. "What's the meaning of this?"

"Exactly what it says. Luna is Dean's biological daughter and that there is Marina's story as recounted by her twin sister Sarina. It's all there in black and white."

Poppy tossed the crumpled letter on Sean's desk. "This is supposition and innuendo."

"You know it's not."

"Well, this is all moot since Dean's mind is a jumbled mess now."

Sean took a deep breath for calm. He wouldn't let her bait him with the spiteful, unkind remark of his long-time client and friend. "Dean came to me with his request to turn over the stock to Luna months ago before his illness manifested into what it is today. No court will refute it. Aside from the fact, DNA proves she's Dean's daughter and his next of kin, he can give his company shares to whomever he wishes. Yes, Poppy, Luna inherits the lion's share of Dean's estate."

Fury simmering, Poppy tossed the document at Sean. "It's still no proof that I did or said any of this."

"We thought you'd say that, so this is an addendum to that. It's a transcript of the conversation between Luna and Britney Dean overheard minutes before Britney's death. It's Britney's confession to Luna." Sean's tone was cool and deliberate. "If you challenge Dean's state of mind, we have Luna to recount the story," he said, although Dean asked for Sean not to reveal his knowledge of the conversation to Luna.

By the time Poppy finished reading the transcript, all color had drained from her face, as had her arrogant, brash attitude.

"Now, none of Britney's confession is legally indictable since moral bankruptcy, unfortunately, is not a crime. But imagine, just imagine if that got out in the public domain. I'm thinking it could do a lot of damage to how you're perceived in philanthropic circles. Not to mention the damage it could do to the Barclay name. Then there's J.R. What will he think of his loving mother using him and sabotaging his relationship with the woman he loves for profit? And I've pondered how your board will react if they got a hold of this information. As a majority shareholder, wouldn't you be violating their code of ethics?" Sean's grin spread from ear to ear.

"You wouldn't dare."

"Try me." Sean flicked defiant eyes her way. "Now, whether this remains from public consumption is up to you. Dean's instructions were only to release these documents if you contested the handover of his shares in West Enterprises to Luna or if you insisted on pursuing possession of J.R.'s stock."

Poppy deliberately tore the document into tiny pieces. "Goddamn him and goddamn you."

Sean shrugged her outburst in a casual dismissive gesture. "The originals are locked away, and it will be solely up to you if they remain there."

Nostrils flaring with each huffed breath like a bull ready to charge, Poppy stormed out of the office.

A small smile played around Sean's mouth as he picked fluff from the lapel of his gray, pinstripe suit and thought there were days when he loved this job. And today was the best one yet.

Chapter 38

OUTSIDE, A SUNSET painted the sky in such beautiful colors it almost seemed unreal. A cold winter wind whistled, and a thick layer of snow covered the grounds, which a few days ago was shrouded in layers of green with scatterings of rust, gold, and copper leaves.

In Dean's living room, a crackling fire made the room warm and cozy. The scent of pine from the ten-foot tree propped in front of the window gave a homey feel. The tree Luna and Sarina cut themselves from the grove hemming the estate was loaded down with lights, tinsel, and ornaments of every color and size. Green garland draped the staircase railing and door entrances. There were five red stockings, one each for Dean, Luna, Sarina, Mrs. Bertinelli, and Maestro, hanging from the mantle.

The festive Christmas atmosphere was what Luna wanted for Dean, who, in a short time, slipped into the fogginess of his disease. It had become more difficult for Dean to communicate coherently, and he struggled to reorder his thoughts. Many were the times his clouded mind failed to recognize his surroundings. However fleeting his moments of recognition became, Luna wanted to fill Dean with the merriment of the season because it may be his last.

Luna turned to Dean when she finished playing a half-botched rendition of Jingle Bells on the baby grand. "Did you like that, Dad? I'm sorry, but I'm nowhere near as good as you."

When Dean smiled, Luna pecked him on the cheek, and as it always did during such shared intimate moments, the thought he'd never call her by name entered her mind. Luna felt an immense sadness. How she wished Dean could see her, see past the vacant look in his eyes that saw everything, yet saw nothing. That, however, was now a long foregone wish.

She had money she never dreamed one person could possess, yet she'd give it all up to have more time with her newfound father. She'd give up every dime to hear him tell her more of his relationship with Marina, the beautiful mother she'd only come to know through his stories and the hundreds of photographs he kept. She wanted more time with Dean to tell him more about Teo, the man who'd been there in her formative years, forming her into the woman she was today.

Luna took Dean's hand and squeezed it. When he didn't fuss or pull away as he so often did, she let his warmth wash over her. To feel so close, yet be as far apart as the earth and the stars, was the most difficult thing she'd had to deal with. It filled her with an immeasurable sadness. During moments like this, although it felt like a lifetime ago, Luna was grateful for the brief time they'd shared. In the few years Dean was a part of her life she'd come to know the father who'd changed her life in unimaginable ways, and made memories with him she'd treasure for the rest of her life.

It made Luna's heart ache to know the man who stared back at her did so through fogged eyes. She'd just begun to get to know him, started to forge a daughter-father bond, and now in his place was a stranger who didn't know her or she him.

Luna wondered if it ever got any easier.

"I'm sure he heard every note, honey." Sarina ladled eggnog into a glass, turned it over to Luna.

"I hope so. Here you go, dad." Luna set the cup into Dean's hands. "It's eggnog with a drop of rum."

"Thank you." The smiling eyes that stared back at her were vacant and distant, had no flicker of recognition. For a moment, Luna watched Dean wondering where his mind set off to when the gleam of recognition in his eyes abandoned him. Luna and Sarina's faces dimpled when Dean winced at his first sip and handed the cup back.

"I'll get you a scotch, Dad. That'll hit the spot."

Eggnog replaced with scotch, Dean sipped and gave a slow approving smile.

"That certainly hit the spot," Sarina said, glancing over at Dean, who with glass in hand and a sleeping Maestro at his feet settled back in his recliner to enjoy his drink and soak in the heat flowing from the fireplace.

"Scotch always does, doesn't it, Dad?"

"You know he's not supposed to be drinking alcohol. It doesn't blend well with his meds."

"It's Christmas. We can overlook a drink or two. Isn't that right, dad?" Luna bent down to kiss him on the cheek. "You relax and enjoy your drink before bedtime. Tomorrow morning we have presents to open, and Mrs. Bertinelli is making a special Christmas Day lunch with all your favorite foods. Afterward, all of us, including Maestro, are going on a sleigh ride at the local farm."

Dean's eyes lit bright. "All right."

"He's always smiling, but I'm not sure whether that's good or bad."

Sarina ladled thick eggnog into her cup. "It's good. He's happy, and I'm guessing that's because of you."

"What do you mean?" On the couch, Luna tucked long legs under her and sipped eggnog.

"Some who suffer from this illness become angry or depressed. Some drink to excess. They drive themselves into an alcohol-induced mean and lash out at everything and everyone around them." Sarina sat next to Luna. "Dino hasn't, and I'm attributing that to you being in his life. He never became that person because he wanted to devote every minute to you, and I think, at some level, he still does."

Luna looked over at Dean. Silver hair slicked back, in a brown cashmere sweater over a blue shirt and chinos, Dean looked handsome and healthy. No one would know about his condition if it weren't for the fact he was conducting an incomprehensible conversation with himself while Maestro listened intently.

"Doesn't seem fair, does it? To have accomplished as much as he has. To have contributed all he has during his lifetime and end up having to deal with the gradual decline of your faculties. It's just not fair." Luna's heart knocked against her ribs.

The formidable man she'd come to know, who'd written hundreds of love songs that touched millions of people's lives and won dozens of awards, who played several instruments—self-taught by ear—had become the shadow of a man who now spent his days walking in a thick fog. That this intelligent, wonderful, loving man didn't remember names, recognize his daughter, or was able to string a rational sentence together was unfathomable. Yet that's how it was now in Dean's world.

"Honey, you're doing exactly what needs to be done. You're here for him, and that counts for everything. You have to stop feeling guilty because in the new year you've decided to get him the professional help he needs. It's what he needs. Besides, we're not abandoning him. We're still going to be here for him." Sarina smiled when Maestro lifted his head to sniff air suddenly perfumed with the scent of Mrs. Bertinelli's freshly baked cookies. After a moment's deliberation, the women watched him bolt on all fours and make his way out of the living room. "I think he's hoping Mrs. Bertinelli's baking him doggie treats along with her Christmas baking."

"If she hasn't, he'll charm her into making them for him. He always does." Luna crossed over to Dean covered a sleeping Dean with a patchwork throw. "You will be here, Mom? You'll stay with me through it all, even when the nurses come in. I don't think I can deal with letting someone else take care of him."

"Of course, I will." Sarina watched Luna open the fireplace screen and add a couple of logs to the fire.

"Thank you, because I don't think I can do this on my own." Luna reached for the poker and moved the wood in place.

"There's nothing to thank me for. I'm enjoying this beautiful home, and Mrs. Bertinelli's cooking, which I'll admit is better than mine is. I will deny that if you so much as give her the slightest indication," Sarina said, to add some levity to the moment.

"My lips are sealed." The crackling of burning wood became deafening when Luna fell into reverent silence. "Thank you, Mom, for bringing us together. I don't think I've thanked you. I know it was difficult and scary for you to do."

"I should have done it long ago. Had I been stronger, had I listened to Teo, you would have had more time with Dino. I'm so sorry about that, Luna."

"Dad said I would understand it better when I have children of my own, but I think I understand the reasoning behind your decision."

"I hope so, Luna. It's been killing me to have taken so much time from the two of you."

"Don't do that, mom. Dad and I were never angry with you. We've spoken about it at length, and we both concluded you did what you thought best under the circumstances."

"Thank you for saying that, Luna. It means a lot to me." Sarina and Luna watched Maestro stroll into the room. A candy cane-shaped doggie cookie in his mouth, he cocked an eye in their direction and then moved on to settle at Dean's feet to feast.

"He does have Mrs. Bertinelli wrapped around his paw." Both women's eyes lit with laughter before Luna turned thoughtful. "You know he loved Mama like crazy. He told me it was because of her he never married. She'd set the bar so high no other woman ever her measured up for him."

Sitting in his favorite chair in front of the roaring fire as flames sparkled amber and red with Maestro at his feet, Luna thought Dean looked like a Dickensian painting.

"Had Marina known he was going to propose marriage, she would have never left Dino. She wouldn't have listened to that bitch Poppy. They could have had a lifetime of happiness together." Sarina's eyes welled, and to divert from the emotions wanting to burst from her, she rose to refill her cup with eggnog. "I wish I wouldn't have been so cynical and steered her back to Dino instead of entertaining her fears, which Poppy put in her head."

"Don't do that, mom. Don't think on the could-haves or would-haves. We can't change the past."

"I know, but we had such a difficult life growing up after our mother, your grandmother, died. Dino would have given her love, financial stability, a comfortable home, the family she wanted. I found that with Teo, and I wanted that for Marina." The familiar choking lump formed in Sarina's throat.

"Let's think about today. I know clinging to anger is simpler than forgiving, but if you let it, it will consume you. And it's not worth it. Poppy's not worth it. I need you. You're the only family I have now. Please forget her, forget everything that's happened."

"You're a better woman than me. I promise I won't mention her again, and I'll try to be the forgiving woman that you are. It'll take some time, though. You know this Latin temper of mine sometimes gets in the way." Sarina flashed an innocent smile. "But in all seriousness, Luna. Don't let what happened to Dean and Marina happen to you and J.R. I know Tom's death is still fresh in your mind, but don't write J.R. off from your life. He loves you, and you love him. Don't throw that away. Don't end up living on regrets."

The statement caught Luna off guard. "There's a lot you don't know, Mom," Luna said as the conversation with Britney she'd pushed back from her mind all these months burst from its locked place and circled in her mind.

"I know you're lonely. I know because of Dino, you and J.R. are now business partners, and eventually, you're going to have to face him. I know you, Luna, are the author of your destiny." Sarina watched a jumble of emotions cross Luna's face.

"There are things Britney told me before she died I don't want to share with J.R., but which I'll feel obligated to do if I come face to face with him."

"Honey, have you not learned anything from Dino and Marina? If Marina had spoken to Dino, opened up to him, their lives would have been happy and fulfilled. You should talk to J.R. Tell him what's on your mind. If he loves you as much as I think he does, it will only bring you closer together." Sarina waved a hand to stop Luna from speaking. "Just promise me you'll think about it. I also want you to think about getting back to your singing."

"I will in time. Right now, dad needs me."

"I guarantee you that what Dino would want is for you to share your talent, your artistry with the world, as he has. He wouldn't want for you to give it all up to sit with him day in and day out," watching him wither away. "Luna, believe me as a parent when I tell you he'd want you to go off and launch the album you, and he worked on and make it his legacy—and yours. Think on that too."

Chapter 39

LUNA HELPED DEAN into his pajama shirt. "There, all buttoned up. Let's get you into bed next to Maestro." At the sound of his name, Maestro raised uneven brows at Luna and nuzzled close to Dean when he slipped under the covers. "Good night, Dad, and Merry Christmas." Luna kissed him on the cheek and clicked off the bedside lamp.

Sitting at the edge of the bed, with moonlight streaming through the window, Luna sang Treasured Memory as she did every night hoping to trigger the slightest memory in Dean. She was on the second verse when Dean stirred and opened his eyes.

"Luna?" Dean's tired voice called.

Unspeakably moved by the simple word he hadn't said in months, Luna's throat constricted. "I'm right here, Dad." She clicked the lamp on as Maestro's brown eyes rose to scan Dean with interest.

"Hello, love," Dean said, his eyes and heart swam with love for the daughter he'd lost, found, and would lose again.

Luna took his hand, holding it in a tight squeeze. "Hi."

Dean looked at her as if seeing her for the first time. Her dark hair spilled around her delicate face. The eyes, a misty lake color with the orange speckles that reminded him of the sunsets he'd watched with Marina years ago sheened with tears. Dean absorbed every nuance of

Luna's beautiful face, taking the picture into his heart, wishing he could preserve it forever in his mind.

"That was beautiful, Luna. Do you sing to me every night?"

"I do."

Dean's eyes holding Luna's, he could see sadness and pain. "I miss you, love."

"I've missed you so much, Dad."

"Please don't cry, Luna." Dean wiped the tears that spilled down her face.

"I'm sorry. I can't help it." She looked away.

Dean slid his fingers under her chin, pinching as he tilted her face to his. "You've been babysitting me?"

"I'm not babysitting. I want to be by your side. I want to take care of you."

Love rolled through him in one fast unrelenting wave, and he put his arms around his daughter to hold her. He loved her more than he imagined the heart could love. She was the perfect child he'd always wanted, borne out of his and Sarina's love for one another. Dean felt a wave of grief flood him at the thought he had seconds with her before he left her again—forever.

Knowing he didn't have much time, Dean rushed to say everything he had to. "Luna, when I fall back into darkness, it's a stranger that takes over my body and mind, and I don't want you wasting your life with him." More tears started flowing down Luna's face, and Dean felt his own eyes fill. "I want you to go off and live your life. I want you to do what you love most. If not for you, do it for me because all I want for you is love, happiness, and music, lots of music to fill your life." How could he expect a child of his blood to be any different? "I know we didn't spend long together, but I hope the time we had will remain in your heart as treasured memories. Fall back on those memories when you think of me. You've been a perfect daughter. You're scored on my heart, Luna, I love you. I always will," Dean said, and as quickly as he'd slipped into the light, he slipped back into darkness.

Luna felt something inside her break, something she knew would never heal, for she sensed this would be their last conversation.

Lying next to Dean, Luna rested her head against his chest. "I love you too, Dad," she said, with tears rolling down her cheeks.

Chapter 40

ON THE THIRD knock, Luna answered the door to her hotel room. "Hi, Marcia." She stepped aside to let her road manager, a leggy brunette with straight-cut bangs that stopped just above long, thick eyelashes, in.

Handpicked by Jean, Marcia and Luna met weeks before the launch of her Com Amor tour and hadn't clicked, but five years in and on their third tour together, Marcia had become an invaluable manager and a good friend. Marcia was fifteen years older than Luna, with the energy and enthusiasm of a twenty-year-old. Large, vibrant brown eyes exuded a shrewdness, and intelligence Luna admired.

"I know it's late, but I had to pass on the good news. You're sold out at all Deep South venues. Georgia, Alabama, South Carolina, Mississippi, and Louisiana sold out in less than two hours. And I'm hearing Florida and the east coast ticket sales are flying. I think the raving article in the Rolling Stones Sheila Buchman wrote about you had something to do with the great sales. I've extended an invitation for her to attend all your concerts—on our dime, of course. Hope you're okay with that"

"It's a great idea." Luna led Marcia to the living room. "It pays to have friends in high places."

Tall and shapely, in slim Levi's and an off-the-rack tapered blouse, Marcia looked as if she'd fallen off a fashion magazine. "Sheila and I were sorority sisters, but she'd never write anything but the facts. Congratulations, Luna, this will be an even better tour than your last three. Not to mention your sales of this album have already surpassed your last two." The smile on Marcia's eyes matched the enthusiasm in her voice. It reminded Luna of Tom's enthusiasm for her successes. Luna wished it wouldn't.

Although Luna believed Britney's account of Tom's transgressions and the wrongs he committed against her was a one-sided account, that there was more to the story, she didn't want the constant reminder of Tom. Partly because of the guilt she still carried for his death and partly because she would never be able to get Tom's side of the story, but mostly because that part of her life was done and over with, and she wanted to put it all behind.

"That's wonderful news, Marcia." Luna crossed to the bar. Her hair tied into a smooth ponytail, a grey tracksuit, and bare feet, she looked as elegant and beautiful as she had hours earlier on stage. "Can I get you a celebratory brandy?"

"Are you going to join me?"

"You know that my drink of choice these days is water."

"I hope to God fizzy water never becomes my drink of choice. I'll take a tall brandy. The taller, the better." Marcia flopped onto the living room couch, and patted the cushion next to her for Bongo, the Maltese who traveled with Luna everywhere, merrily jumped up, and flopped down beside her. "F.Y.I., we've almost finalized your European tour and will start to work on the Australian and Latin American ones afterward. And after a few months rest, if you're up to it, I'd like to work on an Asian one. That'll cover the globe and raise your exposure internationally. You can then take a long overdue rest."

"Count me in on both counts. You've done a great job, Marcia. I'm lucky to have you." Luna handed her the ice clinking glass and sat next to Bongo.

"Your dad would be very proud, Luna," Marcia offered when Luna's gaze trailed off beyond the window to a twinkling night sky. "How is he doing?"

"Not well. He had another mild stroke a couple of days ago. Mom says he's fine, but I know she tries to smooth out the blow for me since I'm far away."

Marcia kicked her flats off, and after flexing her toes, tucked long legs under her. "I'm sorry, Luna, but he's in good hands with her."

Nodding, Luna absently ruffled the fur behind Bongo's ears when he laid his head on her thigh. "Still, I wish I was home with him. I'm only here because of him. It's what he wanted me to do for him."

"Because he better than anyone knows singing is in your blood, and all he wants is for you to be happy. By doing this for him, you've become so emotionally invested in your music, you're channeling those feelings into your songs. Your emotions, raw and real, pour out on stage with every song, Luna, just the way, I believe, your dad knew it would. That emotion transcends to your audience. It speaks to them. Music is not just lyrics and a melody. It's emotion, sensations, you imbed into your audience that becomes so powerful, and wonderful they are transformed into memories they will reflect on forever. Your fans feel those emotions flowing from you for your dad, and they're drawn to you like bees to nectar.

I don't think you need me to tell you any of this, but I think it's worth telling." For a moment, Marcia let her words hang in a crisp silence, hoping they would soothe Luna.

"Dad always said, 'sometimes we're not in people's lives very long, but still long enough to make a difference.'"

"And he'd be so right. Something else worth telling is that J.R. West has called you a million times." Marcia watched Luna turn her gaze back out the window. Luna's face remained blank, but Marcia saw something behind it. She couldn't imagine the horrible thoughts filling Luna's mind as she let her thoughts drift back to her last conversation with Britney. Luna had still told no one of Britney's admission, and as desperate as she was to erase the exchange from her mind, she couldn't—not until she told someone. Not until she told J.R. "Did you hear me, Luna?"

"Yes, I did. Please keep on screening his calls, Marcia. Keep on telling him…"

"You're indisposed. I know." Marcia reached for a doggie treat. When Bongo heard the familiar crinkle of plastic, his tail began to thump wildly on the cushion. "I know it's none of my business, but why not take just one of his calls, Luna. I could be wrong because you know my track record with men, but a man who persistently calls, sends you flowers for the opening of every concert, writes you for five straight years even after all you do is return those letters, is a keeper."

"Haven't you ever heard you shouldn't dip your company pen in the company ink?" Sipping on Perrier,

Luna watched Bongo's tail enthusiastically thumping to the beat of his chews.

"I think there's more than just wanting a dip, and I don't get why…"

"Please, Marcia, keep monitoring him. No calls, no written communication, no visits to my hotel room, and no attendance at the venues I perform. You get the idea."

"I do." Marcia nodded, concluding she was right. Luna was in love with the man she was running from.

COMING OFF THE ROSEMONT HORIZON STAGE in Chicago after another flawless performance, Luna's breath caught on a gasp the moment her eyes locked with the blue eyes aimed her way. Their first encounter, their day on the Seas the Day, his touch, his kiss, the taste of him, his scent, all flooded back in individual drops of memory.

Staring at one another, her heart thudded as quickly as J.R.'s did. The roar from the clapping, cheering audience in the background, faded away into a hummed silence between them. For a long moment, their eyes held as if nothing and no one else existed.

J.R.'s hair was a fall of black against the handsome face. He wore a pale-blue shirt tucked into jeans that were as fit as the body beneath it. How she remembered that toned, warm body pressed to hers. Luna's blood pulsing, her heart pounding, the past and present, and everything in between rushed at her and filled her heart. There was so much love still in her for J.R. it hurt.

J.R. couldn't take his eyes off her. As if he were seeing Luna for the first time, he took in all the details. Her mouth was painted cherry-red. The long, lashed green eyes were wiser. Her dark waves spilled around the beautiful face he envisioned every waking hour of his life. In tight-fitting leather pants and a black fringe top, long, she looked strikingly beautiful.

J.R.'s stomach was in ragged knots. The last time they saw each other was in Rome, what felt like a century ago. After Tom's death, without explanation or reason, she'd distanced herself from him. He dreaded she'd turn away from him now.

"Hi." The internal war of emotions, raw and real, waging inside him, made J.R. realize his love for her had deepened more in the years they were apart.

"I'm sorry, Luna, I know what you told me, but you need to speak to Mr. West right now," Marcia said quickly when she saw the rejection in Luna's eyes.

"I don't need to do anything." Temper showed coldly in Luna's eyes, but J.R. saw something behind them— guilt, fear, maybe regret. He saw eyes damp with emotion and love. She loved him, still, and for now, he'd hold on to that. There were more pressing issues to deal with now. "I have to change." Luna rushed past them. By the time she got to the changing room, tears were stinging her eyes.

Although Marcia heard the ice in Luna's tone, she followed her in. "You really need to speak to Mr. West." Marcia poured the brandy Luna was going to need, handed it to her. "It's about your dad."

Rage turned into a sick and uneasy feeling that rolled in her stomach, and she shot to her feet. "What about dad? Is he okay? I spoke to Mom last night, and she didn't mention anything was wrong."

"Your mom asked Mr. West to come to see you. Can I let him in, Luna?" Marcia asked, and waited for Luna's nod before opening the door and waving J.R. in as she stepped out.

"What's wrong with Dad, Jimmy? Is he okay?"

"I'm sorry, Luna, he's been rushed to the hospital. He's ... he suffered a massive heart attack early this morning. He's in intensive care."

The shell-shocking news sent Luna's mind into a blur. Her knees buckled, and she fell back into her chair. "A heart attack? Intensive care? Why didn't Mom call me?"

How could J.R. tell Luna the prognosis wasn't good when she'd already gone through the painful loss of one father? Knowing first-hand how devastating the loss felt, J.R. said, "She asked me to come to get you. She didn't want you traveling alone. I've come to take you home, Luna."

A hunted feeling crept up her spine. "He's going to die, isn't he, Jimmy?"

How one person could lose two fathers in one lifetime was unfathomable, J.R. thought, and all he could say was, "I don't know, Luna, but we need to get you home right now. My plane is sitting on the tarmac, ready to leave the moment we board."

UNDER A DARK, THUNDERING SKY, THRONGS of people, fans of Dean and Luna's packed St. Mark's church or somberly stood outside under a steady downpour. Luna, Sarina, J.R., Mrs. Bertinelli with Maestro sat in the front pew, dewy eyes never leaving Dean's casket.

Tommy King, the many artists who had Dean to thank for their careers, flew in from all corners of the globe. The hordes of women who had trickled in and out of Dean's life over the years came to say their goodbyes, and Luna didn't mind one bit, because, in her heart, she knew her mother was the only woman he ever loved.

Poppy who wasn't welcome, but who couldn't keep away, stood under the shade of a maple tree in the distance watching on.

Everything inside Luna wept as she sang Treasured Memory and watched Dean's casket lowered into darkness. Although she'd lost him years ago, from the moment his mind sunk into a world she didn't understand, the pain seared in her heart just as it did the first time he didn't recognize her.

The appearance of Dean Ryder in her life heralded changes that steered the course of her personal and professional life to unimaginable heights. Luna ached at the thought of the missed years, the time they could have shared. The father she knew nothing about had come into her life five years ago, and just as soon as he did, she lost him forever. Luna lost him to a world she knew nothing about and was difficult to understand and come to terms with. It was a world Luna hoped never to be a part of, but one she now feared lurked in her future.

It stopped raining, and a guiding light sprinkled from between dark clouds giving way to a blue sky. A soft wind broke through the trees shaking them loose of the moisture dappling their leaves, and the air smelled of September and rich wet earth.

Under the linden tree with its majestic branches hanging over a trickling creek that sounded like a soft flowing melody, Dean was laid to rest next to Marina. Watching the two blue jays spear through the air, land on the linden, and set off on a chorus of chirps, Luna thought it was the perfect place.

The feeling Dean was in a place where his mind would return to the way it once was, unspoiled, creative, thoughtful, and brimming with the memories that once filled it, suffused Luna with a joyful peace.

"Make sure to look up Daddy and Mama in your travels, Dad. Until we meet again," Luna said, laying the music sheet to Treasured Memory on Dean's grave.

Epilogue

LIFE'S PATH IS rarely a straight one. It's often filled with obstacles, some of our creation, others, like random boulders from a collapsing mountain, unexpectedly tumble and make unforeseen, life-altering changes. The boulder that jumped into Luna Lopez's life when she least expected it brought with it unimaginable changes—good and bad. It resurrected a past she knew nothing about. One which lay dormant for two decades, and would have remained secreted away in the annals of time were it not for the simple fact that life takes unexpected twists and turns.

Reaching for the book, Luna opened it and began to read for the umpteenth time. *Sometimes remembering hurts too much, but not remembering hurts worse, for my life—good or bad—is but a collection of memories and without them I am nothing, but a soulless vessel.*

Tears, thick and hot, fell from Luna's eyes at the thought of how perfectly apt the words were. The book read like a fantastic, fictional love story with the making of a best-selling novel or possibly a cinematic masterpiece. But it wasn't meant for any of those things.

For my beautiful daughter Luna, who has brought so much joy into my life, this is my story, our story, and I've written it for you, read the dedication she'd set to memory from the day Sarina set the book in her hands.

"Dean began to write his memoirs for you the night he saw you at Vibe. It has every detail of him and Marina, of their life together, of his life from childhood until he fell into darkness. It documents every minute he spent with you, his love for you, and the joy you brought to his life. It contains a copy of the letter I sent him. He wrote this book for you, honey. He said that when he couldn't remember, someone would remember for him, and it would be you." Sarina told her.

The eight-hundred-page book, Luna treasured like the rare Koh-I-Noor diamond, was all she had left of Dean. Reading it made her feel as if he was walking beside her every step of the way.

Luna wiped her eyes and rose to her feet. Crossing to the bar, she reached for the bottle of brandy to pour into a tumbler. She took it in too quickly for pleasure and refilling her glass, made her way to the large bay window and cast contemplative eyes out to a darkened sky. A round moon, bone-white against a black sky, speckled with stars clear as glass and washed the land in silver. The familiar ghostly outline of the hardwoods that lined the driveway now thickly caped in the fresh greenness of summer swayed to a rhythmic dance under a warm June breeze. Luna watched the two resident raccoons scurrying about, their scavenging eyes luminous in the darkness.

Luna could see why Dean loved this home, which after his death, she made her own with her mother, her husband, her five-year-old twin girls, and of course, Mrs. Bertinelli. Dean would have loved the sound of family, children, and laughter under his roof, she thought.

There were days when Luna felt Dean's presence in the music room, where she spent hours writing the songs to become her fifth album. She sensed his dynamic presence in the recording studio when she recorded her music. There were times Luna heard him in the kitchen in banter with Mrs. Bertinelli.

She'd been blessed with not one, but two wonderful fathers in her lifetime. How lucky was she? They'd both shaped her life, made her the woman she'd become.

"Are we close to having dinner, Mrs. Bertinelli?" Luna asked when she walked into the kitchen.

"I'm done marinating the steaks. Get that man of yours to get his butt off the lounger and set them on the grill." Mrs. Bertinelli ordered turning the tray of meats over to Luna.

Adding mayonnaise to the potato salad, Sarina raised bemused eyebrows at Luna. "Better do it right away, or she's bound not to feed us."

"You got that right." Mrs. Bertinelli snapped with a sidelong smirk.

"I'm starving, so I'm all over this," Luna said, dashing out the door and onto the terrace. The scent of summer and fresh blooms tangled in the air. Luna watched Maestro laze by the pool's edge as Bongo cheerily yapped at the girls when they disappeared below its lit blue waters.

"Honey, Mrs. Bertinelli wants you to get the steaks on the grill, pronto."

"I'd better do it right away, or she's bound not to feed us." He sprinted from the lounge chair and slipped his feet into black flip-flops.

"You got that right," Luna said with a smile.

"That woman terrifies me," he said, dashing to the Napoleon.

Luna's lips curved wider. "Hmm, that sounds so familiar."

"She terrorized Uncle Dean for decades, and now she's made it her life's mission to terrorize me." J.R. flipped the lid on the B.B.Q., turned it on.

Luna's eyebrows winged up. "Terrorize?"

"Yes, terrorize." When Luna's brow raised higher, J.R. said, "Does put me on edge sound better?"

"Much." Luna turned over the tray of steaks, hot dogs, and hamburgers to J.R.

"She used to love me."

"She still does. It's why she treats you the same way she did, Dad."

"Mmm, then, I wish she didn't love me so much."

"Don't tell me that petite, old woman makes my big strong, business tycoon husband so edgy she puts him on edge." Poking out her bottom lip to tease, Luna skated fingers over J.R.'s chest.

"She does, but in a Mrs. Bertinelli way, not in the manipulative way my mother did for years. That is until you opened my eyes. I never realized what a negative force she'd been in my life. What a scheming, greedy, hurtful woman she is." Heat flashed in the pale blue eyes at the thought of what Poppy did to Dean and Marina, to Luna, and him. For all of Britney and Tom's flaws, J.R. blamed Poppy—at least partially—for their misguided actions. A fuse had to be ignited for it to set off the blast, and his mother had always been a hot flame. "Have I ever thanked you for that?"

"Once or twice, but I've told you…"

"Forgiveness is less corrosive than anger. Pain has deep roots, and the only way and to rid yourself of them is to forgive and forget." J.R. quoted Luna's lyrics from her hit *Forgive*, which she wrote with Dean before he succumbed to darkness. "Well, I'm not there yet. I'm not ready to forgive Mother for everything she did." J.R. dropped a few drops of the marinade on the iron grate to test for heat.

"It's hot enough," Luna said, watching the sizzling liquid bounce and evaporate on the hot grate.

"I can't close that door as easily as you have." J.R. lay steaks, hot dogs, and hamburgers on the hot grill, sending a quick stream of smoke upward.

"I haven't completely forgiven Poppy, but she is the girl's grandmother."

"Sarina is the girl's *abuelita*. Now that I have my own children and see how loving and caring a mother, you are to our girls, I recognize what a cold-hearted and uncaring my mother is. I've come to understand she has no love to give. I don't want that toxicity around the girls or me. It saddens me to say, but she's not good for them or me. I function better without her in my life. Even as a child, the rare times I'd see her, I was always anxious when she was around, and I never understood why." Absently, J.R. watched the plume of B.B.Q smoke curl lazily upward until it faded.

"Funny how I can manage a company with thousands of employees, but around her, well, let's just say I always caved in and gave her everything she wanted. It was easier to give in. I'm glad she's put a healthy distance between her and us. Don't get me wrong, she's my mother, and there's an emotional attachment to her, but you, the girls, and your mom, and even Mrs. Bertinelli, are my family now." J.R. kissed Luna with loving tenderness. Feeling his arms around her, the solid reality of them made her deepen the kiss.

"Ewww," Rebel and Reena said in unison when they surfaced and propped themselves against the pool's edge.

"Daddy, Mommy, do you have to do that in front of us?" Rebel, whose name so aptly suited her personality, said crunching her face in disgust.

"Yeah," Reena piped in in support of her older sister.

"You better get used to it, because I like kissing your mother and plan to do it often." J.R. brushed his lips to Luna's.

"That's disgusting, and I choose to look away," Rebel huffed, and dove beneath the luminous water of the pool.

"Me too," Reena echoed following her sister.

"Are you going to be kissing me always and forever, Jimmy?"

Reaching for her hand, he laid it over his heart. "Always and forever."

If you liked The *Forgiving Woman*, look for M.L. Lexi's other novel: *The Guilty Woman*, available as eBook and paperback.

An Excerpt from The Guilty Woman

Prologue

March 1948

THE AIR WAS raw and thick with death.

A river of blood, still red and fresh, flowed from the man's smashed skull soaking and spreading on the ivory carpet like a Rorschach inkblot. Sofas, chairs, tables, and walls were splashed red. Pearl buttons from Francesca's silk blouse lay scattered in the pool of red, looking up like lifeless eyes, staring, judging, condemning. The coffee table Francesca had fallen back on when she'd managed to escape his grip lay upturned. Shards of crystal and glass from shattered tumblers and bottle sparkled like diamonds on polished wood.

The scene before her belonged in a horror movie, not in her living room, Francesca thought as she violently threw up her dinner.

For Francesca's sake, when the sickening smell of warm blood slammed into Father Matthew's gut, he didn't let emotion slip into his eyes or his voice. He'd keep the nerves kicking in his gut like sharp fists making the sour waves of nausea rise in his stomach at bay. With a calm, Father Matthew didn't feel he set the blood-covered candleholder in his hand on the end table before lowering two fingers to the man's neck.

"He's dead," Father Matthew, confirmed when he didn't feel a pulse and wiping his bloodstained hands on his cassock, reached into his pocket for his stole. Kissing it, he draped it around his neck. "*In Nomine* Patris," Father Matthew said, piously crossing himself and launching into prayer.

Watching the ritual performed over the lifeless body, made the taste of sickness claw at Francesca's throat again. She swallowed hard to prevent herself from heaving whatever she had left in her stomach as she stared at her bloody, trembling hands.

"*Deus animae meae miserere.*" Father Matthew begged God to have mercy on his soul before blessing the body and rising to his feet. "It'll be all right, Francesca."

Reeling from the violence she had endured moments ago under the dead man's hands, Francesca's voice trembled when she said, "How's this going to be all right? This is never going to be all right. He's dead on my living room floor." Francesca's eyes shifted to the lifeless body, willing it to come to life. When it didn't, she was glad he lay face down. As much as she believed his demise was the outcome he deserved, Francesca couldn't look into the eyes of death. "What am I going to do?" She let her head drop weakly and let the tears flow.

"It'll be all right, Francesca. I'll be right by your side." Shock flew into Father Matthew's eyes when the face that carried the night's violence rose to meet his. Her face was swollen and raw. Her left eye was puffed shut. There was a deep gash on her cheek where the ringed hand-delivered the fisted punches, and her lip was split open. Blood ran down from both. "You're hurt."

"I'm fine." Francesca pushed away the hand Father Matthew raised to her face with the defiance of a humiliated woman. "What am I going to do?" she asked again, this time her voice sounded defeated.

"Don't worry. I'll sort it." Father Matthew crossed to the telephone. The blood-soaked hem of his cassock painted the floor like a Pollock painting. "Leave everything to me. I'm going to call the police now."

Bolting to her feet, Francesca stepped over the body and crossed to Father Matthew. "You're not calling anyone," she said, tearing the handset from his hand and setting it back in its cradle.

"We need to call the police Francesca." Father Matthew tried to reason.

"No, we don't. We'll take care of it ourselves." The smell of warm blood all at once filled Francesca's lungs, and she began to tremble.

Father Matthew walked a shaky Francesca back to the only unstained chair in the room. When he'd coaxed her into it, he sank to his knees beside her. "Take a deep, calming breath. Do it. Now," he ordered. He watched her breathe in deep, exhale, and repeat when his rolling hand encouraged her to do so. "We can't take care of this ourselves. We have to get the police involved."

Feeling steadier, Francesca forced herself to set emotion aside and set her lawyerly, logical mind to think. Mulling the facts in her head, she said, "Go ahead and call the police, but I don't want you here when they show up.

I'm going to plead self-defense, and I don't want you involved in any of this."

"No, Francesca, I'll admit to the attack. I'll confess my sins to the police." Father Matthew looked down at the motionless body. The gouge in the back of his skull had welled with blood. Father Matthew couldn't begin to imagine the blades of pain the blows to the head inflicted. "God forgive me," he murmured under his breath.

"But…"

"You will say nothing. Do you hear me, Francesca?" Father Matthew firmed his lips in determination. "Nothing."

"I have to. It's my house. It's my husband lying dead on the floor."

"You don't have to say a word. I'll confess, turn myself in. I'll tell them exactly what happened. He was viciously beating you, and I jumped in to stop him. And…" He raised a hand to silence her when she started to speak. "I need to confess, Francesca. Understood?"

The initial shakes had passed, and Francesca laid her throbbing head back against the chair for a moment to let herself think. "All right, but as your lawyer, you do as I say. Understood?"

Nodding Father Matthew murmured *Deus animae meae miserere.*

Coming Soon

The Complete Woman
The Conflicted Woman
The Spiteful Woman
The Tortured Woman

The Relentless Woman Duology
The Relentless Woman
The Vindictive Women

The Unbreakable Woman Trilogy
The Unbreakable Woman
The Brave Woman
The Valiant Woman

Visit or contact us at:

Visit us at www.mllexi.com to read excerpts of upcoming releases.

Email us at mllexiauthor@gmail.com

Sign up to receive emails whenever M.L. Lexi publishes a new book. There is no charge or obligation and your information will remain confidential.

www.ingramcontent.com/pod-product-compliance
Lightning Source LLC
Chambersburg PA
CBHW021351260626
47153CB00024B/146